W9-CCG-244

NEW STORIES
FROM THE SOUTH

The Year's Best, 1999

The editor wishes to thank Kathy Pories,
whose taste, skill, and tact are essential
to this anthology.

Edited by
Shannon Ravenel

with a preface by Tony Earley

NEW STORIES
FROM THE SOUTH

The Year's Best, 1999

Algonquin Books of Chapel Hill

Published by
ALGONQUIN BOOKS OF CHAPEL HILL
Post Office Box 2225
Chapel Hill, North Carolina 27515-2225

a division of
WORKMAN PUBLISHING
708 Broadway
New York, New York 10003

Printed in the United States of America.
ISSN 0897–9073
ISBN 1–56512–247–x

Preface: "Letter from Sister—What We Learned at the P.O." by Tony Earley. Copyright © 1999 by the author. First published in *The Oxford American,* January/February 1999. Presented on a panel for *New Stories from the South* at the Southern Festival of the Book, Nashville, Tennessee, October 1998. Reprinted by permission of the author.

"Little Bitty Pretty One" by Andrew Alexander. First published in *Mississippi Review.* Copyright © 1998 by the author. Reprinted by permission of the author.

"Missy" by Richard Bausch. First published in *Five Points.* Copyright © 1998 by Richard Bausch. Reprinted by permission of the author.

"Miracle Boy" by Pinckney Benedict. First published in *Esquire.* Copyright © 1998 by Pinckney Benedict. Reprinted by permission of the author.

"The Human Side of Instrumental Transcommunication" by Wendy Brenner. First published in *Story.* Copyright © 1998 by Wendy Brenner. Reprinted by permission of the author.

"Booker T's Coming Home" by Laura Payne Butler. First published in *The Distillery.* Copyright © 1998 by Laura Payne Butler. Reprinted by permission of the author.

"Krista Had a Treble Clef Rose" by Mary Clyde. First published in *Boulevard.* Copyright © 1998 by Mary Clyde. From *Survival Rates* by Mary Clyde. Reprinted by permission of The University of Georgia Press.

"Name of Love" by Janice Daugharty. First published in *Story.* Copyright © 1998 by Janice Daugharty. Reprinted by permission of the author.

"Borrowed Hearts" by Rick DeMarinis. First published in *The Antioch Review.* Copyright © 1998 by Rick DeMarinis. Reprinted by permission of the author.

"Quill" by Tony Earley. First published in *Esquire.* Copyright © 1998 by Tony Earley. Reprinted by permission of the author.

"Lunch at the Picadilly" by Clyde Edgerton. First published in *The Carolina Quarterly.* Copyright © 1998 by Clyde Edgerton. Reprinted by permission of the author.

"Beyond the Point" by Michael Erard. First published in *The North American Review.* Copyright © 1998 by Michael Erard. Reprinted by permission of the author.

"Poachers" by Tom Franklin. First published in *The Texas Review.* Copyright © 1998 by Tom Franklin. Reprinted by permission of the author.

"Those Deep Elm Brown's Ferry Blues" by William Gay. First published in *The Missouri Review.* Copyright © 1998 by William Gay. Reprinted by permission of the author.

"Storytelling" by Mary Gordon. First published in *The Threepenny Review.* Copyright © 1998 by Mary Gordon. Reprinted by permission of the author.

"Pagan Babies" by Ingrid Hill. First published in *The Southern Review.* Copyright © 1998 by Ingrid Hill. Reprinted by permission of the author.

"Birdland" by Michael Knight. First published in *The New Yorker.* Copyright © 1998 by Michael Knight. Reprinted by permission of the author.

"Neighborhood" by Kurt Rheinheimer. First published in *The Greensboro Review.* Copyright © 1998 by Kurt Rheinheimer. Reprinted by permission of the author.

"Leaving Venice, Florida" by Richard Schmitt. First published in *Mississippi Review.* Copyright © 1997 by Richard Schmitt. Reprinted by permission of the author.

"Fla. Boys" by Heather Sellers. First published in *Five Points.* Copyright © 1998 by Heather Sellers. Reprinted by permission of the author.

"Caulk" by George Singleton. First published in *Shenandoah.* Copyright © 1998 by George Singleton. Reprinted by permission of the author.

CONTENTS

PREFACE: LETTER FROM SISTER—WHAT WE LEARNED AT THE P.O.

I have a theory—perhaps unformed and, without question, unsubstantiated—that most bad Southern writing is descended directly from Eudora Welty's "Why I Live at the P.O." Welty's story smacks of a certain now-familiar sensibility, rife with caricature, overstated eccentricity, and broadly drawn humor, that has come to represent Southern writing and, through that representation, the South itself.

It would be difficult, if not impossible, to read much Southern fiction and not come upon story after story faithfully cut from our landscape and culture, using the template provided by Welty in 1941. The characters in "Why I Live at the P.O." possess the prototypical, colorful Southern names that, in the musical sound of their regional specificity, have come to promise colorful Southern doings: Papa-Daddy, Uncle Rondo, Stella-Rondo, Shirley-T., Sister. They eat green-tomato pickle and, on the Fourth of July, sport about in flesh-colored kimonos while impaired by prescription drugs. They live in Mississippi. They grow long beards and illegitimate children and mismatched sets of breasts.

In delicious, honey-coated accents they utter the delicious, honey-coated statements, void of any real importance, that fall

sweetly on the ears of book-buying lovers of stereotype everywhere. "Papa-Daddy," Stella-Rondo says, when she's looking to stir
up trouble, "Papa-Daddy! . . . Sister says she fails to understand
why you don't cut off your beard." Uncle Rondo, after he has
donned Stella-Rondo's flesh-colored kimono and illegally ingested
God knows what prescription narcotic (he's a pharmacist), cries,
"Sister, get out of my way, I'm poisoned."

So faithfully have the conventions of "Why I Live at the P.O."
been copied by succeeding generations of writers, so dominant has
the regionally identified literature laid out by the story become,
that Welty might well have titled it "How to Exploit the People of
the Nation's Poorest Region and Get a Really Big Book Advance."
All of which is at least shameful, if not artistically criminal, because
"Why I Live at the P.O." is a bona fide work of genius, not only
one of the best short stories produced by a Southern writer, but
one of the best stories by any writer, anywhere.

The genius of "Why I Live at the P.O." lies not in the story that
the narrator, Sister, tells us — which is, without question, broadly
told, colorful, eccentric, and side-splittingly funny — but in the story
Sister does not *know* she is telling us. In her hysterical attempt to
win us over to her side in a seemingly inconsequential family dis-
pute, Sister inadvertently reveals the emotional and spiritual bur-
dens that she and the members of her family must pull through
their lives. Stella-Rondo has been abandoned by a traveling salesman who might or might not be her husband, leaving her to raise
a daughter who might or might not be illegitimate. Uncle Rondo
is a shell-shocked veteran of World War I who once had a break-
down because one of his nieces broke a chain letter from Flanders
Field. Mama is a tired woman — a widow, one presumes — who
knows that she must spend the rest of her days caring for and keeping peace among the rapidly aging daughters she can't marry off; her
senile father; and her shell-shocked, drug-addled brother. Papa-
Daddy's rages are directed not so much at Sister, but at what a colorful writer who wasn't from around here famously called the "dying
of the light" (Sister tells us he's "just about a million years old").

And Sister, poor Sister. She thinks she is simply justifying to us her reasons for choosing to live in the second smallest post office in the state of Mississippi. But what she doesn't know she is telling us is that she is horribly alone, that she realizes she will spend the rest of her life in a tiny, tiny place, with no chance of escape, unloved and unmarried, dependent upon the charity of her family. Her monologue to us, unbeknownst to her, is at once a comedic tour de force and a heartrending cry in the wilderness.

While these aren't new critical insights, they are, I think, important ones. The bright surface of "Why I Live at the P.O." is so extraordinarily attractive that it is easy to see why it has been so often imitated. But it is also easy to see why, if *only* the surface of Welty's story is imitated, the result is but a shallow and often exploitative parody of a great work of art. It is easy to make up characters who live in double-wide mobile homes, wear beehive hairdos and feed caps, never put a *g* on the end of a participle, have sex with their cousins, voted for George Wallace; who squint and spit whenever an out-of-towner uses a polysyllabic word; who aspire only to own a bass boat, scare a Yankee, have sex with their cousins again, burn a cross, eat something fried, speak in tongues, do *anything* butt nekkid, be a guest on a daytime talk show, and make the next payment on a satellite dish that points toward Venus and picks up 456 separate channels on a clear day. What is difficult is to take the poor, the uneducated, the superstitious, the backward, the redneck, the "trailer-trash," and make them real human beings, with hopes and dreams and aspirations as real and valid, and as worthy of our fair consideration, as any Cheeverian Westchester County housewife.

While I can forgive our brothers and sisters from other parts of the country for taking pleasure in, or even creating, a Southern literature based on stereotype, I find it harder to forgive Southerners who do the same thing, particularly if they are capable of writing with greater understanding but choose not to. What Welty's more cynical impersonators* choose to ignore is that the eccentricities portrayed in "Why I Live at the P.O." are character-specific and not indicative of any larger pattern of regional or cultural behavior or belief. The humor in the words *Uncle Rondo* arises not from the words themselves, but from the way Sister says them.

While the sound of Sister's voice has become the matriarch of all the shrill, self-absorbed voices we hear in Southern fiction, yammering on about nothing at all, we should remember that her voice is also one of agenda and calculation. Sister wants to make her family look bad; she wants us to believe that they are stupid and that, in their stupidity, they have treated her unfairly. What worries me is the possibility that Sister's voice, with all its layers of complexity, will become lost in the din raised by its imitators, and that din will become, if it hasn't already, the only voice we hear in our heads when we think about the nature of the word *Southern*.

I am often asked if I consider myself a Southern writer, and, to be honest, my answer depends on — to borrow a line from Owen Wister's Virginian, one of the most famously one-dimensional Southern stereotypes — whether or not my questioner smiles when he calls me that. If he means, do I make fun of my characters because they are Southern and because there is a bottomless market for that sort of thing, then the answer is no. But if he means, do I consider myself someone who at least attempts to portray the people of my native region in all their complexity and diversity and Christ-hauntedness and moral ambiguity, the answer is yes, I consider myself a Southern writer.

And as a Southern writer — even one who tends to be as thin-skinned, testy, and self-righteous about this issue as I am — I have been tempted to lower the IQs of my characters, name them Something-or-Other Bob, and stick their illiterate backsides to a Naugahyde La-Z-Boy in order to make myself popular and sell some books. The real danger arises when too many of us at once give in to this invidious urge. In creating our own literature, a Southern literature, we often go for the quick laugh, the easy buck, the cardboard character. When we do that, we eat away the foundation of that literature from the inside. My fear is that, eventually, because of our willingness to feed on, without replacing, the tenets and traditions and subjects given to us by our predecessors—Welty, Flannery O'Connor, and William Faulkner most prominent among them—Southern writing will collapse and bury all of us, leaving only kudzu, grits, and a certain vaguely familiar voice to mark the spot.

*I understand that I am committing an act of critical cowardice here by not naming names. My concern is that I might inadvertently indict a writer who is doing the best he or she can do. I would hate to snag the sincere but unsuccessful in a net cast for the cynical. But to those Southern writers who are cynical, mercenary, exploitative, and aware: You know who you are. Shame on you.

PUBLISHER'S NOTE

The stories reprinted in *New Stories from the South: The Year's Best, 1999* were selected from American short stories published in magazines issued between January and December 1998. Shannon Ravenel annually consults a list of one hundred and five nationally distributed American periodicals and makes her choices for this anthology based on criteria that include original publication first-serially in magazine form and publication as short stories. Direct submissions are not considered.

NEW STORIES
FROM THE SOUTH

The Year's Best, 1999

BIRDLAND

(from *The New Yorker*)

Between the months of April and September, Pawtucket, Rhode Island, is inhabited by several generations of a particular African parrot. A millionaire philanthropist named Elgin Archibald brought a dozen or so over from Kenya around the turn of the century and kept them in an aviary built against the side of his house. A few days before his death, in 1907, in a moment more notable for generosity than for good sense, he swung open the cage and released the birds into a wide summer sky. According to eyewitness reports, the parrots, surprised by their sudden freedom, made a dazed circle beneath the clouds and, not seeing anything more to their liking, lighted amid the branches of an apple orchard on the back acreage of Archibald's property. There, following the habit of nature, they flourished, and have continued to thrive for more than ninety years. But in September, when winter creeps in from the ocean and cold air evokes hazy instincts, the parrots flee south for warmer climes and settle here in Elbow, Alabama, along a slow bend in the Black Warrior River, where perhaps they are reminded of waters, slower still, in an almost forgotten continent across the sea.

I know all this because the Blonde told me it was true. The Blonde has platinum hair and round hips, and a pair of ornithology degrees from a university up in New Hampshire. She has a given name, as well, Ludmilla Haggarsdottir, but no one in town is comfortable with its pronunciation. The Blonde came to Elbow a year ago, researching a book about Archibald's parrots, and was knocked senseless by the late-August heat. Even after the weight had gone out of summer and the parrots had arrived and football was upon us, she staggered around in a safari hat and sunglasses, drunk with the fading season, scribbling notes on the progress of the birds. She took pictures and sat sweating in the live-oak shade. They don't have this sort of heat in New England —bone-warming inertial heat, humidity thick enough to slow your blood. She rented a room in my house, the only room for rent in town. At night, we would sit on the back porch, fireflies blundering against the screen, and make love on my grandmother's old daybed. "Tell me a story, Raymond," the Blonde would say. "Tell me something I've never heard before." The fireflies glowed like cigarette embers. The Blonde was slick with perspiration.

"This," I said, throwing her leg over my shoulder, "is how Hector showed his love to Andromache the night before Achilles killed him dead."

Elbow, Alabama, is easy enough to find. Take Highway 14 north from Sherwood until you come to Easy Money Road. Bear east and keep driving until you're sure you've gone too far: past a red barn with the words HIS DESIRE SHALL BE SATISFIED UPON THE HILLS OF GILEAD painted on the planks in gold letters, past a field where no crops grow, past a cypress split by lightning. This is modest country, and nature has had her steady way for years. My house is just a little farther, over a hill, left on the gravel drive.

The only TV around here sits on the counter at Dillard's Country Store. Dillard's has a gas pump out front and all the essentials inside: white bread and yellow mustard and cold beer. Dillard himself brews hard cider, and doubles as mayor of Elbow. He is eighty-one years old and has been elected to eleven consecutive terms. On fall Saturdays, all Elbow gathers in his store to watch the Alabama team take the field: me and the Blonde, Mayor Dillard, Lookout

Mountain Coley, the Foot brothers, and Mae and Wilson Camp, who have a soybean farm north of town. Lookout Mountain Coley is the nearest thing we have to a local celebrity. He grew up in Mentone, Alabama, near the mountain with that name. These days, Lookout stocks shelves and does the bookkeeping in the grocery and mans the counter when the Mayor is in the head, but thirty-five years ago he was only the second black man to play football for the great Bear Bryant. Once, he returned a punt ninety-nine yards for a touchdown against Tennessee. The Crimson Tide is not what it used to be, of course, and we all curse God for taking away our better days. Leonard and Chevy Foot, identical twins, have the foulest mouths in Elbow, and their dialogue on game day is a long string of invective against blind referees and unfair recruiting practices and dumb-ass coaches who aren't fit to wipe Bear Bryant's behind. The parrots perch in pecan trees beyond the open windows and listen to us rant. At night, with the river curving silently, they mimic us in the dark. *"Catch the ball,"* they caw in Mayor Dillard's desperate tones. *"Catch the ball, you stupid nigger."* Mayor Dillard is an unrepentant racist, and I often wonder what the citizens of Pawtucket, Rhode Island, must think when the birds leave us in the spring.

When I was fourteen, Hurricane Frederick whipped in from the Gulf of Mexico, spinning tornadoes upriver as far as Elbow. Dillard's Country Store was pancaked, and a sixty-foot pine fell across the roof of my grandmother's house. My father had been gone almost a year, and we huddled in the pantry, the old woman and I, and listened to the wind moving room to room like a search party. The next day she sent me to town on foot to borrow supplies and see if everyone was all right. Telephone poles were stacked along the road like pick-up-sticks. But the most terrifying thing was the quiet. The parrots were gone, the trees without pigment and voice. We thought they had all been killed, and to this day no one is certain where they spent the winter, though the Blonde has unearthed testimony for her book regarding strange birds sighted in the panhandle of Florida during the last months of 1979. We rebuilt the grocery, and my grandmother turned her roof repairs into a party, serving up cheese and crackers and a few bottles of champagne she'd saved from her wedding. Despite our efforts at good cheer, and exempting New Year's Day, when Bear Bryant licked Joe Paterno in the Sugar Bowl, a pall hung over town until Lookout spotted the birds coming back, dozens of them coloring the sky like a ticker-tape parade.

Our river is named for the Indian chief Tuscaloosa, which means "Black Warrior" in Choctaw, and in the fall, while we sit mesmerized and enraged by the failings of our team, its dark water litters Dillard Point with driftwood and detritus—baby carriages and coat hangers, Goodyear radials and headless Barbie dolls. When the game has ended and I need an hour to collect myself, I wander the riverbank, picking up branches that I later carve into parrot shapes and display in the window of Dillard's Country Store. We have bird-watchers by the busload in season and, outside of the twenty dollars a month I charge the Blonde for her room and board, these whittlings account for my income. But I don't need much in the way of money anymore.

The Blonde doesn't understand our commitment to college football. Ever the scientist, she has theorized that a winning team gives us a reason to take pride in being from Alabama, after our long history of bigotry and oppression, and our more recent dismal record in public education and environmental conservation. I don't know whether she is correct, but I suspect that she is beginning to recognize the appeal of the Crimson Tide. Just last week, while we watched Alabama in a death struggle with the Florida Gators, our halfback fumbled on their twenty-yard line and she jerked out of her chair, her fists closed tight, her thighs quivering beneath her hiking shorts. She had to clench her jaw to keep from calling out. Her face was glazed with sweat, the fine hairs on her upper lip visible in the dusty light. The sight of her like that, all balled-up enthusiasm, her shirt knotted beneath her ribs, sweat pooling in the folds of her belly, moved me to dizziness. I held her

hand and led her out onto the porch. Dillard's is situated at a junc-
tion of rural highways, and we watched a tour bus rumble past,
eager old women hanging from the windows with binoculars at
their eyes. The pecan trees were dotted with parrots, blurs of
brighter red and smears of gray in among the leaves. *"Catch the
ball!"* one of the parrots called out, and another answered, *"Stick
him like a man, you fat country bastard."* She sat on the plank steps,
and I knelt at her bare feet. "Will you marry me?" I said. "You are
a prize greater than Helen to Paris." The Blonde is not the only one
around here with a college education.

She looked at me sadly for a minute, her hand going clammy in
mine. The game was back on inside, an announcer's voice floating
through the open door. After a while, she said, "I can't live here
the rest of my life." She stood and went inside to watch the end of
the game, which we lost on a last-second Hail Mary pass that
broke all our hearts at once.

The Blonde is still working on her book. She follows the birds
from tree to tree, keeping an eye on reproductive habits and the
condition of winter plumage. "Parrot," she tells me, is really just a
catchall name for several types of bird, such as the macaw, the cock-
atoo, the lory, and the budgerigar. Common to all genera, including our African grays, are a hooked bill, a prehensile tongue, and
yoke-toed claws, whatever that means. The African parrot can live
up to eighty years, she says, and often mates for life, though our
local birds have apparently adapted a more swinging sexual culture, perhaps from an instinctive understanding of the necessity of
perpetuation in a nonindigenous environment. Her book will be
about the insistence of nature. It will be about surviving against
the odds.

By the time April came along and the birds began to filter north,
the Blonde and I were too tangled up for her to leave. One day,
the Blonde says, she will return to Pawtucket and resume her studies there. She mentions this when she is angry with me for one reason or another, and leads me to her room to show me her suitcase,
still standing unpacked beside my grandmother's antique bureau.

And the thought of her leaving does frighten me into good behavior. I can hardly remember what my life was like without her here, though I managed fine for a long time before she arrived.

The Blonde won't sleep a whole night with me. She climbs up the drop ladder to the attic, which is where I make my bed, and we wind together in the dark, her body pale above me, moonlight catching in her movie-star hair. When she is finished, she smokes cigarettes at the gable window, and I tell her stories from the Iliad. I explain how the Greeks almost lost everything when Achilles and Agamemnon argued over a woman. I tell her that male pride is a volatile energy, and that some feathers are better left unruffled, but I know she only listens to these old stories for the sound of my voice. She is more interested in the parrots, a few of whom have taken roost in an oak tree beside my house. If there is a full moon, the birds are awake for hours, calling, *"Who are you? Why are you in my house?"* back and forth in the luminous night. According to the Blonde's research, old Archibald was deep in Alzheimer's by the time of his death and was unable to recognize his own children when they visited. She goes dreamy-eyed imagining the parrots passing these words from generation to generation. Before she returns to her bed, she wonders aloud how it is that the birds could have learned such existential phrases in Rhode Island and such ugly, bitter words down here.

Sometimes Lookout Coley gets fed up with Mayor Dillard shouting "nigger" at the TV screen. Having played for Alabama in the halcyon sixties, Lookout knows what football means to people around here, and he restrains himself admirably. But when they were younger men and Mayor Dillard crossed whatever invisible boundary exists between them Lookout would circle his fists in the old style and challenge him to a fight. A couple of times they ended up rolling around in the dirt parking lot, sweat running muddy on their skin. Nowadays Lookout presses his lips together and his face goes blank and hard as if he were turning himself to stone. He walks outside without a word and stares off at the trees across the highway. After a few minutes, Mayor Dillard gets up and follows him. The rest of us focus our attention on the game, so they can have some time alone to sort things out. No one knows for sure what goes on between them, but when they return they are patting each other on the back and making promises that neither of them will keep. Each time, Mayor Dillard offers a public apology, saying he hopes the people of Elbow won't hold this incident against him come election. He buys a round of bottled beers and Lookout accepts the apology with grace, waving his beer at the TV screen so we'll quit looking at him and keep our minds on simpler things.

Her first season in town, the Blonde was appalled by these displays. She is descended from liberal-minded Icelandic stock and she couldn't understand why Lookout or any of us would allow Mayor Dillard to go on the way he does. Once she sprang to her feet and clicked off the television and delivered an angry lecture welcoming us to the "twentieth fucking century." Her fury was gorgeous. She tried to convince Lookout to report Dillard to the N.A.A.C.P. or, short of that, to run for mayor himself, arguing that only a sports celebrity would have the clout to unseat an old incumbent. But Lookout told her he wasn't interested. Though she would never admit it, the words don't offend her so much anymore. You can get used to anything, given time. Some nights, however, when she is moving violently over me, she grits her teeth and says, "Who's the nigger, Raymond? Who's the nigger now?" I don't think her indignation is aimed directly at me. When she has gone, I tangle myself sleeplessly in the sheets and promise never to think another closed-minded thought.

Raymond French was my father's name, now mine. I am the only child of a land surveyor. My mother died giving birth to me, and my dad began to wander farther and farther afield, finding work, until one day he never returned. I was thirteen when he went, left here with my grandmother and the house. She paid for my education, but she was always disappointed with my chosen field of study. "Classics, Raymond?" she would say. "You ought to be studying the future." She loved this town and hoped that I would bring my learning home and give something back. But all I have given unto Elbow is driftwood parrots and the Blonde. Everyone knows she lingers here because of me, and no one is quite sure how they feel about that.

A few days ago, I panicked when I returned from Dillard Point and found an empty house. I waited on the porch and watched the road for cars, but she didn't show. I don't have a phone, so I drove from house to house, stopped by to see Lookout, swung past the Foots' mobile home, whipped the town into a posse. Prowling country lanes, I began to suspect that she was gone for good. Then I spotted her jeep parked beside one of the Camps' fields. This deserted road and vacant field are like horror-movie sets, with a defunct grain silo rising from the ground like a wizard's tower. I called her name, but only the parrots answered. *"Who are you?"* they said, their voices flat and distant. *"Catch the ball."* Then, faintly, I heard her voice, a stage whisper coming from inside the silo, and when I crawled up beside her she shone a flashlight on a nest, so I could see the baby parrots, their feathers still slick and insufficient, heads wobbly on their necks. She threw her arms around me and wept and pressed her lips against my collarbone. The roof of the silo had fallen in years before and stars blossomed in the open space.

One Saturday in the fall and one in spring, the town celebrates Parrot Day. In October, Mayor Dillard stands outside the store, where Lookout has rigged a hand-painted banner, delivers a short speech, and has his picture snapped for the record. He always arranges it so that Parrot Day comes during an off week for the Crimson Tide. This year, we gather in the parking lot and listen to the Mayor give his speech. The parrots jeer him from the trees. *"Run, darkie, run,"* they call, and he pretends not to notice. The Blonde is disappointed with the day. She wants more from these proceedings, wants something meaningful and real, but this year most of us are grateful for a break from football. Six games into the season and already we've lost four. Another stinker and 'Bama is out of contention for a bowl. We'd settle for anything at this point—the Jeep Aloha, the Outback Steakhouse, even the Poulan Weedeater Bowl, over in Louisiana.

All our mail is addressed to Dillard's Country Store, and in the evenings, when the sun is like molten glass over the river, Mayor Dillard hands out our letters and such. Once a month, the Foots hang their heads in a stew of shame because their subscription to *Titty* has arrived. The Camps get postcards now and then from Wilson's brother Max and his other brother, Andre, whose marriage broke up years ago. Lookout gets religious pamphlets and sports-recruiting news, but letters never come for me. I no longer have connections beyond the boundaries of our town. The Blonde dawdles nearby when Mayor Dillard passes out the mail, her hair sweat-damp against her neck. She cracks her knuckles and goes for nonchalance. She has, it seems, applied for a government grant. She wrote the proposal without telling me and will head north in the spring if her funding comes through. We are sitting at a picnic table behind my house eating peanut-butter sandwiches when she announces her intentions. I force down a mouthful and ask her for a second time to marry me, but her answer is the same. She covers my hand with hers, and sends a look of apology across the table. The Blonde holds all history against me. When it is clear that I have nothing else to say, she stands and walks around to the front of the house. I find her staring up into the trees at a pair of fornicating parrots. "Don't mistake this for love," I hear her murmur to the birds. "Don't be talked into something you'll regret." She watches, unblinking, her arms crossed at her chest. I ask her why she stayed last spring, why she didn't follow the parrots when they left Elbow for the season. She tells me she was broke, that's all. She would have vanished if she'd had the cash. I remind her that she paid her rent, that she was never short of cigarettes and oils for her hair. "Shut up," the Blonde says. "I know what you want to hear."

At night, she types her notes and files them away on the chance the government will write. It's warm enough still, even in October, that we can leave the windows open, air grazing her skin and carrying her scent to my chair in the next room. There is something familiar about the way she smells, though I can never place it. I whittle and listen to sports radio and wish I had a phone so I could call all the broadcasters in New Jersey who have forgotten how great we used to be, how we won a dozen National Championships, and how Alabama lost only six games in the first ten years of my life. To listen to them talk, you'd think they never heard that Bear Bryant was on a U.S. thirty-two-cent stamp. I pace the floor when I get agitated and shuffle wood shavings with my feet. I talk back to my grandmother's Motorola portable. When I make the fierce turn toward my chair, I see the Blonde standing in the doorway, her hands on the frame above her. She smiles and shakes her head. "You people," she says. "When are you gonna put all that Bear Bryant stuff behind you? That's all dead and gone." I cross myself Catholic style and look at her a long moment, my heart tiny in my chest. She is wearing a man's sleeveless undershirt and boxer shorts, her hair pinned behind her head with a pencil. I would forgive her almost any sacrilege for the length of her neck or the way she rests one foot on top of the other and curls her painted toes. I remember Calypso casting a spell on the Greeks to keep Odysseus on her island, and I want to teach the birds a phrase so full of magic that the Blonde will never leave.

I want to tell her that the past is not only for forgetting. There are some things, good and bad, that you can't leave behind. According to the record books, Bear Bryant didn't sign a black player until 1970 because the State of Alabama was not ready even for gridiron integration. A decade earlier, however, he had recruited a group of Negro running backs who were light-skinned enough to pass for white. They hid their faces beneath helmets and bunked in a special dorm miles away from campus. They were listed in the program under names Bear himself selected. Lookout's playing name was Patrick O'Reilly.

Every now and then, Mayor Dillard will set up his ancient

reel-to-reel projector on a card table outdoors and, against the rear
wall of his store, show black-and-white movies of Lookout's punt
return. We sit in the grass in the early dark, pressing beer bottles
against our necks to ward off the heat, and watch his image shim-
mering and breaking around chips in the paint. There is Lookout,
sleek and muscled and young, with the punt dropping into his
arms. He shifts his hips side to side and gives a Tennessee defender
a stiff-arm that takes your breath away. The image flickers as he
shimmies toward the sideline, and then he breaks upfield, his back
arched with speed, the rest of the world falling away behind him.
The movie is without sound, and whenever Mayor Dillard rewinds
the film, so we can watch the touchdown over and over, Lookout
goes streaking backward in front of the Alabama bench, past his
exultant teammates and granite-faced Bear Bryant, then forward
again toward the end zone, all swift and silent grace. None of us
have ever done anything so wonderful in all our lives. Chevy Foot,
as if witnessing a cosmic event, whispers, "Old Number Forty-
one, man, you sure could fly."

I ask the Blonde why the parrots keep returning to Elbow, and
she says it's instinct. We are sitting on the riverbank, with our feet
in the water. It's morning on another football Saturday. Downstream, a hot-air balloon hovers on invisible currents in the sky.
The Blonde slips into her academic's voice as she tells me that,
because the birds are native to equatorial Africa, because their food
supply of seeds, nuts, and fruit dries up in the Rhode Island cold,
they are obliged to embark on a southerly migration in order to
survive. "It's a miracle *Psittacus erithacus* endures in this country at
all," she says, and lies back on the ground, crossing her hands
behind her head. There is a parrot perched on a cypress branch
across the river watching us with the side of his head. I find a stone
on the bank and skip it across the water in his direction, and he
screeches and flutters his wings at me.

"But why here?" I say. "They could live anywhere in the world."
The Blonde lifts up on her forearm, her hair falling over her eyes,

and opens her mouth to speak before she realizes that for once she doesn't have an answer to my question.

In the second quarter of the Ole Miss game, a freshman quarterback named Algernon Marquez comes off the bench for Alabama and throws a pair of touchdowns before the half. For nine minutes, as our team works to tie the score, we are beside ourselves, leaping about Dillard's Country Store, pitching our bodies into one another's arms, but at halftime we fall silent, fearing a jinx, and cross our fingers and apologize to God for all the nasty things we have said about Him in the recent past. Even the Blonde wants to bear the suspense in quiet. She carries her cigarettes outside and sits smoking in her jeep. I stand behind my parrot sculptures, and watch her through the window, as she pretends she is above all this.

The second half, God bless, belongs to Alabama. Our defense is inspired, our offense fleet and strong. Algernon Marquez isn't Joe Namath or even Snake Stabler, but he is more a dream than we could have hoped. "A no-name wonder from Boulahatchie," the announcer says, "whose only goal in life was to play for the Crimson Tide." I wonder how it would feel to have achieved all your aspirations by your eighteenth year. I wonder what Lookout would say about that. A busful of Delaware parrot lovers rolls up while the score is 35–17, and Mayor Dillard gives them whatever they want for free.

That night, I tell the Blonde Andromache's story—how she was made a slave to Pyrrhus, the son of Achilles, after Hector's death, but grew to love him a little bit, over time. "She was happy there, even though she never guessed it could be true," I say, sitting on the bed, with my back propped up. We are in her bed now, my grandmother's sleigh bed, which has been in our family since the Revolutionary War; it made the journey down here by wagon from Virginia. The Blonde is on her back, with her feet against the wall beside my head. She is naked, still flushed from our coupling. "I'm pregnant," she says. "I can feel it in my bones." She traces concentric circles on her stomach with a finger, the parrots frantic beyond the windows. Then she sits upright and looks at me, as if she wanted to see something behind my eyes. I'm just about to haul her into my arms and waltz her joyously around her room when she slaps my face, leaving an echo in my head. I watch, too stunned to stop her, while she jumps up and down on the wood floor, landing hard and flat-footed each time, shaking windowpanes, sending ripples along the backs of her legs. She is crying and pounding her knees, and I wrap my arms around her and pin her down. "This is not my baby," she says. "This is not my life." She keeps shouting until her voice is gone, and she cries herself to sleep beneath me.

Morning finds me alone, still sleeping on the floor. I check the house to be sure, but she is nowhere to be found. Her suitcase is gone from beside the bureau, her hair-care products have vanished from the shelf beside the bathroom sink. I sit drinking coffee on the sleeping porch while the parrots call softly, *"Who are you? Why are you in my house?"* It is not quite a new day yet, and I watch the world come to life, winter buds opening in the light, the river far below hauling water toward the sea. I tell myself that I will give up hope at lunch. And though I hold off eating until two o'clock, I keep my promise and carry a melancholy peanut-butter sandwich out into the yard. The grass is cool on the bottoms of my feet. I wonder about the Blonde, see her streaming down the highway in her jeep, sunglasses on her head to keep the hair out of her eyes. I wonder if she will put an end to our baby in a clinic or if she only wants to get some distance between history and the child. I want to tell her that even bland Ohio is haunted by its crimes. I want to tell her, with the air full of birds like this and the shadow of my house still lingering on the yard, that she is exactly what I need. Behind me, as if on cue, the Blonde says, "I drove all night, but I didn't know where else to go." I turn to face her, blood jumping in my veins. There are tired blue crescents under her eyes, and her hair is knotted from the wind. She smiles and smooths the front of her shorts. I am so grateful I do not have the strength to speak. "I took a pee test in Gadsden," she says. "It's official." Then she walks over, grabs my wrist, and guides the sandwich to her lips.

Election day is nearing again, November 17th. Though Mayor Dillard will run unopposed, as usual, he is superstitious about complacency. He pays Lookout overtime to haul boxes of campaign buttons out of the storage shed behind his store and stake DILLARD DOES IT BETTER signs along the road. He visits each of his constituents in person, bribing us with hard cider and the promise of a brighter future here in Elbow. Things are looking brighter for the Alabama team as well. We've won two games in a row and the Yankee radio personalities are beginning to see the light. They say our team has an outside shot at the Peach Bowl, over in Georgia, where we will likely face Virginia's Cavaliers. But we do not speak a word of this in town. We hold our breath and say our prayers because hated Auburn is looming in the distance and one false step could bring all this new hope down around us like a house of cards. At night, the Blonde and I drink nonalcoholic beverages beneath the Milky Way. We have reached an acceptable compromise: spring in Rhode Island, fall back here, until she has finished her book, but she will give birth in Alabama. Elbow will have a new voter in eighteen years, and the Blonde has convinced Lookout to contend for mayor himself. He will not run against his friend, Lookout says. Too much has passed between them. But it won't be long before Mayor Dillard gives in to time, and Lookout Coley can sweep injustice from our town like an Old West sheriff.

My life purls drowsily out behind me like water. Parrots preen invisibly in the dark. I shuttle inside for more ice and listen to the Blonde spin stories about our unborn child. Her daughter, she says, will discover a lost tribe of parrots in the wilds of Borneo, and invent a vaccine for broken hearts. She will write a novel so fine that no other books need writing anymore, and she will marry, if she chooses, an imperfect man and make him good inside. And maybe, if the stars are all in line, our daughter will grow up to be the hardest-hitting free safety who ever lived.

Michael Knight has published fiction in *The New Yorker, Paris Review, Virginia Quarterly Review, Esquire, GQ, Story,* and other magazines. He has won a Henfield Foundation Award, *Playboy*'s 1996 College Fiction Contest, and the Fellowship of Southern Writers New Writing Award. His first two books, a short story collection, *Dogfight and Other Stories,* and a novel, *Divining Rod,* were both published in 1998. Knight, a native of Alabama, is currently residing in Virginia with his wife.

C. JILL SPEARMAN KNIGHT

I stayed up all night four nights in a row the week of my wedding to write the first draft of "Birdland." I was afraid it would leave me if I waited. I made myself ill. I couldn't stop until I had it on paper, and outside of making me sick on my wedding day, this story was pure largesse. I don't know where it came from, except to say that I have been addicted to Alabama football since I was a boy, and I was a Classical Studies major in college, and a friend of mine named Mike McCole once told me a supposedly true story about a band of exotic birds escaping their cage for life in the wild.

FLA. BOYS

(from *Five Points*)

I started driving early. I was twelve. I am a girl. It was not what I lived for.

At first my main fears driving were 1) a dog would run out in front of me and I would crush it and never be able to drive again I would be so upset and 2) my door would fly open and I would fall out and get run over by my own back wheels, my neck tangled hopelessly in the rear axle.

By the time I was thirteen, I was fairly confident on the road. My dad in the front seat, sort of conducting. My uncles once in a while packed into the back seat, their drinks in ice tea glasses. They loaded me with compliments. We didn't see them that often.

Most often it was me driving my dad at four in the afternoon out the two-track to Amber's, where there were chickens and beer and what my father called moonshine but was just regular Gordon's in regular fifths.

Other times I drove to school, and put the car in the teacher lot, and walked in through the front doors. Sometimes I drove the Trail to the ABC, in the morning. Sometimes even the highway when Dad wanted to go downtown for a drink.

Nothing bad happened, except when we got pulled over, and then I did everything my father told me to do, and miraculously, it worked. I cried, and my father had explained we were on the way to the hospital. He just kept talking, and somehow he had made his drink disappear—I still didn't know how he did that. Once the cop ended up giving me money, two damp twenty-dollar bills. Figure that out.

When I was fourteen my father got me a thirty-day restricted driver's emergency license. I would get to drive him to the hospital. Then, I would take care of myself for two weeks. This time, the hospital part was true. I wasn't worried about my father.

"They just take out six inches of colon, Sweetie, it's nothing." His belly was pregnant with fluid—he was huge, and his skin was yellow. We sat in the kitchen drinking—I was having a beer. His little suitcase was on the dining room table. On top of his aqua pajamas, little white cloudy plastic flasks, full.

The license was bigger than a normal license. It was laminated. There was no photo of me. My restrictions were printed on the back in red. A) Operator may only drive 7 A.M.–7 P.M. B) Forty-five miles per hour maximum speed.

The restrictions seemed dangerous. With these instructions I was a slow-moving target.

To get the license, I had driven down to the Orlando City Hall with my father. I drove, illegally, as I did most of the time. He liked to have his gin and tonic going, in his smoky tall glass, a cigarette dangling dangerously above the drink. This was how I learned to drive. You learn to not spill any fluid.

I'd dressed up in my favorite outfit; I was still sure there'd be a photo and I was thrilled—I mean I actually thought this might lead to a modeling portfolio. I clasped purple puka shells around my neck. I had a bitchin suntan, because my father and I had a pool—in the front yard—of our Southside stucco ranch. I wore my white sundress and I loosened the ties at the shoulders so my breasts would look bigger—you couldn't tell really, I thought, if it was the dress flipping around or my boobs. I was thinking, I will invite a guy over to the house, and we will have a little champagne by the pool. I was thrilled to be on my own for two weeks. My father had stocked the freezer in the garage with meat.

"Don't dawdle," my father said, and he held out his palm for the keys. I got out of the car and went to put money in the city hall meter. The palms were scratching together, their fronds like legs. Itch itch.

"Don't fuck with that, I'm right here," he growled out the passenger window.

I turned on my heels and walked up the forty stairs, into the city hall. I pretended I was a lawyer. I was in stiletto Candies, red.

I gave the clerk my fat folder of papers, documenting my father's surgery, the hardship, the loss of work, and giving them a fake address, my uncles' Kissimmee ranch. Farm kids could get the Temporary even without an Emergency.

Here you go, she said.

I wanted it to be harder. I wanted my photo taken. These would be my dominant reactions to many situations for the rest of my life.

When I was a little girl, I would climb into the back seat of my father's car, late late at night, but so bright in Florida, in summer, and I would lie back there on his newspapers and bottles and the fertilizer sacks and papers and carbons and I would pretend a man was making love to me. I don't know where I got that stuff. I guess you just know what goes where.

The next night, when he passed out on the couch, his pale, almost green gaseous belly stiff on top of him, I took his keys and sat in the giant brown Olds out in the green cement driveway, on my side, the passenger side. I had the license in my hand. My sweat was buckling the lamination. I sat out there for hours, and thought of men, and how they drive women around. I didn't need to drive secretly at night, like most kids. I did all that driving during the day.

The next day my father didn't get out of bed. I swam in the lake. I was pretending I was a seal, shooting up from the white mucky bottom of Lake Conway every time a plane came over the blue

lake, and barking *orr orr orr*. Right then the Carrington boys came
by in their Mercury boat and asked me if I wanted to ride around.
I said no.

They sped off and I went down to the bottom. I don't know
why. Their white bathing suits, little flags flapping in the wind,
scared me, like dinner napkins and mothers and rapes and won
races.

That night, I cried out in the Olds. I was so sad I hadn't gone
with those Carrington boys. I started the engine, backed out of
the driveway, hitting the neighbor's curb, and I drove slow and
smooth as Johnny Hartman singing "My Favorite Things" on
88.4, my father's favorite station. I sang loud, and I put on his pilot
sunglasses. I prowled around the Southside in the big car, pretending I was a pimp, or a Colonel or a cat or a woman with small
children or a woman with no children at all.

The last night before he went in to Orange Memorial I was
completely happy just to sit in the driveway with my hands on my
father's sticky steering wheel. It was like I was hiding and everyone I knew had quit looking for me.

I was fourteen. I didn't even own a wallet yet. The Emergency
license sat in my red plastic purse alone, among my lip gloss and
eyeshadow and concealer and tiny plastic Hallmark calendar and
calculator and Troll doll, all the things I would get to keep forever.

I drove him to the grocery store. It was his last day.

"Monday dinner," I said, just to get him thinking on it. I
threaded us between the cars, trolling and idling and parked in
places that weren't even really places in the Winn Dixie parking
lot. I worked around broken bottles, and grocery carts and a large
St. Bernard who looked to be suffering a heat stroke out by the
cart corral.

"Why do you want to park in bum-fuck Egypt?" he said.

"Is there something wrong with your legs?" I said.

"As a matter of fact," he said.

And he bought me everything I wanted that day, and finally I wanted some things. More makeup. A giant pink iced angel food cake. A tiny bottle of champagne. I don't even know if it was real or play.

And the ABC, we stopped there, and he sat inside at the revolving bar for one hour and twelve minutes while I waited in the car, reading *Seventeen* and staring at the men who went in and out. Everything was fine except I was melting inside, I was so worried he would die of cancer. And he was. He was to have his ear cut off and six inches of colon taken out.

"I'll tell you what to worry about," he said. He was frying fish that night. Dad always made us wonderful dinners, chop suey and chicken Buck. Buck is my father's name, Buck Jackson, and chili. He could do Mexican, he could do Indian, he could do steak and potatoes. Everything he cooked tasted so good.

"Thanks for making this wonderful dinner," I said, most unworried voice.

"Jesus, who the fuck can't cook," he said. "If you can follow directions, you can cook."

I didn't point out that he didn't follow any directions at all, he just seemed to stumble around throwing things on the counter and making an enormous mess. My job was to clean up that mess. I didn't point out that one of his refrains was "people in this world can't follow goddamn directions."

We ate out on the patio in the purple starlight. He threw his bones into the pool. Bones float sideways.

Then it was the morning of Tuesday, June 7th. I drove him to the hospital. He told me again where I was born, pointing five floors up to a dirty greenish window.

"You looked like Rocky Marciano." He always said this. And he laughed in a sad way, like it was the end of something, my birth, his seeing me like Rocky.

"How much did it hurt my mother?" I wanted to say. I was having trouble keeping my eyes on the road, much less doing the circle of rotations between the road, the rearview, and the siderear, duh, duh, dunh. *That my face was so flattened then. Did she scream?*

Was sex worth this? Why was a baby so big? Couldn't it start off much smaller, much much smaller, something to fit in your palm, something the size of a penis, something appropriate for the woman? Couldn't we find a way to grow them out here, in the open, an easier way?

I looked at my father, transmitting my questions to him subliminally, as always. He didn't like to be asked things, unless he asked you to ask.

"Ask me if I fucking care." "Ask me how to wire a goddamn house, I will fucking tell you. Hell I will fucking show you." "Ask me what you should do with your life, Georgia. Ask me."

I didn't ask him, never about her. He'd left her and taken me with him, and he had what he called mixed feelings. This always made me think of cement. Mixed feelings. Our lives, the products of mixed feelings.

"Turn around back. Not here. This whole part is for ambulances. Damn it."

She was in Wisconsin, so who knew what was what. This was not the day to ask my father particulars. We were into the Emergency period. He was getting cancer out of his colon. He was getting the colon out of his system. When you live with an alcoholic, if you are fourteen, you learn quickly and sweetly. You learn that many things can be put off. You learn how to stay in a place of not-knowing. You never would consider asking prognosis, odds, or how much money there is. Not-knowing. You learn to find this somewhat relaxing.

Earlier in the morning he had showed me how to fix the toilet, that creepy rusty water, the green corroded chain, and how to load his gun, those slimy shells—he didn't think there was anything else I ought to need to know. A gun and a commode is what I had to hold me through the next two weeks. Hormel tamales and fourteen frozen cube steaks. Onions in our yard. Enough muriatic acid for the pool for a year. And the Emergency License.

I was driving perfectly, around the back of the hospital, up into the parking garage, wrapping around, not gunning the engine at this very low speed—I was going two miles an hour, not spilling a drop, even though inside I thought my father would die during this operation, I would never see him again, I would drive to his funeral with an expired Emergency license.

We didn't have the radio on. He was nervous, but he was always nervous. He always had a lot going on. He was drinking the whole way down to the hospital, long drinks out of his smoky gray glass.

He looked hard into his fist, which had just swallowed his cigarette, his eyebrows untamed wires, his complexion yellow from the colon blockage, his eyes sweating, his blue jumpsuit unzipped too far. He had gotten all skinny in the face and shoulders and legs and arms. His middle was more enormous, as if he were pregnant way past the time, like sixteen months or something.

On level three, I braked and gas-pedaled at the same time I think. My legs were all mixed up, the car chortling, my father coughing, and I wanted to just take a breather at this four-way stop, I just really wanted to stop and not think, just pause the world for the moment, a big moment. It spilled. It spilled, my father's fist, around his drink, the drink was on the floor, and ice slid around, and I lurched through the intersection and somehow the Olds was spinning, a wide circle, like how guys drive on purpose, at night, doing their donuts, sometimes. Spinning, and then Buck socked me in the throat. He socked me hard. The parked cars slipped past my windows. We lurched on through. I could make no noise. Up to level five.

I concentrated on the burning on my neck and the red golf cart in front of me, with its pails of paint stacked like white heads.

"Sorry about that," he said. He had ochre eyes, always wet. "Get going. Now, get going. You're going to get rear-ended. And in a couple of hours I'm getting out six inches of my colon. Get vehicle out of goddamn intersection. Go up to the top."

My hands tingled on the steering wheel. My stomach whooshing. This was pretty much my constant state.

"We oughta get em to put it in formaldehyde so we can display my contribution on the mantel. What do you think about that as a conversation piece, baby?" My dad smiled and you could tell he was seeing a crowd of people around our mantel and all of us talking and laughing.

I pulled up to the Admitting doors at the top of the parking garage.

There was no plan.

"Just let me out," he said. He didn't have the suitcase. Standing in the sun, he drained the rest of the bottle, a jug of gin he had in the back seat. There wasn't a lot left.

"Dad," I was going to say, "are they going to cut you open? Is it going to hurt? Will you know when they are inside you? Will you not be able to feel them?" But my throat hurt from where he hit me and I just turned on the radio, I didn't know the tune, and he walked into the building.

I waited, idling for a few minutes, like moms do when they drop you off at school or dance lessons.

How do you know what gets inside of you? Why was I born? How could you ever figure out something like that? How could you not? I wanted to drive into the lake behind the hospital. By way of a cure.

I didn't know much about cancer. What it was. It seemed like stones. I knew about guns and toilets and making drinks, mimosas, molotov cocktails, his favorites. I knew about butt-fucking. My father's pornography collection was vast and specific.

I didn't know any people who had died. I didn't know that many people.

My mother and brother had moved to Wisconsin seven years ago. I had a memory block from age twelve to age seven. And what can you remember before age seven? Wanting stuff made out of sugar or plastic and crying and some ducks at a park. I remembered my kid brother's hair. It was cute and white, like the Christmas angels my mother hung around our kitchen. It was so white you wanted to taste it, it was so shiny.

My dad didn't come back out. He hadn't forgotten anything, not anything that he had, anyway.

He'd said the cancer of the colon thing was nothing. It was good to get rid of your excess colon. You had two hundred feet of the stuff. What he was getting rid of was just excess. It wasn't anything. He said that about everything—him not going to work, finding me still asleep in the back of the car in the afternoon, stunned in the sun, the Florida room flooding and the television in water sparking, cops at the door at five in the afternoon, a woman trying to stab him on our patio on his birthday, me drinking beer and floating in the pool so that I could drown. It wasn't anything. None of it was anything.

I believed that I was going to be okay while I had the E. L.

I circled down out of the parking garage, pretending I was twenty-seven years old. I put on some more lip gloss, and my father's sunglasses. I changed the radio station to WDIZ, Rock 100, and it was Van Halen and I knew the song. "Pretty Woman." Ah, I said. "Oh Baby." That was a shame, because those words hung around in the car with me.

I drove down the Orange Blossom Trail, with the radio on really loud. I was looking for a drive-thru liquor window. I was going to try out the credit card I had been given by my pops.

The Olds was chugging funny. I wondered if spinning out, if losing it back there in the parking garage, had that hurt the car? He'd told me to take the car to Earl if I had any trouble. Earl at the Shell station was always trying to feel me. Earl had a cot behind the Coke cooler and a mattress in his Rescue Van. The misnomer of the century.

"Hey baby you sure look wonderful," a guy on a motorcycle yelled into my open window at the red light on Bumby.

"Oh, thank you," I said. It was so funny to me how no one knew what you had just done.

I wanted to use up this part of my life driving on the highway. I decided to take the Beeline to the beach, to Daytona Beach. I would just sit there in the sun. I was wearing diaper shorts. Those shorts that are printed with parrots and palm trees, of thin cotton, that you wrap up between your legs, and then the ties wrap around your waist. And my pink tube top. I looked pretty cute and skinny and tan and significantly older than fourteen. I could just sit on the beach on my diaper shorts, and if they got wet, I had on great underwear, that could just be my bathing suit and I could drive home in that easily.

The shins always lost their color first. I would get my shins back even with my arms and thighs. The tan was important.

I hurtled up the I-4 access ramp and took the Beeline Exit, a cloverleaf that I handled like an expert, and I loaded myself onto the highway. It felt like roller skating, going this fast after having been limited to low speeds for all these weeks. The rumble in the engine disappeared and I started breathing better. I sped up. I went a little faster than the speed limit, like everybody else. Something my father would never let me do.

Highway 50 draws a neat straight line across Florida, like a belt from the sea to the gulf. It was Tuesday in the middle of the afternoon. It was hot and salty, and the palms and the crotons and the oleanders planted along the sides of the highway looked scratchy and tired and somewhat poisonous, which they were. The sky was a washed-out blue, and I had tears in my eyes. I liked my highway—no other cars. I liked my lane. It made a rhythm like my heart.

I headed to the sea.

I started steering with one hand. I powered down all the windows to one-half.

But then I changed my mind. I would go back and make myself a mimosa and sit in the pool, keep an eye on the Olds, and watch the stars come out and reheat some of the chicken Buck left for me in the microwave and then watch the Clint Eastwood channel. I didn't want to get stuck at the beach hungry and then have to drive back home in the dark. I didn't want to get stuck anywhere at all.

I pulled over, to a Fat Joe's. Gas. I needed gas. You always need gas if you have an Olds. They are true gas hogs. But I didn't want to buy gas at that juncture. I wanted to go right home and reset my head, break through the walls.

Highway 50 had quickly become peculiar to me. I couldn't tell which way was back to my dad's house, couldn't tell which way went on out to the ocean or the gulf. I went a ways and then, no, wrong way. To get back I had to go east. I looped around on the median, ten miles back the other way and then I would do it scared all over again. I kept passing the Fat Joe's. There were no signs that were useful to me. I must have turned around ten times. I was lost on a straight line.

I was lost on a straight line. The town back over in the marsh was Christmas. In Christmas, Florida, a town of 1,322, I was lost. I was lost, crying, then screaming. My throat hurt on both sides, like I had a scalpel there in my neck. The same kind of Florida scrub—palmettos and sword bushes passed in my windows. I couldn't read the sky. I couldn't figure it out.

One thing I remembered from my mother, the death scream. It's just a scream you can do when you are really upset and you want people to back off, to give you some room to work in. I screamed her scream, pleasant little legacy. Then I was shaking the car by the steering wheel, by the neck it seemed—everything was coming loose, the sky was one big blue eye and I could hardly see, soaked, red, a puff—let go and screamed thinking I'd fall. My dad's Olds rolled into a ditch.

My head didn't hit the windshield when the car banked and rocked over, so I slammed it against the windshield myself. It didn't crack. The jug of empty gin rollicked up to my feet, lay there like an accusation, a destiny. I pitched it out the window.

I was so wet between my legs I thought I had had an accident, or a female emergency, but it was just sweat. I thought, well, the back seat. A little sleep. But I was too sideways and I couldn't get back there. I had to sit on my own door. I had no idea which way to go. I wanted to walk down the highway with the steering wheel. That would be funny. Straight to the hospital, please. I did want to just share a room with my father. We could be together now.

I waited. No blood. I was just soaked with sweat. I kept looking at my face and head in the rearview mirror. No one came. I
turned the rearview mirror to me so I could stare at myself without having to crane my neck. No contusions arose to the surface
like lovely rose tattoos.

It was so hot. No cars passed me. Would I be a person walking
into Christmas? I was sticking to the vinyl bad. It was hard not to
think about Earl and his creepy van and my dad and his colon like
a sausage in brine on our mantel. You can't get stuff like that out
of your head unless you are willing to sacrifice years of memory
around it, and at my age, that would pretty much wipe me out.

The pine trees were only about a foot outside the ditch. Their
needles were so green, so dark, they seemed like ink up there,
through my dad's window.

"Shut up, trees," I said. I spoke out loud. "Good-bye," I said, and
turned the rearview mirror around so to face them, those scaly
trees, and not me anymore. "Bad bye," I shouted. "How don't you
do!"

Nothing seemed wrong, except the crowd was missing, and I
knew my dad had been asked to lie down and breathe in a blue gas,
and he was not thinking about me. There were dirty magazines at
home on the dining room table. There was porn in the suitcase and
both bathrooms. So I needed a boyfriend somewhat older than the
Carrington boys and their innocent red boat with its sharp white
flags.

Keep it on the road. I knew what he meant by that now.

In my next little dream he lived. And I died because I went off
the road and that was the last thing. No one would know! This
was my constant fix. I wanted to live in order to tell people, but in
order to be interesting my good stories required my death.

I started screaming again, out loud or not, I don't know. Three
big green Publix trucks passed fast and I felt my car wiggle and
shudder, even though it was locked into mud. You know how
some people start laughing to keep from crying, or so they say, I've
never really seen anybody do that. I do the opposite.

In a ditch, in an Olds Delta 88, in Christmas, Florida, so sweaty I am smelling like formaldehyde, I started howling harder maybe than I have ever howled, and I have howled, because everything takes so long when you are a kid. I started screaming so hard my whole body hurt. I tried to rip my short blue shorts, but there wasn't a way to get a good grip on the denim. I was wet and huge mucous was everywhere. I was screaming red screams and scratching my face. No one came. There weren't that many people in Christmas. A cougar escaped from Circus Land two weeks ago, and they hadn't caught it yet. It was kind of a flat jungle. There aren't that many people in Florida. I know it must seem like it if you just see Florida on television, but the crowds here are clustered in pockets. It is mostly trees, cows, bushes, and bugs and more field scrub, a cougar or three. Not that many people. Fat Joe's. I didn't see the cougar.

I got out by opening up the passenger door, my dad's door now, and climbed out like from a box. Like the lady out of the cake. I said "Hello" when I got out. The car was so hot, like an eye on your stove. Man. My thighs sizzled. My diaper shorts were scooched up into my butt. Adjusting, I slid off of the car. It was hurt pretty bad. It made me think of an abandoned jungle gym, the brown knot of it.

I hopped down into the reeds.

I wiped my face off on the soft weeds, cattails, in the ditch. I threw my Emergency License and then my whole purse into the hyacinths because I would never ever be driving again. No one could make me.

I was lost, ankle deep in humus. It was noon, and the sky just kept going higher and higher, like each breath I took puffed my clean blue blanket off of me a little bit more.

I felt naked in my tube top and my parrots shorts. They were so short when you sat down it was like a bathing suit up around your thighs, tight and into the skin.

On my way up to the highway, I saw a baby alligator in the

water in the ditch with my car, sunning on a stick in the muck—
they always look like they are smiling, and I felt just like him. I
wanted to slip into his mud with him, stay small and soft and have
little bright teeth like that.

He couldn't remember a thing. He couldn't know why my car
was lodged like a spaceship on his nest. He couldn't care less. He
wasn't even really grinning.

It's like I was in a fog, but without the fog. Not that I was slow.
I went to a special school called PEP. You had to be smart and you
had to have some kind of problem. The same kids had always
known me. One had a rod in her back, Sara. She'd been my best
friend since I was seven, she said all the time to everyone. She
made me wear her jewelry and her flower blouses over my halters.
The others that went to PEP were all boys, brilliant nerds with
epilepsy or hemophilia or something else like attention deficit dis-
order, something that didn't really show up to us or seem at all
important. Me and Sara tied their shoes together while they did
enormous and tormented math problems. We were supposed to
teach each other. Sara and I taught the boys how to love us, how
to be our lovers. I did all of this without speaking or remembering. The boys taught us how to balance checkbooks and exactly
what the gonads were capable of. We had to translate Dolly Par-
ton's measurements into metric. They were interested in learning
that kind of thing. They liked the idea of taking pi out to the mil-
lionth digit, working it out on rolls of toilet paper. They got into
fist fights over infinity and the Big Bang and the size of the largest
mammalian penis.

"It's not the elephant. It's the guy from Austria in the *Guinness
Book of World Records.*"

"It's a shark."

"Well, how are we defining largest? Length, bulk, circumfer-
ence, or total cubic volume when erect?"

"You have to factor in flaccid weight, or you are an asshole, butt
face."

Blue whale, I didn't say.

You will write us a love letter every morning, first thing when you get to school, okay boys? Sara had them all churning the stuff out. Now, we move to roses, she said. She actually said that. Next, promise rings! We'll make em, and you just give them to us when I say.

It was a great school.

We were allowed to write on the walls and to play the stock market in theory. The teacher talked on the phone all day, selling real estate.

I played along but I wasn't happy to receive presents from Sara's hostages. It didn't feel like love, it felt like school. I just wanted to cheat.

I wasn't really interested in anything except the film room down the hall because it was dark. There was only one movie in all those tin circles—*Michelangelo: Tragic Genius*. I was allowed to go there on Fridays and only if Sara came with me. We watched it and watched it and watched it on the wall. None of the boys were allowed in there with us. It was too much focus on the breast, Mr. Rose said, with Michelangelo, the tragic genius. I loved the stealing corpses part. I just loved it that you had to have an arm in order to draw an arm.

All those boys liked me and they made me the Queen of Dogs before school let out. They would follow me around the PEP classroom on their all fours, and bark and I spoke my secret language— "Zimba Marton. Cray Cray." They went crazy rolling at my feet. Sara got mad when I was made Queen, especially at her fiancé John Trombley rolling around and barking and salivating at my feet, the one she loved best, but you know she'd never marry him. She was just playing eighth grade. She would be different next year.

Now Sara Simko was the type who would go over to Fat Joe's and call the police, I think. She wasn't allowed to ride motorcycles or wear bikinis because of the rod in her back. She was a police caller. But I was scared to call. I was always a criminal-feeling girl.

Like when the coffee money was stolen from the teachers' lounge at PEP I wondered: could it have been me? It wasn't, but I always worried.

I creeped over to that Fat Joe's, making it seem like I was just walking on in from any old direction.

I cried by the pumps. Maybe I would just get in someone's car. I walked up to the little booth with the money woman in it and pulled my shorts down better. They were hiked and wrinkled and all wet. I couldn't see the car and that was good. It was just below the horizon. Like the little yellow alligator, I couldn't see what happened.

The woman in the booth at the pumps gave me some questions, and tried to be helpful.

"Where you trying to go, Sweetie?"

I explained that I lived in South Orlando, and I had a car, not far away, and I was just lost.

"Oh sugar, it's okay, you want a Coke?" I didn't. She gave me directions to my subdivision. It was just a line she drew, a line that was also an arrow, and she put an "x" where my house was, at the end of the line. It angered me, this map. It was not what I needed. How was I supposed to figure out which way to hold that arrow? You could turn it an infinite number of directions.

"No, thanks," I said. My throat hurt like it had had something jammed into it.

I just wandered off across the parking lot, over to the line of pumps where truckers filled up their tanks. I mouthed the words "Taxi Cab" into the sky, and then I started humming Van Halen. Little bit of a dance, a sexy dance.

I stepped in front of a large red truck with a man filling two gas tanks, one on each side. His engine was running. This was illegal. I stood in front, aligning myself with where he stood in the back, looking into his grille, which had a piece of a bird, a pigeon, caught in it. The wing was fine, but the rest was a smeary mess. I looked at the road, and could tell I wouldn't ever know which way to go.

I said I was lost.

"Are you lost, girl?"

"My horse ran away," I said. "Our best paint." I fell onto him, and tried to cry. I wondered if maybe I should ask him to take me to a hospital, an orderly well-run mental hospital, but then how could I pick my dad up in two weeks, how could I keep the toilet on track?

His name was Michael it said on his shirt in red writing. He had hair like the fake icicles that hung on the gas pumps, dried-out white hair, salt and sun hair, but he was young. He had all kinds of deer horns and fish bait cartoons and turtle shells laid out across his dashboard. I thought of my egg. All this stuff. All this life that he had, all this that never spilled. I sat on the edge of the sofa-like seat in his truck while he paid and got me a Coke and him a carton of Marlboros.

"I can't find my way home." I had let the map blow off, even though there was no wind. I had no pockets. No change of clothes. I had no purse, no bra, not a dime, even the Emergency License was not on me. My long blonde hair was all around my hot pink tube top, like waves.

"Well, what's your name?"

"Georgia," I told him. "Like the state."

He smiled. "Where are you trying to get?" His lips were thin and white and his eyes were like horse's eyes, big and brown.

I liked it that he didn't ask where I was coming from.

"I don't know," I said. I knew this was the most radical thing I had done, even more radical than putting my dad's Olds in that deep wet ditch. It was a lie. A public lie. I thought it was a little sad that my lying debut had to take place at Fat Joe's in Christmas. But I was driving off the road, fast and hard. I had already spilled.

That afternoon, late, red, orange, and blue, in Room 2-7, in a hotel by the beach, a Daytona 500 truckers' hotel with no name, two stories, and long black railings wrapping around the second floor like a little prison or a Spanish condo, an odd long hour away from Orange Memorial Hospital, Michael showed me how much money he had on him. We went through his boots, $500 in each. His wallet on a chain, pictures of kids, $100 bills behind each of them, and $1000 in a secret pocket. We went through his shirt together, and there were secret inside places with $100 bills.

I wanted to lay it all out on the little round table and get all of the heads facing the same way. I pushed some of the bills towards each other, a little family of Franklins.

"Don't even fuck with me, not once, or I will kill you."

"Thank you," I said. "I won't." I felt I was doing well.

I got under the covers. I pulled the white sheet up to my neck and lay there with my arms at my sides. This made me think of my father. I smiled. This was my life! The brown scratchy bedspread smelled like cigarette smoke and when Michael sat down on the end of the bed, the smoke smell puffed and made me cough. He leaned forward, lit a cigarette with his silver lighter, and changed the channels on the television.

"You sure are quiet, girl," he said. He didn't look back at me. He had cartoons on really loud. "Let's get ourselves hungry," he said.

He put the cigarette in his mouth backwards, and pulled his shirt, a button shirt, over his head. His slim wrists slipped through the cuffs, and he threw the inside-out shirt on the television and kicked the cigarette back out. The arm of the shirt draped over the cartoons. He slid his belt out, and said, "What are you lookin' at?" in a mean voice but he was smiling. "Your hair looks so beautiful, gold on white," he said. "Against the sheets. My God," he said. "This is not what I was expecting when I woke up this morning. Angel hair."

"Where do you live?" I said. He turned up the air conditioner.

"To block out noise," he said, and I didn't follow up or imagine or do anything except take my diaper shorts off under the covers, and push them with my feet down to the end of the bed, under the spread, where things were heavy and tight.

"You never fucked a nigger, I hope," he said.

"No one," I whispered to him when he lay down next to me, on top of the spread. I could hardly move. I could feel my legs sweating and between my legs spreading. The light in the room was blue and although it was stuffy and close and strange, I liked it. I liked being away from the car, far from the freezer of chuck steak, the hospital. I liked not having my purse.

"I wish I had a photograph of you," I said.

"Why don't you get out from under there and let me look at you," he said. "Let me see a little bit more of ya." His voice was soft and sweet. He was watching television, the part you could see around the sleeve, while he talked to me, but it wasn't like my dad. He wanted to see me.

"No," I said. And Michael looked at me then, his white icicle hair didn't move, but he did. He took me in his arms and laughed. "You get down in here with me," I said. And I started kicking and kicking the heavy brown spread, making smoke smells puff into the room, and I got the stuff over him at last, and I said, "Let me take off your pants."

"What. Are you my angel?" he said and I was glad I was under the covers, in the brown tent, because I would have started laughing or maybe I would have burst into tears had I seen his face when he said *that.*

I unzipped his pants slowly, and then I started scooting them down his slim hips, over his funny bent hipbones. This is much harder to do than you would think. You have to really yank. It's nothing like a doll, which is smooth and plastic and purely dry. His skin looked older and his hair was blonde, all the way up his legs, curlier and curlier as you got to his gray underwear. The smell was of acid and lemons and sulfur. It was like playing tent with my brother when we were little, except for that complex smell.

I could not tell if he had a hard-on or not. I started kissing his knees, pulling the hairs with my teeth, and licking and kissing the skin, which was salty and fearless. And I worked my way up to the above-the-knee.

His hands came down under the covers like two cheerful squids.

I was happy to feel them. He kneaded my butt and stroked me like I was a car, then a bird, then a saddle.

I was so wet it was like I had my period, and it was gross and strange and wonderful under those covers. I could hardly breathe, so I sounded like I was panting with pleasure, which I thought was a good thing.

"Are you my angel? Am I going to fall in love with you?" Woody Woodpecker made his famous noise, and it was like Woody talking to me. I had my eyes open and could only see the wall. I was licking the white scratchy sheet. I was numb from the waist down. I couldn't feel anything. My feet were sweating buckets, though. I could tell that.

"I hope not," I said as softly as I could talk which was very very soft.

We had shrimp dinner down at the pier late that night and he bought me a rose from the girl with them in her little white plastic basket.

"She's gorgeous," the girl said. "And you're going to get ten years. They have laws, Tackett," she said, laughing. I had this feeling they knew each other, but I had that feeling about every single set of people I encountered ever since I got my memory back. I liked the rose. It had black edges, and it was a tight bud.

It would never open. I knew that. Just looking at it.

"That will open up really nice in the next few days," he said. He was building River Country, part of Disney. He got paid in cash at the end of every day. He had cement poisoning, and I felt sure I was going to get it on my legs too. He had a woman on his crew. He wouldn't be able to hire me on. There were too many problems with this one woman. She couldn't carry two buckets. She was willing to make two trips, but it wasn't fair. The men all hated her ways.

"I know what an Allen key is," I said. "I can fix a toilet. I know I could be very useful at River Country."

"Oh, you could be useful," Tackett said, and he put three shrimp tails into his mouth and crunched them in. "Ah," he said. I thought, the joke is on me. But, I didn't care. I wanted anything. Just to have more to think about than my dad, that life. People always are saying teenagers are difficult and crazy. We just want something other than the trouble we have.

We sat on the mess of bedcovers like we were in a nest. He was skinny without his clothes, a true stick. Like my dad without the pregnant belly, but this man was hard, whip thin, yellow-eyed, but a hard yellow, not that watery yellow. We watched cartoons on television for a long time, not talking. I put on his blue work shirt and snapped it up to the top of my neck. He made me take it off and go shower and dry off really good before he let me put it back on. He didn't say anything about the way I handled things. Maybe it had gone okay. It was easy to forget. It was so easy to know that things had always been this way.

He fell asleep with the television on at 10:33 P.M. I smelled him while he slept. The ceiling had a stain on it in the exact shape of the sausage-curled head of Marie Antoinette.

Sometime late in the night, the cartoons had turned to a black-and-white movie that didn't have any cars in it, just women who yelled out all these beautiful sentences at the men in a tiny office, big women in suits with big buttons, yelling but in the most sexy way you could imagine, like trumpets, many notes all spilling out at once—it was wonderful but it was too many words. I kept fearing a car would come on screen, or a car commercial, or even a horse-drawn carriage. I couldn't understand who was who or what the point was.

Michael Tackett was sleeping like a stick would sleep. Stiff and straight with his arms at his sides. Not a leaf stirred. I got up quick like a snake and put on his jeans. They had so much stuff on them. Dirt and writing and clots of cement. I felt like a building in progress. White streaks of caulk and sand in the pockets. I emptied his pockets. I didn't want to get killed.

I didn't want anything to happen. I didn't want one single

moment anywhere in the world to go forward. Not because I was so happy, but because it seemed this was a good place to stop. Everything as yet undiscovered but completely changed—that was how I wanted to stay, but that isn't a way that can stay.

The door made a sucking sound as it locked behind me. I had the feeling I was leaving something behind, but I realized I was always going to have that feeling. That was the car, that was my dad, that was my dinner, and that was my stomach. That was my memory block, that was my brother in Wisconsin with our mother, that was the Emergency License. I walked outside, tip-toeing on the Astroturf into the parking lot.

It could have been anywhere in the whole world of Florida, I thought. The light was my same old lonely no-lover back seat of the car light at way past midnight in my dad's driveway light. The ROOMS $20 SEA PEARL L UNGE OPEN sign blinked in gold and peach letters and I looked back at the motel, all those dark windows like a hospital. Down the strip I could see more neon problems. BUG BOY. IMPER   GARDEN.

As I walked away from the hotel, his truck, down to the highway, I thought—everyone is going to be able to see me now. I am no longer invisible.

Right after he drifted off, he had started rolling his lips, saying "Shelley, Shelley, Shelley," over and over. It was hard to tell if he was mad at her, having sex with her, or she was driving, or what. I knew she would be the mother of the kids in his wallet, the hundred-dollar-bill kids. Then later he was humming emotionlessly.

He'd told me things about women and I kept thinking of those things, those shapes, those quantities, those colors, those holes, those words he said, all he knew.

I worked towards the highway where trucks were passing with the same noise that I always felt in my stomach, the whooshing. In a while, those trucks, they would pass by the yellow shiny baby alligator and my dad's yellow car in the ditch, as they closed in on Orlando. I started walking that way. The pavement was still hot from yesterday and my sandals were already wet and salty from my sweaty feet. The pines were all inky and sharp and salty alongside me. I touched my face—it had lines deep into it, from the coarse sheets, scratching. I smelled like cigarettes. His pants, now my pants, shifted around my body as I walked, like in a denim barrel, chafing. His shirt felt like a pelt on me.

I felt like my self was a vital organ beating, somehow staying alive inside an ancient husk that was not my own. My hair stuck to itself. A truck's horn blasted me off the highway, like it was the first sound I ever heard, the siren I had been waiting for all this time. It was a good kind of frightened to death.

The road, that straight line, was a geometry lesson. The air, its salt making me a kind of chemical reaction I cannot even describe. That new space inside of me.

It scared me, all of it. As much as the thought of the next thing.

———

Heather Sellers earned her doctorate in English at Florida State University. She was born and raised in Orlando, and lived in Florida for nearly thirty years. Her work has appeared in *Five Points*, *The Indiana Review*, and *Field*. She teaches creative writing at Hope College in Holland, Michigan.

I don't like to look at this story. To write, I had to blurt it out.

It's a blurt which has gone through two dozen drafts, several workshops, and lots of rejections. It was a hard story to get on top of. So I got under it, and let it have its way.

I set the story in the landscape I am most acquainted with: a backside, no-place strip of Florida, between Bithlo, Christmas, and Narcoosee. That setting—flat and scrubby, unseen by outsiders—seemed a perfect metaphor for the adolescent girl body.

I am attracted to these vulnerable, exposed characters: the girl who dismantles herself in order to, she hopes, I think, rebuild from the bottom up. The father who thinks he is the essence of freedom but who is the opposite. The ceremony with the stranger man, all this stuff you just don't want to know about the inner workings of girls and the inner workings of truck-stop hotels.

You don't want to, but you have to look in there.

Clyde Edgerton

LUNCH AT THE PICCADILLY

(from *The Carolina Quarterly*)

We're in the nursing home parking lot. Aunt Lil and me. She's behind her walker. She pushes it way out in front of her. Arm's length. Humped way over and all fell in the way she is, and weighing less than ninety pounds, her arms look longer than brooms. To see where she's going she has to look up through her eyebrows.

"Is that my car?" she says.

"Yes ma'am. I washed it."

"Well, it looks good."

She's wearing a striped jacket, Hawaiian shirt, tan slacks, gold slippers, silver wig, and a couple of pounds of makeup.

"I'll let you try to drive it after we eat," I tell her, knowing damn well she ain't able to drive. I've been putting it off—letting her practice her driving, that is—by driving my truck when I take her to lunch instead of her car. She keeps asking me when she can practice her driving and I keep putting it off. Because for one thing, as far as when she's going to get out of this place, I don't think it's going to happen. And she won't be able to drive again in any case, and it's my job to tell her. I'm it. It's one of the most worrisome things in my life because I'm about all she's got left, as far as people. Everything is pretty much up to me.

But today we've got her car, and after I let her try to drive after lunch, in the mall parking lot there at Piccadilly's, for just a minute or two, I'm going to tell her she can't drive anymore. It's past time to just break the news.

I get her walker fitted in the back seat, get her in the passenger seat—her head about as high as the button on the glove compartment. Her car is a 1989 Oldsmobile, kind of a maroon color, with a luggage rack on the trunk lid. She drove it seven years before her problems and it ain't got but 21,000 miles on it. She's always had something kind of sporty in cars. Back in '72 she had a 1967 two-door Ford Galaxie with fender skirts. White with red interior, and she let me drive it to my prom.

We park on top of the two-deck parking lot at the mall. It's mostly clear of cars. I tell her that after lunch I'll let her drive around up there a little. Mainly, I'm simply going to let her prove to herself that she can't. Can't drive. That will make it lots easier for her to take the news, which I will probably deliver as soon as she makes her first mistake, which might even be before she cranks up.

We get inside Piccadilly, and since it's only 11:30 there's not a real long line, but on the way past the food toward the trays and silverware where the line starts she wants to stop and take a look at what they're serving today. Right here I want to say, Aw, come on Aunt Lil, you'll get to see it in a minute. But I'm thinking, Be patient. Be good. She's in the hardest time of her life.

We get the trays, silverware. She gets a bowl of Chinese stuff without the rice. I get it with the rice. I'm trying not to help her. Let her do what she can. It's going to be bad enough when she sees she can't drive. Aunt Sara, before she died, said stopping driving was the worse thing she ever went through, including Uncle Stark's death.

Down at the cash register a small black man, maybe sixty years old, takes Aunt Lil's tray and leads us to a table. She wants the smoking section. She smokes Pall Malls. He puts her tray down. She says thank you and starts getting all settled in. She can't figure out where to put her walker. I move it over against the wall.

All she's got on her tray is this bowl of Chinese stuff and a biscuit and iced tea and a little bowl of broccoli with cheese sauce. I got the Chinese stuff over rice, fried okra, string beans, fries, cucumber salad, pecan pie, and Diet Coke. She reaches for my little white ticket slip and puts it with her own. She'll get me to pay with her Mastercard.

She says, "That was Larry," talking about the man that brought her tray over. "Let me get him a little something," and she starts looking around for her pocketbook.

I'm thinking, Oh no, the quarter tip.

"You know," she says, "he's lost some weight." She finds her pocketbook, but can't get it open. I help her.

"He'll be back," I say.

"He's been working in here for twenty years at least," she says.

Here comes Larry, walks right by before I can say anything. I check his name tag. It says LEWIS CARLTON. "There he goes," I say. She raises her hand, misses him. "His name tag said Lewis," I say. "Lewis Carlton."

"No, it didn't."

"I think it did. 'Lewis Carlton.'"

"Then it's *Larry* Lewis Carlton," she says. She sort of twists around in her seat, like a buzzard in makeup looking over its shoulder. "There he comes back. Larry! Larry, come over here."

The man, Mr. Carlton, comes over.

"Here, I want you to have this." She hands him a quarter.

"Thank you, thank you." He steps back a couple of steps, starts to turn.

"You've lost some weight, ain't you?" says Aunt Lil.

He frowns. "Oh, no ma'am."

"You've lost at least twenty pounds."

"No ma'am, I, ah, been at one sixty for quite a few years now."

"Well, I remember when you weighed a lot more than that."

He looks at me, kind of smiles and backs off.

"He's been here a long time," she says. "I don't know if they want you to tip them or not, but I always do."

Yeah, I'll bet he's glad to see you coming. "Say he's lost some weight, huh," I say.

"Oh yes, he used to be a great big old thing."

So we eat along, and talk about the normal things.

Last time we were in here, a woman named Ann Rose wanted to carry Aunt Lil's tray from the cash register. Aunt Lil saw her coming and said to me, "Lord, she'll talk your head off." Aunt Lil shunned her, but Ann Rose took the tray anyway, said she'd saved Aunt Lil a table, but Aunt Lil don't want no part of it. Said she wanted to sit someplace else. So Ann Rose looked at me with this nod of understanding. I'm staying out of it. Later at the end of the meal, Aunt Lil says, "Go tell Ann Rose to come on over here. I don't want to make her feel bad." So Ann Rose came over, sat down, and started right in about how she worked forty-four years at the cigarette factory—American Tobacco—and they'd all told her that whenever *she* finally left they'd have to close it down, and sure enough she left in June of '91, and then in *July* they announced they *were* closing it down, and then there was a woman had been working there got cut loose, then joined an accountant firm that came right back and was doing an audit of the very people who'd just let her go, and "I want you to know they lost one hundred retirement checks and only one showed up and that was at somebody's P.O. box and nobody knows how in the world that happened, that all the ones with regular addresses got lost, and blah blah blah blah blah. Like to drove me crazy.

Just about every other time we come in here, somebody comes over. Because Aunt Lil made all these friends, coming up here all these years. I like it when they don't come over.

It's one of those giant two-decker parking lots, about the size of a football field, with a couple of ramps going down to the ground-level deck below it.

We drive to the far end of the lot, where it's away from the mall and empty. I stop, get out, get her out of the passenger side, the walker out of the back seat, and she plods around the back of the car in her walker.

This all started when Aunt Lil fell in her tub, twice on the same night, same bath, a couple of years ago. Then not long after those bathtub falls her back started breaking on its own—from gravity, you know, just broke and broke, then broke some more and the awful thing is that you could see so clear and fast the way it bent her right over. The worst thing was the pain it caused her. She cried a couple of times, and I'll tell you she is not the crying sort. The first few minutes in the nursing home, after she got off the van, she was following her walker—real slow, you know, with it ten feet out in front of her, and it hurt her just to walk. She sat down in her little room with her roommate—I helped her—and she said I don't know what I'm going to do and she started crying right there. It was almost like one month she was standing as straight as an arrow, walking as classy as a model, one foot in front of the other—eighty-seven years old I'm telling you—and then in a few months there she was with a walker and all bent over like that, crying.

I got my own business and can get off work when I need to, and this was say three o'clock in the afternoon and when she finished crying, she said to her roommate, "Don't you wish you had a nephew who'd do for you like this one?" and her room-mate, name of Melveleen, says, "I got *two* nephews. *They* both work." Melveleen.

So, anyway, I help her in. I get in the passenger side, hand her the key, she puts it in the ignition, turns it, starts the car right up, and kind of looks around. I'm feeling a little sad about it all. This is it. This is the last time she'll ever do this. I'm about to break the news. She will not like what I have to tell her.

"Where's the exit?" she says.

"We're just going to drive around up here on top for a few minutes and let you get the feel of things."

"I got the feel of things."

Yeah, you got about one minute left in your driving history on earth, Aunt Lil. And I'm the one about to break the news.

She pulls it into drive and we're off—in a little circle.

"Where's the exit?" she says.

"We're going to stay up here on top, Aunt Lil. You can drive over toward those other cars if you want to. Maybe a little slower." We do.

All of a sudden, she says, "There's a exit!" and swings the car to the left, right down this down ramp. Because the sun is so bright up top, I can't see. I assume she can't either. I'm straining to see straight ahead, one hand on the dashboard. Then I see the curb on each side of the car—about two feet high, thank goodness. Aunt Lil is drifting left. I think about pulling the hand brake, but decide against it. She needs to see, to prove to herself what she can't do. We scrape the curb with the front left tire, or bumper, I can't tell which. She slows to a stop.

"We drifted left," I say. "Let's pull on straight ahead, on down there beside that column and I'll take her back over." This is all the proof I need. The proof I want her to know for herself. She is unable to drive anymore—the time has come. I will have to break the news to her—as soon as we stop.

The top of her head is even with the top of the steering wheel. She starts out slowly, drifts left, and runs against the curb again.

"What's wrong," she says.

"You keep running up against the curb."

"Oh," she says. She looks over at me, her hands up on the steering wheel. "Am I driving?"

"Yes, yes. You're driving. Pull straight ahead there and I'll take back over."

"I need a little more padding under me, she says. "I'm too low in this seat."

"I don't think that's the basic problem, Aunt Lil."

"And I need a little more practice. That's all." She pulls straight ahead and stops. We sit there. This is the time to tell her, I think, but I'll just wait until I'm back behind the steering wheel with everything under control.

"Okay," I say. "Put it in park."

She does.

Then for some reason she presses her door lock switch and locks us in.

"It was unlocked," I say. "Now it's locked. You need to unlock it."

She touches the window button and her window starts down.

"That's the window," I say. "Press where you just pressed it."

"Where?"

"Right there where that lock button is—the top part of what you just pressed on the bottom. You locked it. Now you need to unlock it. Right there, above where you pressed it."

She looks up into the ceiling, her hand in the air like she's waving at somebody.

"This one right here." I point to my lock button.

Finally, she gets it right, unlocks the doors, then opens hers. I get out to go around and help her out. I'm sort of preparing my speech. I want to make it as easy as possible, to kind of set it up so she might make the suggestion herself, set it up in a way that if she doesn't take the bait, then I can say, Aunt Lil, I think you're just going to have to give up driving. And then I'll say something like, That way you won't have to pay car insurance and all that. That's costing you over a thousand dollars a year.

I open the back door, get out her walker. As I pass around the back of the car, I see her head leaning into the middle of the car, looking down at something. As I come around to her side I see her feet hanging out the open door. I can't remember if she put it in park.

"Be sure it's in park," I say.

This is where she pulls the gearshift from park down into drive, and off she goes, them gold slippers hanging out the door. There she goes, very slowly at about two miles an hour, her door and the passenger door wide open. I open my mouth. Nothing comes out. She's going in a big wide circle, missing one of those big columns, then another, circling around. I see her head now. I think she's steering. I decide to just stand and wait, because it looks like she might come on back around. All I have to do is wait. Something tells me if I holler at her she'll try to get out. She's not going fast. I must remain quiet.

She's now traveled one half of a large circle, missing everything. There are about five or ten cars in this area and many thick concrete columns. If I stand still I think she'll be back around. She must be holding the steering wheel in one position. I hope she doesn't straighten it out. But if she does, maybe she'll start up the ramp and the car will choke down—that thought crosses my mind. But then she'd roll backward. Her foot is not on the gas because I can see those two little gold slippers. She misses another column, then another. I will wait.

Here she comes. I believe she's steering. I move so that I will be on her side of the car when she comes by. Both doors are wide open. I see those gold slippers. I see her eyes above the steering wheel. Here she comes. I start walking beside her; fairly fast walk. "You need to put it in park," I say. I put my hand on the door. She's looking straight ahead, frozen. The passenger door hits a column and slams shut. "Put it in park, Aunt Lil."

There is a tremendous explosion and pain to my body and head. I've walked into a column. I stagger backward, catch myself, and head out after the car. By God this proves she can't drive anymore. I run to the passenger door, open it, jump in, grab the hand brake between us, and pull it up slowly and firmly. We stop. I put the gear lever in park. Because her feet are out the door, she can't turn her head all the way around to see me, but she tries.

"Is that you, Robert?" she says.

"Yes ma'am. It kind of got away from you there, I believe."

"I was doing okay," she says.

God Almighty. "Let's get you out, and I'll drive us on back."

"I would have got out," she said. "But I couldn't reach that seat belt thing."

"What would have happened to the car, Aunt Lil—if you'd got out?"

"You could have caught it. Just like you did."

I figure that as soon as we get back and sit down in her room and kind of recover and eat a couple of Tootsie Rolls, I'll break the news to her. She keeps Tootsie Rolls for everybody that comes in. I buy them for her, along with bananas and other stuff. It's not going to be easy, but I'm just going to have to tell her like it is. Her driving days are done and over. Ka-put. End of story.

Clyde Edgerton grew up in rural North Carolina and now teaches in the MFA program at the University of North Carolina at Wilmington. He is the author of seven novels, including *The Floatplane Notebooks* and *In Memory of Junior.* His stories have appeared in *New Stories from the South* and *Best American Short Stories.*

*T*his story came about after I offered to let my aunt drive her car for what was her last drive (I think). That drive resembled the drive in the story up to the point where Robert gets out of the car. I made up the rest. I sent it to a reader who said it wasn't a story, but was rather an anecdote. So then I made up the reluctance of the main character to bring up the dreaded subject of stopping driving, and stuck that here and there so the piece might then be thought of as a story—it seemed to me to deepen the whole thing a bit. I've yet to figure out what a story is—and that helps keep the effort of writing them interesting.

William Gay

THOSE DEEP ELM BROWN'S
FERRY BLUES

(from *The Missouri Review*)

I heard a whippoorwill last night, the old man said.

Say you did? Rabon asked without interest. Rabon was just in from his schoolteaching job. He seated himself in the armchair across from the bed and hitched up his trouser legs and glanced covertly at his watch. The old man figured Rabon would put in his obligatory five minutes then go in his room and turn the stereo on.

It sounded just like them I used to hear in Alabama when I was a boy, Scribner said. Sometimes he would talk about whippoorwills or the phases of the moon simply because he got some perverse pleasure out of annoying Rabon. Rabon wanted his father's mind sharp and the old man on top of things, and it irritated him when the old man's mind grew preoccupied with whippoorwills or drifted back across the Tennessee state line into Alabama. Scribner was developing a sense of just how far he could push Rabon into annoyance, and he fell silent, remembering how irritated Rabon had been that time in Nashville when Scribner had recognized the doctor.

The doctor was telling Rabon what kind of shape Scribner was in, talking over the old man's head as if he wasn't even there. All this time Scribner was studying the doctor with a speculative look

49

on his face, trying to remember where he had seen him. He could almost but not quite get a handle on it.

Physically he's among the most impressive men of his age I've examined, the doctor was saying. There's nothing at all to be concerned about there, and his heart is as strong as a man half his age. But Alzheimer's is irreversible, and we have to do what we can to control it.

Scribner had remembered. He was grinning at the doctor. I've seen you before, ain't I?

Excuse me?

I remember you now, the old man said. I seen you in Alabama.

I'm afraid not, the doctor said. I'm from Maine and this is the farthest south I've ever been.

Scribner couldn't figure why the doctor would lie about it. Sure you was. We was at a funeral. You was wearing a green checked suit and a little derby hat and carryin a black shiny walkin stick. There was a little spotted dog there lookin down in the grave and whinin and you rapped it right smart with that cane. I hate a dog at a funeral, you said.

The doctor was looking sympathetic, and Scribner knew he was going to try to lie out of it. Rabon was just looking annoyed. Who were you burying? he asked.

This confused Scribner. He tried to think. Hell, I don't know, he said. Some dead man.

I'm afraid you've got me mixed up with someone else, the doctor said.

Scribner was becoming more confused yet, the sand he was standing on was shifting, water rising about his shoes, his ankles.

I reckon I have, he finally said. That would have been sixty-odd years ago and you'd have to be a hell of a lot older than what you appear to be.

In the car Rabon said, If all you can do is humiliate me with these Alabama funeral stories I wish you would just let me do the talking when we have to come to Nashville.

You could handle that, all right, the old man said.

Now Scribner was back to thinking about whippoorwills. How Rabon was a science teacher who only cared about dead things and books. If you placed a whippoorwill between the pages of an enormous book and pressed it like a flower until it was a paper-thin collage of blood and feathers and fluted bone then Rabon might take an interest in that.

You remember that time a dog like to took your leg off and I laid it out with a hickory club?

No I don't, and I don't know where you dredge all this stuff up.

Dredge up hell, the old man said. I was four days layin up in jail because of it.

If it happened at all it happened to Alton. I can't recall you ever beating a dog or going to jail for me. Or acknowledging my existence in any other way, for that matter.

The old man was grinning slyly at Rabon. Pull up your britches leg, he said.

What?

Pull up your britches leg and let's have a look at it.

Rabon's slacks were brown-and-tan houndstooth checked. He gingerly pulled the cuff of one leg up to the calf.

I'm almost sure it was the other one, Scribner said.

Rabon pulled the other leg up. He was wearing wine-colored calf-length socks. Above the sock was a vicious-looking scar where the flesh had been shredded, the puckered scar red and poreless and shiny as celluloid against the soft white flesh.

Ahh, the old man breathed.

Rabon dropped his cuff. I got this going through a barbed-wire fence when I was nine years old, he said.

Sure you did, the old man said. I bet a German shepherd had you by the leg when you went through it, too.

Later he slept fitfully with the light on. When he awoke, he didn't know what time it was. Where he was. Beyond the window it was dark, and the lighted window turned the room back at him. He didn't know for a moment what room he was in, what world the window opened onto. The room in the window seemed cut loose and disassociate, adrift in the space of night.

He got up. The house was quiet. He wandered into the bathroom and urinated. He could hear soft jazzy piano music coming from somewhere. He went out of the bathroom and down a hall adjusting his trousers and into a room where a pudgy man wearing wire-rimmed glasses was seated at a desk with a pencil in his hand, a sheaf of papers spread before him. The man looked up, and the room rocked and righted itself, and it was Rabon.

The old man went over and seated himself on the side of the bed.

You remember how come I named you Rabon and your brother Alton?

Yes, the man said, making a mark on a paper with a red-leaded pencil.

Scribner might not have heard. It was in Limestone County, Alabama, he said. I growed up with Alton and Rabon Delmore, and they played music. Wrote songs. I drove them to Huntsville to make their first record. Did I ever tell you about that?

No more than fifty or sixty times, Rabon said. But I could always listen to it again.

They was damn good. Had some good songs, "Deep Elm Blues," "Brown's Ferry Blues." "When you go down to Deep Elm keep your money in your shoes," the first line went. They wound up on the Grand Ole Opry. Wound up famous. They never forgot where they come from, though. They was just old country boys. I'd like to hear them songs again.

I bought you a cassette player and all those old-time country and bluegrass tapes.

I know it. I appreciate it. Just seems like I can't ever get it to work right. It ain't the same anyway.

I'll take Brubeck myself.

If that's who that is then you can have my part of him.

It's late, Papa. Don't you think you ought to be asleep?

I was asleep. Seems like I just catnap. Sleep when I'm sleepy.

Wake up when I'm not. Not no night and day anymore. Reckon why that is?

I've got all this work to do.

Go ahead and work then. I won't bother you.

The old man sat silent a time watching Rabon grade papers. Old man heavy in the chest and shoulders, looking up at the school-teacher out of faded eyes. Sheaf of iron-gray hair. His pale eyes flickered as if he'd thought of something, but he remained silent. He waited until Rabon finished grading the paper he was working on and in the space between his laying it aside and taking up another one the old man said, Say, whatever happened to Alton, anyway?

Rabon laid the paper aside ungraded. He studied the old man. Alton is dead, he said.

Dead? Say he is? What'd he die of?

He was killed in a car wreck.

The old man sat in silence digesting this as if he didn't quite know what to make of it. Finally he said, Where's he buried at?

Papa, Rabon said, for a moment the dense flesh of his face trans-parent so that Scribner could see a flicker of real pain, then the flesh coalesced into its customary opaque mask and Rabon said again, I've got to do all this work.

I don't see how you can work with your own brother dead in a car wreck, Scribner said.

Sometime that night, or another night, he went out the screen door onto the back porch, dressed only in his pajama bottoms, the night air cool on his skin. Whippoorwills were tolling out of the dark and a milky blind cat's eye of a moon hung above the jagged treeline. Out there in the dark patches of velvet, patches of silver where moonlight was scattered through the leaves like coins. The world looked strange yet in some way familiar. Not a world he was seeing, but one he was remembering. He looked down expecting to see a child's bare feet on the floorboards and saw that he had heard the screen door slap to as a child but had inexplicably become an old man, gnarled feet on thin blue shanks of legs, and the jury-rigged architecture of time itself came undone, warped and ran like melting glass.

Naked to the waist Scribner sat on the bed while the nurse wrapped his biceps to take his blood pressure. His body still gleamed from the sponge bath and the room smelled of rubbing alcohol. Curious-looking old man. Heavy chest and shoulders and arms like a weight lifter. The body of a man twenty-five years his junior. The image of the upper torso held until it met the wattled red flesh of his throat, the old man's head with its caved cheeks and wild gray hair, the head with its young man's body like a doctored photograph.

Mr. Scribner, this thing will barely go around your arm, she said. I bet you were a pistol when you were a younger man.

I'm a pistol still yet, and cocked to go off anytime, the old man said. You ought to go a round with me.

My boyfriend wouldn't care for that kind of talk, the nurse said, pumping up the thingamajig until it tightened almost painfully around his arm.

I wasn't talkin to your boyfriend, Scribner said. He takin care of you?

I guess he does the best he can, she said. But I still bet you were something twenty-five years ago.

What was you like twenty-five years ago?

Two years old, she said.

You ought to give up on these younger men, he said, studying the heavy muscles of his forearms, his still-taut belly. Brighten up a old man's declinin years.

Hush that kind of talk, she said. Taking forty kinds of pills and randy as a billygoat.

Hellfire, you give me a bath. You couldn't help but notice how I was hung.

She turned quickly away but not so quickly the old man couldn't see the grin.

Nasty talk like that is going to get a soapy washrag crammed in your mouth, she said.

With his walking cane for a snakestick the old man went through a thin stand of half-grown pines down into the hollow and past a herd of plywood cattle to where the hollow flattened out then climbed gently toward the roadbed. The cattle were life-size silhouettes jigsawed from sheets of plywood and affixed to two-by-fours driven in the earth. They were painted gaudily with bovine smiles and curving horns. The old man passed through the herd without even glancing at them, as if in his world all cattle were a half-inch thick and garbed up with bright lacquer. Rabon had once been married to a woman whose hobby this was, but now she was gone, and there was only this hollow full of wooden cattle.

He could have simply taken the driveway to the roadbed but he liked the hot, astringent smell of the pines and the deep shade of the hollow. All his life the woods had calmed him, soothed the violence that smoldered just beneath the surface.

When he came onto the cherted roadbed he stopped for a moment, leaning on his stick to catch his breath. He was wearing bedroom slippers and no socks and his ankles were crisscrossed with bleeding scratches from the dewberry briars he'd walked through. He went on up the road as purposefully as a man with a conscious destination though in truth he had no idea where the road led.

It led to a house set back amid ancient oak trees, latticed by shade and light and somehow imbued with mystery to the old man's eyes, like a cottage forsaken children might come upon in a fairy-tale wood. He stood by the roadside staring at it. It had a vague familiarity, like an image he had dreamed then come upon unexpectedly in the waking world. The house was a one-story brick with fading cornices painted a peeling white. It was obviously unoccupied. The yard was grown with knee-high grass gone to seed and its uncurtained windows were opaque with refracted light. Untrimmed tree branches encroached onto the roof and everything was steeped in a deep silence.

A hand raised to shade the sun-drenched glass, the old man peered in the window. No one about, oddments of furniture, a wood stove set against a wall. He climbed onto the porch and sat in a cedar swing for a time, rocking idly, listening to the creak of the chains, the hot, sleepy drone of dirt daubers on the August air. There were boxes of junk stacked against the wall, and after a time he began to sort through one of them. There were china cats and dogs, a cookie jar with the shapes of cookies molded and painted onto the ceramic. A picture in a gilt frame that he studied until the edges of things shimmered eerily then came into focus, and he thought: This is my house.

He knew he used to live here with a wife named Ellen and two sons named Alton and Rabon and a daughter named Karen. Alton is dead in a car wreck, he remembered, and he studied Karen's face intently as if it were a gift that had been handed to him unexpectedly, and images of her and words she had said assailed him in a surrealistic collage so that he could feel her hand in his, a little girl's hand, see white patent-leather shoes climbing concrete steps into a church, one foot, the other, the sun caught like something alive in her auburn hair.

Then another image surfaced in his mind: his own arm, silver in the moonlight, water pocked with light like hammered metal, something gleaming he threw sinking beneath the surface, then just the empty hand drawing back and the muscular freckled forearm with a chambray work shirt rolled to the biceps. Somewhere upriver a barge, lights arcing over the river like searchlights trying to find him. That was all. Try as he might he could call nothing else to mind. It troubled him because the memory carried some dark undercurrent of menace.

With a worn Case pocketknife he sliced himself a thin sliver of Apple chewing tobacco Rabon didn't know he'd hoarded, held it in his jaw savoring the taste. He walked about the yard thinking movement might further jar his memory into working. He paused at a silver maple that summer lightning had struck, the raw wound winding in a downward spiral to the earth where the bolt had gone to ground. He stood studying the splintered tree with an old man's bemusement, as if pondering whether this was something he might fix.

Say, whatever happened to that Karen, anyway? he asked Rabon that night. Rabon had dragged an end table next to the old man's bed and set a plate and a glass of milk on it. Try not to get this all over everything, he said.

Scribner was wearing a ludicrous-looking red-and-white-checked bib Rabon had tied around his neck, and with a knife in one hand and a fork in the other he was eyeing the plate as if it were something he was going to attack.

Your sister, Karen, the old man persisted.

I don't hear from Karen anymore, Rabon said. I expect she's still up there around Nashville working for the government.

Workin for the government? What's she doin?

They hired her to have one baby after another, Rabon said. She draws that government money they pay for them. That AFDC, money for unwed mothers, whatever.

Say she don't ever call or come around?

I don't have time for any of that in my life, Rabon said. She liked the bright lights and the big city. Wild times. Drinking all night and laying up with some loafer on food stamps. I doubt it'd do her much good to come around here.

I was thinkin about her today when she was a little girl.

She hasn't been a little girl for a long time, Rabon said, shutting it off, closing another door to something he didn't want to talk about.

Past midnight Scribner was lying on top of the covers, misshapen squares of moonlight thrown across him by the windowpanes. He had been thinking about Karen when he remembered shouting, crying, blood. When he pulled her hands away from her face they came away bloody and her mouth was smashed with an incisor cocked at a crazy angle and blood dripping off her chin. One side of her jaw was already swelling.

Where is he?

I don't know, she said. He's left me. He drove away. No telling where he's gone.

Wherever it is I doubt it's far enough, he said, already leaving, his mind already suggesting and discarding places Pulley might be.

Don't hurt him.

He gave her a long, level glance but he didn't say if he would or he wouldn't. Crossing the yard toward his truck he stepped on an aluminum baseball bat that belonged to Alton. He stooped and picked it up and went on to the truck, swinging it along in his hands, and threw it onto the floorboard.

He wasn't in any of his usual haunts. Not the Snowwhite Café, the pool hall. In Skully's City Café the old man drank a beer and bought one for a crippled drunk in a wheelchair.

Where's your runnin mate, Hudgins?

Bonedaddy? He was in here a while ago. He bought a case of beer and I reckon he's gone down to that cabin he's got on the Tennessee River.

Why ain't you with him? The old man did not even seem angry. A terrible calm had settled over him. You couldn't rattle him with a jackhammer.

He's pissed about somethin, said he didn't have time to fool with me. I know he's gone to the river though, he had that little snake pistol he takes.

The night was far progressed before he found the right cabin. It set back against a bluff and there was a wavering campfire on the riverbank and Bonedaddy sat before it drinking beer. When Scribner approached the fire, Bonedaddy glanced at the bat and took the nickel-plated pistol out of his pocket and laid it between his feet.

Snake huntin? the old man asked.

These cottonmouth hides ain't worth nothin, Bonedaddy said. Nobody wants a belt made out of em. Too muddy lookin and no pattern to speak of. I mostly shoot copperheads and rattlesnakes. Once in a while just whatever varmint wanders up to the fire.

Scribner was watching Bonedaddy's right hand. The left clasped a beer bottle but the right never strayed far from the pistol. The hand was big and heavy-knuckled and he couldn't avoid thinking of it slamming into Karen's mouth.

You knocked her around pretty good, he said. You probably ain't more than twice her size.

She ought not called me a son of a bitch. Anybody calls me that needs to have size and all such as that into consideration before they open their mouth.

The old man didn't reply. He hunkered, watching the hammered-looking water, the farther shore that was just a land in darkness, anybody's guess, a world up for grabs. He listened to the river sucking at the banks like an animal trying to find its way in. He saw that people lived their own lives, went their own way. They grew up and lived lives that did not take him into consideration.

I don't want to argue, Bonedaddy said, patient as a teacher explaining something to a pupil who was a little slow. Matter of fact I come down here to avoid it. But there's catfish in this river six or eight feet long, what they tell me. And if you don't think I'll shoot you and feed you to them then you need to say so right now.

The hand had taken up the pistol. When it started around its arc was interrupted by Scribner swinging the ball bat. He swung from the ground up as hard as he could, like a batter trying desperately for the outfield wall. The pistol fired once and went skittering away. Bonedaddy made some sort of muffled grunt and crumpled in the leaves. The old man looked at the bat in his hands, at Bonedaddy lying on his back. His hands were flexing. Loosening, clasping. They loosened nor would they clasp again. His head looked like something a truck had run over. Scribner glanced at the bat in mild surprise, then turned and threw it in the river. Somewhere off in the milk-white fog the throaty horn of a barge sounded, lights arced through the murk vague as lights seen in the muddy depths of the river.

He dragged Bonedaddy to the cabin then up the steps and inside. There was a five-gallon can of kerosene and he soaked the floors with it, hurled it at the walls. He lit it with a torch from the campfire. With another he searched for blood in the leaves. Bonedaddy's half-drunk beer was propped against a weathered husk of stump, and for a reason he couldn't name Scribner picked it up and drank it and slung the bottle into the river.

He stayed to see that everything burned. When the roof caught, an enormous cedar lowering onto it burst into flame and burned white-hot as a magnesium flare, sparks rushing skyward in the roaring updraft, like a pillar of fire God had inexplicably set against the wet, black bluff.

Hey, he said, trying to shake Rabon awake.

Rabon came awake reluctantly, his hands trying to fend the old man away. Scribner kept shaking him roughly. Get up, he said. Rabon sat up in bed rubbing his eyes. What is it? What's the matter?

I killed a feller, Scribner said.

Rabon was instantly alert. What the hell are you talking about? He was looking all about the room as if he might see some out-stretched burglar run afoul of the old man.

A feller named Willard Pulley. Folks called him Bonedaddy. I killed him with Alton's baseball bat and set him afire. Must be twenty years ago. He had a shiny little pistol he kept wavin in my face.

Are you crazy? You had a bad dream, you never killed anybody. Go back to sleep.

I ain't been asleep, Scribner said.

Rabon was looking at his watch. It's two o'clock in the morning, he said, as if it were the deadline for something. The old man was watching Rabon's eyes. Something had flickered there when he had mentioned Willard Pulley but he couldn't put a name to what he had seen: anger, apprehension, fear. Then it all smoothed into irritation, an expression Scribner was so accustomed to seeing that he had no difficulty interpreting it.

You know who I'm talkin about?

Of course I know who you're talking about. You must have had a nightmare about him because we were talking about Karen. He did once live with Karen, but nobody killed him, nobody set him afire, as you put it. He was just a young drunk and now he's an old drunk. It hasn't been a week since I saw him lounging against the front of the City Café, the way he's done for twenty-five years. You were dreaming.

I ain't been asleep, Scribner said, but he had grown uncertain even about this. His mind had gone over to the other side where the enemy camped, truth that had once been hard-edged as stone had turned ephemeral and evasive. Subject to gravity, it ran through the cracks and pooled on the floorboards like quicksilver. He was reduced to studying people's eyes for the reaction to something he had said, trying to mirror truth in other people's faces.

In the days following, a dull rage possessed him. Nor would it abate. He felt ravaged, violated. Somewhere along the line his life had been stolen. Some hand furtive as a pickpocket's had taken everything worth taking and he hadn't even missed it. Ellen and his children and a house that was his own had fallen by the wayside. He was left bereft and impotent, dependent upon the whims and machinations of others. Faceless women prodded him with needles, spooned tasteless food into him, continually downloaded an endless supply of pills even horses couldn't swallow. The pills kept coming, as if these women were connected directly to their source, so that no matter how many he ingested there was always a full tray waiting atop the bureau. He pondered upon all this and eventually the pickpocket had a face as well as a hand. The puppeteer controlling all these strings was Rabon.

At noon a nameless woman in a dusty Bronco brought him a Styrofoam tray of food. He sat down in Rabon's recliner in the living room and prepared to eat. A mouthful of tasteless mashed potatoes clove to his palate, grew rubbery and enormous so that he could not swallow it. He spat it onto the carpet. This is the last goddamned straw, he said. All his life he'd doubled up on the salt and pepper and now the food everyone brought him was cooked without benefit of grease or seasoning. There was a compartment of poisonous-looking green peas and he began to pick them up one by one and flick them at the television screen. Try not to get this all over everything, he said.

When the peas were gone he carried the tray to the kitchen. He raked the carrots and mashed potatoes into the sink and found a can of peas in a cabinet and opened them with an electric can opener. Standing in the living room doorway he began to fling handfuls of them onto the carpet, scattering them about the room as if he were sowing them.

When the peas were gone he got the tray of pills and went out into the back yard. The tray was compartmentalized, Monday, Tuesday, all the days of the week. He dumped them all together as if time had no further significance, as if all days were one.

Rabon had a motley brood of scraggly-looking chickens that were foraging for insects near a split-rail fence, and Scribner began to throw handfuls of pills at them. They ran excitedly about pecking up the pills and searching for more. Get em while they're hot, the old man called. These high-powered vitamins'll have you sailin like hawks and singin like mockinbirds.

He went in and set the tray in its accustomed place. From the bottom of the closet he took up the plastic box he used for storing his tapes. Wearing the look of a man burning the last of his bridges, he began to unspool them, tugging out the thin tape until a shell was empty, discarding it and taking up another. At length they were all empty. He sat on the bed with his hands on his knees. He did not move for a long time, his eyes black and depthless and empty-looking, ankle-deep in dead bluegrass musicians and shredded mandolins and harps and flattop guitars, in old lost songs nobody wanted anymore.

Rabon was standing in the doorway wiping crushed peas off the soles of his socks. The old man lay on the bed with his fingers laced behind his skull watching Rabon through slitted eyes.

What the hell happened in the living room? Where did all those peas come from?

A bunch of boys done it, Scribner said. Broke in here. Four or five of the biggest ones held me down and the little ones throwed peas all over the front room.

Do you think this is funny? Rabon asked.

Hell no. You try bein held down by a bunch of boys and peas throwed all over the place. See if you think it's funny. I tried to run em off but I'm old and weak and they overpowered me.

We'll see how funny it is from the door of the old folks' home, Rabon said. Or the crazyhouse. Rabon was looking at the medicine tray. What happened to all those pills?

The chickens got em, Scribner said.

The going was slower than he had expected and by the time the chert road topped out at the crossroads where the blacktop ran it was ten o'clock and the heat was malefic. The treeline shimmered like something seen through bad glass and the blacktop radiated heat upward as if somewhere beneath it a banked fire smoldered.

He stood for a time in the shade of a pin oak debating his choices. He was uncertain about going on, but then again it was a long way back. When he looked down the road the way he had come, the perspiration burning his eyes made the landscape blur in and out of focus like something with a provisional reality, like something he'd conjured but could not maintain. After a while he heard a car, then saw its towed slipstream of dust, and when it stopped for the sign at the crossroads he was standing on the edge of the road leaning on his stick.

The face of the woman peering out the car window at him was familiar but he could call no name to mind. He was wearing an old brown fedora and he tipped the brim of it in a gesture that was almost courtly.

Mr. Scribner, what are you doing out in all this heat?

Sweatin a lot, Scribner said. I need me a ride into town if you're goin that far.

Why of course, the woman said. Then a note of uncertainty

crept into her voice. But aren't you . . . where is Rabon? We heard you were sick. Are you supposed to be going to town?

I need to get me a haircut and a few things. There ain't nothin the matter with me, either. That boy's carried me to doctors all over Tennessee and can't none of em kill me.

If you're sure it's all right, she said, moving her purse off the passenger seat to make room. Get in here where it's air-conditioned before you have a stroke.

He got out on the town square of Ackerman's Field and stood for a moment sizing things up, getting his bearings. He crossed at the traffic light and went on down the street to the City Café by some ingrained habit older than the sense of strangeness the town had acquired.

In midmorning the place was almost deserted, three stools occupied by drunks he vaguely recognized, bleary-eyed sots with nowhere else to be. He sat down at the bar, just breathing in the atmosphere: the ancient residue of beer encoded into the very woodwork, sweat, the intangible smell of old violence. There was something evocative about it, almost nostalgic. The old man had come home.

He laid his hat on the counter and studied the barman across from him. Let me have two tall Budweisers, he said, already fumbling at his wallet. He had it in a shirt pocket and the pocket itself secured with a large safety pin. It surprised him that the beer actually appeared, Skully sliding back the lid of the cooler and turning with two frosty cans of Budweiser and setting them on the formica bar. The old man regarded them with mild astonishment. Well now, he said. He fought an impulse to look over his shoulder and see was Rabon's rubbery face pressed to the glass watching him.

You got a mouse in your pocket, Mr. Scribner? a grinning Skully asked him.

No, it's just me myself, Scribner said, still struggling clumsily with the safety pin. He had huge hands grown stiff and clumsy and he couldn't get it unlatched. I always used one to chase the other one with.

I ain't seen you in here in a long time.

That boy keeps me on a pretty tight leash. I just caught me a ride this mornin and came to town. I need me a haircut and a few things.

You forget that money, Skully said. I ain't taking it. These are on the house for old time's sake.

Scribner had the wallet out. He extracted a bill and smoothed it carefully on the bar. He picked up one of the cans and drank from it, his Adam's apple convulsively pumping the beer down, the can rattling emptily when he set it atop the bar. He turned and regarded the other three drinkers with a benign magnanimity, his eyes slightly unfocused. Hidy boys, he said.

How you, Mr. Scribner?

He slid the bill across to Skully. I thank you for the beer, he said. Let me buy them high-binders down the bar a couple.

There was a flurry of goodwill from the drunks downbar toward this big spender from the outlands and the old man accepted their thanks with grace and drank down the second can of beer.

We heard you was sick and confined to your son's house, Skully said. You look pretty healthy to me. What's supposed to be the matter with you?

I reckon my mind's goin out on me, Scribner said. It fades in and out like a weak TV station. I expect to wake up some mornin with no mind atall. There ain't nothin wrong with me, though. He hit himself in the chest with a meaty fist. I could still sweep this place out on a Saturday night. You remember when I used to do that.

Yes I do.

I just can't remember names. What went with folks. All last week I was thinkin about this old boy I used to see around. Name of Willard Pulley. I couldn't remember what become of him. Folks called him Bonedaddy.

Let me see, now, Skully said.

He's dead, one of the men down the bar said.

Scribner turned so abruptly the stool spun with him and he almost fell. What? he asked.

He's dead. He got drunk and burnt hisself up down on the Tennessee River. Must be over twenty years ago.

Wasn't much gone, another said. He ain't no kin to you is he?

No, no, I just wondered what become of him. And say he's dead sure enough?

All they found was ashes and bones. That's as dead as I ever want to be.

I got to get on, the old man said. He rose and put on his hat and shoveled his change into a pocket and took up his stick.

When the door closed behind him with its soft chime, one of the drunks said, There goes what's left of a hell of a man. I've worked settin trusses with him where the foreman would have three men on one end and just him on the other. He never faded nothin.

He wasn't lying about cleaning this place out, either, Skully said. He'd sweep it out on a Saturday night like a longhandled broom but he never started nothin. He'd set and mind his own business. Play them old songs on the jukebox. It didn't pay to fuck with him though.

The old man sat in the barber chair, a towel wound about his shoulders and he couldn't remember what he wanted. I need a, he said, and the word just wasn't there. He thought of words, inserting them into the phrase and trying them silently in his mind to see if they worked. I need a picket fence, a bicycle, a heating stove. The hot blood of anger and humiliation suffused his throat and face.

What kind of haircut you want, Mr. Scribner?

A haircut, the old man said in relief. Why hell yes. That's what I want, a haircut. Take it all off. Let me have my money's worth.

All of it?

Just shear it off.

When Scribner left, his buzzcut bullet head was hairless as a cue ball and the fedora cocked at a jaunty angle. He drank two more beers at Skully's, then thought he'd amble down to the courthouse lawn and see who was sitting on the benches there. When he stood on the sidewalk, the street suddenly yawned before him as if he were looking down the sides of a chasm onto a stream of dark water pebbled with moonlight. He'd already commenced his step and when he tried to retract it he overbalanced and pitched into the street. He tried to catch himself with his palms, but his head still rapped the asphalt solidly, and lights flickered on and off behind his eyes. He dragged himself up and was sitting groggily on the sidewalk when Skully came out the door.

Skully helped him up and seated him against the wall. I done called the ambulance, he said. He retrieved Scribner's hat and set it carefully in the old man's lap. Scribner sat and watched the blood running off his hands. Somewhere on the outskirts of town a siren began, the approaching *whoop whoop whoop* like some alarm the old man had inadvertently triggered that was homing in on him.

All this silence was something the old man was apprehensive about. Rabon hadn't even had much to say when, still in his schoolteaching suit, he had picked Scribner up at the emergency room. Once he had ascertained that the old man wasn't seriously hurt he had studied his new haircut and his bandaged hands and said, I believe this is about it for me.

He hadn't even gone in to teach the next day. He had stayed in his bedroom with the door locked, talking on the telephone. Scribner could hear the rise and fall of the mumbling voice but even with an ear to the door he could distinguish no word. It was his opinion that Rabon was calling one old folks' home after another trying to find one desperate enough to take him, and he had no doubt that sooner or later he would succeed.

The day drew on strange and surreal. His life was a series of instants, each one of which bore no relation to the one preceding, the one following. He was reborn moment to moment. He had long taken refuge in the past, but time had proven laden with deadfalls he himself had laid long ago, with land mines that were better not stepped on. So he went further back, to the land of his childhood, where everything lay under a troubled truce. Old voices long silenced by the grave spoke again, their ancient timbres and cadences unchanged by time, by death itself. He was bothered by the image of the little man in the green checked suit and the derby hat, rapping the spotted dog with a malacca cane and saying: I just hate a dog at a funeral, don't you? Who the hell was that? Scribner wondered, the dust of old lost roads coating his bare feet, the sun of another constellation warming his back.

He looked out the window and dark had come without his knowing it. A heavy-set man in wire-rimmed glasses brought a tray of food. Scribner did not even wonder who this might be. The man was balding and when he stooped to arrange the tray, Scribner could see the clean pink expanse of scalp through the combed-over hair. The man went out of the room. Scribner, looking up from his food, saw him cross through the hall with a bundle of letters and magazines. He went into Rabon's room and closed the door.

Scribner finished the plate of food without tasting it.

He might have slept. He came to himself lying on the bed, the need to urinate so intense it was almost painful. He got up. He could hear a television in the living room, see the spill of yellow light from Rabon's bedroom, the bathroom.

His bandaged hands made undoing his clothing even more complicated and finally he just pulled down his pajama bottoms, the stream of urine already starting, suddenly angry at Rabon, why the hell has he got all his plunder in the bathroom, these shoes, suits, these damned golf clubs?

Goddamn, a voice cried. The old man whirled. Rabon was standing in the hall with the *TV Guide* in his hand. His eyes were wide with an almost comical look of disbelief. My golf shoes, he said, flinging the *TV Guide* at Scribner's bullet head and rushing toward him. Turning his head, the old man realized that he was standing before Rabon's closet, urinating on a rack of shoes.

When Rabon's weight struck him he went sidewise and fell heavily against the wall, his penis streaking the carpet with urine. He slid down the wall and struggled to a kneeling position, trying to get his pajama bottoms up, a fierce tide of anger rising behind his eyes.

Rabon was mad too, in fact angrier than the old man had ever seen him. He had jerked up the telephone and punched in a series of numbers, stood with the phone clasped to his ear and a furious impatient look on his face, an expression that did not change until the old man struck him in the side of the head with an enormous fist. The phone flew away and when Rabon hit the floor with the old man atop him, Scribner could hear it gibbering mechanically at him from the carpet.

The hot, clammy flesh was distasteful to his naked body but Scribner had never been one to shirk what had to be done. With Rabon's face clasped to his breast and his powerful arms locked in a vise that tightened, they looked like perverse lovers spending themselves on the flowered carpet.

When Rabon was still, the old man got up, pushing himself erect against Rabon's slack shoulder. He went out the bedroom door and through a room where a television set flickered, his passage applauded by canned laughter from the soundtrack, and so out into the night.

Night air cool on his sweaty skin. A crescent moon like a sliver of bone cocked above the treeline, whippoorwills calling out of the musky keep of the trees. He stood for a moment sensing directions and then he struck out toward the whippoorwills. He went down into the hollow through the herd of plywood cattle pale as the ghosts of cattle and on toward the voices that called out of the dark. He came onto the spectral roadbed and crossed into deeper woods. The whippoorwills were drawing away from him, urging him deeper into the shadowed timber, and he realized abruptly that the voices were coming from the direction of Brown's Ferry or Deep Elm. Leaning against the bole of a white oak to catch his breath he became aware of a presence in the woods before him, and he saw with no alarm that it was a diminutive man in a green plaid suit, derby hat shoved back rakishly over a broad pale forehead, gesturing him on with a malacca cane.

They're up here, the little man called.

Scribner went on, barefoot, his thin pajama bottoms shredding in the undergrowth of winter huckleberry bushes. Past a stand of stunted cedars the night opened up into an enormous tunnel, as wide and high as he could see, a tunnel of mauve-black gloom where whippoorwills darted and checked like bats feeding on the wing, a thousand, ten thousand, each calling to him out of the dark, and he and the man with the malacca cane paused and sat for a time against a tree trunk to rest themselves before going on.

———————

William Gay was born in middle Tennessee. After traveling extensively in his youth, he returned to and now resides in rural Tennessee near his birthplace. His work has appeared in *The Missouri Review* and *The Georgia Review*, and a novel, *The Long Home*, is forthcoming. He is currently at work on another novel and a collection of short fiction.

RENEE LEONARD

*A*n old man with Alzheimer's was telling me a story about a place he had once lived. In his mind he could see it with great clarity, the way the light fell, the flowers his late wife had planted. I asked him where the place was, and he grew confused. He didn't know. The memory seemed cut off and isolated. Nothing led up to it, nothing led away. He became frustrated, and finally angry at his own impotence. I felt an enormous empathy for him, and the same sense of impotence. Maybe that feeling of empathy and impotence seeped into the story. I hope it did.

Richard Bausch

MISSY

(from *Five Points*)

One catastrophe after another, her father said, meaning her. She knew she wasn't supposed to hear it. But she was alone in that big drafty church house, with just him and Iris, the maid. He was an Episcopal minister, a widower. Other women came in, one after another, all on approval, though no one ever said anything —Missy was six, and seven and eight, and he wanted her to make judgments for him about who he would settle on, who would be her mother. Terrifying. She lay in bed in the dark, dreading the next visit, these big women looking her over, until she understood that they were nervous around her, saw what she could do. Something hardened inside her, under the skin. It was beautiful because it made the fear go away. Women with large bosoms and a smell of fake flowers about them came to the house. She threw fits. She was horrid to them all.

One April evening, Iris stood out on the back stoop, smoking a cigarette. Missy looked at her through the screen door. "Your daddy's a nice Southern gentleman," Iris said. "Might as well be 1952." She laughed as if it wasn't much fun to laugh. She was dark as the spaces between the stars, and in the late light there was almost a blue cast to her brow and hair. "You know what kind of place you livin' in, girl?"

"Yes."

Iris blew smoke. "You don't know *yet.*" She smoked the cigarette and didn't talk for a time. But she kept staring. "Girl, if he settles on somebody, you ain't gonna have me around no more. You gonna be sorry to see me go?"

Missy didn't answer. It was secret. People had a way of saying things to her that she thought she understood, but couldn't be sure of. She was very precocious. Her mother had been dead since the day she was born. It was Missy's fault. She didn't remember that anyone had said this to her but she knew it anyway, in her bones.

Iris smiled her white smile, but now Missy saw tears in her eyes. This fascinated her. It was the same feeling as knowing that her daddy was a minister, but walked back and forth sleepless in the sweltering nights. If your heart was peaceful, you didn't have trouble going to sleep. Iris had said something like that very thing to a friend of hers who stopped by on her way to the Baptist Church. Missy hid behind doors, listening. She did this kind of thing a lot. She watched everything, everyone. She saw when her father pushed Iris up against the wall near the front door and put his face on hers. She saw how disturbed they got, pushing against each other. And later, she heard Iris talking to her Baptist friend. "He ain't always thinkin' about the savior." The Baptist friend squealed, then whispered low and frightened-sounding, but still trying not to laugh.

Now, Iris tossed the cigarette and shook her head, the tears still running. Missy curtsied without meaning it. "Child," said Iris. "What you gonna grow up to be and do? You gonna be just like all the rest of them."

"No." Missy said, just to say it. She was not really sure who the rest of them were.

"Well, you'll miss me until you forget me," said Iris, wiping her eyes.

Missy pushed open the screen door and said, "Hugs."

When Iris went away and swallowed lye and got taken to the hospital, Missy's father didn't sleep at all for five nights. Peaking from her bedroom door, with the chilly guilty dark looming behind her, she saw him standing under the hallway light, running his hands through his thick hair. His face was twisted; the shadows made him look like someone else. He was crying.

She didn't cry. And she did not feel afraid. She felt very gigantic and strong. She had caused everything.

———————

Richard Bausch is the author of twelve volumes of fiction, including the novels *Good Evening Mr. & Mrs. American and All the Ships at Sea* and *In the Night Season* and four story collections. A new collection of stories, *Someone to Watch Over Me,* is due out in April 1999. His short fiction has appeared in *The Atlantic Monthly, Esquire, The New Yorker, Playboy, Harper's,* and other magazines and has been widely anthologized. Recently elected to the Fellowship of Southern Writers, he is Heritage Professor of Writing at George Mason University and lives in rural Virginia with his wife Karen and their five children.

This story started as an exercise — to see if I could tell a story in only 750 words or less. I confess that I have never really liked the concept of so-called "sudden" fiction. I once asked readers of an anthology review I edited to imagine sudden sex as an analogy, and said I preferred the slow hand. I liked — and still like — long stories, what Peter Taylor once called "an evening's entertainment." But if there's one thing I've learned over the years (and it may indeed be the only thing), it's that one shouldn't shut off any avenues of exploration when it comes to writing prose fiction. So I wrote several of them, one of which is "Missy" — and discovered that when a story is compressed so much, the matter of it tends to require more size: that is, in order to make it work in so small a space, its true subject must be proportionately larger. At least I found that to be so.

George Singleton

CAULK

(from *Shenandoah*)

Elaine insisted on more silicone, and I stood my ground at least twenty-four hours on how she didn't need it. I said there was a reason for honest ventilation, for breathing, and that too much silicone would hamper this process. I mentioned how it would be obvious to her both winter and summer, when everything unnatural in the world either contracted or expanded. This was fall—late October—in South Carolina. At noon the temperature got up to the mid-seventies, but the humidity was a low 60 percent. There existed no other time to paint a house.

"If you don't caulk right then you'll have to do the job again before the year's out," Elaine said. "I know what I'm doing, Louis. Remember—I lived in Mexico City the spring semester of my junior year in college."

I didn't get the connection. We stood outside. I held a caulk gun in my right hand, with about half of the tube gone. It was the first one of the third case. I turned the lever down so no silicone spilled out, so caulk didn't exude out on my beat-up nonamebrand tennis shoes, making me undergo flashbacks of a time at the Auto Drive-In with my first high school girlfriend who almost gave it up. I said, "I've caulked every goddamn seam, Elaine. I've caulked boards that were welded together—that were petrified, by God—and needed caulk about as much as a goat needs a can opener."

Elaine held nothing. She stood with her hands on her hips and looked at the soffit and fascia. She looked at a point twenty feet off the ground and said, "You didn't smooth that bead down. You missed a spot."

This was near dusk. Elaine had come home from work hoping to find me—I know—not working on the house like I'd promised. Some time earlier in the week I'd been drinking, and as drinkers might be wont to do, I'd said the house needed painting unless we wanted someone like Andrew Wyeth hanging out in the front yard thinking we lived in a weather-beaten barn, and that I didn't have much else to do seeing as I'd gotten mad at my last boss and quit a job driving oxygen cannisters around to hackers and wheezers. Elaine said, "It needs to be scraped and caulked hard, Louis. Why don't you let me hire someone to do the job right. There's no need to even talk about it if you don't feel committed to do the job right."

Of course I took all her talk to be a challenge, and didn't understand that she knew how to wind me up like a cheap metal mouse that skitters across linoleum floors. I said, "Why would a complete painting stranger care about how this house turns out?" I felt my one eye starting to travel off. We stood outside, still. I pretended to check the soffit and fascia, too. I said, "Personally I think I'm ready to paint tomorrow. If you want, I'll go over the whole house again with caulk."

And I meant it. In my mind, a person scraped flaked paint and caulked up holes, buckled seams, roof flashings, door casings and paid special attention to window frames. That's what I did the first day. The goddamn house was airtight, but if she wanted more caulk, then I'd do it.

Elaine said, "You weren't drinking up on that ladder, were you?" She took my caulk gun, turned the lever 180 degrees, and shot an invisible indention underneath one of the living room windows. Elaine rubbed it four directions, then handed the tube back.

"There's no telling what somebody might charge to paint this place. I don't even know anyone who knows an honest painter.

They say to never let a roofer around your wife, and never let a painter near your liquor cabinet." I felt my eye wander back even with the other. I'd drunk about half a bottle of Old Crow during the day. There are two theories: don't drink and don't fall off the ladder, or go ahead and drink hard so it won't hurt so much in case you do fall.

I've tried both in the past. The second's best. When I worked construction one summer in college sober, I pulled back a shutter where a small but nervous clan of bats nestled daytime. They flew out. I fell off. This is no lie: on the way down the entire history of French literature passed before my eyes. When I hit the ground I got out the "Bo" from "Baudelaire," but nothing else.

Most times when Elaine went off on two-day business trip seminars in order for her to push what she pushed, namely new and improved kitchen accessories—there are more conventions held on blenders and whatnot than the average person thinks—I'd either find a way to get time off from my job delivering oxygen, or I'd stay home looking out the venetian blinds to see if Elaine hired a detective to see if I left or invited dancing escort women over. But this last time I didn't get an invitation to go with her, even though I'd quit my job and had the time.

"We're doing a fair in Atlanta," Elaine said. "We got I don't know how many rooms downstairs at the Omni to show off the new products. They're saying every new micro-brewery pub is sending someone to check out our line of mid-sized Hemingway sampler stemware."

I said, "Huh. Not to mention the zucchini thing." What else could a caulking boy say? Elaine's company had developed a slicer/dicer/skinner mechanism that worked so clean and easy they thought it might change Americans' attitudes and diets. Me, I couldn't tell the difference between zucchini, cucumbers, or dill pickles. I didn't care to cook or eat any of them, either. As far as the Hemingway line—I'm glad Elaine's company didn't market a set of *shot* glasses.

I said, "Well you have a good time, dear. Don't go down to Underground Atlanta all by yourself. Don't show up at the Cheetah 3 with your friends just because women get in a strip joint free."

Elaine rolled her eyes. She said, "I won't have any time off, Louis. And if I did—like maybe if there's a blackout and we can't showcase our wares—I'd find a museum."

"If there's a blackout it might be hard to look at art," I said. It just came to me, fast. Sometimes I thought that maybe those oxygen cannisters leaked, and gave me extra brain cells or something.

Elaine said, "Caulk. Don't start painting until I get back. I'll call you when I check in at the hotel."

She kissed me on the mouth, but didn't mean it. This happened once a month. I knew she had cutlery on her mind. Me, I could only get out, "If you're going to talk the talk, you better caulk the caulk," like an idiot.

I'd still be married if it weren't for the weather. As any reputable caulk tube will point out, caulk cannot be used at temperatures below 5 degrees centigrade, which is 40 degrees Fahrenheit. In a way, Canada's to blame. If that big arctic swoop they show during the weather map segment had moved south of Appalachia while Elaine went to Atlanta, then we'd still be together, I'm sure. Whereas it got down to the low 20s in places like Johnson City, Tennessee, it stayed in the low 70s in the upstate of South Carolina—prime caulking weather.

Elaine went off, and I got to work. I finished the last eleven tubes of the third case, and then I called a local hardware joint and got them to deliver another dozen cases and put it on Elaine's bill. I brought Jason the delivery boy inside and we feasted on canned smoked oysters and Bloody Marys before I got back to work on the house.

I said, "My wife seems to think a wooden house needs a layer of caulk before it gets painted," and handed him some ground *habañero* peppers for his drink. Jason looked like a college kid going to a Baptist school, but this was a Friday morning and he

wasn't in class. Later on I thought how he looked a little like someone I saw on television who was a member of a white supremacy mi-
litia group.

"A lot of people use primer," he said.

"Exactly! You prime the wood, and then you paint it," I said.

This is no lie: Jason poured a quarter teaspoon of ground *habañero* on his thumb, then snorted it. Jason said, "Pain. Pain's good
so you remember pleasure. That's one of my mottoes."

I poured another drink and put it away. I poured another drink
and put it away. I'd made a pitcher, and made a mistake. I didn't
want a delivery boy dead on my hands with hot peppers up his
nose. I said, "Prime, paint."

"Well, technically, you only prime new wood, man. Or new
sheetrock. After your house's been painted, I wouldn't prime it
again. Maybe that's just me," Jason said. I looked across the table
at him and thought, How can a twelve-year-old get a job as a delivery boy? Jason said, "I only work weekdays, you know. I help
out my friends doing jobs they're doing—not as a gopher, either.
If you need help caulking and you're willing to pay, I'd be glad to
help you out. I can get you references." He nodded up and down
ten times.

I poured the last of the pitcher and said, "Am I the only delivery
you have today? Here." I handed Jason ten bucks for a tip. I said,
"No. This job is something I have to do myself."

Jason sat there with his first drink still full and a red powdery
stain on his upper lip. He said, "I understand, dude."

I said, "Say, do you have any other mottoes?"

He didn't blink. He said, "Paining others gives pleasure, too."

That night I slept without my wife. Every light, television, radio
and appliance stayed on. The evening low was 52 degrees.

I cut half of the nipples down two inches, and the others only
a half centimeter. I needed thick, thick beads and I needed ones
so thin I could've worked in Hollywood as a makeup artist for vil-

lains and swashbucklers. I put the twenty-foot extension ladder up at the far gable and set my stepladder against the front of the house. There was no need for dropcloths.

When I got four feet down the house, squeezing wide rows of caulk, I'm sure the bees showed up only because they thought it was the biggest albino hive ever. There are different caulks, I'm sure, but I stuck with siliconized acrylic white. If I'd've used a gray color, then wasps would've shown up, thinking our house was one big paper nest.

My right forearm hurt and pulsed like the furthest moon of Jupiter, and at times I thought the four triggering fingers I used might cramp into a claw so hard no middle-weight boxing champion would have a chance with me. I did not think of Elaine flirting with men from Minnesota who owned slight restaurant chains, with men who didn't come so much for the spectacular as they came for the spectacle—let me say now that I know my wife got hired for her physical attributes more than she did for her culinary or home ec. prowess. Elaine majored in anthropology, for Christ's sake, and I know for certain she spent her first year in college as a pom-pom girl.

Our house was thick and white, is what I'm saying, by Sunday night when Elaine came back. She only got a sweeping glimpse of it when she turned her car into the driveway. At the door I said, "Hey! You got back safely. You cheated Death again."

Elaine said, "There must've been too many cars coming my way in the opposite direction. You didn't paint the house all white, did you?"

I grabbed my wife's suitcase. I shuttled her inside as quickly as possible. This was the exact moment when I thought maybe I'd gone too far, out of meanness. I said, "Did people like y'all's products?"

"The house looked really white," Elaine said. She tried to turn around, but I pushed her toward the inside. "I could see our house from way far away," she said. "There's a glow."

"Life in the big city," I said. "Boy, that really seems to change your way of looking at things. Of seeing things. Of your outlook on what is real and what isn't."

I held my wife's suitcase. She held a handful of her company's pamphlets. Ten minutes after I closed the door it got steamy in the house, for reasons other than a wife returning from a business trip.

Elaine saw nothing wrong the next morning. When I awoke due to a cramp in my forearm, Elaine stood above me in her robe at an hour past dawn. She held an eight-inch-wide brush in her hand and said, "You can start now." In her other hand, she held a blazer outfit she always wore to work, as if she went out to either sell real estate or lead a group of drunks from intervention to commital.

I said, "It's supposed to rain today." It's the first thing that came to me.

"No it's not. I just watched the local news while I dried my hair. It's supposed to be warm again." Elaine brushed something invisible from her jacket.

I said, "How could you hear the weather report with a blow-dryer on? I think you heard wrong. There's no way you could hear anything right with a blow-dryer on."

Elaine smiled, but didn't show her teeth. She grinned. She said, "I went outside to get the paper. I bet it's ninety degrees out now."

Lookit: I swear it doesn't get 90 degrees at dawn in South Carolina during October. There might be 90 percent humidity. It might get to 90 degrees by two o'clock in the afternoon, but not before sunlight. One time my grandmother on my father's side said it reached 110 and rained simultaneously on Christmas day, 1950, but at that point she'd gone through both radiation and chemotherapy—she liked to pull the top of her dress down and show the cavity where one breast had existed, then say how smoking was bad for you.

I got up and said to my wife, "Did you look at the house?"

"I'm so happy you gave in," she said. "Let me say now that I thought I'd come home and find that you hadn't done anything since I left. I'm sorry. I didn't think you'd caulk the house right." Elaine walked into the laundry room.

I stood in my boxer shorts, sober. I said, "It's a joke, you idiot! I caulked every square inch of the house. It looks like a Dairy Queen treat from the road. Yesterday an Eskimo family happened by and asked me the name of our contractor—they said they'd been looking for an igloo like ours ever since they left Lapland, or wherever."

Understand, I caught myself hyperventilating, and my bad eye strayed off even though it was morning and I'd not partaken yet. Elaine came back in the room wearing a pair of bicycle shorts so tight she showed camel-lips. I didn't realize that everything was out of sync. Why did she take a shower and wash her hair before exercising? Elaine held five-pound weights in her hands and said, "What? One-two, one-two, one-two."

I came inside from almost painting to find Elaine on the telephone with her college roommate Amy. They planned their tenth reunion. Elaine laughed too much, I thought, as I came up from behind her. Elaine said, "Well I wouldn't know how to react to an uncircumcised man, either. I've only seen one once."

I tried to step back out of the room, but made a noise. The floor creaked, is what I'm saying, and you'd think somebody who lived there—namely my wife, Elaine—would've thought to have caulked the area.

Elaine hung up without saying good-bye or anything. She just put down the phone. To me, my wife said, "Hey," and smiled. She could've done a commercial for toothpaste or dental floss.

I said, "Is there a problem with the phone lines? If you want me to do it, I'll call the telephone company and say our phone's gone out."

Elaine stood up erect. She'd put on the business suit. "That's okay," she said.

"I couldn't call the telephone company if our line was out, stupid!" I said.

Elaine said, "Louis, there're men who don't play this game always. I thought you were outside painting the house."

What could I say? I knew there were other men out there—younger, better-looking men—who didn't have the advantage of taking a logic course on the college level. I don't want to come off as superior or anything, but I've noticed how people without four-year college educations tend to buy more mobile homes percentage-wise, and how people like me have noticed that acts of nature, viz. tornadoes, knock over trailers. Of course they didn't scrape, caulk, and paint wood, granted.

I said, "So you looking for a man who ain't circumcised, is that what you want? I guess that's what you want." I'd put minibottles in the gutter the night before. I said, "Four fat men stopped by thinking our house was a shrine to the Michelin man. Did you, by any chance, know that the word *caulk* comes from the word *caucus,* which means just a faction of a political party? It's Greek. It means the whole goddamn house doesn't need doing." This wasn't exactly true, but it sounded right. I was pretty sure the word *caucus* came from some Greek word.

Elaine said, "You're full of crap. Caulk comes from a 304 milliliter tube, which is approximately 10.3 fluid ounces."

I said, "Does Amy have a 10.3 fluid ounce uncircumcised caulk tube she's worried about? Is that what y'all were talking about, Elaine?"

My wife actually giggled. She turned her back towards me. She said, "Uh-huh." Then she went to work, finally, running late.

It's impossible to roll paint right across concentric horizontal loops of siliconized acrylic caulk. After Elaine left I put the brush aside, and rummaged around in the garage until I found an old roller with a nap meant for rough surfaces. My wife wanted the house a hue the paint company paint-namers tabbed Saharan Winter Sand, which most sane individuals outside of the house-painting business would call *tan.* I took my roller and pan and aluminum extension handle outside, and climbed up the long ladder. The beads of caulk were stuck so thick it felt like driving over a Wal-Mart parking lot of speed bumps, one after another. It didn't take me one hard roll up and down to have a flashback of little league baseball and that feeling of bees in the hands when you swing and hit a pitch on the handle. The sound which emanated was not unlike a stick dragged across an expensive, tightly-picketed fence.

"That's a nice mural of the Riverside dirt track stands after a muddy Saturday night," some guy in a Camaro yelled out at me as I stood in the middle of the front yard not admiring my work. I turned around and waved. I laughed, and even thought deep-down how this guy probably knew exactly what I had done to get back at my wife. I watched him ease by slowly, and paid attention to his mouth sag, and thought to myself, now there's a man who's had destiny knock on his forehead more than once before he thought about answering the door.

I thought how maybe the same could be said about me, too, for about three seconds. Then I looked up at the sky for rainclouds, and wondered if rain might wash Saharan Winter Sand down over caulk lips over and over until one smooth façade showed that might satisfy wife, real estate agent, and prospective buyer alike. A thunderstorm wasn't in the forecast, just as Elaine told me. I yelled back, "Come here and tell me that," like fighting words. I knew this guy—I'd seen him over at Compton's store—and he always meant business one way or the other. He was one of the Shirley boys who ran an auto body shop nearby, pushing and pulling dents out of car panels and hoods. Ray Shirley also ran dirt track at Riverside in the modified division. One time I took Elaine over there and everyone jumped out of the stands holding their faces. I said, "Someone farted." What happened in fact was that there was a drunk guy raising hell below us, this old woman had a cannister of mace, she blew the thing in the drunk man's direction and then all hell broke loose. Much like that Canadian arctic wind not showing up on the weather screen, this woman didn't understand how the wind blowing towards her might send spray backwards.

That's what happened. Elaine and I stood there while everyone ran from the bleachers. Elaine said, "What the hell?" like that. We smoked cigarettes and didn't smell or feel a thing. This old guy in a wheelchair up top with us shook his head and said, "Again. It's happened again. When will people understand stock car racing?"

I thought about the double-amputee in the wheelchair at the race track when I returned to the ladder, after the Shirley boy drove off. I thought to myself, there's a way caulk might make his life bearable, if one of those companies came up with a more pliable prosthetic limb.

I got up on the ladder and got my face close, is what I'm saying. This is no lie: I caught myself wondering why a Supreme Being didn't invent regeneration for human beings. And at that moment something picked me off the ladder and threw me to the ground.

I almost broke my hip at age thirty-three.

"You did it all on purpose, Louis. Don't lie to me," Elaine said when she got home. "What'd you do, jump off the ladder? I bet you had to go up that thing ten times and dive off to get a swelling that bad."

I was in a tub of Epsom salts with an ice pack on the side of my ass. It had been years since I'd bruised myself, and I couldn't remember if heat or ice came first. One time ten months before, I crashed the oxygen delivery van into the front of some old guy's house and tore up my knees. This was winter and I'd lost control going down his driveway. He came outside with his walker and handed me two Darvons. I sang in the ambulance, later.

"Is it raining outside yet?" I asked Elaine.

"What did you do to paint the house? Did you get out a little watercolor brush and draw lines?" she asked.

My ice melted. For a second I wondered if I could create a thunderstorm in the bathroom with enough ice and hot water. I said, "I used a roller instead. Then on top of the ladder I looked up and saw these buzzards circling. They thought they'd found a dead polar bear rolled over, I bet. I leaned back, and then fell off, I swear. Help me out of here."

Elaine walked away. I struggled around, then finally slid out over the edge. When my wife returned she said, "Good. I found six fine red sable brushes from when I took that painting class in college. Fill in the gaps, Louis." I think she might've meant that in a double-entendre kind of way, now.

She did. Elaine didn't come back that night, or even the next morning to pick up clothes for work. I waited until noon the next day to call her at work, and then only got an answering machine message about what number to call to order the new chinois with beechwood dowel and stand. Of course I went outside with my tiny brushes and started filling in the white indentions by hand. I knew later that the job wouldn't be so difficult if I'd've only used the eight-inch brush instead of the roller.

Ray Shirley came by and said, "I seen you fall off the ladder. I seen you in the rearview mirror and felt it was part my fault for breaking your concentration."

I said, "My foot slipped." I felt like an idiot holding the artist's brush.

Ray said, "You aim to fill in every spot you missed with that little thing? Goddamn, boy, I didn't think you'd be good on detail work, what with the way you caulked the whole place."

My hip hurt. I'd put Icy-Hot on it earlier, which burned my fingertips, and made it hard to hold the brush, which felt like a thin branding iron in my hand. I said, "Originally I only planned on teaching my wife a lesson. I think she left me, though."

Ray stood on the ground, looking across the street. His Camaro idled chugging in my driveway. He said, "I'm on my third. The first two didn't understand racing. Third one's half blind. She don't get scared watching me ever."

I started to say how I could've used a blind wife—and even got my mouth open to say so—when some hand reached down again and pushed me. I almost broke my other hip, then. Ray stepped out of the way without looking up. He got me to my feet and held my arms over my head so I'd get my breath back. "You seem to be the kind of fellow what needs a job on the ground, son. Hell, you need a job below the ground, like a miner, or a grave digger."

I tried to say, "Or a cave guide," but couldn't get it out.

Out of meanness I finished painting the fouled front of the house, then the rest of it, with the regular paintbrush sideways. The place looked pretty good when I finished. From afar—like maybe two miles away—the ripples weren't even noticeable, and up close it only looked like I'd bought wood cut with dull and wiggly band saws from a lumberyard.

This process took me less than a week. I forget meteorological lingo, but it may have been an Indian summer. What I'm saying is, it was the end of October and early November, and still warm enough to paint at night. There was no need for spotlights. I'm no geologist or chemist, but I bet siliconized acrylic caulk has some kind of phosphorescent properties that make it glow in the dark. I almost needed a welder's mask to see what I did and where I'd been.

In my mind I saw Elaine driving by the house at dawn, checking to see if I covered the caulk adequately. When cars passed by I never turned around for two reasons: I didn't want to make eye contact with my wife, and both my hips seemed fused to the point of petrification. I think there's some kind of toy where this guy goes up and down a ladder, stiff, and I could've modeled for it. I didn't turn around, but I did yell out "Dead man caulking!" more than once, I swear.

Understand, I didn't call Elaine up at work, and made a point not to look in her closet to see if somehow she'd returned while I went out for booze or cigarettes so she could scavenge up all of her low-cut blouses and slit skirts. I didn't pace back and forth, seeing as how I couldn't. Not once did I get on the telephone and call Elaine's parents, her boss at home, her old roommate Amy, various clients I knew she kept an ongoing customer relationship with, the police, or that guy who has a show on TV about missing persons. Somehow I thought maybe Elaine was going through a seven-year itch thing known usually to people like me, and that she'd return in time all apologetic, spiritual, calm, and ready to patch up anything wrong in our relationship. She didn't.

Somehow I knew my wife had given up and left her job. She'd learned about quitting from me. I thought about that poor kid Jason with his mottoes, and wondered if he knew Elaine.

My wife called once and when I said "Hello," she hung up, not remembering we'd gotten that Star 69 device. Elaine had left everything we'd accumulated in order to live with Amy, the woman worried about what uncircumcised people might mean to her future. My wife had moved to *Delaware,* of all places.

I sat in the living room and thought about how this house now stood caulked beyond what full-time caulkers might agree upon.

Ray Shirley finally showed up again and I waddled to the front door and let him inside. He said, "I got people working the pits who don't care as much about life as you do."

"What?" I said.

"I want to ask you if you're working anymore in a real job," Ray said. I know you're not working a real job getting paid and all."

I'd been thinking about oxygen. I'd been thinking about how someone out there needs to start up a business as an oxygen tent caulker, just in case. I said, "I'm working. I don't get paid, but I'm working. It's hard to explain, man."

Ray looked out the front window where my eight-foot stepladder still stood. He said, "I have one word for you."

I said, "Uh-huh."

"Pitman," he said.

My whole life flashed before my eyes, with the exception of the time Baudelaire came to me in college. I said, "Right, pal."

Ray said, "My boy I had working for me down at the garage just quit. He worked Saturday nights when I raced, too. I think you the man I need for the spot he left."

I nodded. There was no way I could afford my tan igloo another year without a job. I'd called my oxygen boss drunk and begging, but he'd found someone stupid and reliable to fill my place. I said, "I don't know anything about cars."

He shook his head sideways. Ray Shirley mentioned how I needed to get over Elaine, and nothing could do it better than learning the intricacies of carburetors, pistons, valves, and timing chains. He said there weren't enough people out there who could fill holes left wide and inviting by people who ran four-way stop signs, or followed too closely. I limped each step outside towards his car, on my way to find my new job, the one he said God called upon me to do.

These days I sit on an upside-down dry-wall bucket, waiting for customers to offer their dinged and dented vehicles. Let me say that I'm not the first person to notice how modern science should've invented a Bondo of sorts by now, to smooth over damage we've done to what still flutters on beneath the rib cage.

George Singleton's fiction has appeared in *New Stories from the South 1994* **and** *1998, Writer's Harvest 2, Shenandoah, Playboy, The North American Review, The Southern Review, New England Review, Carolina Quarterly, The Georgia Review,* **and elsewhere. He lives in Dacusville, South Carolina.**

I said to Glenda, the woman who's put up with me for seven-plus years, "I'll paint the house in September," because I'd kind of quit a teaching job on the spur of the moment — which turned out, probably, to be a hazardous decision but at the time seemed perfectly rational to me — and she said, "Okay."

I got to work. I scraped and rubbed this house down with Clorox. I caulked every hairline gap in the wood. Glenda came home and said, "You didn't caulk enough," and pointed at what looked to me like mere wood grain. I caulked. I spelled things out on the front of the house for when she came home from work.

I thought things up while stranded on the ladder, and the story developed each morning before I went to the hardware store for extra tubes of silicone.

Rick DeMarinis

BORROWED HEARTS

(from *The Antioch Review*)

L eon woke up smelling the past. The past smelled rank, a
funky odor: sex, sweat, and broth, a foul, soupy cafeteria
smell, or worse. He needed to remember it, the time and place
where the smell originated, but could not. It was important, cru-
cial, but it was impossible. He felt like crying, and then he did cry.
He choked back the sobs, but could not hold back the tears. He
was wracked with pointless nostalgia and then by free-floating re-
morse. It made no sense.

He rolled toward Maisy, his wife, thinking she might be the
source of the smell. She was sleeping on her back, snoring lightly
with her mouth open. He leaned close to her face and inhaled
her breath. He slid the blanket down and sniffed her body, beginning with her armpits and moving to her neck and breasts. He
sniffed her navel and pubic tuft. He sniffed her knees, and finally
her feet. But he smelled nothing, not even her sweat. She woke
up, muttering, "What are you *do*ing, Leon? Stop that. Where are
my blankets?"

"Sorry," he said.

"You have to see a doctor," she said. "I mean it."

"It's not medical," he said. "It can't be just a medical thing."

"It *is* medical. It *is* a medical thing."

Maisy got out of bed and found her robe. She grappled with it, looking for the armholes. Leon still desired her, though her belly in recent years had gotten large. It fell like a roll of silver-white dough over the long horizontal scar from a decades-old hysterectomy. The fine geometry of her face was becoming obscured by thickened flesh. Her hair was thin and mostly gray and her eyes had lost the startling blue urgency they'd had when he first met her thirty years ago. Even though she was sixty-six, time's relentless anvil had not been completely punishing. She still evoked the image of the woman he'd married—the dancer with the long-legged twirl, her lean back descending in a subtle arch to the abrupt hillocks of her firm rump, the wide, generous breasts, the smooth neck, and the classic planes and hollows of her lovely face.

The smell that woke him up was fading. It had not come from his wife, he knew that now. Alone in bed, he smelled himself, his pits, his wrists and hands. He was still limber enough to pull his pale white feet up to his nose, but he had no odors at all. The odors—*fumes*, really—that he had smelled hadn't come from anything in his present surroundings. They had come to him from the past, like a memory, a memory without images. The odor lacked a name and the feeling that if he could only pin it down—soup, sweat, candle wax, glue, sulfurous tar, the gamy residue of sex—then something momentous would be revealed to him, something linked to a past event of pivotal importance. But it remained abstract, and by the time he got out of bed and brushed his teeth, it was reduced to a memory of a memory, insubstantial as a pointless dream. None of it made sense.

He joined his wife in the kitchen. She'd already finished making coffee and was reading the paper at the table. He poured himself a cup and sat down. He inhaled the steam rising from his cup but could not smell the good coffee aroma. He went to the pantry and found the can of coffee and removed the plastic lid. He inhaled deeply, his nose almost touching the rich, dark grounds, but he smelled nothing.

"It's completely gone, isn't it? Your sense of smell," Maisy said, studying him now.

He sat down, sipped his coffee. "I could smell it even after I was awake," he said. "It lasted about a minute, then it went. Same smell, every morning. I can't pin it down, but it's so real."

"Something's not right."

"It can't amount to much, Maisy."

"You walk around the house trying to smell things. The other day I saw you light a match and inhale the sulfur. Only someone who couldn't smell would do a thing like that."

"Maybe it's just an allergy, a temporary thing," he said, making a show of inhaling coffee steam with unrestrained pleasure. "The mulberry trees are budding out now. You know how bad that pollen can be."

Maisy sighed. "I don't like being waked up like that, Leon. I don't want you smelling me every morning. It gives me the willies. Something's wrong with you."

"Nothing's wrong with me," Leon said. "I feel fine. A lot of people lose their ability to smell things. I'm sixty-five. I can't see as well as I could twenty years ago, either."

"But you smell phantoms. I want a doctor to look at you just in case. I'm thinking a neurologist."

"It isn't a medical problem," he said. "How could it be a medical problem?"

"Milder symptoms than that are medical. I'm going to call the clinic." Maisy had been an army nurse, and had served in Korea and then again, after an interlude as a surgical nurse in Tucson, in Vietnam.

Leon chuckled, shaking his head, but it was an act. He felt like crying again. It was frightening, this sudden deprivation of one of his senses. He remembered being inducted into the army, a hundred naked boys bending over and spreading their cheeks for the examining doctors, the overpowering anal stink misting his eyes and making him gag. Oh! if only he could smell those scared young sphincters again!

The loss was frightening, but it was more frightening that he would receive powerful smells in his dreams, smells that were so

insistent that he woke up with them still present, his heart pounding and his mind reaching back for something in the distant past
that cried out for recognition. It was like a blind man waking up
from strongly textured visual dreams in which an unidentifiable
scene from his past presented itself and continued to present itself
in the minutes after he was fully awake, mimicking restored sight.

Maisy opened the morning paper. "I think you're having seizures of some kind," she said, scanning headlines.

Leon put on his sweats and walked down to the work-out room,
angry at Maisy's casual diagnosis, a diagnosis that implied a serious
medical condition. He looked forward to working out his anger on
the weight machine. One of the reasons they had moved to this
new retirement community—Sierra del Monte—was the splendid
exercise facilities. A personal trainer was available, but Leon preferred to work out using his own routine. The trainer held group
sessions in the afternoon. Leon worked out in the morning.

Dick Drake was standing in front of the universal gym when
Leon arrived. Dick was a big man with long, scraggly white hair
that still showed shocks of red in random patches. He stood like a
stone image contemplating, it seemed, the lat machine. Leon knew
him well enough to give him a nickname. He called Drake "Rasputin." Drake, in turn, called Leon "Captain." Leon assumed this
was because of his silver crew cut and for the pressed khaki slacks
he wore exclusively.

Drake, in his early seventies, had had a recent heart transplant
and was exercising now under his doctor's orders. He was broad-
shouldered, slim-hipped, and tall, a one-time college basketball
player. He enjoyed his special status as a transplant patient. He told
the details of his operation to anyone who would listen—how the
heart-lung machine's connection to his aorta had failed and how
his blood left red slicks on the operating room floor. Drake was full
of life and bravado and endless talk. He had neither self-pity nor
conceit, which, Leon thought, ennobled him. Leon liked Dick
Drake; Maisy did not.

"I'm defibrillating," he said to Leon's greeting. "I've got to stand still."

Leon sat down at the leg press and started exercising. There was too much weight on the rack, but he didn't stop to change it. After half a dozen presses, he quit. Drake was still standing in front of the lat machine as his defibrillator hammered spikes of voltage into his misfiring heart.

"Son of a bitch," Drake said, touching the bulge in his side where the defibrillator had been implanted.

"You okay?" Leon said.

"Sometimes I feel like I'm on a high wire stretched over Niagara Falls."

Drake's forehead was yellow as wax. His grand nose hooked out of his face like a damaged keel. He grinned, his pale eyes alive and merry under shaggy gray eyebrows. "What do you say we trash this for today and go out for a plate of bacon and eggs?" he said. He raised his arms and flexed the biceps. The lumpy muscles bucked erratically under the sagging skin. "I'm in good enough shape to miss a day. What do you say, Captain?"

Maisy wouldn't go with them. She didn't want to hear Drake describe his operation again. Leon showered, put on his gabardine slacks and a Hawaiian shirt, then walked to the Lanai room, one of three cafeterias in the Sierra del Monte complex. Drake was already there, seated at a table. He hadn't changed out of his sweats. Leon pulled out a chair and sat down.

"You didn't have to dress up for me, Captain," Drake said.

"I didn't," Leon said.

A pretty waitress came by, a girl just out of high school. Leon ordered corned beef hash and poached eggs. Drake asked for the fruit plate.

"Damn," Drake said, leaning sideways to watch as the girl moved briskly between the tables. "Doesn't that make you want to start the nonsense all over again, Captain?"

"She's a baby, Rasputin," Leon said.

"I was a baby once, too," Drake said gravely. His collapsed lips drooped into a sad inverse smile.

"What's wrong?" Leon said.

"I feel so goddamned useless. How come Dick Drake gets a brand new heart when he can't do anything with it anyway? I'm just waiting to die, like the rest of us. Seems like a waste."

Drake never talked like this. "Something's bothering you," Leon said.

"I think the Nigerian wants his heart back, Captain."

Leon knew that Drake's heart had come from a Nigerian cab driver, killed in a head-on collision in Washington, D.C. The Nigerian was twenty-eight years old at the time of his death. His heart was flown to El Paso from D.C. in four hours. Except for the heart-lung machine problem, it had been a perfect transplant.

"Fibrillating again?" Leon said.

Drake shrugged. "Off and on. Nigerians are big on ghosts. Maybe the cabby feels he can't break away from the earthly bonds until his heart is buried, too."

"Mumbo jumbo, Rasputin," Leon said, though he did not think Drake's superstitious fear was unreasonable. He was tempted to let apparitions, visitations, or vibrations in the ether account for the phantom odors he woke up to every morning.

Drake raised his napkin to his face. He coughed and something came up. He folded the napkin and put it on his plate. "I'm okay," he said. "Sometimes when I retch I can put pressure on the vagus nerve. That makes it quit."

The young waitress came by and leaned over their table. "Is everything okay, guys?" she asked.

Her thick auburn hair, electrified by the dry desert air, fell inches from Leon's face. He closed his eyes and breathed in, nostrils flared, but he could not smell her fragrance.

"I was as good as dead," Drake said to the waitress. "Now look at me." He opened his shirt and showed her his smooth, wide scar.

He raised his arms and made the gnarly biceps leap. The shadow of melancholy and doubt that had obscured his optimistic nature had passed. "I'm going to live forever, honey," he said.

Leon got up and went into the men's room. He stood in front of a urinal. Before he unzipped he tried to smell the powerfully astringent deodorant bar that lay next to the drain. He knelt in front of the urinal and breathed in the fumes. His eyes watered but he smelled nothing.

A man in a wheelchair rolled into the men's room. "Are you okay, buddy?" he said.

Leon stood up, embarrassed. "Fine," he said. "I'm fine."

Age had not made Maisy lose interest in sex. Leon was capable, but had little staying power. "Sorry," he said, breathing hard. He rolled away from her. "I'm short on wind these days."

"Don't worry," Maisy said. "I'm not going to start trolling the playgrounds for teenage distance runners."

They both laughed. It had been a good marriage. They had no children and were content with that. Maisy had been thirty-six when they got married, Leon thirty-five. Ten years before that, Maisy had been married briefly to an army officer.

They took a shower together. Leon put his face directly under the spray. He smelled roses in the steam. The showerhead overwhelmed him in fragrance. He stepped back, startled. "Is that your shampoo, Maisy?"

"What are you talking about?" she said. "I'm not shampooing yet."

It was roses and more than roses. He could almost remember the place—a river bank, maybe a lake, a fine house in the country. And there was a gathering of some kind, people he knew but could not name. There were voices among the roses, by the river or lake, and the familiar house, a handsome place tucked in green hills, was full of music and roses, thousands of roses. *He's here,* he heard someone say. Someone else said, *Sure enough.*

He fell to a squat on the tiles, shaking. Maisy turned off the water and left the shower. When she came back she toweled him dry. "I've called for an ambulance," she said.

"I'm okay," Leon said, standing up. "I almost remembered it that time, Maisy." Tears rolled down his face and his voice shook.

"There's nothing to remember," she said. "You had a seizure, a bigger one this time."

"Maybe heaven," he said. "Maybe heaven smells like flowers and the houses are full of roses and music and the people are sweet."

"Take it easy, hon," Maisy said. "They'll be here in a minute."

It was an aneurysm. A bulging vein, dangerously fragile, had pressed hard against a branch of the olfactory nerve. The pressure the aneurysm had exerted on the brain had also stimulated the seizures. The seizures—the nostalgia-rich odors of nowhere—stopped after the operation. And after a while his sense of smell came back. Leon was able to smell ordinary, everyday things again, but his dreams were odorless. Stripped of fragrance, they no longer had the power to draw him into haunting and familiar landscapes where people he recognized but did not know welcomed him. He missed this, which was foolish, and made no sense.

He wore a cap to hide his shaved head. A long red arc traveled from his right temple, across the top of his skull, ending just over his left eye. He wanted to show Dick Drake his scar, wanted to bore him with the details of his surgery—Rasputin had it coming, after all—but discovered that Drake had been taken back to the hospital where he'd received his heart transplant.

Leon visited him. Drake's Nigerian heart was failing rapidly and he was waiting for a new donor.

"Jesus, I hope this time they give me the heart of a goddamn Swede. Swedes don't believe in ghosts, do they, Captain?"

Leon went along with it. "You want a *Swiss* heart, Rasputin. The goddamn Swiss only believe in money."

They were out in an open-air plaza between buildings. Fast-moving springtime clouds moved them in and out of shade. Dick

Drake sat bundled in a wheelchair. He looked thin and wasted, but his spirits were high.

"The Nigerian's calling it in," he said. He looked up, as if he could see the Nigerian cabby gesturing among the clouds. "He can't travel without his heart."

Leon stopped at a flower shop on his way home. He bought a dozen roses for Maisy, a mix of reds and yellows and pinks. The roses filled the car with perfume. It was a happy smell, the fragrance of optimism and hope, a fragrance that would be welcome in anyone's idea of heaven.

He knew he did not need to, but he wanted to win her heart again. He wanted to win her heart every day for whatever time they had left together. It made no sense, but it didn't have to. Nothing had to.

———

Rick DeMarinis has published six novels and six collections of short stories. *Borrowed Hearts: New and Selected Stories* was released this year. He teaches writing at the University of Texas at El Paso. He has received two NEA grants, and a literature award from the American Academy of Arts and Letters. Two of his short stories have been selected for inclusion in *Best American Short Stories*.

UCIR / STEVEN KIP

*S*ome of the medical oddities in "Borrowed Hearts" come from first-hand experience. In 1994 I was diagnosed as having a benign brain tumor. Among my symptoms were olfactory hallucinations and false memories. I'd wake up smelling something familiar but unable to put a name to it. The smell was connected to a memory. I was convinced that if I could identify the smell, I'd remember the circumstances that gave rise to it. The memory felt important, centered on some pivotal experience in my life. These *hallucinations were compelling and disturbing. The neurologist who discovered the tumor told me that I was merely suffering brain seizures. There was no smell, no memory, just a cerebral spasm. After a surgeon removed the tumor, the hallucinations died. The surgery also wiped out my sense of smell. I can't smell flowers or taste food as it ought to be tasted. The aromatics — herbs, spices, garlic — don't get through. It was a big loss. What I gained was material for a couple of fictions based on my symptoms. An old man in this story, a young woman in another. It's all grist.*

Wendy Brenner

THE HUMAN SIDE OF INSTRUMENTAL TRANSCOMMUNICATION

(from *Story*)

Greetings, and welcome to the third annual Conference of the Instrumental Transcommunication Network. We are delighted to see such a large turnout; surely our growing numbers indicate that verifiable communication with the dead through the use of electronic instrument systems will soon be recognized by even our most outspoken critics.

I would now like to share some thoughts about the meaning of this year's conference theme, "The Human Side of Instrumental Transcommunication." For myself, founder of this network, the answer to the question "Why attempt to use tape recorders, televisions, and computers to communicate interdimensionally with spirit beings?" has always been a highly personal one.

My involvement in the field began four years ago in St. Augustine, Florida, where I was vacationing with my wife and son, Nathan—who at that time was the only person in our family with a particular interest in recording equipment. Then seven years old, he already owned a dozen miniature tape recorders, and more cassettes than crayons. When he was only a baby he had discovered my wife's little Panasonic portable from her journalism school days, digging it out of a box in the basement and screaming when we tried to pry it away. Thereafter, we bought tape recorders for him wherever we saw them, at thrift stores, flea markets, garage sales we happened to pass. They were cheap, we reasoned, too big to swallow, and Nathan couldn't seem to get enough—he carried them around like hamsters and wouldn't sleep without one or two in his bed. On his first day of kindergarten an entire wing of his school had to be evacuated when the tape recorder he kept in his windbreaker got stuck on fast-forward in the coatroom and was believed to be a ticking bomb.

He just had a way with those little machines. He could rewind or fast-forward any cassette to the exact spot he wanted on the first try, without using a counter device, and on long car trips my wife and I took turns requesting songs from the middles of tapes to keep him busy. He would sit on the floor under the dashboard and put his ear up next to the tape deck like a safecracker, and then his whole face would light up as though someone had flipped a switch behind it when he hit the right spot, pressed the play button, and my wife's favorite song came on once again, perfectly cued to the beginning. He never missed, and like any good magician, he never told his secrets.

Interestingly, though, despite his love for junky cassette players, Nathan didn't care at all for the brand-new Walkman my wife's mother bought him. His love was for making tapes, not listening to them, we discovered, so we allowed him to make as many as he wanted. He recorded himself talking in different voices, acting out dramas he made up himself that were full of coyotes, opera singers, helicopters, Mack trucks, nuclear-emergency alert sirens, hives of angry bees. In his stories people had frequent arguments, and there were many slamming doors, much shouting to be let in or out.

He was so enthusiastic about his sound effects, he tended to neglect things like plot and logic, jumping from one sensational noise to another without explanation, rushing through dialogue and mixing up his voices so that half the time you couldn't understand what any of his characters were saying, or even what was going on. "You'll have to slow down and enunciate," my wife, ever the good editor, would tell him, "because whatever you just said there is not a word." But Nathan paid no heed. "If it's not a word," he argued, "then how come I just said it?"

Of course he could not have understood how meaningful that offhand remark would come to be, to so many of us. He was saying, of course, that *the act of communication is of greater significance than the legitimacy of the means used to achieve it*. Who among us today has not felt deeply that very sentiment?

On our trip to St. Augustine, I will always remember, Nathan wished for three things: to visit a Spanish war fort, to find and bring home an unbroken sand dollar, and to get the hotel maid to talk into his tape recorder. This was his first stay in a hotel since he was a baby, and he grew very excited when we explained to him that a lady was going to come into our room while we weren't there and make our beds and leave clean towels for us. "A lady we know?" he asked, and when we told him no, a strange lady, he concluded it was the tooth fairy, or someone just like her, perhaps her friend. This was where they probably lived, he said—in Florida. We tried to explain the truth without letting on that the tooth fairy wasn't real, but Nathan only grew more certain in his belief. Every morning before we left the room to go down to breakfast or the beach, he set up one of his tape recorders on the dresser with this note:

> Dear cleaning lady,
> Please press Play and record at the same time and then read this message out loud, begin Here.
>   Hello, this is the cleaning lady coming to you live from the hotel. Today will be hot and sunny.
>   Now, back to you.
> When you are done press Stop.

Unfortunately, the woman never responded. Every night when we returned to the room Nathan ran to the recorder, but it had never been touched, and he grew more disappointed every day. We had already photographed him waving down at us from the parapet of the war fort, and he had not one but several perfect specimens of sand dollars wrapped in Kleenex like cookies and tucked for safety in our suitcase pockets. Yet these successes seemed only to make him more frustrated, as if this were some fairy tale where he had to satisfy an angry king. "Why didn't she do it, why?" he cried to us, night after night. It was possible the cleaning lady didn't speak or read English, we told him, or, more likely, she didn't want to disturb the belongings of guests—or perhaps she never even saw the note, or realized it was intended for her.

Privately my wife and I discussed tracking this woman down and talking to her, or finding another hotel employee who would cooperate, or even disguising one of our voices and recording the message ourselves. We *had* written little notes to him from the tooth fairy, my wife said, and wasn't this the same thing? But in the end we decided it was best to leave the situation to chance. Since we knew the maid was a real person capable of responding, we wanted her message, should it come, to be genuine. My wife eventually came to question this decision, but, as all of us here today understand, in such a situation integrity cannot be compromised, regardless of how desperately our hearts might long for different outcomes to our experiments.

Consider, for example, the pioneers in our field: Dr. Konstantin Raudive, who made over one hundred thousand separate recordings after hearing a single mysterious voice on a blank, brand-new tape; or Friedrich Juergenson, who abandoned his successful opera-singing career so he could investigate voice phenomena full-time after one of his tapes mysteriously recorded strange voices speaking Norwegian. Falsifying results was never an option for these scientists, as it should never be for us.

Yet despite our faithfulness to the scientific method, we must not ignore the human side of instrumental transcommunication. The personal relevance of the message, when it finally comes, is often what establishes authenticity. Those of you who have already received such messages report that the sender will often use, as a kind of password, a phrase or nickname or piece of information that only he and you, the recipient, could know. Who can forget

Dr. Raudive's own unexpected communication from the other side, which came through one night at home on the clock radio of the researcher who had been tirelessly advancing Raudive's cause after his untimely death: "This is Konstantin Raudive. Stay on the station, tune in correctly. Here it is summer, always summer! Soon it will work everywhere!" It almost seems that the deceased answer the calls of the living, rather than vice versa, as is usually assumed.

In light of these considerations, I strongly contend that my wife and I were justified in not faking the maid's voice on Nathan's tape. We could not have known what was about to occur.

For those of you not familiar with my story, which was reprinted in last month's newsletter, the paramedics who so heroically attempted to revive my son gave his cause of death as "generalized childhood seizure," meaning he had lost consciousness before he went underwater, rather than afterward. My wife, who was swimming not far away at the time, agrees; otherwise, she says, he would certainly have splashed or kicked, or cried out for help. She maintains she certainly would have heard him. We did recover the tape recorder in a Ziploc bag he was carrying so he could record underwater sounds, but he hadn't sealed the bag properly, the whole thing was waterlogged, and the cassette yielded nothing.

It might have been restored, of course, but my wife allowed the bag and its contents to be thrown away at the hospital—an oversight which some of us might find difficult to comprehend, but again, how could she have known? At that time, I knew nothing about instrumental transcommunication, not even that it existed, that great men had devoted their whole lives to the study of it. I knew nothing of the hours of research already completed, the extraordinary messages already received, the elaborate devices created by scientists and by ordinary men, like myself.

It was later that evening that the first seeds, as they say, were planted. To get back to our hotel we had to go through St. Augustine's cobblestoned sidestreets, past the crowded displays of artisans; one fellow dressed as a blacksmith called out to us, "Smile! It can't be that bad!" The very quality of the day's light seemed different, smoky, like a film stuck on one frame, the edges burning and closing in. When we got back, my wife went into the bathroom and shut the door. Our room still smelled cheerfully of bananas and Sea & Ski. The TV was on, for some reason, muted and tuned to the closed-circuit bulletin board. A message was running across the bottom of the screen: *If you like what you are hearing, tune in 24 hours a day . . . If you like what you are hearing, tune in 24 hours a day . . .*

That's when I noticed the recorder on the dresser, the one Nathan had left for the maid. It was black and silver and shining in the TV's cold blue light. But there was something off about it, I thought, as if it had been touched or moved by someone. Not the way he'd left it. Then, like a punch in the stomach: Of course! The maid's message! She would have done it this time. *Of course.* I saw it all at once, in simple, clear progression, our lives laid out as in a comic strip, with everything—not just each day of our vacation, each day the maid had not responded, but each day of Nathan's life, our lives, our parents' lives before ours—leading up to *this,* this final square, this *joke.*

I had to hear it anyway. I pressed play and held my breath because it suddenly seemed too noisy, not right, and with my breath stopped I felt the air around me stop, the molecules stop popping, everything stop moving, so I could hear this awful answer, this stupid woman speak the words my son had written for her, too late. Instead, there was silence. Then, ever so faintly, something else, something so small, so familiar it seemed to come from my own body—but it could not have. It was breathing—Nathan, breathing. I waited for him to speak, to begin one of his stories, but he went on breathing, as if he were just sitting there, reading his Sesame Street book, or lying on the floor, battling with his action figures. But *breathing.*

My wife was in the bathroom with the door closed. And my son, my son who I knew was dead, was breathing in my ear.

Like a deejay, God plays the impossible for us. I cannot speak for others, but that was how it began for me. I did not mistake the sound on the tape that night for the aspirations of a ghost, a message from the other side—but when I heard it, I knew such things were possible.

My wife was not there to receive the message. Was that only a fluke? Had she not been in the bathroom at that moment, I wonder, would she have heard it, too? Or did she leave the room on purpose, following some premonition, practicing a kind of willful deafness, the selective hearing of parents? It is impossible to say. Later, I brought home books for her—every study I could find that proves instrumental transcommunication is real, every seminal text in the field—but she refused to look at any of them.

At the time of our divorce, we catalogued Nathan's tapes and stored them in a safe-deposit box so that I could continue my research, and so that she could listen to them for what her lawyer called "sentimental reasons"—an accusation, apparently. *I* am not the sentimental one, is the implication, not *human,* she has said. Yet it is she who refuses to take her own son's call, a call I have no doubt he will make, is perhaps preparing to make this very moment. I am ready. Upstairs in my room in this hotel the most sensitive and sophisticated equipment available—thanks to many of you here today—is in operation even as we speak, poised and ready to receive and safeguard the most tentative inquiry, the faintest nudge of sound.

We are not spoon-benders, I tell my wife and others like her, not flimflammers, but scientists and engineers, scholars and teachers and builders, fathers, many of us, and mothers. We wait like any line of people at a pay phone: impatient, hopeful, polite. What will he say when he calls? We can only imagine. It may not sound like English—it may not be English. We still have much work to do in the areas of clarity and amplification. On a typical recording, "soul mate" sounds like "sailboat," "father" may be indistinguishable from "bother," "Nathan" might come through as "nothing."

Still, we wait. We listen like safecrackers, we listen like sleuths. We remember the words of those listeners who came before us, the brave ones who started this whole thing. *Stay on the station, tune in correctly. Here it is summer, always summer! Soon it will work everywhere!*

Wendy Brenner is the author of *Large Animals in Everyday Life,* which won the Flannery O'Connor Award. Her stories have appeared in *CutBank, Mississippi Review, New England Review, Plough-shares, The Oxford American, Story,* and elsewhere. This is her third appearance in *New Stories from the South.* She teaches creative writing in the MFA program at the University of North Carolina at Wilmington.

CAROLINE NIKITAS

I visited a friend whose seven-year-old son was obsessed with tape recorders, and I remembered feeling the same way as a child — that basic thrill of communicating technologically, saving and transmitting messages on my low-tech 1970s-model Panasonic portable, which seemed high-tech at the time. It was a way of making one's voice (and whatever one had to say) "official." Later, I came across a lot of information about electronic voice phenomena on the Internet, and felt moved and compelled not so much by the "science" as by the way the people talked about their involvement in it — the language was very scientific and technical, but the underlying pull to communicate, to make official one's voice and message, came through strongly.

Ingrid Hill

PAGAN BABIES

(from *The Southern Review*)

G oing door to door down Zita Street, Molly Andree could
see right through most of the houses. They were "shotguns," in which the rooms lined up like railroad cars, without even
a hall. The front room opened into the next one, a bedroom,
which led to the next bedroom, then to the kitchen. Molly Andree was soliciting donations for the Society for the Propagation
of the Faith, and she carried a dull dark-blue folder that Sister Edwardine had given her, with several sheets of stamps carefully
tucked inside.

She did not want to sweat on them: then they would all stick together. She did not want to dog-ear them: customers—or contrib-
utors more properly—deserved perfect stamps in exchange for
their donations. The stamps were beautiful. The donations went
to save pagan babies, and the stamps pictured, in beautiful brown
and gold, crimson and blue, chubby-cheeked African infants and
slit-eyed, gold-skinned Asian babies in beautiful wraps of exotic
cloth.

Sister Edwardine said that they all were orphans, and the stamp
money went to support missionaries who ran clean and wonderful orphanages where the babies were saved from their heathen
fates. She said their mothers had died from terrible diseases they
got from river miasma and witch doctors' poison-root poultices.

A girl in the class had moved to New Orleans from somewhere north, maybe Missouri. She had gone to a Bible church when she was little. She raised her hand and asked Sister Edwardine if they were saving the babies from being passed through the fire. Sister Edwardine said she was not sure what that meant. The girl said she had learned that they used to burn babies up, *barbecue,* to make the pagan gods happy, that was in the Bible, and did they still do that? Sister Edwardine shuddered. She didn't know what to say. So she said, "I hope not," in the same tone she had said, that morning, that she hoped no one would pick their noses or their chickenpox scabs when the archbishop came for May Crowning the following week.

The girl said, "Are we saving those there pagan babies from getting barbecued?" Sister Edwardine said then she was sure that we were, but she did not sound solid on that. Sister Edwardine was only twenty years old.

For each donation of a penny, a donor got one stamp. Molly Andree thought this quite a bargain. Stamps to mail letters cost triple that, and were not beautiful, just dull blue profiles of some dead American president.

The houses on Zita Street all were a lusterless, peeling white. They reflected the harsh sun as if they were built of damp chalk. There were no trees, as there was no room for trees. Between houses ran alleyways so narrow that the fat uncle of one of Molly Andree's classmates had gotten stuck between his own house and his neighbors' and had to be pried loose by firemen. No one looked out the windows, because all there was to see were the shutters and curtains of the people next door, their windows uniformly positioned all the way from the front to the back.

Most of the houses had their front doors open, because it was hot today. It was the second of June, and even though school had closed the week before, Molly Andree had asked Sister Edwardine whether she could please keep collecting for pagan babies and bring what she collected to the convent at the end of the week. She wanted to finish Zita Street, end to end. She wanted to get all the way from the school to her own house on Marillac. She lived on the second floor, over a grocery.

Chloe, the black maid, had told Molly Andree that the family's house had once been the grocer's family's house, and that they must have been grand people for their day, to judge from the chandeliers. The rooms were arranged end to end, just the same as the more modest one-story shotguns, but the house was twice as wide, with tall ceilings and those crystal chandeliers with teardrop-shaped crystal hangings, a hundred, a thousand teardrops on each chandelier. It seemed to Molly Andree she must be richer than these people in these small shotguns, but she could not see it, did not feel it. She envisioned the rows of dark-brown and pale-gold pagan babies, glowing with health on their mission cots, that she would save, and her heart burned with wanting them milk-filled and blanket-wrapped children of God.

She climbed the five steps to the next house and knocked on the soft, peeling wood of the doorframe. The door was wide open. The screen smelled of dark rust and bulged out, disfigured, in several places. It was ripped at the corner and taped with shiny gray tape. She peered into the house. It was cool with shade. She could see no one. She called in: "Hello? Anyone home?" But the huge window fan kept on making its rubber-belt thucking noise, masking her call. Then a figure moved out of the shadow in the archway into the bedroom, and she caught her breath. It was a man's shape, the kind that at night in the doorway looked more like a bear's.

For a moment she thought it was her father, and caught her breath again, but the silhouette moved and turned into a rumpled man in belted trousers and a vest undershirt. The man came to the door. His eyes were watery, and he smelled as if he had been working with metal, a whiff of galvanized something—nails, fencing—that lifted off his skin through the screen.

"Would you like to help save pagan babies?" asked Molly Andree. "On far continents?" The man blinked, attempting to register this. He seemed still to be thinking about metal fenceposts or

garden-gate latches. "I am collecting for the Society for the Propagation of the Faith," Molly Andree said. "For my class. At Queen
of Martyrs School, you know, um, over—" she motioned behind
her, somewhat grandly, proprietarily, as if she were an explorer
who had sailed up the Mississippi River and climbed the muddy
bank to claim this land for some distant monarchy, "over *there*."

Again the man blinked. "Oh," he said finally. "Da Catlicks."

Molly Andree blinked in response. She felt as if she were hearing a foreign language, but she knew she was seven blocks from
home.

"F'om the Catlick school," said the man.

Molly Andree understood. Somehow until now she had
thought everyone in the city was Catholic. Even the girl from Missouri was, now. Suddenly she remembered a number of other
churches she had seen, the white stucco Presbyterian church with
the actual lawn out front, the shadowy little no-color church of
some kind on the avenue that she walked past on her way home
from school, where the sidewalk was covered with acorns, and
where she walked more slowly and crushed them, with great and
deep pleasure, with her saddle-oxford heels.

"They're saving the babies," she said.

From the shadow inside came a voice, someone sitting in the
unlit living room. "Tell da chile to come in, hon," the voice said.
"We tryin' to watch this ting on da TV."

The man opened the door to let Molly Andree in. On the sofa
sat a baggy woman with her hair in a thick pink hairnet. The elastic band bit into the flesh of her forehead. She was obviously this
man's wife: their softnesses, like overcooked vegetables' in soup,
matched. Beside the woman sat a little girl Molly Andree thought
probably just short of school age. In a straight-backed rocking
chair next to the sofa was a bony grandmother, crocheting a doily
and cocking a wiry gray eyebrow to listen.

"For every penny you give you get one of these beautiful
stamps," Molly Andree said. "Look. Aren't these beautiful babies?"

"I want them!" the little girl said. "I want stamps!"

"For *what* now?" the woman said. "These stamps is for *what?*"

"In the Congo and places like that," Molly Andree said. "It is all very primitive. There are witch doctors and swamp fever, and all the mothers and fathers die."

The little girl's eyes were wide with wonder.

"So all of these babies are orphans, and if you buy stamps—or more like, if you *give* a donation and I *give* you stamps—they have money to save all of these pagan babies."

"Hush, y'all," said the crocheting grandma. "I can't hear the TV man talk. The parade is on. The man's esplaining it."

All eyes turned to the TV, its screen the size of a school notebook page. Indeed there was a parade, dark horses with plumes and coaches like something out of a fairy tale. Then Molly Andree remembered: it was the coronation day of the Princess Elizabeth, elegant over the sea in England, where nobody looked like cooked vegetables, where everyone sat in drawing rooms and had umbrella stands by their front doors, where people drank tea with their pinkies up, and babies rode in mysterious, cozy conveyances called perambulators. Molly Andree had read that in a book and found the idea irresistible. Today Princess Elizabeth, who was barely grown up, would become the queen. Molly Andree had put the coronation out of her mind in her concentration on getting to as many houses as she could. Now she wanted to watch.

The soft-vegetable mother saw this in Molly Andree's eyes. "Sit down, hon. You could watch wid us. This here is something. Just think! She's getting crowned queen! Little Princess Elizabeth! Remember when she was a chile. Look at them horses. So beautiful." The father sat down by the mother, and Molly Andree sat next to the little girl.

The girl snatched a sheet of stamps from Molly Andree and petted them on her lap, running her open hand over the silky stamps, dozens of perfectly identical pictures of groupings of pagan babies, cupped in some soft fabric like a nest. Everyone stared at the small television screen. The parade rolled on. There were clop-clopping sounds of horsehooves and the sounds of herald trumpets in the distance. A commentator was talking about other times like this, the crownings of other queens and kings—in England and the rest of the world.

Molly Andree had a vision of herself as Princess Elizabeth, with all the wealth of the world—or whatever kingdom or queendom England was part of—at her fingertips. She would ride in that carriage on Sundays, with its top down—she could not imagine it raining on Sunday in England—collecting all the pagan babies from all the homes where the mothers and fathers had died, and she would bring them to the palace. They would each have a perambulator and a nanny.

She would not be as beautiful as her own mother, who everyone said looked like Joan Fontaine, though she would have long braids wound about her head as Joan Fontaine had done in some movie once. She would not be as little as Princess Elizabeth. She would be tall like her father, too tall for anyone to want to marry, which would be just fine, and her face would be not like her mother's or father's but honest and shining as that of Sister John Vianney, the nun who taught the other third grade and knew how to make flower crowns for May processions. She would probably be something like a nun herself, a queen without a prince-husband or king-husband.

She would eat creole cream cheese with a silver spoon for breakfast every day. Her initials would be on the spoon, whose handle would be as ornate as her best special-occasion crown, not the crown she would wear every day. She would take turns relieving the nannies with the perambulators, each of them bearing the royal crest—she could not quite picture this, as she did not quite know what perambulators looked like—and wear her everyday crown walking the babies in the royal gardens. She would always be twenty years old, and the babies would always be babies. Perhaps if there were too many orphans she would sell her crowns and wear floral coronas like Sister Vianney's.

On the television they were coming to someplace. The carriages were pulling into a grand driveway.

"Get me my pills," said the grandmother. Molly Andree looked over at her. It was unclear who was being addressed. Molly Andree looked back at the television. "I said get me my pills," the grandmother repeated. No one else moved. Molly Andree stood up and looked a question at her: where? The woman gestured toward the sideboard. There were piles of bills, a vase of pink plastic roses with a coating of fine, fuzzy dust, and several brown medicine bottles. Molly Andree walked to the sideboard and picked all the bottles up between her hands. The grandmother made a sound of disgust, as if she should have known which bottle. Making a slight curtsey, Molly Andree set the bottles down. She did not know what else to do. She went back to her seat. The coronation party was processing into a grand doorway. The cameras shook slightly, and there were too many shadows to see clearly just what was happening.

"How do they *save* them, these babies?" the father said.

Molly Andree realized that she didn't know. She made a face of stupidity. She tried to think of a logical answer. She didn't want to attempt to explain about barbecue, because she wasn't sure that was the answer. Instead, she said, "Each of these sheets is worth fifty cents. Five rows of ten."

The father shrugged and seemed somehow satisfied.

Molly Andree wanted to stay here and turn into a fat, cooked cross-section of carrot in the soup of this family. She wanted to be Queen Elizabeth, or one of the pagan babies. She did not want to go home. Her mother would be out getting a manicure and would come home with glistening dark red nails. Chloe did not come today, and Molly Andree missed her. The house was far too big and too empty this afternoon. She could not tell when her father would come home. He sold cars in a big, shiny showroom, and you never could tell what his hours would be. She moved closer to the little girl, who smelled like fruity shampoo.

On the TV, the procession seemed to have gotten somewhere, the scene of the real action.

"Do you want to play tea party?" said the little girl.

"No, thank you," said Molly Andree.

The little girl nodded, pleased, as if she had said yes, and went and got small plastic cups with blue flowers and green leaves on their sides. She went into the kitchen and brought back a bottle of root beer. She handed it to Molly Andree.

"It's *hot*," Molly Andree said. "Root beer's supposed to be cold."

"That's all right," said the girl. "We'll pretend it is tea."

"And I don't have an opener anyway," said Molly Andree.

The girl went to the kitchen and brought back an opener. Its handle was pearlized and said JAX BEER in beautiful scrolly-script letters. Everyone else watched the TV, absorbed. Molly Andree wrenched the top from the root beer as if she were an expert. She had never opened a bottle alone before. The liquid frothed up and spilled hot root-beer bubble-drool onto the worn flowered rug. No one cared. Princess Elizabeth was being crowned.

Molly Andree and the little girl drank their hot root beer from doll cups. "Delicious," the little girl said, smacking her lips delicately. She seemed to be more truly Molly Andree's small sister than these vegetable-soup people's daughter. Perhaps if she could not be crowned Queen of England, Molly Andree would run away to Chloe's house in the batture at the bend in the river behind the church, the dried-mud wilderness between the first levee and the disaster levee. If there were a real flood, Chloe's house would be washed away. But in the meantime, the three of them could be quite happy.

One day a couple of months before, Molly Andree had been helping Chloe spring-clean the chandeliers. This involved three buckets—soap-water, rinse-water, vinegar-water—and old diapers that had to have been Molly Andree's own, dug from some remote closet to wipe and polish the dangling crystals. Molly Andree stood in her sock-feet on the dark, heavy dining-room table, taking down the crystals, hook by hook. The wood of the table felt waxy and dangerous through her socks.

She thought she might slip, hit her head, and die. She wondered whether there would be a funeral, as she was sure that no one but

Chloe would come—her mother did not like funerals, and her father had to work almost every day—and she was not sure Father Bergeron would let a colored girl into his church. Chloe sat at the end of the table and dunked the crystals in soap-water, scrubbed them clean, dunked them in rinse-water and then in vinegar-water. "And what is the vinegar-water for?" Molly Andree asked, a dozen crystals into the chandelier. "Sparkle," said Chloe. "Shine. After that vinegar gone, you see. That when it squeak. When it shine."

When Chloe went into the kitchen to dump the rinse-water, Molly Andree stuck a sharp-faceted, vinegar-wet crystal into her mouth and sucked all the vinegar off, as if perhaps she were a two-year-old or did not know any better. Chloe came back quicker than Molly Andree expected and saw her pulling the long, fat crystal dangler, pensive and slow, from her mouth. She shook her head. "You one crazy white child," Chloe said. Then she laughed very big, and Molly Andree admired the rosy skin inside her mouth and the grand, solid ivory sheen of her teeth. After they finished the chandelier, Chloe went home. Before her parents returned from whatever they were doing, separately, Molly Andree turned the lights off and sat in the dining room playing a flashlight through the crystals, dazzling the glass in the dark.

Molly Andree and the little girl were drinking tea-set cup after cup of lukewarm root beer and saying, "Dee-*lee*-ci-ous!" in unison as all this went through her head. On the television the coronation continued. "What is she sitting on?" the little girl squealed. "A potty?" She clapped her hands in great glee at seeing a princess on the toilet on television.

The grandmother snorted in disgust. The father said, "They call that thing a throne, honey." The mother, distracted, said, "What did she say? Her *throat*? Her throat hurts?" No one answered.

Molly Andree remembered a dream she had had the week before. In the dream she had something in her mouth, and she did not know what it was. It felt like a stone, but it was too smooth, more like glass, like an egg, like an egg that was a jewel. She pulled out the egg and looked at it. It seemed that there was something inside, but in the dream she would not be permitted to know what that was until she had sold all her stamps.

Princess Elizabeth's crown looked far too big for her. Or, Molly Andree thought, if she had that crown already on her head perhaps she wasn't *Princess* Elizabeth anymore. "Queen" seemed less lovely somehow. For a moment Molly Andree resolved that she would not metamorphose to Queen after she was transformed into Princess. But then there was something awry in that, she couldn't figure what.

She looked into the bedroom of the vegetable mother and vegetable father. An overbright picture of Jesus as the Sacred Heart hung above their bed. Gold beams like spikes of a porcupine radiated from his very pink heart, which was the color of cube steak, raw. The bedspread was pink chenille and had a design of orange flowers with green leaves worked into the center of it. The pillows looked flat and dispirited tucked underneath the top edge of the spread. She thought of her mother's bedroom with its quilted silk coverlet, its throw-pillows like valentine hearts plumped in a careful pile against the pickled-oak headboard. She looked at the cube-steak heart of Jesus over the little girl's mother and father's bed.

Her own father slept on the far side of the stairs, in the room she called the Scary Room. They had once had a boarder, a middle-aged woman named Mrs. Hodge who smelled like disinfectant and Pepto-Bismol, who had died there. She had been Christian Scientist. She had made a point of telling that fact to Molly Andree one morning when they met by accident in the kitchen. She said Christian Scientists did not take medicine. Molly Andree asked well then what about Pepto-Bismol? Mrs. Hodge said, as if it should be obvious, that was on a par with cough drops, which were pretty much just hard candy, and so the rule did not apply. Mrs. Hodge very rarely came into contact with the rest of the family, going about her business with an air of slow urgency, receiving no mail, never needing to use the phone.

Molly Andree had seen her—again, by accident—one day when she had gone downtown on the Saint Charles streetcar to meet her mother at Godchaux's. Her mother wanted to buy her a nylon seersucker dress she had seen in the department store window on a mannequin with a blond pageboy hairdo. The dress was printed with tiny crowns and fleurs-de-lis. Molly Andree felt perfectly indifferent about the dress, though she tried it on and twirled for the salesgirls as her mother asked, and she could tell that her mother was quite disappointed in her. As the streetcar passed, Molly Andree saw Mrs. Hodge standing outside the Christian Science Reading Room with her umbrella half unfolded, looking up at the sky. Then the streetcar moved on toward Lee Circle.

Mrs. Hodge had caught cancer and died. No one would tell Molly Andree how one could catch cancer. Chloe said she didn't know, that colored people probably did not get it, that her kin died of other things. She regaled Molly Andree with the story of a growth on the side of the face that her uncle in Opelousas had had, and the two-headed baby that got stuck and killed her aunt Bertholine.

Mrs. Hodge refused to call a doctor. She just lay in that room getting smaller until finally Molly Andree's mother called the hospital and told them to come get Mrs. Hodge, that she just couldn't stand all this Christian Scientist business one minute more.

She went into Mrs. Hodge's room and told her in no uncertain terms that the ambulance was coming. Mrs. Hodge made a very small puckered mouth. Her eyes shrank and darkened with anger or some kind of bedridden Christian Scientist resolve. Molly Andree's mother had Chloe pack Mrs. Hodge a bag. "*Any* bag," she said to Chloe, in clear earshot of Mrs. Hodge. "I just want her out of here."

Molly Andree and her mother and Chloe sat in the dining room and played cards on the lace tablecloth to distract themselves while the ambulance was coming. Molly Andree knew her mother had to be *very* upset if she would resort to such a measure. Asking the maid to play gin rummy with them when the ironing was piled high in both baskets and Chloe had just cooked a new batch of pale-blue starch in the aluminum pot on the stove made no sense otherwise.

Molly Andree liked the scraping sound of the wooden spoon on the pot bottom as Chloe heated the starch. She had sat at the table listening to it, pretending to be busy with spelling words. She wrote them out ten times each: *ache, cable, mountain.* She knew them already but didn't mind practicing penmanship. Her mother had an autographed eight-by-ten glossy photo of the dimple-faced, swaggering Clark Gable hung on her bedroom wall. It was good to have penmanship skills. One might someday be Vivien Leigh, or the Princess of England, and have to sign who knew what.

Mrs. Hodge had been dead when the ambulance came, as ferocious as that. The little inky-black shrink of rebellion that had filled her eyes when Molly Andree's mother told her the plans for the hospital seemed to have grown, become a dark vacuum, and swallowed her whole. She lay dead on the bed looking straight at the door with her eyes open, furious. Molly Andree's mother had sucked her breath in and let her knees go out from under her. The ambulance attendants assisted her to her heart-pillowed bed at the far end of the house, and then took Mrs. Hodge's body away.

Molly Andree's father slept in Mrs. Hodge's old room now. Her mother said it was better that way, so he wouldn't wake her when he left very early or came in late. The Lysol and the pink, minty medicine smell of Mrs. Hodge were not totally gone, but remained, ineradicably Christian Scientist or something like it, in an ethereous layer beneath the scents of her father's hair wax and shave lotion, which filled the first layer of the air of the room now. Sometimes her father asked Molly Andree to come in and visit with him. She recalled stepping into the room twice or three times, but just stepping into it, not talking, not anything else except the sound of the lock clicking behind her.

In back of Princess Elizabeth—now apparently queen—stood a dozen or so dignitaries. One was jut-jawed and ecclesial, cloaked in brocade, a great cross hanging down on his belly. Several wore ermine about their shoulders; some had crowns of various sorts; one seemed to be holding a sword erect in an uncomfortable way.

The grandmother balanced herself on her elbow on the chair arm, lifting her bony left buttock off the seat, and released a long, terrible flatulent bleat. The mother and father kept watching the TV. The little girl looked over at Molly Andree and made a gagging face, waggling her tongue in disgust. The room filled with the smell, which resembled the odor Mrs. Hodge's room had had in late morning when she left the door open to air it out.

Molly Andree peered into the shadowy, snowy approximation of reality on the screen of the TV. The man behind the new queen had a face like her father's. Her heart skipped a beat. She remembered the time—when? Mrs. Hodge was already dead, she knew that—in the dark must-and-gasoline-smelling garage when her father had come up behind her in his boxer shorts without making a sound.

Molly Andree had been looking for a small can of green paint to retouch a worn spot on her dollhouse roof. Her mother was at the hairdresser's, and it was Chloe's day off. She remembered her father's hand coming flat over her mouth. There were calluses on his palm, and she felt them like horn or sandpaper against her cheek.

She remembered the clammy feel of the skin of his belly as he forced her hand down inside the waistband of his shorts. She remembered the sweet, awful floury smell of his parts, which she never had seen or remembered she'd seen, only inches away from her face as he urged her to open her mouth wider, wider, to show him the cavity—lower left—that had been filled with cool silver the previous week. She remembered him calling her Princess. And that was all she remembered.

Next to her on the sofa, the little girl squirmed. The grandmother's fart still lingered, and the porcupine heart of the front-bedroom Jesus was all she could see. It filled her eyes. Something filled her own heart: a desire to stay very small, to grow smaller, to become twins with this little girl, to shrink to the size of the black pupils of Mrs. Hodge lying dead on her bed, to vanish. She felt her throat tighten.

She wanted to grow up, but of all the grownups she knew, only Chloe was worth growing up to be, and she couldn't grow up to be Chloe.

"I guess I should go," she said to the parents. Her voice did not sound like her own, or as if it meant anything of what it said. Her voice seemed to want to stay here and offer to help, some way, any way. Maybe she could bring the grandmother medicine all day long. She wanted them to ask her to stay, to adopt her. Queen Elizabeth moved forward, her skirts and cloak stately, her crown still too large, and all the courtiers moved as one with her. The man who looked like Molly Andree's father was nowhere to be seen. Molly Andree thought, yes, she would like to be queen.

The father said, "Hey, lemme buy some a dem stamps off a you." He gave Molly Andree a quarter.

She laid all the stamps she had on the coffee table, several sheets. There was no set price, really, so this was technically OK. They were all sold, if she'd sell them that cheap. That would be a relief. She was sure God could save all the pagan babies in French Equatorial Africa with just one quarter if he so desired. It was the best she could do.

As she left the house, the screen door squeaked slowly and stopped before closing completely. Looking back, she saw the mother and father and little girl leaning forward to look at the beautiful sheets of stamps she had left for them. The grandmother was squawking that she couldn't see, let her see, let her see. On the TV, Elizabeth, Queen of the Empire, would be climbing into her coach, going home to a new life.

Molly Andree turned left, toward Chloe's house. She would wait there, sitting quiet and still on the low, squeaky bed until Chloe came home, in the dusk. There were no lights in her little shack, no electric wires. Molly Andree would sit in the semi-dark, breathing the comforting smells of molasses, moss mattress, and the very heavy old coverlet, which smelled as human as anything ever could. She could get in with no problem. She had been to Chloe's house many times. Chloe's house had no locks. She remembered that clearly.

———————

Ingrid Hill has published stories in *The Southern Review, The Michigan Quarterly Review, Shenandoah, North American Review, Louisiana Literature,* and *Story;* and a collection of fiction, *Dixie Collection Interstate Blues.* She explains, "I grew up in New Orleans but—perhaps because I was born in a blizzard in New York City—I write best about the South from a distance, from places where it snows: the more the better. I'm currently in Iowa City."

*O*ften *I dream of houses. One recurrent dream-setting is a dwelling over an old grocery store at the corner of Carollton and Sycamore in New Orleans, where I lived from the age of seven to the age of nine. I wanted to summon the atmosphere of this house: ornate chandeliers, spooky roominess, a sinister room on the far side of the stairs. I had also thought I'd like to write about my childhood experience of selling "pagan babies" stamps door-to-door. What utterly astounded me was Molly Andree's taking over the story, wrenching it into a place I had never intended, by sucking on those chandelier crystals. Both Molly Andree and I sank into a very dark place I had never known.*

Richard Schmitt

LEAVING VENICE, FLORIDA

(from *Mississippi Review*)

Dave and me were sitting in Betty's Elephant Car Cafe a couple of weeks after I'd hitched down from New England. We were at the counter on chrome stools covered with cracked red vinyl, and we weren't talking much because the night before Dave had told me he was sick. Said he'd been to a doctor, and they wanted to cut him open. To look around, they said. Nothing serious. But it sounded serious the way he said it, and he said he wanted me to go with him to the hospital in Sarasota. "When?" I said.

"Tomorrow," Dave said.

"Dave," I said, "I can't stand hospitals."

Behind the counter Betty, the retired circus trouper, both waitress and cook, was fixing a couple of Ring Two Specials — poached eggs on wheat toast with home fries or grits for $1.45. Dave hadn't said anything about being sick on the phone. He said he'd started a car cleaning business in Venice, Florida. It was January and I was doing nothing but freezing in a room in Boston. Dave said I'd be a full partner. I pictured palm trees, girls in bikinis, large drinks with flowers in them.

Turned out not to be a big business, and Venice was a bus stop, but we'd grown up together and hadn't seen much of each other since quitting high school in '69, so I didn't hold it against him.

The bell over the door sounded and two guys walked in. One was tall with a handlebar mustache, the other small with a pointed face, thin skin over sharp bones. They took stools at the counter, and the big guy nodded at us and talked real friendly to Betty. She wiped her hands on a corner of her apron, then ran one hand over the counter in front of where they sat. They hadn't been there before. Dave's shop was just down the road, and he knew everyone who ate at Betty's. The big guy ordered a Center Ring Scramble—three scrambled eggs with onions and black olives served in an iron skillet for $1.65. The little rat-faced guy had a water. Big guy told Betty he was looking for a car wash, and she glanced over at Dave.

"That your van?" the guy said to us.

I turned my stool to look through the plate-glass window. Parked next to Dave's van with the plastic magnetized sign on the side—Dave's Auto Detailing—was a white Buick Riviera. The guy said his dog had been hit by a car and had died on the way to the vet. He was interested in having bloodstains removed from the interior. "Is it a white interior?" Dave said.

"It was white," the guy said.

Dave went outside with the big guy while I sat sipping coffee and eyeballing the rat-faced guy, who looked jittery. He continuously flicked his thumb against the filter of his cigarette and glared at me whenever I caught his eye. I thought I'd seen him the night before climbing out of the Dumpster behind the Showfolk's Lounge. There were only three bars in town, and Dave and me were kicked out of two of them. Only place would let us in was the Showfolks. In the other places if you threw up on the floor or something they kicked you out fast. None of the places had large drinks with flowers in them.

When Dave and the big guy came in they had a deal. Dave told the guy two hundred bucks would clean the car and said it would take the whole day. The guy handed him two brand-new one-hundred-dollar bills. Said we could hold the car overnight as long as we parked it inside.

On the way back to the shop, Dave said the carpet looked like burnt toast. "Had to be a big dog to produce that kind of crust," he said. "Had to be a big gutted dog."

The shop was an end unit in a strip of garages. An open space with water for one hundred and fifty dollars a month: cement floor, roll-down door, toilet, small piece of tarmac out front. It was a neighborhood of transmission joints, self-storage areas, welding shops, places vacated by people after dark. Except us. Dave pulled his van inside at night and slept in it. I had a sleeping bag and the bench seat of a Chevy pickup. We were only a block from the police station, so after dark we pulled the door down and kept quiet or else drove out of there in the van, which we didn't like to do because coming and going after hours attracted attention. Dave was sure we'd be taken for burglars. Dave was also sure the landlord did not intend that the units be used as homes.

We were in high spirits holding over a month's rent on a single job, so we stopped at Jax Liquors to restock the beer cooler and bought a quart of Canadian Mist.

The car was parked in the sun on the tarmac outside the shop. Dave had the van wired so we could blast rock 'n' roll while we worked. He took the leather seats out of the Riviera. Underneath, the blood was caked in smooth, cracked wafers like a dried-up mudflat. "Must have been a huge dog," Dave said. He pulled the carpet out, and the steel floor was wet with blood. I wanted to run the hose right inside the car, but Dave said there was no way to drain it without drilling holes in the floor. So I took off my shoes and shirt and squatted inside the shell of the car and squeegeed the muck from side to side with a dustpan. When I got a panful, I scooped it up and tossed it out the door. Outside on the tarmac Dave hosed off the carpet and the seats and sprayed them down with bleach. On his hands and knees he scrubbed the carpet with a brush, then stood and hosed a pink river down the driveway into the street. I sprayed some rinse water around inside the car and sucked it up with the wet-and-dry vacuum. We took regular cigarette and beer breaks, sitting in our wet shorts on plastic lawn chairs with the cooler between us, listening to music, chasing the beer with occasional sips from the whiskey bottle. By late afternoon the floor was clean and the carpet dried on a line strung across one side of the garage.

"Dave," I said, "there is no dog that big."

We sat watching our neighbors pull down their garage doors and drive off. They had homes to go to, and that was always a sad time for us. We had to decide whether to head out to the bar or pretend we were working late. The sun was low in the sky when we got it into our heads that it would be a great idea to drive the Riviera down to the beach. "What the hell," Dave said. "We got chairs." So we set the cooler in the car between the lawn chairs, and Dave rolled two huge joints, locked the van inside the shop, took his box of tapes, and backed the Riviera down the driveway. Dave drove pretty well, but he had to take the corners real slow otherwise the chairs shifted around. He had the wheel to hang onto, but I fell over backwards twice until I turned my chair sideways and held onto the door.

We drove down Main Street past the police station and the Showfolk's Lounge with music blasting through the Riviera's speakers and drove on out of town where there were no cars. We drove over the intracoastal waterway bridge and took a dirt road through the scrub pines by the circus winter quarters. There was a shortcut to a beach that few people used. In the mid-eighties, after Venice had grown up, the place became a notorious nude beach with cops dragging naked women over the sand and men without a stitch on waving their arms and yelling. But when Dave and I drove between the dunes of sand and saw grass, down to the water, it was wild and unknown.

We sat on the hood with our backs to the windshield in the best part of the Florida day with the sun spreading out into the gulf and the sky in the west gone the color of pink champagne and the breeze keeping the mosquitoes moving and the joint burning even when we forgot about it and held it too long between our fingers. And lions were roaring. It must have been feeding time at the winter quarters. Lions or something like lions huffed loudly over the sound of low waves, and we were stoned enough to wonder what they wanted. Did they roar for horse hocks, rib cages, slaughterhouse scraps? Or did they eat some kind of Purina Lion Chow? Dave said a large part of his small intestines might have to be cut out. "What do they do with that stuff?" He wanted to know. "What do hospitals do with people's parts?"

"Dave," I said, "hospitals make me sick." But he wouldn't stop talking about his small intestines and with those damn lions roaring all I could think about was catgut. Catgut wooden tennis rackets Dave and me had used when we were kids. My dad had them in the basement, they must have been made in the forties, catgut strings and warped wooden frames. Dave and me used them in the road between our houses until the catgut fell away loose and broken and the shellac on the frames dried and flaked away like old skin. Dave said chemo made all your hair fall out. Said he'd never have children.

We stayed on the beach until well after dark, and there was an inch of backwash left in the whiskey bottle which neither of us had any intention of drinking but would not throw away. We'd smoked both joints but still had beer, which we used to try to get normal enough to drive back to the shop. We drove between the dunes with the lights off, following the sandy road which glowed in the moonlight. The lions were quiet; I imagined them gnawing viciously on bloody bones, and decided right then that I was not going to any damn hospital.

Reaching the main road we saw the lights from the winter quarters a mile or so away. Dave switched on the headlights, and we turned toward town.

Just after the intracoastal waterway we passed him. I had my chair turned toward the door with my arms and head out the window, so I looked right at him. "Who was that?" Dave said.

"The rat-faced guy!"

"He see us?"

"We went right by him."

"But did he see us?"

"He looked right at me."

Dave twisted his head around to see behind him, and I guess that's how he lost control of his lawn chair, because the next thing I knew he crashed to the floor still holding onto the wheel with one hand, which turned the car sideways to the road. The car fishtailed hard and the two of us, with chairs and cooler, clattered back almost into the trunk. When the rear wheels hit the sandy ditch the car stalled out and came to a halt. We were afraid to move, as if the car were teetering on the edge of a cliff, but then we remembered the rat-faced guy and crawled toward the door. It was an uphill crawl because the car was buried to the frame, the rear wheels stuck in the ditch with the front wheels on the pavement. On both sides of the road were tall dark pines and low palmetto bushes. No sign of the rat-faced guy.

We stashed the beer in the palmettos and walked around the car for a long time, shaking our heads, saying, if only we had front-wheel drive or a couple of stout boards and some rocks and a place to stand or a tractor with nine guys and a rope. We were miles from town and nobody drove this road unless they were going to the winter quarters. "Where was that rat-faced guy going?" I said.

"Where did he go?" Dave said. We walked up the road to where I first saw him, but there was nothing except the drawbridge, the pines, and palmettos. No houses, no sounds, and no lights except across an expanse of low scrubland the winter quarters lit up like a small city.

"What we need is an elephant," I said.

"Hey!" Dave said. "We can walk over there. They've got stuff to pull us out."

"Elephants?"

"Someone should stay here," he said.

"You stay here, I'll go."

"I don't even have a license," he said. "What if a cop comes?"

"You're the proprietor of a business, Dave. Say someone stole the car and you walked here and found it." He held his head and walked around in the road. I wanted to bed down in the ditch and sleep till daylight, but I knew he'd start walking if I didn't, and I saw for the first time a change roll over his body. Blood took leave of his face, and he gripped his midsection with both arms as if to wring the pain from his body like a sponge. It was at least a mile to the winter quarters. "Dave," I said, "let me walk over there."

I began walking up the middle of the road. The bridge was a hump with a glass booth. Inside I saw a telephone. I thought about breaking the glass. But who would I call? The police? A tow truck? The hospital? I'd say a man in need of surgery was stranded on the winter quarters road, then hide in the woods and watch them take him away. Again I felt the urge to simply lie down under a bush and sleep. Looking back I saw the white car halfway across one lane, front wheels on the pavement, back end buried to the frame. It was too dark to see Dave.

Past the bridge I left the roadway and walked on a wide path of trampled sand that cut through palmettos. Light streaked toward me from vapor lamps on telephone poles in the winter quarters. I walked slowly in the center of the path, watching for snakes, and came to a dirt parking lot next to a building that looked like an aircraft hangar. I stood in the shadow of a thick pine. Behind the building was an open area the size of a football field surrounded by a chain-link fence topped with three strands of barbed wire. A number of low buildings backed up to the fence, some were horse stalls, others were aluminum trailers. Farthest from the main building were two large green tents. People moved about on foot and drove strange blue vehicles pulling brightly painted wagons. I heard voices. Next to the main building was a guardhouse and gate. A short, stocky figure in a guard's hat dragged one leg behind him as he paced in the road under a vapor lamp waving and shouting as people drove in and out. Later, I learned this was Backdoor Jack, and had I approached him that night, things would not have worked out.

I walked away from the guardhouse, kept to the shadows, until

I came to a break in the fence behind one of the green tents. A man in coveralls rolled a wheelbarrow of steaming bowling balls across a makeshift bridge, planks over mirrors of vile black liquid, to a pile of manure. I was no expert on crap, and not thinking clearly, but I suspected whatever let loose crap of those proportions had to be big. I suspected elephants.

I slipped through the gap in the fence behind the wheelbarrow man and followed a path of hard-packed dirt between the tents. They were old damp-smelling canvas tents surrounded by trenches of seeping juice the color and consistency of used motor oil. Around front I mixed with busy people and no one challenged me. There was an old guy sitting on an overturned bucket. I sidled up to him. He held a Coke can with both hands.

"Lookin' to get on?" he said.

"Maybe."

"Hilmer's the man."

"He around?"

"Somewhere." He took a sip off the Coke can. This didn't seem like the guy I needed to help me get the car off the road, so I stepped away and moved inside the tent flap.

Elephants. Massive. Silent, active, and close. They were chained side by side, chained by one back foot, swinging their trunks and whipping their club-like tails, rocking their heads back and forth, lifting one foot then the other, repeating each step in turn like some demented dance. I saw their eyes on me, acute, not missing a beat of their dance. Then there was a compact man in front of me wearing tight blue jeans and knee-high turquoise boots, no shirt, and teeth like Chiclets. Chiclets chewing gum right out of the box. He had bleached blond hair over his shoulders and he said, "*Ja? Ja?* What do you want?" He looked like a picture torn from a glossy magazine and tossed to the gutter. All I could think of was George Armstrong Custer.

"The guy out front," I said. "He said I might get on."

"You been on bulls?"

"Bulls?"

"We're loading out," he said. "Tell Martin to set you up." Then he was gone before I had a chance to say I knew Elephant Car Betty. I stared at the elephants again. There were other people in the tent, men and women moving about, lugging large trunks with leather handles to wagons lined up outside. None of them spoke to me or even looked my way.

I cut back through the tent flap to the old guy with the Coke can who was still sitting on the bucket.

"You Martin?"

"You get on?"

"I guess so."

"Been on bulls?" I didn't answer. It took me three days to figure out for sure that elephants were called bulls.

"Got a hook?" he said.

"Hook?"

"How 'bout a smoke?"

"I got nothing," I said. The guy leaned so far forward I thought he would fall on his face, then hocked a blood-red gob of spit between a pair of dry cracked wingtips with curled toes. He tilted the bucket to one side, reached underneath and brought out a bottle of Everclear grain alcohol, unscrewed the cap and tipped some into the Coke can. He put the bottle back and slowly stood, flat-footed and swaying, like he was riding on a subway. When he had his bearings, he turned and ambled off toward one of the low aluminum buildings, waving me after him with his Coke can.

The building was crowded with men and women packing stuff into boxes and bags, odd leather stuff, nylon, canvas and rubber stuff with brass rings and silver chains, steel buckles and studded straps. Elephant stuff. Martin rummaged for a club and handed it over. "Yours while you're here," he said. "You leave, you leave it." It was a sledgehammer handle wrapped in black electrical tape. Embedded in one end was a vicious-looking steel hook, a bullhook.

I guess it was the bullhook that really knocked me off course. I hadn't forgotten Dave, but for the moment I felt swept along, as if the plans I had coming over here had no life once I slipped through that fence. I'd been taken up, given a part, and playing it seemed the easiest thing to do.

Outside, I wandered around carrying the bullhook, trying to look on-duty, expecting someone to tell me what to do. No one did. I set my hook down and rolled bulltubs to wagons. When the wagons were full and the doors clamped shut, someone roared up in one of those strange blue vehicles, "unimugs" Martin called them. They had large steel pinhole hitches on both ends, two steering wheels and a revolving driver's seat. Their sole function was to push or pull. Dave would be impressed if I showed up with one of these things. I held the tongues of the wagons for the drivers to back into and tried to catch their attention, but they backed up fast, dropped the pin into the hole without leaving their seats. One driver nodded to me, so I stepped up close to his steering wheel and said, "I have a problem." He drove off fast.

The center of activity was the brightly lit building across the lot. Two sliding doors big enough to roll planes through were open, and inside ropes and cables hung from the ceiling and gray canvas bags cluttered the arena floor. People lifted, carried, pointed, and pulled. Shouts rose and died. Steel poles clanged, and clattered as men grimed with sweat slid them into wagons and slammed the doors. The wagons were immediately taken up by unimugs and towed around the corner and out the gate where Backdoor Jack stood. I watched from under the bleachers and tried to formulate a plan. I decided Dave should come here. I'd go get him, and we could both get jobs on bulls and the hell with that white car. But Dave had his van, and his wet-and-dry, and some other stuff. Dave had baggage, something growing in his gut, that hospital appointment in the morning.

Everyone in the building hustled around, and people began to eyeball me standing under the seats with a bullhook, so I went back to the elephant tent. It was close to midnight. The only person sitting was the old Coke-can guy, Martin, so I slid up to him and tried to get information. "What time do we knock off?" I said.

He stared at me through eye slits like pencil lines and took a hit off his Coke can.

The blond guy, Hilmer, grabbed my arm. "You come in here." He dragged me behind him into the tent. "Next town you see Huffy," he said. "Huffy in the pie car. Tell him you're on bulls." He took my bullhook, handed me a pitchfork, and I spent the rest of the night scraping soiled straw from beneath elephants. I watched and copied the other guys. You timed your work to the elephant's dance, dodging swinging tails and trunks. When the left front leg came up you grabbed a sodden forkful and backed off, then the right rear, the right front and so on. They seemed okay with me, but their eyes left no doubt, they knew I had no idea what a bull was.

Before we finished, Hilmer came in yelling. Everyone put up the forks and began unchaining feet. The chains were shackled on a rear leg, and each shackle had a pin which had to be unscrewed. This happened fast with a lot of loud jabbering by Hilmer. Within minutes they moved out of the tent. Each beast took delicately with its trunk the tail of the one preceding it. They moved with strong snorts of breath on round padded feet and lined up facing an identical group from the adjoining tent. The men stood between them, even Martin was on his feet, bullhook in one hand, Coke can in the other. I mimicked the other guys, trying hard not to do anything stupid in the close proximity of forty loose elephants and a dozen men with clubs.

We were loading out of winter quarters. I wondered where we were going, but it didn't occur to me until later, after I'd seen the train, that all of us—elephants and their stuff, unimugs and wagons, worlds of people, animals, and things that I had no notion of, but had somehow become caught up in—were leaving Venice, Florida.

Hilmer hollered and both lines of elephants moved at once. I moved as the guys near me moved. We walked at the left hind leg, the way horse people walk at the left shoulder, we carried our clubs prominent. The beasts were not to break the trunktail hookup, that was gospel, if one let go of the tail our job was to hook the inside back leg and say "Tail!" If the tail wasn't picked up immediately the role of the bullhand was to take a full roundhouse swing with the club and bury the hook in the leg. This took something more of an adjustment than I'd been able to muster that night, but luckily the beasts were compliant, they knew their role, fell readily into it, and did not test mine. They seemed happy to be moving. I pictured myself a native in a safari movie.

The impetus of the movement, the focal point, was Hilmer. Each man and beast watched Hilmer and he watched everyone. He moved along the line and spoke in a way I could not at first understand, spoke in what I thought was a foreign tongue, but once we'd gone through the gate, past Backdoor Jack, and out onto the same sandy path I'd taken across the palmetto field, I heard what he was saying were the names of the elephants.

He wasn't talking to us but to them. Moving slightly faster than the herd, he cooed the name of each beast. They had regular girl names: "Ellen, Jenny, Cindy." He said their names slowly and affectionately and he looked each one in the eye as if they had his personal assurance that everything was under control, that they would be fine, that there was nothing to worry about. That reassured me, too. I saw that in this world bull and bullhand were not that different, both had a place, both were taken care of. I nurtured a state of helplessness about Dave, pushing guilt behind fantasy, and felt better the more confusing things became. The world shifted, I was caught in the afterwind, and went with it because it was the easiest thing to do.

The eastern sky had gone peach over the black horizon. At the rate we moved we would pass the car in broad daylight. I could bail out of the line. I knew that. I could simply stop walking, hand my bullhook to Martin as he went by, and everything would be the same as the night before. Why not? Nothing would stop the line, that much was clear, if I fell down dead they'd walk on over me. But nothing else was clear to me. I didn't want to stop. I wanted to walk to Africa. I didn't want to clean bloody car floors, sleep in garages, wait in hospitals, watch Dave double over and not get up. I wanted to be a bullhand. The problem was not the car, or even Dave. But rather, could I abandon a dying man? I felt like I could. In fact, a dying man felt like the best kind to abandon. Dave would understand that. Only a captain goes down with the ship, and clearly I was no captain.

We made it onto the road when the sun was just breaking over the tree line and the inland waterway was beginning to steam. From the drawbridge I saw the car. The herd padded silently in pairs straight down the double yellow. As I got close to the car, I hunkered tight against my elephant's leg, moving with her, but as we went by I peeked back under the tail and saw Dave's head sticking up in one of the windows, his eyeballs wide as telescope lenses. He never saw me.

Shortly after, we turned onto a dirt road and came upon a white train parked in the woods. Brilliant white. Freshly painted white. With large red and blue letters on the sides. It sat there waiting for us. For me. I was stunned. Never in my life would I have considered the idea that there was a white train in the world.

Richard Schmitt is a graduate of the MFA Program for Writers at Warren Wilson College in North Carolina. He has published stories in *The Mississippi Review, Flyway, Puerto del Sol, The Marlboro Review, Flying Horse,* and others. "Leaving Venice, Florida" won the 1997 *Mississippi Review* short story contest. He lives on a horse farm in Central Florida, where he is currently at work on a novel.

CHELSEA SCHMITT

I never lived in Venice, Florida, but I had a close friend who did, years ago when the gulf towns between Sarasota and Fort Myers were just green signs on old Route 41. Now they're monotonous crossroads of the new interstate. My friend still calls I-75 "the new interstate" even though the road has been there two decades. Once I asked him, with genuine curiosity, what activities could possibly keep him busy in a place like Venice. "Well," he said slowly. "There's only three bars in town and I'm kicked out of two of them." That told me everything I needed to know, and I pretty much wrote the story from that one line. I knew about circus winter quarters in Venice, and I knew some circus people, and the whole thing kind of took off on its own (on a train actually).

Mary Gordon

STORYTELLING

(from *The Threepenny Review*)

I went to Florida to see my brother Ted because I was tired of reading and writing. I'd just finished the first draft of a novel—a labor of two years. I knew what was wrong with it—everything that was wrong with it—but I couldn't think of how to fix it, or even how to take the first step. It came upon me that I had misspent my life: all those years laboring over words, words, words, and for what? What difference did it make to anyone? Who cared what I had to say? I had lost the appetite for telling.

I wanted to visit Ted because, whatever else shifts in my life, one thing is constant: I have always loved my brother. Is this really so unusual or does it just seem so to me, that there should be a person you have loved and been loved by your whole life? What does this say, my finding it so unusual, about the age we live in, or the way I live?

Perhaps it isn't love I'm talking about, constant love, but rather constant enjoyment, which is even more rare. I guess there must have been times in childhood when Ted and I didn't get along, but I don't remember them. I remember always a sense of safety with him, a safety of a rather special kind, because although he was older than I, he wasn't the oldest child. Our parents had, in effect, had two families: three older children who were like aunts and uncles to us, whom we seemed hardly to know, who had moved out of the house and married before we started school, whose children were a bit of an embarrassment to us, and whom we embarrassed.

Our parents were worn out by the time we came and it seemed to me later (though it's nothing I would have thought of as a child, or even while they were alive: they died when Ted and I were in our twenties, in a car accident) they were a little abashed by our existence, proof as it was of their untimely fecundity. They tended to us—we were physically well cared for—but they had no interest in our entertainments. Mostly, they left us alone. We had the orphan's luxury without the orphan's anxiety. We understood that our parents didn't think about us much, and so we couldn't go to them for understanding. Ted guessed, though I don't think it dawned on me, that our parents couldn't be looked to as a source of pleasure, either. We divided the world up, then, into kingdoms or protectorates of which he and I were in charge. His domain was pleasure; mine was understanding. That meant that the smooth movements of home life—that which made it more than bearable: decoration, desserts, no hurt feelings, no anger that lasted after sundown—were his charge. He made things happen and later I would suggest what they had meant.

He was popular in school, an astonishing social success, but his grades weren't good. I had no friends but was valedictorian. So he went to a poor state school and I to Radcliffe on a scholarship.

We were proud of each other in those years, but our orbits didn't touch. Happily, I watched him drive by in convertibles, picked up for tennis or for swimming by bronzed gods, their golden hair absorbing more than its fair share of light. Sweetly, every year he drove me to Cambridge in our sky-blue Rambler, the only family car. Then after college he came back to New York and worked for an advertising agency, where he met Pete.

It would be wrong to say that Ted came out to me: there was no need. That he would have a man seemed to me unremarkable. That we could keep it from our parents the expected thing. Pete and I liked each other; we liked to laugh at the same things, and we both loved Ted. Ted was twenty-five when they moved to Fort

Lauderdale and opened a wallpaper business. They've been there ever since. Twenty-five years.

They enjoy their comforts. And I travel to see them when I want comforting. Their house (which, as Ted says, is a living hymn to wallpaper) looks over a golf course. It has all the things I enjoy that I wouldn't think of having: a refrigerator with crushed ice that appears, magically, through the door, a swimming pool, a hot tub, a shower as big as my Upper West Side kitchen.

Ted picks me up at the airport. He takes my winter coat: "You still own one of these?" He carries my bag, complains about the weight of my laptop.

"We'll bury all this under a palm tree while you're here. But I'm not even going to give you the time to unpack. We'll lock everything in the trunk. We're having lunch by the water. I want to introduce you to Jean-Claude."

"So who's Jean-Claude?"

"Jean-Claude is an expert on bathroom lighting. Particularly boat bathroom lighting. He works on our upmarket jobs. That's where we met. He's from Grenoble. If he's not from outer space. I'm never quite sure. There's something a little extraterrestrial about him. But as our grandmother would have said, he's good for what ails you. At the very least, he's awfully pretty."

He pointed to a table where a man was sitting alone, a man of about our age, fifty or so. He was attractive, certainly, but I wouldn't have called him pretty; there was nothing fine or fresh about his looks, and nothing girlish. His hair was thick, dark brown with a few strands of gray. His eyes were bluish green and gave the simultaneous appearance of being hooded and alert, as if he couldn't decide whether to succumb to something or spring for its throat. His shirt was Polo, navy blue, tucked into khaki trousers. He wore loafers without socks.

"So," he said, before I had sat down. "You're wondering whether to start coloring your hair. Don't. I love the silver. It makes you look experienced. People aren't going to want to take advantage of you. But with that wonderful skin, those fabulous eyes, of course they'll be intrigued. And, you begin dyeing, it's nothing but enslavement."

"This is Jean-Claude," said Ted.

"I'll bet you want her to color her hair," he said. "So you look younger."

"I want her to start when I start."

"Edward, please. I can't begin to tell you the calamity of someone with your complexion embarking on such a course. So, you're depressed," he said to me. "What happened? Have you lost your lover?"

"I don't have a lover," I said. "I've been married for twenty years."

"And how old is your husband?"

"Fifty-eight."

"You need a lover."

"My problems aren't about love. They're about work. I'm tired of my work."

"I understand completely. Then you must travel. When I'm tired of my work, I go somewhere completely new. That's how I got to America."

The waiter came by and took our drink order. Jean-Claude ordered Beaujolais nouveau, which had just arrived that week.

"Tell me about your coming to America," I said. Recognizing that I was feeling curiosity, I realized how long I'd gone without.

"Yes, tell me," my brother said. "I've never known."

"First, we take a moment to appreciate the beautiful young waiter. If you're young, you don't have to do anything. Just your health and youth is beautiful. Look at the fresh color of his lips, even his gums are beautiful when he smiles. Because everything of him is healthy it says, 'Nothing will grow old and sick and dead.'"

"How's Ray?" my brother said.

"Terrible. Suffering. Dying."

"Jean-Claude volunteers with the AIDS Crisis center. He takes people to their doctors' appointments, helps them with meals. This guy Ray that he helps is, what is he, Jean-Claude, twenty-three? You're very good to him."

"Well, what I am feeling is it's the least I can do. It's my way of saying 'Thank God,' when I am spared. I am not sick, and really I deserve to be sick, so much more than these other people. I mean, I was really promiscuous. Not only that, I made a living off it."

"Being sick isn't something anyone deserves," I said.

"I know what you mean. But I did all the things you are supposed to do to get it. And I'm spared. So I do this in gratitude."

"You were telling us how you came to America."

"Well, of course, it starts in Grenoble. I'm a bastard, I mean literally. Let's say that right away, because it isn't something that bothers me or something I try to hide. It's like the color of my eyes: just something that's there, that I was born with. So why try to hide it? My mother was very young when I was born and she left for Canada with a man when I was six. My grandparents were kind and good, but too old for a wild boy like I was.

"Probably now, I'd be called A.D.D. I couldn't stay still in school and all the teachers hated me. I was bored, so I made trouble to entertain myself. Doesn't everyone do that, do anything to entertain themselves when they're bored? I swear people do the most unbelievable things because they're bored. I never had any teacher who liked me. Not one. I wonder what would have happened if I did. That's why I never learned how to read very well. Do you know I've never read a whole book in my life? Not one. And here I am talking to you, a real writer, who's written so many books. But it doesn't matter, does it? Because we're just people, talking, enjoying each other. It would matter if we were bored, but we're not bored so it doesn't matter."

I thought how odd it was that he was right, that it didn't matter. And that I didn't know what I felt about his never reading a book, and what that meant about his life. I wondered whether or not I should be sad for him, and I didn't know why I was so insistent on introducing a note of sadness when Jean-Claude told the story of his life with so little self-pity, such an easy sense of "once upon a time," "and then this happened and then that," such a peaceful sense of proceeding without thoughts of "The End."

"Perhaps if some teacher had taken an interest in me I would have been different. Now I make up this story about this retired teacher who moves onto my street. One day I see her having trouble carrying a heavy package from her car, and I offer to help. She invites me for tea. She plays the piano for me. We become friends. I help her around the house. She gives me books to read and helps me with my reading. We go to the opera. In the summer we go on vacation, where we go to museums and read books in the hotel. But when I was young I never met anyone like that, or maybe I wouldn't have ended up on the streets of Paris at the age of fourteen. But if I hadn't gone to the streets of Paris, I wouldn't be here, having lunch with you in the sunshine by the pine trees and the beautiful green sea. Maybe I'd be a grandfather now, working for the telephone company in Grenoble, with a fat wife getting varicose veins. Your legs are great, by the way, you still have a girl's legs."

"Why do you think you'd have a wife?" I asked. "Haven't you always liked men?"

"I've had two wives already."

"Jean-Claude," said Ted, looking amazed. "You've never told any of us that."

"Well, all right, I haven't had two wives, only one, according to the law. But I lived with a woman I wasn't married to for six years."

"This is incredible," Ted said.

"She had great legs, too, but not like yours. Hers were very long, very strong, like trees. Like a man. And she gave great blow jobs, as good as the best man, which is very unusual, most women just don't get it. We had a restaurant together. Well, a café, more of a bar. When I met her she was already pregnant. I went to the hospital with her. Her son called me daddy. I was always the one who got up with him and then took him to school. She was a lousy mother. She started picking up men in the restaurant. Then she threw me out, so one of them could move in. He beat her up, he hit the kid. The kid came to me, trying to get away from them. I was living with a rich American then, and he wanted to take me to America. But I'd have given it up and stayed in Grenoble if she'd let me have the kid. She said if I ever came near the kid again she'd have me arrested as a pedophile. I saw him ten years after that, he was nineteen, a complete mess, greasy hair, missing teeth, sitting in a filthy hamburger place drinking wine, he already had a kid. We had nothing to say to each other."

"What happened with the rich American?" I asked.

"I went to America with him, but it didn't work out. So I made my way to Aspen. I'm a great skier, of course everyone in Grenoble is, and I got a fabulous job on the ski patrol. With a lot of good tips from lonely widows. That's where I met Penny. She was a waitress there and we got married for the green card. We were great friends, but the fucking was no good. I don't know why, because we really liked each other."

"How did you get here?"

"A Cuban guy brought me to Miami. I learned bathroom lighting. Then I met George. I went home with him because I thought he was rich, but even when I found out he doesn't have shit, I stayed with him. I guess we're in love. Maybe that means I'm getting old. I don't feel old, but I could never support myself by my cock any more. That's over."

"Well, it's too dangerous nowadays," I said.

"What do you think about the waiter? Would he like to go home with you or me?"

"Probably with someone his own age," I said.

"Are all your books depressing?" asked Jean-Claude.

"I think I write about life as it is."

"Why would you do that when what everyone wants is to forget about it? Why don't you write something funny? Something romantic. Something about the waiter who meets his long-lost father the oil sheik who's dying and is going to leave him ten million dollars so he buys a house for himself and this older guy who's the love of his life."

"That's not the kind of story I can do."

"Anyone can do any kind of story if they want to," he said.

My brother called for the check. He and I fought over it. Jean-Claude looked at the palm trees, or the waiter, or the boys, bare-chested, rollerblading down the middle of the street.

On our way to the car, my eye fell on a dress in a store window. Gray wool, sleeveless, a jacket trimmed in Persian lamb.

"Remember grandma's Persian lamb coat?" I said to my brother.

"You must try it on," Jean-Claude said. "It will be very elegant for you."

He was right. I did feel elegant, although it seemed odd to be trying on gray wool when, fifteen yards away, people were dressed in almost nothing, in neon colors, their bare arms and legs absorbing the last of the October sun.

The dress was more than I could afford. But I'd been working hard, and no one else I knew was going to treat me to anything in the foreseeable future. I shook off the self-pity that was ready to drown my sense of well-being about how good I looked in the dress. I looked at myself carefully from all angles, partly hoping in one of them I wouldn't look good, so I wouldn't have to spend the money, or take the risk on so much pleasure, partly praying that when I turned I'd still look as good as I had a few seconds before.

"Magnificent," said Jean-Claude.

"Terrific, honey," said my brother.

Jean-Claude came by with a black-velvet-and-silk scarf, velvet flowers embossed on the silk plainness. He wound it around my neck. The dress, already a success, was transformed into something entirely other; it turned from a success into a triumph. I looked at the price. The scarf was $300.

"That's higher than I can go," I said, handing the scarf back to Jean-Claude, trying to keep my spirits from being dashed.

I was happy with the dress, and Ted kept telling me I was doing the right thing, the dress was a luxury, but it was clearly worth it;

the scarf might make me feel bad in the end. I know I'd be happy when I got back to New York, but at that moment all I could do was mourn the scarf.

"You two go on ahead," Jean-Claude said to me and my brother. He caught up with us in half a block.

"So," he said. "You're happy with your dress."

"Oh, yes," I said.

"But you're sad about the scarf."

"Well, it doesn't really matter."

"Bullshit," he said, and threw a small bag at me.

I opened the bag. The scarf was wrapped in aqua-colored tissue.

"Jean-Claude," I said. "Don't be ridiculous. You can't afford this."

"Baby," Ted said. "It's a lovely gesture, but you can't afford it. You're up to your ass in debt as it is."

"Of course I am, you idiot. Of course I can't afford it. Do you think I'm an idiot like you? I didn't pay for it."

"You stole it?"

"What do you take me for? I've been many things, but not a thief. No, I didn't steal it. All I did was tell him that you and Ted were married but what you didn't know was that this would be the last shopping you'd do for some time because Ted was leaving you for me tomorrow. That I was terribly guilty, but we couldn't live without each other. So I told the guy who owned the store that he should give you the scarf because your life was about to be ruined, that I would buy it for you, but I had no money, the money was all Ted's, and he was a monster but I loved him and what could I do?"

"So he gave you the scarf?"

"Of course. For a while I was trying to decide whether to tell the story as I did or to say that you and I were running away, that you were leaving Ted for me because you loved me and what could I do. I had to figure out whether the guy was straight or not, and I had to do it quickly because the way I told the story depended on it. I have trouble telling which way these guys from the Islands go.

But I liked his ass and I'm usually not into straight men. I decided he was one of us. Thank God I was right. I knew everything was riding on my telling the right story."

"Jean-Claude," I said. "You must bring the scarf right back."

"Of course I won't," he said. "Why should I? I earned it. And everyone gets something they want. You get the scarf. The guy from the Islands gets something to think about, and a warm feeling inside, like he's the Good Samaritan. I get to give you the gift I want for you and can't afford. Only Ted didn't make out so well. But, what's the difference, he's got love and money. Life is good for him. And one day, you'll write something and Ted will be the hero of the story and you'll let everybody know how wonderful he is. Then he'll be paid back for not looking so great in my story. And one day, you'll write something about me."

"Jean-Claude," I said. "No one would believe me."

"Of course they will, if you do your job."

When we got home, Ted put my bags and laptop into the spare room, the one that looked out on the golf course. I said I needed not to be disturbed. I put the scarf around my neck, sat at the desk, and wrote all night. I didn't move until the sun came up, a garish red over the flat, prosperous green where soon real humans would appear, to my astonishment, alive beyond the rim of my invention.

Mary Gordon's works include best-selling novels—*Final Payments, The Company of Women, Men and Angels, The Other Side, Spending*—and a memoir, *The Shadow Man.* She has published a book of novellas, *The Rest of Life,* a collection of stories, *Temporary Shelter,* and a book of essays, *Good Boys and Dead Girls.* Her most recent collection of essays, *Seeing Through Places,* will be published in January 2000. She has received the Lila Wallace–*Reader's Digest* Writer's Award and a Guggenheim Fellowship. She is a professor of English at Barnard College.

JOYCE RAVID

I wrote this story sitting with my cousin (who is like my brother) and a friend of his by the Fort Lauderdale waterfront. My cousin's friend is an enchanting fabulator, and he began spinning tales. Then we went shopping. What happened in the story did not really happen, but it could have, as my cousin's friend is capable of outrageous, miraculous acts. It occurred to me that he and I are in the same profession—both of us are storytellers—only I get paid for it.

Mary Clyde

KRISTA HAD A TREBLE CLEF ROSE

(from *Boulevard*)

Anne and Nicole at Lunch

Perched on bar stools at Johnny Rockets Diner, Anne tugs at the lettuce ruffle of her sandwich; Nicole smears a puddle of ketchup with a French fry.

"We're freaks," Anne announces. She says it mildly. Though she believes it, she's said it before.

"We are." Nicole's slow nod accelerates in agreement.

Poster teenagers, they call themselves, though they're not. Still, they are aware it's only the survivors who get to represent their disease.

A girl in cutoff jeans and combat boots pauses in front of the frantic shapes of a mall theater's movie posters.

"Cute hair," Anne whispers. She straightens the turquoise shopping bag resting by her sandaled feet. Inside is a clam comb of imitation tortoiseshell and wands like chopsticks to twist up her hair.

Nicole says, "The anesthesia made my hair fall out. I've got three hairs left. I'm playing up my eyes." She bats them as proof. Then, "Dr. Stafford is the cutest of the junior doctors. Don't you think? He told me I reminded him of his sister-in-law."

"Except when he pulled my wound drain, he didn't warn me."

Nicole sighs. "The Jackson Pratt drain."

They wince and smile, knowing smiles of well-tended teeth.

148

Nine months ago, they were Garden Grove Honor Cotillion Debu-
tantes. Anne had giggled when she told her mother about her nomina-
tion because wasn't she just exactly not the type? But wasn't it a kick to
be one?

Anne now says, "My dad wants to buy me clothes. Suddenly, he can't
buy me enough clothes."

Nicole says, "My mom will say, 'Would you like something to eat,
sweetie?' Then doesn't even blink. Brings it like some genie and stands
there watching me eat."

"They feel guilty."

"It's no one's fault."

"We're not going to die, not now."

"Saved by stomas."

"Ileostomies," Anne says, a word that suddenly sounds like a flying
dinosaur.

Anne's Boyfriend

Anne's boyfriend, Jeff, left for college while she was still in the
hospital. Before he left, he visited her often and brought roses in
a vase. Like a wedding anniversary or an apology for forgetting
one. Florist flowers, but all different colors, which showed he had
no taste. Part of why she liked him, that he didn't pretend he did.

When an alarm sounded, he ran to get the nurse. "It's just a
pump," Anne called, but he was already in the hall. He played ice
hockey; he was fast even without his skates.

They went for walks in the halls. Jeff pushed the IV pole and
kept a wary eye on the pumps. He was prone to giving himself ti-
tles: Amazing Microwave Chef, Consumer Math Repeat Kid.
"Supreme IV Pole Navigator," he now said. His smile looked like
his old smile, goofy and a little shy. It made her miss him and understand how that part of him was already gone.

Once they rode the elevator to the cafeteria. The cashier spotted
some label on Anne's equipment and radioed for help. It came in
the fast-moving form of an efficacious Asian nurse.

"Must not leave floor," she scolded, wresting the IV pole from the startled Jeff. "Never, never. You N.B.M."

Nothing by mouth. It sounded contagious, deadly.

Anne said, "You think I'd eat something?"

"Been done," the nurse said, commandeering the IV pole.

Jeff looked as if he might cry.

What to Wear in the Hospital

As her condition worsened, Anne abandoned her appearance. She quit plucking her eyebrows, didn't bother with her contact lenses, sent her makeup and earrings home and her nightshirts with a prostrate Snoopy and Jesus Christ as a superstar.

It took concentration to stay alive. She wore hospital gowns because of their utility and as an admission of how sick she was and because she now belonged. Soldiers wear fatigues. She rolled up her sleeves, lost the knack of good looks, forgot the need.

When she came home from the hospital, just shaving her legs exhausted her.

Anne's Father and Mother

After, she heard her father whisper in the hall, "Do you think she understands?"

Her mother said, "Do you?" It sounded fierce.

The Psychiatrist Visits

The psychiatrist told her about his brother who had been hospitalized with the same thing when he was a young boy. "They took him off food, too." The psychiatrist untangled her IV tubes, expertly. He said he didn't want to see the photographs of her ulcerated colon, but the way he said it was kind, and made Anne hope the pictures weren't as important as the doctors made them out to be. "My brother watched TV all day. It was when McDonald's was just introducing Chicken McNuggets. All he talked about was how when he got out he'd get some. It helped him get through it, gave him something to look forward to."

(Talk to him, her mother had pleaded before he came in. "Annie, just try. He can help you.")

Tubes brought things into Anne's body, other tubes took things out. It seemed like math, a hospital story problem: If a teenager is not responding to medication and has two tubes for feeding and one tube for blood, and if the tube in her nose . . .

"Anne," the psychiatrist said, "visualize a healthy colon."

Anne and Nicole Go Shopping at J. Crew

Anne buys a high-waisted dress of fluttery fabric with the colors and spots of overripe bananas.

"Is it too short?" she says.

Nicole shakes her head. "You've got great legs."

"Look how my calves go in. Right there. Look how deformed."

Nicole holds out her freckle-doused arms. "You think that's bad? Look at my fat arms." Anne has seen Nicole's mother; she has seen these arms before. And my knees are kind of baggy." Nicole pinches her knees where Anne notices they sag, something like a zoo elephant's.

What to Expect Before Surgery

The enterostomal therapy nurse will visit your hospital room to mark the ileostomy site. The placement is based on several factors: skin creases, scars, navel, waistline, hipbone, how you sit, and where you wear the waist of your clothes. Proper location makes ileostomy care easier after the surgery.

Food Dreams

Frequently: mashed potatoes—fluffy innocence, the gastrointestinal patient's last food friend.

Occasionally: Chocolate Cornflake Crunchies. Anne's mother hadn't made them since kindergarten. Anne thought she'd forgotten them, didn't remember even liking them, now she had Chocolate Cornflake Crunchy fantasies. A steep yearning, sweet as homesickness.

Recurring nightmare: Popcorn—salted, buttered, white-cheddar-cheesed, carameled, balled, pink-candied. She'd been told she could never eat popcorn again, which scared her and proved her vulnerability as nothing else quite had. Because who could be undone by popcorn?

Krista had a treble clef rose, a tattoo three inches long on her thigh, because she was going to major in music.

Jen had blown out her knee cheerleading, but she refused to have it operated on until after basketball season. As a concession to her parents she wore a brace for tumbling.

Richard said he'd been born with an extra finger. Its ghost helped him catch. It gave him ESP.

Anne's Father at the Hospital

Sometimes her father seemed as difficult as the illness. He washed her undriven car and replaced the burnt-out taillight. He bought her Rolling Stones CDs. Mick Jagger looked desperate.

He brought Misty, their sincere Golden Retriever, who stood beneath Anne's hospital window, dismayed by the circumstances. She sniffed the humid air. When a doctor knelt to pet her, she gratefully wagged her tail.

When Anne's pain was intense, she thought no one else could have ever experienced anything like it. She learned what morphine demanded in exchange for its not-quite-heroic rescue. She worried about becoming addicted.

Her father's experience with pain medication included the nitrous oxide from the dentist and Tylenol with codeine from the time he broke his leg skiing. "I heard it snap," he said, still in fond disbelief.

"Annie, what can I do for you?" he said.

Out of kindness, she or her mother came up with errands: lo-tion from home? a blanket from the warmer? He forgot them. In-stead, he wired her hospital room for stereo sound from the VCR and replumbed the bathroom shower.

"This way," he yelled over the clank of his tools, "when you're ready for a shower, you can direct the spray."

Hospital Routine

The hospital gave medication, recorded vital signs, changed linens, and offered sponge baths on a rigid schedule.

Unscheduled but with frequency, Anne bled, cursed, wept, vomited, and prayed. Whatever she did the staff called her brave, and she understood how saying it helped them.

The Boyfriend Leaves for College

Anne wore white surgical support stockings and two hospital gowns. Jeff wore a baseball cap. The logo was NO FEAR. They walked by the surgery waiting room, where the occupants re-garded their progress with ill-concealed anxiety or baby's-first-step encouragement.

Back in Anne's room, Jeff sat in the chair one of her parents slept in at night. He stroked the IV pole and told Anne about work at the furniture rental store. How his dad kept asking what kind of people have to rent *furniture*. Anne realized a boyfriend was an ex-hausting luxury like reading or crossword puzzles.

Jeff didn't talk about how he was going away to Florida State, which proved to her how badly he wanted to talk about it, how eager he was to go. He didn't talk about Anne either, but she knew he watched her carefully to see what she expected or wanted from him and if she were in any way still the same.

She thought, *we are in love* and also, *this relationship is probably over.*

* * *

Anne and Nicole Shop at the Sports Watch Counter

Nicole says her goal is to kiss a guy of every race. Every religion, too. "But with a system," she says, "like starting with boys from extreme far-right religions and going to extreme-left. Or from short guys to tall ones. Something to make it challenging."

The watch Anne is looking at doesn't have numbers, but has weird geometric shapes instead.

"Or older men to younger," Nicole says, taking the watch from Anne. "That way I'd be shocking when I was young fooling around with old men and again when I was old, kissing young guys."

Anne says, "Do all religions allow kissing?"

"Who could be against kissing?"

"I don't know. Amish? Do they?" Anne says.

"Yuck, who'd want to kiss some Amish guy?"

Anne takes the watch back. "Do you think after I got used to this watch, I'd be able to tell time on it?"

"I mean he'd never forget me, an Amish boy. He'd be so grateful."

Mother of pearl makes one watch face appear chaste. Another is no bigger than an aspirin.

Anne says, "I'd like something plain, but gorgeous."

Nicole's Mother

Nicole's mother banned popcorn from the house, as if it were responsible. When the popcorn ads were flashed before movies, Nicole said her mother clucked her tongue and said, "Honestly!" the same as she did for cigarette or beer ads. Popcorn became a vice.

Nicole's parents were divorced. Her father moved to New Mexico and kept urging her to join him, telling her how the fresh mountain air and exercise could help her. Once her mother yanked the phone out of Nicole's hand. "Rodney," she screamed, "she doesn't have tuberculosis!"

Anne's Mother

Anne found even if she didn't respond to her mother, her mother continued to talk to her. She jabbered cheerfully. Anne hadn't thought her mother was a jabberer. Sometimes she didn't bother to listen while her mother changed her hospital gowns or shampooed her hair. She looked away when her mother bathed her, her earlier modesty forgotten. Once, she thought, this must have been how she spoke to me when I was a baby before I learned to talk.

Then one day Anne heard her: "Anne," she said, "where are you when you don't answer us? Where is it you go?"

Anne looked at her mother then, saw how bruised her eyes looked; how she'd lost weight. She is suffering, Anne thought, and it frightened her.

"Sometimes I just don't feel like talking," Anne said, but she thought, I'm holding my breath, balancing on life's thin edge.

Coach hung Richard's jersey from where the rafters would be if the high school gymnasium had them. He said the team would finish the season playing in his memory. In all his years of coaching, he'd never seen anything like what Richard could do to an opposition's defensive line. Coach hugged his clipboard to his chest and swore it: Richard could just plain read their freaking minds.

Nicole

Nicole threatened her brother when he wouldn't give her the TV remote control. She said she'd show him her bag. "You use what you've got," she explained sensibly to Anne. "It's what America is all about."

Nicole said she's never flying on an airplane, because what if the bag explodes? Nicole said stoma means mouth. Nicole's scar was purple. It puckered thick as masking tape.

A Letter from Anne's Boyfriend

> Dear Anne,
> I tested out of freshman English. Awesome! I've got
> a great roommate. He's from around here and knows
> about everything.

He signed it *love,* not *love you.* Anne guessed it mattered, wondered what she could do.

Nicole's Mother and Aunt

Nicole's mother and aunt stayed with her in the hospital. Nicole's aunt called Nicole's mother *sis* or *sister.* "Sister, you need some coffee." "Sis, it's high time we got the doctor in here." Anne asked Nicole if her aunt sometimes got grossed out. "No," Nicole said, "she's a Republican."

The Jackson Pratt Drain

Anne read about it. "Drains remove fluid from the surgical sites. Once the draining decreases, they will be removed." It sounded simple enough, hardly brutal.

But cute Dr. Stafford knew better. She wondered what he *should* have said when he pulled the drain shaped like a lawn mower starter from the surgically punctured hole in her side—a lawn mower starter with a long, long deeply embedded cord.

But she couldn't find a warning that would not have alarmed her, a caution with the right amount of sympathy, words that would have bolstered her courage and respected the suffering that had come before and was about to be inflicted.

But: "This will sting a little?" No, not that.

Finding the Perfect Gown

Your cotillion dress must be pure white. Because of its variability in color, silk is not allowed. It must be sleeved. A cap sleeve is flattering and feminine. It must not have detracting decoration, such as feathers, sequins, beads, or pearls. A pearl necklace, however, is acceptable.

Anne's dress was drop-waisted cotton brocade. Nicole's had a sweetheart neckline. It was taffeta. She said she thought the rustle of it sounded sexy and cheap, undermining the whole virgin-maiden thing. They wore slips, layers and layers of white netting.

Anne said, "If my period starts, I'll kill myself."

Nicole said, "If your period starts, you'll never find it."

Possible recurrence hangs heavy as a stage curtain.

Hospital Visitors

Batman, with a plastic pectoral chest and a cape that swished like Nicole's cotillion dress. He gave Anne a picture of himself signed "With Bat wishes."

The team mascot for a minor league ball team, a shaggy bull who kept banging his horns on the door frame. He gave her a blue-and-white pom pom and a red baseball bat. He was led around by a uniformed bat boy.

Raggedy Ann from the Ice Capades, whose real red hair stuck out from under her red yarn hair. "Lose this place, babe," she said in a husky whisper.

Anne's grandmother. She left a plate of peanut butter cookies, Anne's favorite, long after everyone else seemed to have forgotten Anne had ever eaten. Confused by Anne's mother's explanation of her condition, she sighed. "I don't understand what you're saying to me."

Leaving the Hospital

Going home from the hospital you get ostomy bags, one or two piece—like swimming suits. You get ostomy wafers, a spray-on skin barrier, an ointment to heal the skin the skin barrier misses, adhesive for the ostomy wafers, solvent for the adhesive. You get instruction from the enterostomal therapy nurse, long-suffering as a piano teacher. You get a subscription to *Ostomates*.

Nicole wore clear bags. Anne wore flesh-colored bags. She said she thought they were more feminine.

"What?" Nicole said. "You think they're more what?"

Johanna had ridden her bike late at night along the canal. Her killer folded her clothes neatly beside her. Johanna had signed Anne's yearbook, "See ya this summer!"

The Psychiatrist Visits

The psychiatrist tugged on his soaring-and-diving-seagulls tie and told Anne about a young woman in his parish who had the surgery, how glad she was to be well. "Anne, visualize your return to health. Visualize no more pain or bleeding."

The psychiatrist actually had the disease. It wasn't just his brother. He told Anne's mother in the hall, who told Anne after he'd left.

"Why didn't he just tell me himself?" Anne said.

"Maybe he thinks it would undermine his authority," her mother said.

"Because I'd know he got sick?" Anne was being what her mother called petulant. But she knew she'd slipped, like Alice, into a world with its own nonsensical rules.

"How sick?" she said. "Can he eat popcorn? Does he wear a bag?"

"Can't you call it an appliance?" Her mother turned toward the window.

Personal Ads in *Ostomates*

Female, 32. Diagnosed with colitis at 18. Colon cancer discovered two years ago. Had ileostomy and pull-through. Having rough time right now. Enjoy poetry, movies, my cat Spike. Will answer all letters.

I am a girl, 15. Just diagnosed and had surgery. I had never heard of it before. I like music and love to dance; take gymnastics. I don't care about your age or anything. Am scared.

Single male, 32, from Seattle area. Would like to hear from any female interested in friendship and support. I'm a great listener.

Anne's Colon

After the surgery, the surgeon asked Anne's parents if they would like to see Anne's colon. Anne's mother, who had never yet looked away, said, "I couldn't." But her father looked, so he could say what he now says: that Anne is better off without it. He also calls it names, says, "more holes than Swiss cheese," "craters deeper than the moon," "pockmarked," "pitted," "ravaged," *"U-G-L-Y."*

The surgeon's hands were red and cool. He stood next to a bobbing balloon bouquet and talked to Anne about colons. He said they are inelegant. Big, dumb organs whose agility is limited to spasms of contraction and whose perception of pain is dim and inaccurate.

But Anne thinks of them—of hers, as shy. A mole, maybe. Loathsome, but gentle. A homely animal taken out and shot. And her stomach, her heart—whatever they've left inside—hurts with the cruelty of it.

Anne and Nicole Shop at the Cosmetic Counter

They are walking past the wooden gleam of a bookstore and a pyramid of soaps, multicolored and clear like Jell-O in the window of a bath shop.

"I almost fell on the cotillion runway," Nicole says, referring to a time Anne thinks seems long ago as counting sheep with Bert and Ernie or begging to wear a bra. "Eric gave me his right arm, instead of his left, and it threw me off. I kind of wobbled."

"I didn't see a thing," Anne says. She is lying—recalling the gracelessness of it—because what are friends for?

The mannequins have erect nipples but no facial features. A glass el-evator rises as if with grace. They walk by Surf, Sea, and Swim where empty bathing suits float disembodied in the blue-tinted display. (Visu-alize, Anne thinks, a red bikini, sun glistening off the baby oil of an un-seamed abdomen.) Escalator teeth endlessly recycle. They hear the patter of the computerized water fountain, brown-bottomed with penny litter. At a table in front of Coffee Breaks, a woman says to a young girl, "But everyone uses a napkin."

"How's Jeff?" Nicole says.

"Fine." Anne makes a face to say like it matters. *It's a save-face face, in case she needs it when he comes home.*

Nicole says, "I've been feeling ugly as a dog dish. Let's get some new makeup."

"I saw this eye shadow that goes on white and changes color in the sun."

"Have you seen that lipstick? Black ice? It's dark but light at the same time."

They rearrange their bags and retrace their steps, heading for Dil-lard's cosmetic counter. Anne tries to remember the name of the eye shadow. Glimmer Glow? They pass the movie theater: Nicole points to a coming-soon poster, says while she's kissing, she wouldn't mind kissing Johnny Depp. Does Anne happen to have any idea what religion he is?

From the snack bar comes an explosive burst of popcorn, as well as its urgent smell.

"Christian Scientist?" Anne says. "And I think he might also be part Indian."

Nicole grins, as if it's all but done.

In the Music Box Company, someone is trying one out. Anne and Nicole hear the mechanical plunking of "Camp Town Races," a tune they do not know.

Mary Clyde's work has appeared in *The Georgia Review, Boulevard, American Short Fiction*, and elsewhere. Her short story collection, *Survival Rates,* which won the Flannery O'Connor Award, was published this year. She currently lives in Phoenix with her husband and five children.

JOHN HALL

*T*he summer I watched my daughter suffer in the hospital, I realized that someday I would write about it. Salman Rushdie — who should know — writes, "A writer's injuries are his strength." Of course as the weeks went by I didn't care about anything beyond the frantic yearning for my daughter's life. When she came home, looking and feeling for all the world like a Phoenix Children's Hospital POW, we rejoiced with banners and a goofy new puppy. We still can't drive down the hospital's street without the sense of a desperate near-miss. We dodge.

What surprised me about the story when I came to write it was that it emerged not from the mother's point of view, but the daughter's — as if she wanted to claim her own story. I believe it assumed the fragmented structure in part to spare the reader, to give her a chance to look away from the pain, but also because suffering — perhaps more than any other situation — determines its own strange time and shape.

Laura Payne Butler

BOOKER T'S COMING HOME

(from *The Distillery*)

I discovered my own little postage stamp of native soil was
worth writing about and that I would never live long enough
to exhaust it.

—William Faulkner

When Booker T, our papa, died this past year, the whole
town of Quincy, in fact the entire Gadsden County,
seemed to come out, untangling themselves from amidst the deepest vines in the woods south of Jefferson Street to get him up a
big old-fashioned coming home ceremony. They called around
and wrote letters like mad until they rounded up all of us, his children, from the cities we fled to so many years ago. "You simply
must come home to Quincy and look toward the Heavens from
your saintly departed mama's Mt. Zion," Brother Theo's wife
wrote to us.

We smiled and shuddered as this letter quietly made the rounds
among all of us who endured the years and hours more of sitting
on the sweat-slippery pews up front under flying-spit-and-lather
sermons of Theo's own dead papa, old Brother Damon. Those
years of our mama, fanning away flies and the devil, and us wondering how come our own papa was exempt from the torture of a
Sunday morning at Mt. Zion African Methodist Episcopal Church;
we wished, as we scratched mosquito bites under the rim of our
stiff white socks folded neatly around our ankles, that we could get
on down to the river with our papa and listen to him talk about

the sport and fun of life. In fact, we actually tried praying to Jesus on occasion, just to see if old, decrepit Brother Damon might be correct in his predictions and mighty assertions that the Lord up above Mama Eleanor's Mt. Zion was listening intently to every individual prayer. *Please, Jesus. We've been good. Just let old Brother Damon feel poorly today so as we might go on down to the river with our papa instead of spending the heat of the morning at church. We'll think much of you. Booker T will, too.* We prayed in unison, all of our eyes shut tight as we attempted a forceful prayer through number and conviction. We weren't strong enough; Brother Damon remained the healthiest preacher in Gadsden County, and we hangdogged to church with Mama Eleanor.

Booker T—we always called him by his Christian name—walked on past our bedroom door and out the front, down the steps and through the yard. Every last morning of our childhood, we peeked through the cracked door and rolled on our beds, hoping the creak from the rusty springs might draw his attention to us and he just might, once, take us along.

"Get on out," Mama Eleanor bellowed to us while following on his heels. Her voice drowned out our rollings around. "Come on now. Quit peeking at me and get to your chores; school's waiting. You children is going to try and sleep right through this day the Lord's done given you. And I ain't abiding by that." Booker T went on down to his river.

Mama Eleanor taught us from before we could comprehend the lesson to get out of bed with the energy of puppies and scamper over to Dr. Woodard's house and accomplish chores for shiny quarters. Mama Eleanor worked for the Woodards as their house-keeper all our young lives. After each school week full of afternoon chores, we marched on into the front house—it was really a mansion of sorts by Quincy's standards. We hid behind our mama's large form and peeked at the doctor as he once-a-week checked off tasks on a yellow legal pad and slowly opened his top drawer to pull out a roll of coins. As small children, we were frightened by the cool headiness of the leather and ashen book dust of his library.

The ceiling seemed to reach up to heaven, and we wondered if Dr. Woodard wasn't really Jesus's papa.

"Now, children, you had better get downtown and put that money into the bank. Someday, you'll need to educate yourselves, be a credit to your community," he commanded us as he slowly doled out coins, one blinding blink of nickel after another. At times, if one of us contracted some fever or cough at school, he looked down our throats with a soft, wooden compress that tasted like the wooden stick from the middle of ice-cream bars Mama Eleanor occasionally bought us down at the drugstore to com-memorate special Friday afternoons.

Indeed, we later walked on down to First Bank of North Florida every Friday afternoon. Staunch and erect, each of us stood in line, not looking around but straight ahead, slight smiles on our faces. We put our shiny quarters in our accounts and were rewarded with free popcorn. Mama Eleanor never let us touch our small reward until we were safely seated on a courthouse square bench under the shady darkness of what she called "Gadsden County's authen-tically historic oak tree branches."

"Babies," she commanded, "count in, very carefully, that deposit. Be sure you ain't cheated none. Can't depend on nobody else's honesty but your own. Unless you is a fool, and I ain't raising no fool babies."

Mama Eleanor always wore her very best day dress and elegant hat those trips downtown; she reserved her antiquated "just for good" outfit for bank day and Sunday going-to-meeting. The ensemble never seemed to wear out, although the hat gathered North Florida dust that clung to the netting with the sweat of summer afternoons on the square.

Dr. Woodard's big house loomed over Quincy, just a block to the north of the square, but Mama Eleanor treated Friday after-noons with the deference of a true sacrament. We held our dark red savings books tight in one salt-greasy fist and counted fortunes in twenty-five cent increments, content and cool.

* * *

When Mama Eleanor died, we were not surprised the whole town of Quincy came out. We were not even shocked at the showing from Havana, Gretna, and even Bainbridge, Georgia. We had moved away to various, faraway places years ago, and, ourselves, come back home to send her to her savior. She had pushed us mightily out of the Quincy nest and on to vaster skies of cities with universities and opportunities. We then came home in a rush of sniffles to hold hands and once again stand in line and not look around too much. We felt gratified to be so envied and praised by our home community.

"Mama Eleanor's children done growed up and made something of theirselves," exclaimed Brother Theo's wife in a mid-eulogy stage whisper.

"Oh, Lord. She must have done died one contented woman. Mmm-hm," replied her companion, a small, very black-complected woman none of us could recall.

They catalogued our accomplishments amidst fanning off the fever of eulogy: one doctor, two educators, one journalist, one wife to a doctor—a mother to future doctors. They fanned all around us, wiping the sweat of the coming home ceremony onto ironed, worn handkerchiefs, then placed the damp cotton squares, folded to slightly browned creases, back into breast pockets. The women continued to fan and gush.

We sat up front at Mt. Zion AME Church and listened as Brother Theo—old Brother Damon had long since died and left his calling to his son—eulogized our mama's loyalty to her employers and mostly to her community. He preached to us, her children who had gone off to the west and to the north, about forgiveness and about pride. He yelled in sweat and saliva: "We all need to give honor to our dearest Lord, up above, as we honor the memory of Mama Eleanor: A woman who single-handedly raised up her own precious children amidst the weighty responsibility of also raising the esteemed white family, the Woodards."

A woman behind us murmured, "Amen, Brother." We sat still and straight as Mama Eleanor taught us in childhood and smugly thought what fools these country folk could be not realizing that Mama Eleanor herself was a fool for wasting so much more time than her wages compensated on those Woodards. Dr. Woodard had endowed a scholarship in his own name—reserved for Mama Eleanor's children—over in Tallahassee at Florida A&M University, and we dispersed with hardly a genuine "thank you" to the embodiment of the endowment. We perfected our slight smiles in those long lines as children, but not even Mama Eleanor could try and teach us to supplicate ourselves below our pride. Upon leaving, we didn't, any of us, look back hardly once.

Until her coming home ceremony where, once again, like so many Sundays of years past, we sat there, up front, on the sweat-slicked pew, showered by yet another preacher's sweat and saliva. And we took our medicine, slowly, incomprehensibly steaming at the lowness of coming home to Quincy and finding ourselves peeking around for our papa.

Booker T didn't seem to show his face at Mama Eleanor's funeral although some of us claimed to have caught a peek of him in the sun-dusted shadows. People talked, of course, but we envied him more than we hated him. Behind their soggy handkerchiefs, the ladies of the church auxiliary beat their gums in hushed tones, just loud enough for the entire congregation to hear, clear as a bell, that we were poor fatherless waifs and our getting up right was no thanks to that ingrate Booker T Goldwire.

"That storm-buzzard didn't know nothing about nothing unless it had to do with juice, canepoles, and boiled peanuts. Here, Eleanor had loved him as if he was God himself. She doted on him all her poor, pitiful life long, and he don't even take a morning off from his own Beluthahatchie old river and wish that angel-wife a little luck in the great reward. Jesus, please have mercy on his soul as you usher him down into the fiery depths of West Hell."

We listened to preacher and congregation alike, calmly, and we avoided actual conversation or eye contact as much as possible, figuring all the while that Booker T was still down at the river minding his own. None of us acted to particularly mind or blame him.

Nor did we dare to walk on down there and see for ourselves how our papa was doing. We decided, perhaps, we simply couldn't muster enough curiosity in those days of cities and careers.

Booker T seemed so far away, a sleepy dream-walker from our childhood, no more real than our dusty memories. We knew now how he had never legally been married to Mama Eleanor. Only some of us had traceable physical features on our faces and bodies to the man, but we all felt confident that Mama Eleanor adored Booker T. She gave him enough of us so that she could feel, herself, the maternal pride and fulfillment of giving a man a houseful of children. A gift. It didn't matter in her world whether the man asked for that present or not. It was expected.

Booker T rarely reacted to the expected, and Mama Eleanor never settled him down into our family. We wondered at times: If she could have managed to move our house from out back in the shade of Dr. Woodard's mansion down to the bank of the Ochlocknee River, could her relationship with Booker T have fared a bit better for her. As was, our lives progressed; Booker T came and went out the back screen door of Dr. Woodard's kitchen and through the front screen door of our parlor in the dusk of evening and the midst of morning. We thought he smiled at us when we were tiny. He might have even told us stories as we got ready for bed.

We sat at his feet, and he showed us how to crack the shells of boiled peanuts, suck out saltwater, spit out shell, and enjoy the meat, all in one moment. It took years and many stories of fishing and backwoods jukes to perfect the motion. We were afraid if we let Booker T know that we were quite proficient at eating boiled peanuts he might not stay up late and tell us racy stories while Mama Eleanor finished cleaning up the supper mess over at the Woodards'.

When we finally got old enough, we begged Mama Eleanor to let us accompany Booker T down to the river in the mornings.

"I don't never want to hear you even thinking out loud such sinful things. I didn't raise any of you none to be a breaking my poor heart like such. Booker T Goldwire may be stuck down there, but that don't mean none of you is having no business down on the banks of a stenchful sin-hole."

She forbade us to ever even think about wandering down to the river, and, if she heard anything about us going, her poor heart would break into more pieces than the particles of muddy sand of the river bottom. She cried for the rest of the week and on through Sunday service. Old Brother Damon even had to come spend Sunday afternoon sipping sweet tea and preaching to us about the degradation of liquor and loafing one's life away, all the while spitting shells of Booker T's boiled peanuts right onto the steps of our plank-wood porch floor.

After that, Booker T rarely appeared in the evenings to tell us stories and give us peanuts. He took to slipping in and out of our house in the darkness of night, not so much as peeking through the crack in our door to see about our sleep anymore. We all felt pretty lonely for him and angry at Mama Eleanor. We couldn't understand why she would want so bad to deprive us of this man, but we were still very young and much too afraid of the forces behind Brother Damon and Dr. Woodard to ever question her to her face. Brother Damon, full of Sunday ham, greens, and salty, boiled peanuts, even threatened us one afternoon on Mama Eleanor's own front porch: "If you so much as think about trekking down to that river, Dr. Woodard hisself will be forced to perform a operation on each of you; remove the degradation and sin so it can't breed on to his own family none," he bellowed, spitting saliva and sweat in front of his angry words. "He'll perform this need operation in his own library, right up in his mansion, he will. And I'll be there to oversee the spiritual awakening."

We trembled and shifted uncomfortably around the shells dusting the planks as he warmed to his predictions and continued.

"Jesus will have commanded Dr. Woodard to cut you all open, remove the ornery parts. Badness live on down in your intestines, and, when it drives us completely to sin, it must be cut out like it is a snake. You hear me clear and true, now. Your Mama Eleanor says you all is acting like little devils and planning to do bad. You may think that no one on God's earth knows, but Jesus knows everything inside and outside your hearts and minds. And I is in cahoots with him on keeping Mama Eleanor's babies going to the light."

We believed Brother Damon and quaked in our sheets, thinking we might actually die of heat strokes but also suspecting that was better than Brother Damon's predictions. We only missed Booker T real bad when we hid our heads under goosedown pillows within the pitch of midnight. Booker T passed through our little house that looked outwardly so much like Dr. Woodard's right there in his backyard, and we almost smothered to death, all missing him in the dark.

None of us came back to Quincy, nor to Gadsden County, after Mama Eleanor's funeral. Much too old to hold a grudge against anyone, we said amongst ourselves. It wouldn't seem too practical to blame an entire town or even a county for our own unhappiness, but we never looked back. We all secretly wanted to be angry against Booker T and maybe even Mama Eleanor. Instead, we found other interests and found our own new families on which to shower attention. Quincy, Florida, became a faraway story to tell our own babies about—babies who called us mama and papa and didn't know anything about a mama who spent more time praying than loving and a papa who traveled through a house like a dream shadow.

When the phone calls and letters began arriving telling us that our papa, Booker T Goldwire, had passed and was being held at Williams Funeral Home, waiting for his children to make arrangements, we quietly sent messages around in cards and brief phone calls. Finally, we converged together, stranded at the Quincy Motel just east of the courthouse square on Jefferson Street, in the shady midst of our childhoods.

After Mama Eleanor's death, we lost track of the Woodards and of Booker T. We supposed and did not care that the Woodard family had tragedy and death, birth and laughter, like every other family. Booker T, we heard from Mr. Williams, the funeral director, still fished down at the river and had moved into some backwoods shack. He said it used to belong to a woman named Alice, some old friend of our papa's. We knew nothing of this and shrugged off the news as if it were the slow sweat of the afternoon. We felt a surge of youthful jealousy that this old shack surrounded our mystery just as the night had draped Booker T's comings and goings in our youth. We smiled back at Mr. Williams's talk, all the while protecting our wonderment and longing.

Lou Woodard, Dr. Woodard's only child, showed up at the funeral home claiming she was the only one, really, with any supposed family connection to Booker T. "I want to pay for the service, for all of it. Please, I have to do this for Booker T. He was my friend," she insisted, crying as if Booker T was her own father. We all felt uncomfortable with her. Mama Eleanor hadn't liked us to spend too much time visiting Lou Woodard when we were small, and we had gone to different schools. We knew her as wild and untamable, and we heard rumors about her and Booker T, but Mama Eleanor had told us they were all malicious lies told by lowdown people with only jealousy in their hearts. We backed away from her memories. Hers were alive and colorful, much like Booker T's stories in those long-ago evenings on Mama Eleanor's porch, rocking on splinters and spitting dry hulls in the light of the moon. We refused Lou Woodard's money; we signed checks and listened and smiled.

So when the entirety of Gadsden County came out to see our papa Booker T go deep into the earth, we were quite surprised as we could be. Masses, mostly black, but some white, seemed genuinely saddened at his passing, and even the folks down at Mt. Zion AME Church acted as if they sincerely wished the best journey for his coming home. Ladies proclaimed they could feel Mama Eleanor waiting with her heavy arms outspread, welcoming Booker T home to her never-dying love. Old men weaved intricate yarns of fishing tales all complicated with stitches of whiskey and strangers. We listened and pulled our families close so that they, too, could hear these stories. Some of the tales we had even heard before from Booker T himself and delighted at their familiarity. Women we called "aunties" as children pointed out which of our own children looked like Booker T and which looked like Mama Eleanor.

Lou Woodard had seemed disappointed that we would not allow her to pay for our papa's funeral, and we reminded her that because of her own papa, Dr. Woodard, we all had plenty of money. She insisted on holding the wake at her father's old mansion, closed up for years. We said we were honored and welcomed her to sit with us, her and her sons, on the front pew of Mt. Zion African Methodist Episcopal Church for the coming home ceremony. She accepted and cried wet tears that dripped profusely onto the sweat-slicked pew. We felt sadness for her.

Along with the rest of Gadsden County on this confusing day, Lou Woodard tried to crack our smiling facade and tell us stories about Booker T. And up there on that front pew on which we had suffered countless Sundays of stiff hardness and sliding sweat, we stopped smiling for just a prayer's length and listened. We couldn't determine why she got through to us when no one else's stories particularly could, but later we decided that perhaps it was the same oddness of this white woman stranger who was raised up just a yard away and a world of difference from us by the same two people: Mama Eleanor and Dr. Woodard. She told us things we had no idea about, things that for one reason or another Mama Eleanor and the rest of our town had wanted to protect us from: how Booker T befriended her as a small child, a lonely little girl with a workaholic father and a drunk mother. She told us that he taught her to live for herself and never allow people who thought themselves on a higher bank to push her off her own rivers and to never, ever go against the current. He taught her that the act of flailing upstream would rob her of her life. Booker T introduced her to her own husband, and when he warned her off from him, she recounted how she left Booker T and broke his heart. She said that her own heart broke, too, especially now that it was too late to tell Booker T she knows he was right about everything.

Lou Woodard seemed so low down through the whole funeral weekend. We hurt for her and even settled on burying Booker T down by the river on her insistence. The ladies of the auxiliary acted scandalized and whispered how Mama Eleanor "certainly might never rest peaceably again." But the river seemed fitting, and we finally trekked down to our father's world to lay him down in the plain pine box with a soft and prickly pine needle bed like he had told Mr. Williams he wished to be buried. The day was peaceful, broken only with the chirping of birds and an occasional whine, then deadly slap, of a mosquito. We were struck by the lapping of the current as it rolled lazy and quiet, not stopping to pay homage to one of its disciples, but simply flowing past.

We left Brother Theo up at the church. In fact, we left mostly the entire county—all the people who surprised us by coming out for the funeral—up there. They all went on to wait in the grand parlor of Dr. Woodard's mansion while we interred Booker T deep in the soft black dirt just off the bank of the Ochlocknee River. Lou looked at us and smiled serenely. She told us we must be pleased at our gift to our papa. She said she felt at peace now, that she figured he might just forgive her for not understanding after all these years. We had allowed her to bring him home. The sounds of the gravedigger hit into the soft dirt as he shoveled and moved sand that slid and pounded in our ears. We left Lou to watch over him, and we ourselves went up to wait in Dr. Woodard's mansion.

We all left the next day, packed up our belongings and our families and returned to our real lives. We felt less connected to Quincy, to Gadsden County, and to our papa after this coming home. This was not our time to mourn, it seemed. It was our time to continue to wonder at this man and his river and to drive away, dispersed and distracted, to the varied directions from which we had come.

Laura Payne Butler is a Ph.D. candidate in the
Creative Writing Program at Texas Tech
University, where she was the 1998 recipient
of the Robert S. Newton Award for Creative
Writing. Her stories have appeared in *The
Distillery* and *Concho River Review*.

*"Booker T's Coming Home" is part of a short-story
cycle inspired by my experiences working on a
small-town weekly newspaper called* The Gadsden
County Times. *Right out of college and bumming around without
direction, I moved to North Florida, a strange and wonderful part of the
world, at the invitation of my Southern maternal family, who have lived
there many years. I quickly found myself fascinated with the peculiarities of
place and people as I learned about my heritage while also being introduced
to the histories of many other people. A particular voice exists out in the North
Florida jungle, a voice which reverberates cross-culturally between past and
present.*

*One hot and muggy afternoon, as I stood outside the Suwannee Swifty gas
station filling up my car, an old brown Impala pulled up next to me. Cane
poles hung out the glassless back window, and as the motor grumbled to a
painfully extended off, a small, dark-skinned man climbed out from the
driver's side and confidently strode right up next to me. He fished in his
pocket for loose change, smiled a toothy smile, looked me up and down, and
said, "Baby, I be getting your gas." His name became Booker T Goldwire,
and that moment began a fictional journey I continue and will continue
until, like Booker T, the voice "comes home."*

Michael Erard

BEYOND THE POINT

(from *The North American Review*)

That summer when we were looking for something, we used to congregate at the Big House at South Point. We'd come down off the highway straight toward the coast, then along the small roads of Maryland's Eastern Shore dotted with vegetable stands where we'd buy fresh vegetables for dinner, corn and tomatoes and watermelon, and then we'd keep driving south until we reached the pillars that announced the estate, then down the driveway through the rows of elms, down the hill, to the end of the Point, curling to a stop and parking at the Big House's double front doors.

The host of the parties, a young man named Chris, lived in the mansion, so it was his in practice, but it was the legal property of his grandfather, a former U.S. senator who had walked out of the house one day with his wife and died in a car accident on an icy road in New England. The tragedy left the house, the pier, the boathouse, the tennis courts, the elm trees, and the lawn suspended between owners. Chris's father was the only heir. He might have said that he was letting his son live in the house in order to keep it heated in the winter and dry in the summer; everyone else figured, correctly, that it was Chris he was keeping out of trouble. What Chris's father didn't know was that Chris lived there because he had inherited his grandfather's senatorial elegance, and though he was only twenty years old, he was already displaying the charisma of an older man, and he'd come to need the Big House, as it was called, as a tragic keep for his precious magnanimity. That was why he resisted all efforts to sell the house or demolish it, and why, no matter how far he traveled, he always came back. His father, a small-town lawyer, was undecided: he hoped that if the house would blow away in a hurricane, Chris would finally go to college. For Chris, it was the only place he'd ever loved. You could imagine him camping next to the wreck in his van. So the tale, if there were one to be told, was about family duty and geographical piety, an epic poem whose unraveling strands you could sometimes glimpse but never fully understand, particularly if you weren't from the area.

Often it wasn't what we'd come for, but for some of us it was enough to marvel at the long, rambling two stories of the house. The insides were remarkably preserved, a museum to the man who'd owned it. Everything that had hung on the walls and rested in cupboards was as the way he left it when he walked out the door that day in January. The photos of him with the President, with Frank Sinatra, with John Glenn, with the Governor, with Nelson Mandela. The study's executive desk studded with pens and festooned with miniature flags. The sunporch off the master bedroom lined with hatboxes. The shining tools in the breezeway. China dinner sets, heavy and awkward silverware, stemware, thick starched napery: the accoutrements of a fine life. *World Book* encyclopedias, 1960; stacks of *National Geographic*s and *Life;* liquor in the bar. The closets in the long upstairs hallway had stacks of matching towels with embroidered borders, and all the beds in the eight bedrooms where we slept were covered with thin cotton blankets.

When you inspected it for the first time, you expected to trip over velvet ropes. You expected to encounter elderly docents snoozing in the corners. But the husk of the house still kept a presence— you half expected to hear the senator's booming laugh as he whipped up the driveway in a convertible.

But there were no ghosts. The house was ours.

We were fishermen, lifeguards, T-shirt stand operators, waiters and waitresses, phone operators, motel managers, dishwashers, gas station attendants, boat mechanics, newspaper reporters, chefs, fishing boat captains, ferris wheel operators. We lived in Berlin, Ocean City, Salisbury, Rehoboth, working just for the summer or staying all year round, in small inland apartments or mooching off friends and family. For us, the Big House was a getaway, a retreat, from the thousands of tourists from Baltimore who stripped off their clothes and took their vacations sunburning on the beach, asking a lot of questions, drinking beer, and spending their hard-earned money, giving it to us, or rather, to our bosses. We weren't only looking for a break from these jobs; amidst the luxury, or what was by then a luxury remembered, we lived out our fantasies. Chris's invitations were more than to visit, but to live, and prodigally; we responded to his magnanimity, not by visiting, but by staying, participating, finding in one or two nights the generous amounts of world and life that had been disproportionately allocated by the universe to the house on the bay.

Some of us harbored anarchist dreams. The revolution had been unleashed, and we were partisans living off the fat of the toppled aristocracy. We had invaded Martha's Vineyard, Bethesda, Beacon Hill, Farmington Hills, La Jolla, Newport, whatever area we associated in our minds with large houses we could not enter and would never hope to own. Sitting in shorts and sandals, drinking beer in rooms appropriate for Kennedys, we imagined that we had always deserved such splendor and had now come into our own.

Still, we never destroyed anything, except perhaps symbolically. Rock and roll was appropriate: thrash bands, Grateful Dead cover bands. Once a second-rate Baltimore guitarist in tight Spandex pants played dinosaur licks at dinosaur volumes late into the night in the living room with French doors open agog and the furniture pushed aside and the foundation shifting imperceptibly and the nematodes contorting in their tunnels in the walls.

We ate sit-down dinners at linened tables, if the group were small, eating off the china with the heavy silverware and drinking wine out of crystal goblets. We used cloth napkins. We toasted each other endlessly. We piled watermelon seeds in empty butter dishes. We were drunk before dessert. No one thought about dessert. Who had room? So we drank more beer to cleanse our palates. We lounged around the table and talked, each with one fist apiece on the table. We were playing at something; we had taken something for now that we might never have again; but this, also, wasn't what we were looking for.

In the salt-damp mornings we woke up whenever we did, untangled ourselves from whomever we'd ended up sleeping with, and went down to the kitchen to make coffee and begin cleaning up. The pans from a dozen cooking projects, the stemware and the china, filled the double sinks. We sipped coffee and rolled up our sleeves and started the hot water, worked through the piles of dishes, the first za-zen of the day. Someone had remembered doughnuts; these we ate with the coffee while other people, now friends, took our place at the sinks. Other people filtered through, reappeared, and helped or did not; sometimes we hadn't remembered when they had come, sometimes we did not remember meeting them at all. The mornings were already hot, that early, as we cleaned up, and when the kitchen and the dining room were rearranged and wiped down and the furniture in the living room pushed back into place as if in anticipation of a caterer who would later in the afternoon set up for the senatorial reception that evening, we prepared to swim or sail or go crabbing off the pier.

Those mornings, Albert, the black caretaker, who lived in a shack next door, would come over to collect beer cans. He had been left behind by the senator too, and no one in Chris's family knew what to do with him either. Because we wanted to help, we collected the cans from around the house and piled them on the counter in the kitchen, and then he came and bagged them and brought them to his shack and washed them and set them out on the crumbling tennis court to dry. When we had the patience to throw crab traps into the water, his young son, a boy nine or ten years old, would come by and we would give him a few crabs, what we could manage, only two or three—we weren't catching too many ourselves. Albert was thin and his teeth were broken. His presence reminded us that we enjoyed our luxuries at a cost, that our egalitarian weekends were incomplete dreams. But we hadn't come to the Big House to be reminded of truths that had been denied in the Senator's time.

You didn't drive all this way to pretend that you were rich or to realize that you weren't. And you hadn't come so far just for a party. It was more than that. At the Big House, you had to touch all the dark poles of your emotions, your fears and elations. If you didn't achieve this, you had to be sad. This will not last. This is beautiful. It had an awful transience, and telling about it the morning later was talking into a void. At a point, all talking dissipated; there was no one there.

In our time that summer, other friends took the time to lounge by the indoor pool. Couples slumped in the moldy cushions of the furniture, weaving unresolved incidents into relationships. They were looking for connections with other people. Do you remember when she told me? Well you know why she was saying that? It's because he had gone over there when she had just. And so that's when it happened.

Some of us braved the mosquitoes and took off our clothes at the end of the pier and swam naked in the warm shallow water of the bay. You could stand, your feet in the soft mud and your unwitting toes uncovering clams, and you could walk into the bay for a mile. Enclosed by the water, you could find what you were looking for.

Sometimes there were dozens of us there. Once maybe a hundred, though it would have been difficult to count all the heads drifting off their individual or paired ways past the limits of the glare of the Big House's spotlights, moving away from the land and the buildings and the costs and the pains, moving away from the dishes in the sink, away from the angry landlord, the waves of

summer tourists at the beach resorts, the misunderstanding boyfriend, the elusive girlfriend, the rattly car, the possibility of school
you couldn't afford in the fall, and a million other responsibilities
of our civilized lives.

We moved with a singular idea in mind, away from the electrical light. Returned to amniotic baths, naked as we'd come. This
was what we wanted.

We moved even further out, where the plankton and jellyfish
live, we waved our hands through the water at our sides and acti-
vated the million diamond points of the bioluminescent plankton,
the supernovas of jellyfish which were as large as golf balls, scattered explosions of light we could not feel in the dark water because they gave off no heat.

We were as numerous as plankton. We'd been looking to become multiple for a long time.

If you didn't start over like this, you'd misunderstand your life's
vividness, which was always about to begin.

From the water, like creatures in the water, from somewhere beyond time, we watched what people remained in the house moving in the windows. They seemed very far away. They seemed like
the last part of a bad idea that you wanted to forget, except that it
was part of the experience to remember the idea's failure, in order
to be able to say that you'd learned from your mistakes.

If you didn't disperse, you wouldn't know what it meant to be
together.

So we waded out further, by ourselves or clinging to another
person, further and further, beyond the last of the floodlights' soft-
ened glow, beyond ennui, beyond anticipation, toward the places
where we wanted to be, in the lapping dark seamed with glitters
above and below.

There, like legions of God's angels, we thought about life on
earth, and we were sad together.

Michael Erard is a graduate of Williams College and currently teaches at the University of Texas at Austin. His stories and essays have been published in *North American Review* and *The Texas Observer.* His essay "Millenium, Texas" appeared in *The Year 2000.* He is writing now about supermarkets.

"Beyond the Point" was supposed to be about the time Edward was trying to sleep during a memorably endless Big House party, and so he popped the circuit breaker. I never got around to writing that part, though. A draft of the story stayed on my hard drive for a long time, until one restless summer night, when I opened the file and realized that it didn't have one person or event at its center but instead traced a scene of collective desperation. In that flash, the story revealed what it wanted to be.

Pinckney Benedict

MIRACLE BOY

(from *Esquire*)

Lizard and Geronimo and Eskimo Pie wanted to see the scars.
Show us the scars, Miracle Boy, they said.

They cornered Miracle Boy after school one day, waited for him
behind the shop-class shed, out beyond the baseball diamond
where the junior high's property bordered McClung's place. Miracle Boy always went home that way, over the fence stile and across
the fields with his weird shuffling gait and the black-locust walking stick that his old man had made for him. His old man's place
bordered McClung's on the other side.

Show us the scars. Lizard and Geronimo and Eskimo Pie knew
all about the accident and Miracle Boy's reattached feet. The newspaper headline had named him Miracle Boy. MIRACLE BOY'S FEET
REATTACHED IN EIGHT-HOUR SURGERY. Everybody in school
knew, everybody in town. Theirs was not a big town. It had happened a number of years before, but an accident of that sort has a
long memory.

Lizard and Geronimo and Eskimo Pie wanted to see where the
feet had been sewn back on. They were interested to see what a
miracle looked like. They knew about miracles from the Bible—
the burning bush, Lazarus who walked again after death—and it
got their curiosity up.

Miracle Boy didn't want to show them. He shook his head when they said to him, Show us the scars. He was a portly boy, soft and jiggly at his hips and belly from not being able to run around and play sports like other boys, like Lizard and Geronimo and Eskimo Pie. He was pigeon-toed and wearing heavy dark brogans that looked like they might have some therapeutic value. His black corduroy pants were too long for him and pooled around his ankles. He carried his locust walking stick in one hand.

Lizard and Geronimo and Eskimo Pie asked him one last time—they were being patient with him because he was a cripple—and then they knocked him down. Eskimo Pie sat on his head while the other two took off his pants and shoes and socks. They flung his socks and pants over the sagging woven-wire fence. One of the heavy white socks caught on the rusted single strand of bob-wire along the top of the fence. They tied the legs of his pants in a big knot before tossing them. They tied the laces of the heavy brogans together and pitched them high in the air, so that they caught and dangled from the electric line overhead. Miracle Boy said nothing while they were doing it. Eskimo Pie took his walking stick from him and threw it into the bushes.

They pinned Miracle Boy to the ground and examined his knotted ankles, the smooth lines of the scars, their pearly whiteness, the pink and red and purple of the swollen, painful-looking skin around them.

Don't look like any miracle to me, said Eskimo Pie. Miracle Boy wasn't fighting them. He was just lying there, looking in the other direction. McClung's Hereford steers had drifted over to the fence, excited by the goings-on, thinking maybe somebody was going to feed them. They were a good-looking bunch of whiteface cattle, smooth-hided and stocky, and they'd be going to market soon.

It just looks like a mess of old scars to me, Eskimo Pie said.

Eskimo Pie and Geronimo were brothers. Their old man had lost three quarters of his left hand to the downstroke of a hydraulic fence-post driver a while before, but that hadn't left anything much to reattach.

It's miracles around us every day, said Miracle Boy.

Lizard and Geronimo and Eskimo Pie stopped turning his feet this way and that like the intriguing feet of a dead man. Miracle Boy's voice was soft and piping, and they stopped to listen.

What's that? Geronimo wanted to know. He nudged Miracle Boy with his toe.

Jesus, he made the lame man to walk, Miracle Boy said. And Jesus, he made me to walk, too.

But you wasn't lame before, Geronimo said. Did Jesus take your feet off just so he could put them back on you?

Miracle Boy didn't say anything more. Lizard and Geronimo and Eskimo Pie noticed then that he was crying. His face was wet, shining with tears and mucus. They saw him bawling, without his shoes and socks and trousers, sprawled in his underpants on the ground, his walking stick caught in a pricker bush. They decided that this did not look good.

They were tempted to leave him, but instead they helped him up and retrieved his socks and unknotted his pants and assisted him into them. He was still crying as they did it. Eskimo Pie presented the walking stick to him with a flourish. They debated briefly whether to go after his shoes, dangling from the power line overhead. In the end, though, they decided that, having set him on his feet again, they had done enough.

Miracle Boy's old man was the one who cut Miracle Boy's feet off. He was chopping corn into silage. One of the front wheels of the Case 1370 Agri-King that he was driving broke through the crust of the cornfield into a snake's nest. Copperheads boiled up out of the ground. The tractor nose-dived, heeled hard over to one side, and Miracle Boy slid off the fender where he'd been riding.

Miracle Boy's old man couldn't believe what he had done. He shut off the tractor's power-takeoff and scrambled down from the high seat. He was sobbing. He pulled his boy out of the jaws of the silage chopper and saw that the chopper had taken his feet.

It's hard not to admire what he did next.

Thinking fast, he put his boy down, gently put his maimed boy down on the ground. He had to sweep panicked copperheads out of the way to do it. He made a tourniquet for one leg with his belt, made another with his blue bandanna that he kept in his back pocket. Then he went up the side of the silage wagon like a monkey. He began digging in the silage. He dug down into the wet heavy stuff with his bare hands.

From where he was lying on the ground, the boy could see the silage flying. He could tell that his feet were gone. He knew what his old man was looking for up there. He knew exactly.

Miracle Boy's old man called Lizard's mother on the telephone.

He told Lizard's mother what Lizard and Geronimo and Eskimo Pie had done to Miracle Boy. He told her that they had taken Miracle Boy's shoes from him. That was the worst part of what they had done, he said, to steal a defenseless boy's shoes.

The next day, Miracle Boy's old man came by Lizard's house. He brought Miracle Boy with him. Lizard thought that probably Miracle Boy's old man was going to whip the tar out of him for his part in what had been done to Miracle Boy. He figured Miracle Boy was there to watch the beating. Lizard's own old man was gone, and his mother never laid a hand on him, so he figured that, on this occasion, Miracle Boy's old man would likely fill in.

Instead, Lizard's mother made them sit in the front room together, Lizard and Miracle Boy. She brought them cold Coca-Colas and grilled cheese sandwiches. She let them watch TV. An old movie was on; it was called *Dinosaurus!* Monsters tore at one another on the TV screen and chased tiny humans. Even though it was the kind of thing he would normally have liked, Lizard couldn't keep his mind on the movie. Miracle Boy sat in the crackling brown reclining chair that had belonged to Lizard's old man. The two of them ate from TV trays, and whenever Miracle Boy finished his glass of Coca-Cola, Lizard's mother brought him more. She brought Lizard more, too, and she looked at him with searching eyes, but Lizard could not read the message in her gaze.

By the third glassful of Coca-Cola, Lizard started to feel a little sick, but Miracle Boy went right on, drinking and watching *Dinosaurus!* with an enraptured expression on his face, occasionally belching quietly. Sometimes his lips moved, and Lizard thought he might be getting ready to say something, but he and Lizard never swapped a single word the whole time.

Miracle Boy's old man sat on the front porch of Lizard's house and looked out over the shrouded western slope of the Blue Ridge and swigged at the iced tea that Lizard's mother brought him, never moving from his seat until *Dinosaurus!* was over and it was time to take Miracle Boy away.

Geronimo and Eskimo Pie got a hiding from their old man. He used his two-inch-wide black bull-hide belt in his good hand, and he made them take their pants down for the beating, and he made them thank him for every stroke. They couldn't believe it when Lizard told them what his punishment had been. That, Geronimo told Lizard, is the difference between a house with a woman in charge and one with a man.

Lizard saw Miracle Boy's shoes every day, hanging on the electric wire over by McClung's property line, slung by their laces. He kept hoping the laces would weather and rot and break and the shoes would come down by themselves, and that way he wouldn't have to see them anymore, but they never did. When he was outside the school, his eyes were drawn to them. He figured that everybody in the school saw those shoes. Everybody knew whose shoes they were. Lizard figured that Miracle Boy must see them every day on his way home.

He wondered what Miracle Boy thought about that, his shoes hung up in the wires, on display like some kind of a trophy, in good weather and in bad. Nestled together nose to tail up in the air like dogs huddled for warmth. He wondered if Miracle Boy ever worried about those shoes.

He took up watching Miracle Boy in school for signs of worry. Miracle Boy kept on just like before. He wore a different pair of shoes these days, a brand-new pair of coal-black Keds that looked too big for him. He shuffled from place to place, his walking stick tapping against the vinyl tiles of the hallway floors as he went.

I'm going to go get the shoes, Lizard announced one day to Geronimo and Eskimo Pie. It was spring by then, the weather alternating between warm and cold, dark days that were winter hanging on and spring days full of hard, bright light. Baseball season, and the three of them were on the bench together. Geronimo and Eskimo Pie didn't seem to know what shoes Lizard was talking about. They were concentrating on the game.

Miracle Boy's shoes, Lizard said. Geronimo and Eskimo Pie looked up at them briefly. A breeze swung them first gently clockwise and just as gently counterclockwise.

You don't want to fool with those, Eskimo Pie said.

Lectrocute yourself, Geronimo said.

Or fall to your doom, one, Eskimo Pie said.

Lizard didn't say anything more about it to them. He kept his eyes on the shoes as they moved through their slow oscillation, and he watched the small figure of Miracle Boy, dressed in black like a preacher, bent like a question mark as he moved beneath the shoes, as he bobbed over the fence stile and hobbled across the brittle dead grass of the field beyond.

The trees are beginning to go gloriously to color in the windbreak up by the house. The weather is crisp, and the dry, unchopped corn in the field around Miracle Boy and his old man chatters and rasps and seems to want to talk. Miracle Boy (though he is not Miracle Boy yet—that is minutes away) sits on the fender of the tractor, watching his old man.

Soon enough, Miracle Boy will be bird-dogging whitewings out of the stubble of this field. Soon enough, his old man will knock the fluttering doves out of the air with a blast of hot singing birdshot from his 12-gauge Remington side-by-side, and Miracle Boy will happily shag the busted birds for him. When the snow falls, Miracle Boy will go into the woods with his old man, after the

corn-fat deer that are plentiful on the place. They will drop a salt
lick in a clearing that he knows, by a quiet little stream, and they
will wait together in the ice-rimed bracken, squatting patiently on
their haunches, Miracle Boy and his old man, to kill the deer that
come to the salt.

Lizard made a study of the subject of the shoes. They were hung
up maybe a yard out from one of the utility poles, so clearly the
pole was the way to go. He had seen linemen scramble up the
poles with ease, using their broad climbing slings and their spiked
boots, but he had no idea where he could come by such gear.

In the end, he put on the tool belt that his old man had left behind, cinched it tight, holstered his old man's Tiplady hammer,
and filled the pouch of the belt with sixtypenny nails. He left the
house in the middle of the night, slipping out the window of his
bedroom and clambering down the twisted silver maple that grew
there. He walked and trotted the four miles down the state highway to the junior high school. It was a cold night there in the
highlands of the Seneca Valley, and he nearly froze. He hid in the
ditches by the side of the road whenever a vehicle went by. He
didn't care for anyone to stop and offer him a ride or ask him what
it was he thought he was doing.

He passed a number of houses on the way to the school. The
lights were on in some of the houses and off in others. One of the
houses was Miracle Boy's, he knew, a few hundred yards off the
road in a grove of walnut trees, its back set against a worn-down
knob of a hill. In the dark, the houses were hard to tell one from
another. Lizard thought he knew which house was Miracle Boy's,
but he couldn't be sure.

His plan was this: to drive one of the sixtypenny nails into the
utility pole about three feet off the ground. Then to stand one-
footed on that nail and drive in another some distance above it.
Then he would stand on the second nail and drive a third, and so
on, ascending nail by nail until he reached the humming transformer at the top of the pole. Then, clinging to the transformer,

he imagined, he would lean out from the pole and, one-handed, pluck the shoes from the wire, just like taking fruit off a tree.

The first nail went in well and held solid under his weight, and he hugged the pole tight, the wood rough and cool where it rubbed against the skin of his cheek. He fished in the pouch of nails, selected one, and drove it as well. He climbed onto it. His hands were beginning to tremble as he set and drove the third nail. He had to stand with his back bent at an awkward angle, his shoulder dug in hard against the pole, and already he could feel the strain grinding to life in his back and in the muscles of his forearm.

The next several nails were not hard to sink, and he soon found himself a dozen feet up, clinging to the pole. The moon had risen as he'd worked, and the landscape below was bright. He looked around him, at the baseball diamond, with its deep-worn base path and crumbling pitcher's mound and the soiled bags that served as bases. From his new vantage point, he noted with surprise the state of the roof of the shop shed, the tin scabby and blooming with rust, bowed and beginning to buckle. He had never noticed before what hard shape the place was in.

He straightened his back and fought off a yawn. He was getting tired and wished he could quit the job he had started. He looked up. There was no breeze, and the shoes hung as still as though they were shoes in a painting. He fumbled another nail out of the pouch, ran it through his hair to grease the point, mashed his shoulder against the unyielding pole, set the nail with his left hand, and banged it home.

And another, and another. His clothes grew grimy with creosote, and his eyes stung and watered. Whenever he looked down, he was surprised at how far above the ground he had climbed.

McClung's Herefords found him, and they stood in a shallow semicircle beneath the utility pole, cropping at the worthless grass that grew along the fence line. This was a different batch from the fall before. These were younger but similarly handsome animals, and Lizard welcomed their company. He felt lonesome up there on the pole. He thought momentarily of Miracle Boy, seated before the television, his gaze fixed on the set, his jaws moving, a half-eaten grilled cheese sandwich in his fingers.

The steers stood companionably close together, their solid barrel bodies touching lightly. Their smell came to him, concentrated and musty, like damp hot sawdust, and he considered how it would be to descend the pole and stand quietly among them. How warm. He imagined himself looping an arm over the neck of one of the steers, leaning his head against the hot skin of its densely muscled shoulder. A nail slithered from his numbing fingers, fell, and dinked musically off the forehead of the lead steer. The steer woofed, blinked, twitched its ears in annoyance. The Herefords wheeled and started off across the field, the moonlight silvering the curly hair along the ridgelines of their backs.

The nail on which Lizard was standing began to give dangerously beneath his weight, and he hurried to make his next foothold. He gripped the utility pole between his knees, clinging hard, trying to take the burden off the surrendering nail as it worked its way free of the wood. A rough splinter stung his thigh. He whacked at the wobbling nail that he held and caught the back of his hand instead, peeling skin from his knuckles. He sucked briefly at the bleeding scrapes and then went back to work, striking the nail with the side of the hammer's head. The heavy nail bent under the force of his blows, and he whimpered at the thought of falling. He struck it again, and the nail bit deep into the pine. Again, and it tested firm when he tugged on it.

He pulled himself up. Resting on the bent nail, he found himself at eye level with the transformer at the pole's top. Miracle Boy's shoes dangled a yard behind him. Lizard felt winded, and he took hold of the transformer. The cold metal cut into the flesh of his fingers. There was deadly current within the transformer, he knew, but still it felt like safety to him. He held fast, shifted his weight to his arms, tilted his head back to catch sight of the shoes. Overhead, the wires crossed the disk of the moon, and the moonlight shone on the wires, on the tarnished hardware that fixed them to the post, on the ceramic insulators. These wires run to every house in the valley, Lizard thought.

He craned his neck farther and found the shoes. Still there. The shoes were badly weathered. To Lizard, they looked a million years old, like something that ought to be on display in a museum somewhere, with a little white card identifying them. SHOES OF THE MIRACLE BOY. The uppers were cracked and swollen, pulling loose from the lowers, and the tongues protruded obscenely. Lizard put a tentative hand out toward them. Close, but no cigar.

He loosened his grip, leaned away from the pole. The arm with which he clung to the transformer trembled with the effort. Lizard trusted to his own strength to keep him from falling. He struggled to make himself taller. The tips of his outstretched fingers grazed the sole of one of the shoes and set them both to swinging. The shoes swung away from him and then back. He missed his grip, and they swung again. This time, he got a purchase on the nearest shoe.

He jerked, and the shoes held fast. Jerked again and felt the raveling laces begin to give. A third time, a pull nearly strong enough to dislodge him from his perch, and the laces parted. He drew one shoe to him as the other fell to the ground below with a dry thump. He wondered if the sound the shoe made when it hit was similar to the sound he might make. The shoe he held in his hand was the left.

In the moonlight, Lizard could see almost as well as in the day. He could make out McClung's cattle on the far side of the field, their hind ends toward him, and the trees of the windbreak beyond that, and beyond that the lighted windows of a house. It was, he knew, Miracle Boy's house. Set here and there in the shallow bowl of the Seneca Valley were the scattered lights of other houses. A car or a pickup truck crawled along the state road toward him. The red warning beacons of a microwave relay tower blinked at regular intervals on a hogback to the north.

Lizard was mildly surprised to realize that the valley in which he lived was such a narrow one. He could easily traverse it on foot in a day. The ridges crowded in on the levels. Everything that he knew was within the sight of his eyes. It was as though he lived in the cupped palm of a hand, he thought.

He tucked Miracle Boy's left shoe beneath his arm and began his descent.

When Lizard was little, his old man made toys for him. He made them out of wood: spinning tops and tiny saddle horses, trucks and guns, a cannon and caisson just like the one that sat on the lawn of the county courthouse. He fashioned a bull-roarer that made a tremendous howling when he whirled it overhead but that Lizard was too small to use; and what he called a Limber Jack, a little wooden doll of a man that would dance flat-footed while his father sang: "Was an old man near Hell did dwell, / If he ain't dead yet he's living there still."

Lizard's favorite toy was a Jacob's Ladder, a cunning arrangement of wooden blocks and leather strips about three feet long. When you tilted the top block just so, the block beneath it flipped over with a slight clacking sound, and the next block after that, and so on, cascading down the line. When all the blocks had finished their tumbling, the Jacob's Ladder was just as it had been before, though to Lizard it seemed that it ought to have been longer, or shorter, or anyhow changed.

He could play with it for hours, keeping his eye sharp on the line of end-swapping blocks purling out from his own hand like an infinite stream of water. He wanted to see the secret of it.

I believe he's a simpleton, his old man told his mother.

You think my boy wants anything to do with you little bastards?

Lizard wanted to explain that he was alone in this. That Geronimo and Eskimo Pie were at home asleep in their beds, that they knew nothing of what he was doing. Miracle Boy's old man stood behind the closed screen door of his house, his arms crossed over his chest, a cigarette snugged in the corner of his mouth. The hallway behind him was dark.

I don't necessarily want anything to do with him, Lizard said. I just brought him his shoes.

He held out the shoes, but Miracle Boy's old man didn't even look at them.

Your mommy may not know what you are, Miracle Boy's old man said, and his voice was tired and calm. But I do.

Lizard offered the shoes again.

You think he wants those things back? Miracle Boy's old man asked. He's got new shoes now. Different shoes.

Lizard said nothing. He stayed where he was.

Put them down there, Miracle Boy's old man said, nodding at a corner of the porch.

I'm sorry, Lizard said. He held on to the shoes. He felt like he was choking.

It's not me you need to be sorry to.

Miracle Boy appeared at the end of the dark hallway. Lizard could see him past the bulk of his old man's body. He was wearing canary-yellow pajamas. Lizard had never before seen him wear any color other than black.

Daddy? he said. The sleeves of the pj's were too long for his arms, they swallowed his hands, and the pajama legs lapped over his feet. He began to scuff his way down the hall toward the screen door. He moved deliberately. He did not have his walking stick with him, and he pressed one hand against the wall.

His old man kept his eyes fixed on Lizard. Go back to bed, Junior, he said in the same tired tone that he had used with Lizard before.

Daddy?

Miracle Boy brushed past his old man, who took a deferential step back. He came to the door and pressed his pudgy hands against the screen. He looked at Lizard with wide, curious eyes. He was a bright yellow figure behind the mesh. He was like a bird or a butterfly. Lizard was surprised to see how small he was.

Miracle Boy pressed hard against the door. If it had not been latched, it would have opened and spilled him out onto the porch.

He nodded eagerly at Lizard, shyly ducking his head. Lizard could not believe that Miracle Boy was happy to see him. Miracle Boy beckoned, crooking a finger at Lizard, and he was smiling, a strange, small inward smile. Lizard did not move. In his head, he could hear his old man's voice, his long-gone old man, singing, accompanied by clattering percussion: the jigging wooden feet of the Limber Jack. Miracle Boy beckoned again, and this time Lizard took a single stumbling step forward. He held Miracle Boy's ruined shoes in front of him. He held them out before him like a gift.

Pinckney Benedict grew up on his family's dairy farm in the mountains of southern West Virginia. He has published two collections of short fiction—*Town Smokes* and *The Wrecking Yard*—and a novel, *Dogs of God*. His stories have appeared in a number of magazines and anthologies, including *Esquire, Pushcart XXI: Best of the Small Presses, Zoetrope All-Story, Ontario Review, Story,* and *The Oxford Book of American Short Stories.* His awards include the 1995 Steinbeck Award, the *Chicago Tribune*'s Nelson Algren Award, and a James Michener Fellowship. He is an associate professor in the Creative Writing Program at Hollins University in Roanoke, Virginia.

RICHARD BOYD

When I was a kid, I was always bombing around the farm on a tractor with my father, either riding up on a fender beside him or hanging on to the three-point hitch at the back. It was fun, because I was with my old man, I was outside, and the tractor was noisy and powerful. But it was also terrifying, because I could see how easy it would be to fall off—the tractor was always bouncing over rocks or dropping into holes—and we were generally pulling some implement behind us, the silage chopper of the haybine or the hay rake, and I knew I'd be mangled if I did fall off. I guess it was about this time that doctors started to be able to reattach limbs that had been torn off in accidents, the sort that you see a lot of in agricultural communities. We read in the newspaper what we'd never read before, about these kids who had lost their feet or their arms or what have you and then had gotten them back, and we said, "Now if that isn't a miracle, I don't know what the heck is."

Kurt Rheinheimer

NEIGHBORHOOD

(from *The Greensboro Review*)

The Boys

The boys understand the air. They are nine or ten, and stand in the infield of the baseball diamond as the late-summer afternoon carries a set of distinct and important scents to them. Most constant is the faint smell of spent fuel from the airplane engines that are tested, day and night, on the little peninsula where they live. The war has been over since just before they were born, but the testing continues. More immediate is the chalky smell of the dust-dry field itself, where they have played a hundred games over the summer. And that smell is countered by the rich, oily scent of the leather of their gloves, which they rub and bend and smell and spit into almost incessantly. The gloves, deepened in color by repeated over-applications of neat's-foot oil, are their most treasured and intimately known possessions — the scent lingering on their fingers through the night.

Into that close smell comes another, at first distant and unwelcome. It is the scent of a hundred suppers being cooked all at once inside all the identical houses not far from the baseball field, along pleasant short-blocked streets with names taken from the trees left standing when they were built. The suppers are heavy and immediately postwar in substance, anchored with porkchops or thick cuts of beef, or macaroni and cheese, with potatoes and corn and bread alongside. The scents from the meals drift out of the open-windowed houses, where domestic air conditioning has not yet been heard of, and are at first fended off by the boys, and then at last received as evidence of hunger. Afraid to miss an at bat, they ignore calls of their names a time or two, and then all run home at once so they can eat at the same time and get back to the field before it's too dark to play.

Especially during the after-supper resumption of the game, the big airplanes take off on the company runway just across Bay Drive from the field, and roar over their game—overcoming all other sound, and stopping play. The planes are so loud and low that they make the boys feel they should duck. It is a ritual that, at the moment a big belly of plane passes over, the boy holding the ball will reach back and throw it straight up at the plane. But no one has ever hit a plane, and despite the legend that the aircraft company guards will arrest people who try to attack U.S. aircraft, no one has ever said anything to the boys about throwing baseballs at airplanes. Their favorite plane—viewed with an awe usually reserved for major league baseball players or cowboy legends—is the Seamaster, a huge experimental seaplane the company is building for the navy. But of course the Seamaster does not take off from the runway, but from the water. Its size and amphibiousness make it perhaps the most magical thing in the world for the boys, even though big airplanes have been taking off and landing around them all their lives. They were born in the mid-1940s, just as the war ended, and as fathers came home, or as fathers who worked for the aircraft company got married, or felt comfortable enough with the future to begin families. As the boys stand in the field in the late-summer air, they are fully unaware of that history. They can think back four or five years if someone asks them to, and can remember nothing before. They have no inkling that this community was built for them, that the man who founded the aircraft company also helped design the housing his company put up around the peninsula, that he left a huge green space at its center, and that he put two baseball diamonds in the middle of the green space, as if thinking with a boy's mind and assuring that as the boys resumed their game, they would be surrounded by a hundred mothers washing the grease off the supper dishes, and by a hundred fathers fiddling under the hoods of shiny American sedans parked out in front of the little houses.

But the boys on the field, now hurrying their game in anticipation of dusk, have come to love all that the community of Victory Cape has to offer them—the long stretches of shoreline along the coves and inlets, the Beach Club, where their mothers began taking them before they could walk, the woods that are just large enough to go into and get away from the neighborhood without feeling lost. It is as if the neighborhood was built for boys. The girls their age are more prone to stay in the houses, listening to little transistor radios or helping their mothers. Except for the Beach Club, no part of the community draws the girls the way the woods and the shoreline and the baseball field draw the boys.

On this evening in 1956, they still have six players on each side. It is a good turnout for this late in the day, this late in the summer. Six to a side means no hitting to right field. Each team has a pitcher, a first baseman, a shortstop, a third baseman and a left and center fielder. Anything hit to the right of second base is foul, but doesn't count as a strike. For left-handed hitters, they shift all the infielders to the right side, ignoring the unfairness of having three infielders to cover one side of the infield. The game as they play it holds an intricacy of structure and detail which seems far too sophisticated for boys of ten who, in other contexts, have no care for such complexity. Their chatter is boyish, imitative, and high-pitched. "No stick, no stick" is their favorite call to the batter. At the plate, they go through extended rituals in finding their stances, imitating Stan Musial or Ted Williams or the Orioles' Gus Triandos. They are all in love with the Orioles, a team as young and gawky as they are.

As the first layer of twilight begins to cover the field and the boys have a long discussion about whether a ball that hits third base and then goes foul in front of it is fair or foul, there is suddenly a huge booming sound, followed by a sustained engine noise that is far too loud. This stops the discussion immediately. There have been innumerable plane noises throughout the game, but this one is different. The players look at each other, toward the sky, and then toward the direction of the sound. It has come from the far end of the thicker finger of the double-ended peninsula, where the quicksand pits are, and where the company does most of its testing. The fielders start to edge toward home plate as they listen.

"It's down at the end of the point," Brian Hardin says at last, and then they all begin to run in that direction, moving like a small gathering of tandem-flighted birds headed south. They leave bats, ball, and gloves in a careless scattering across the field. They cross Bay Drive—the main road that connects their community with schools and doctors and stores—and then run down Marshy Point Road, where they sometimes camp overnight in the big woods just before where the aircraft company guards would chase the boys away if they saw them and felt like it at the time.

As they run, they speculate among themselves, shouting above the noise. It is six B-52s warming up at one time. The Seamaster has crashed again. The Japanese have invaded. Brian Hardin thinks maybe the whole big plant at the end of the point has exploded and caught on fire. They shout these guesses to each other through a noise so thick and loud that it seems to be sucking them toward it. They speed across the meadow of waist-high grass, feeling as fast and sure as if they were on pretend motorcycles. They run along the edge of the woods and then make the turn in the road, running full speed. Then they stop, with almost cartoon suddenness. Before them—as if in a dream coming true—is the stunning manifestation of all their unending speculation and exaggeration about some huge strong object meeting an unimaginably horrible fate. They stand, their mouths and eyes open so wide as to again give them a cartoonish appearance, in a close cluster. It *is* the Seamaster. It really *is*. They look at each other, now without words, as if to verify that what they see is really what they see. Of all the giant things they love and admire and fear—sea turtles, Gus Triandos, rocket engines, and high school boys—it is the Seamaster that captivates them most. It is, after all, as big as twenty houses and top secret and indescribably loud, and it has already crashed twice. They have all heard rumors from their fathers or friends of their fathers that it is too dangerous to fly. It tends to sink even though it was designed to land on water. It is costing three times as much as it was supposed to. The navy is going to cancel the contract with the aircraft company and the company will lay off half its workers.

And now, on a warm evening in late summer, when the boys are content to satisfy their needs for strength and size by pretending to be major league baseball players and by throwing their ball at unreachable airplane bellies, the Seamaster is right here in front of them, captured by the land it has hit. The word SEAMASTER itself is written in big white letters across the giant blue nose of the plane, and the whole front section—as big as a department store—is pushed up into the land. There is a long, deep gash in the soil, and a new hill of weeds and grass has been created. One wing sticks up high into the air at an angle like a roof, but higher than any Brian has ever seen. Only a short part of the other wing is visible. The rest is stuck down into the water, and where the wing goes in, there are big, furious bubbles gurgling up, as if the water were boiling. The bubbles are fifty times as big as the ones in a pot on the stove. And muddy looking. No one is around the plane as the boys stand panting and watching it. As the sirens begin to rise into the air behind them, they realize they are the first people to see it—one of the objects of their nightmares and dreams is actually before them. But once they hear sirens in motion, they know they need to hide, and they move as a group, again like birds in flight, toward the woods. They do this without words, moving quickly and never taking their eyes from the riveting presence of the monstrous blue seaplane, and then scattering slightly to find spots behind trees, just as they do when they play hide-and-seek, or cops, or army. Soon, as the bubbles continue to rise to the top, and the noise of the engine screams on, there are both fire trucks and police cars. Not the red volunteer fire trucks from the neighborhood or the white county police cars, but two short white fire trucks from the aircraft company, and five or six jeeps painted camouflage colors. All of the vehicles drive right across the meadow toward the plane, whipping through the tall grass with a blurry speed that impresses the boys greatly, causing them to exchange glances of approving wonder and to remember their own speed through those weeds, well ahead of the jeeps.

Men get out and leave doors open, moving toward the airplane and then stopping short, their mouths wide open the same way the boys' had been when they were that close. Within the engine noise, there is the occasional crackle of a radio as the men shout into little boxes held in their hands. At the fire trucks, men unroll long white hoses and point them toward the plane. But nothing comes out of the hoses, and some of the men from the jeeps are shouting at the men from the fire trucks to back away from the plane. By now the noise of the sirens is almost as loud as the noise of the airplane.

In a short time, when it is nearly dark, there is a sudden decrease in the noise from the airplane, even though no one has squirted it or even gone near it. Then, for a brief moment, flame shoots up with the bubbles from the wing that's underwater, as if there's a dragon down there. And then the huge blue plane falls silent. As it does, the boys shrink back farther into their hiding places, worried that the sudden silence exposes them to the men and trucks and jeeps in the field. Now there are regular cars trying to come down Marshy Point Road too. They get only a short distance and are then turned back by some of the men in the jeeps. The boys, aware of being first and far closer than anyone would ever have let them go, avoid looking that way very long, knowing their parents will be looking for them. Then, as a cluster of parents forms up at the new roadblock, there are loud, urgent calls of some of the boys' names. They shrink back from the trees, and then turn and run through the deep part of the woods, speeding down familiar paths.

They emerge at Bay Drive, and cut back through one of the numbered streets to the field to get their baseball equipment. That's the end of the Seamaster, Brian Hardin thinks on his way home. He's heard enough grownups say if it crashed once more, they would stop working on it forever. Melt it down for scrap.

The Fathers

Though they did not know it as they watched the crashed plane, the boys in 1956 were looking at an airplane whose pilot was the father of one of the boys they went to school with. The pilot was in the plane while they watched it lean and bubble, but he chose not to come out just then. The boys, along with the rest of the neighborhood, came to learn that the pilot had stayed in, hoping the plane would explode. He had been inside it one of the other times it had crashed, and the aircraft company had been telling him that the problems were not with the design of the aircraft, but with the manner in which it was being operated.

Now, at the end of the 1960s, the aircraft company has shrunk to less than half the size it was when the founder was still alive and running it, and the boys who saw the plane first are enrolled in good colleges along the eastern seaboard. They have left behind their passions for huge and frightening things, and are now obsessed with new things: girls, growing their hair long, and folk-protest song lyrics which verify for them the corruptness of the world—a world that still builds warplanes right next to neighborhoods. They are scruffy, bearded young men who listen to Bob Dylan and Joan Baez and Frank Zappa and read comic books in which cats and pigs cuss and smoke marijuana and perform sex acts. The boys make good grades at college, but back home they are rash and unpredictable.

It is the fathers who are most affected and disturbed by the bluntness of the sons. The fathers are now well into their forties, and most have left the aircraft company as it has shriveled in its presence on the peninsula. Where once there were six huge buildings busy twenty-four hours a day, with hundreds of shiny cars filling the lots outside, now the big plants have been repainted and sold to trailer manufacturers and aluminum siding companies and auto parts suppliers. The men who built the airplanes in the 1940s now work at the steel mills or the state highway department. In a period of just over ten years, their lives have completely transformed. Where once they saw the little houses as perfect starter homes, they now view them as the places they may live the rest of their lives. Some have built on a bedroom or two to accommodate another son or daughter, and have put enough into the houses that they are reluctant to sell, despite regular and serious urgings from their wives to move out into one of the pretty new subdivisions farther north of the city. The neighborhood seems to have changed little over the years, except for the additions. Few people have moved, and so, few new people have come in, and yet in the stasis there has been change. The water in the coves has become dirty to the extent that certain kinds of fish no longer live in it, and there are fewer members at the Beach Club. And the tree-shaded sidewalks, once maintained by the aircraft company, show the same pattern of cracks and lines as the skins of the men who worked at the plants. Even the baseball diamonds, for years resodded each spring, have become lumpy in spots.

The fathers carry some vague awareness that the neighborhood is slowly deteriorating, as if in tandem with the willful seediness of their sons or their own resignation to aging, but they don't know what to do about any of it. They can gain no control over the neighborhood or the sons, who occasionally call them rough, ugly names like "capitalist warmonger," and who ask, with mean tightened eyes, just how their fathers could have a conscience and still have worked on airplanes *consciously designed* to kill people.

The fathers feel the sons laugh at them for all they do. On Friday evenings the men gather at the Beach Club to play cards and drink beer. They have been doing this for perhaps twenty years, but suddenly find themselves looking over their shoulders for the opinions of their sons, who sneer about the old farts getting smashed every Friday night. Even the Victory Cape Fire Department, one of the best in the county, is derided by the college boys. They talk among themselves about their fathers loving to have an excuse to drive their cars, Mustangs and Darts and Corvairs, across the dry baseball field to the firehouse just to feel the speed and see the dust as they race to what are most often false alarms.

The inner family workings—the parents' generation is one that will largely miss women's liberation, but the mothers, women just now discovering their own intelligence, do assert more and more control—have minimal impact on the neighborhood. Divorces, though no longer shocking, are still rare, and the community remains firmly traditional—aside from the aberrational boys—in its attitudes about sex, abortion, war, patriotism, and the centrality of comfort and convenience in the American dream. Indeed, perhaps in part by virtue of its peninsula-imposed isolation, Victory Cape is behind as the nation's attitudes begin to change. The fathers seem not particularly aware of the changes. They are unaware of themselves as part of sociology. They are not reflective enough by nature to think much about these things, and the trend of newspapers and magazines to document demographic events is just beginning, and the focus is almost entirely on the sons and their huge community of peers all over the country.

Each fall, on the last Saturday in August, the fathers of Victory Cape hold their annual oyster roast to raise money for the Victory Cape Volunteer Fire Department. They treat the task—creating beds of coals in several car-size roasting racks, buying kegs of beer and taking care of the napkins, utensils, and trash containers—as if they are undertaking a major state function, fighting small, intense turf battles that are never acknowledged verbally.

The volunteer fire hall, where the siren goes off every day at one o'clock, sits to the far side of the baseball diamonds, and the roast takes place next to it. The men are early, parking their cars back at the edge of the lot and starting the coals sooner than is necessary. They joke with each other about tapping a keg before noon, which they do, and about the weather, which is cool but clear. They worry about the turnout, but shortly after noon the traffic begins to build, and by two they are afraid they will need more oysters and more help. Some have asked sons or daughters to help, but few daughters and even fewer sons have obliged. Among the boys are Brian Hardin and David Conley. Brian's father has never had anything to do with the fire department, but Brian and David are there because David's father has demanded that David help. The two boys—still pimply faced as they prepare for their second year in college—are alternately helpful and surly, as if they do not mind being around the men until they suddenly think that maybe they *should* mind. Among the girls is Kathy Kelley, a skinny girl Brian has known all his life but has not spoken to at all since about the eighth grade, when he became aware of girls in a new way. He is surprised to see her, and watches her furtively as she helps at the roasting pit. She has a small spot of sweat on her light blue shirt, in the little space just between and beneath her small breasts. At one point she burns a finger and the men cluster around her, giving her more attention than she deserves, it seems to Brian.

Not long after that, an unexpected source of help arrives, someone who has not been active in the VCVFD for a decade. Even in the crowd and activity, Brian sees his car immediately as it crackles across the rock lot and is parked at a slightly odd angle near the baseball diamond. The driver gets out slowly as they all watch. He is about the same age as the men sweating over the fires, but appears perhaps fifteen years older. Back in 1956, three weeks after the Seamaster ran a big gouge into the land—a grassed-over scrape that remains—the pilot and the airplane were retired. The airplane was melted down to make new airplane parts. The pilot has melted down more slowly, with less potential for reuse. After a year of sympathy from the neighborhood and of unending self-torture, he took a job as a salesman for a pharmaceutical company. Over the years since then, he has wrecked three or four cars and has stopped drinking completely for several weeks once or twice a year. But since 1963, when his wife at last divorced him, things have gotten steadily worse. He now makes no pretense of working, and goes for months at a time with a completely routinized day, arriving at the Victory Cape Inn at opening time, remaining jovial through the early afternoon, and then being taken home and put to bed soon after supper. To many of the rest of the fathers, he is sort of a justification for their own lives. They may be too heavy or drink a little too much or not be ambitious enough or cheat on their wives, but they are nothing at all like the man who is walking determinedly across the rock lot from his blue Mustang. He comes toward them with an exaggerated ironic smile of greeting, as if to say, *Hey, I know I've missed a few years, but here I am today.* The rest of the men exchange apprehensive glances, and several of them move forward to meet him, to judge the level of his intoxication from the strength of his breath and then steer him away from the danger of the pit. He protests that he's fine and wants only to help, but they are not convinced. For a few moments there is uncertainty among the men as to whether or not to let him stay. Brian wants him to stay. "Maybe he's really getting better," he tells David, who agrees that he should get a chance. But it is Kathy who is afraid. Kathy, who never saw the plane crash, is the one who convinces the men that the pilot needs to go. "He could burn himself," Brian hears her tell her father. "It's just too dangerous."

In the end they take him inside the fire hall and fix him a plate of food. They offer him a Coke or coffee but he waves off all offers, saying he's not drinking *anything* these days. Within an hour he is irritated and quarrelsome, and they do not try to stop him when he gets in the Mustang and drives it across the baseball diamond in the direction of either the Cape Inn or his house.

One Woman

It is late summer. The recent evolution of the neighborhood is nowhere more visible than on the baseball diamonds. The backstops are rusted and leaning, carrying an atrophied appearance, with weeds reaching up out of the infield. In the outfield are ruts cut diagonally by informal motorcycle races run some afternoons by boys in their early teens. Organized recreation for the younger children of the neighborhood now takes place off the peninsula, at one of the elementary schools. The demographics of Victory Cape have changed to the extent that its current makeup is very much like that of the depressed, older areas of the city itself. Perhaps a quarter of the houses are still occupied by their original owners, men who came north in the forties to work for the aircraft company. They are now well into their sixties and seventies, and keep tidy lawns and drive ten-year-old Dodges and Chevrolets. They are retired, but their wives still work part-time in the new malls or the day-care centers toward town, where they are astonished at the language and daring of the children they help tend.

This generation—the people who founded Victory Cape—is now surrounded by people they describe as trash. These new people have no feel for the houses they live in, no inkling that the yards they use for parking lots were once filled with pretty ornamentals —that forty years ago, people worked hard at the soil to make this into a neighborhood, not a parking lot for hot rods. These people have no sense that the rooms they fill with loud, incomprehensible music and half-dressed children were once loved and cared for by old friends of the people who remain. The anger of these older people is constant and pervasive. It is as if the Cape is being stolen from them, much as real objects—shovels, garbage cans, car parts, wheelbarrows—are sometimes taken when they are at the grocery store. They talk to each other as if it is just a phase, as if the old days of good jobs at the aircraft company, of streets lined with round-shouldered Buicks and Fords, and people who help each other build piers out into the little coves, will come back soon enough.

The angry sons of the sixties are gone too, having never returned from college. They live farther out in the county, or in counties outside other big cities along the East Coast, where they have become stockbrokers or lawyers or accountants. They have abandoned their rebelliousness and now raise families and advance careers. The sons almost never come back to the Cape, preferring

that their parents come to visit in quiet subdivisions just now beginning the march through neighborhood evolution. This inter-
rupts the continuity of life on Victory Cape, leaving little that connects the community's rushed utilitarian beginning, its happy
unacknowledged midlife, and its isolated deteriorating present.

Brian Hardin is an exception. He lives at 1418 Oak, less than two
blocks from where his father bought a new house in 1943. His parents divorced in 1970 and moved in toward the city. He is a
roundish balding man well over forty and has for the past five years
worked for the vestigial remains of the aircraft company that built
the community several years before his birth. It no longer makes
anything close to full airplanes but builds small obscure parts that
go into planes built by larger companies in Connecticut and
Florida. Brian Hardin is in bonding and tells people he started
putting airplane parts together with glue when he was seven, and
is still doing it—in the same place. He has no wife or children and
lives close to the aircraft company, so he moves around the neighborhood on foot or by bicycle. He is known to both the children
and the old people. Many Saturdays he takes a walk down toward
the tip of the Cape, to visit with Kathryn Kelley Pelletier, now a
twice-divorced woman slightly younger than Brian who left the
Cape after college and has come back to live because she always
wanted to own waterfront property and this is the only place she
can afford it. She is a somewhat depressed woman who keeps a
varying number of cats and dogs. Their relationship ranges from
nearly intimate—their childhood memories interlock in many
places—to nearly indifferent. She is increasingly amazed at the
destruction of the Cape, an attitude which strikes Brian as exaggerated, and this helps him subvert his own worries about the
Cape and his feelings about her. He still remembers her as a queer
sort of girl, and now in adulthood she is perhaps more so. But she
is a good companion on her little sailboat and can talk about
almost any topic he can think of, except professional sports.

As he walks, Brian is stopped by older people out in front of their
houses. They stand on the cracked sidewalks and make him talk

about the neighborhood and the company. Or they talk about the pool going in at the Beach Club, reveling in the irony of the water being so dirty that they have to build an artificial swimming hole to keep the club open. They ask Brian about the plant, and he is deferential or indirect, knowing the exact blend of generality and vagueness that will reaffirm their memories and rekindle their loyalties. Then Brian compliments their gardens and moves on. He stops often on these walks at the bumpy, broken-down diamond to play for a brief time with a group of boys who are eight or ten years old. They don't play nearly as well as the boys did when Brian was that age, or so it seems. But then they have disadvantages. Grounders bounce unpredictably over the infield, and in the outfield they have to watch their feet as much as the ball when they go back on a fly. The boys do not seem to know the sad brokenness of the field, have no knowledge of its glory days thirty years earlier when there were nine boys on a side and the infield hops were true and the backstop sturdy and silver colored. And Brian does not tell them. He hollers out infield chatter for them to imitate, and chastises himself good-naturedly when he boots one, so they can learn it's okay.

As the boys break away from the field and get on small racerish bicycles that are too shiny to fit with their torn, dirty clothes and unwashed hair, only two acknowledge Brian at all, telling him to *hang in there* and to *lose a little weight*. He waves easily at them, and starts back on his way to Kathryn's. As he starts, he feels the first real hint of fall at the small sweat spots under his arms. When he makes this walk, he chooses Third Road for its friendly dogs and its relative stability. Its five blocks, by some quirk, have more long-term owners than any of the other numbered streets.

In one of the yards in the first block is an old circus carousel, its once bright paint still distinct next to a tall hedge, where it has been for perhaps thirty years. Brian rode it as a boy, at the fire department carnival, when Mr. Riordan was a busy young man who drove an ice-cream truck and a school bus, provided carnival rides all over the county, and taught Sunday school. He has become angry and defensive in his old age, and put up a chain-link fence just inside his hedge, as if it will keep out the noises of the night that frighten him and his wife. Where once airplanes roared out of the darkness, lending a certain security in their sustained loudness, the noises are now sudden and unpredictable: the accelerating screech of a motorcycle along a residential street where the speed limit is fifteen, the crashing doors and panicked screams of a full-moon fight between a man and a woman at 3 A.M. Aren't they ashamed? the older people ask Brian when he walks by on Saturdays, as if he will have an explanation. We all have our fights, they tell him, but isn't there some call to keep it till morning, or at least inside the house?

As Brian walks along Third Road, nearly all the houses are known to him. He was inside many of them as a boy, when his playmates lived along here. Each house was identical inside, and when he went into a new friend's house, he knew where the bedrooms were, where the refrigerator would be, even where they hung the towels in the bathroom. It was as if, by living in one of these small houses, he had automatic access to the whole community—it all belonged to him almost as much as his own house did. Brian tries to picture the insides of the houses now—populated by frightened old people and rash young people—and while he knows they must look the same, he cannot make his mind bring the rooms into exact focus any longer, as if the changes in the people have changed the form of the rooms.

In the last block of Third Road the peninsula hooks, and as if in deference to geography, the numbered streets stop and are replaced by curvy unnamed lanes with rock surfaces. The last house before the change is the worst in the neighborhood. It belongs to Pete Draper, the pilot whose career and life and the Seamaster all smashed into the soil at the edge of the water that day while Brian was playing baseball. Draper's house, built onto when Brian was a boy and Draper was trying to rebuild his family, has fallen ever further into disrepair over the last twenty years. Draper has been in and out of detoxification wards and has lived for periods of time with one of his sons, but has never sold the house. As Brian gets near the house, he sees that the back door is open. This does not surprise him because he has closed the door many times over the years. He goes through the yard, avoiding a stack of roofing tiles that have gone through their life cycle sitting on the ground waiting to be used. At the door he looks inside, into a room where he and David Draper used to push toy cars and plan excursions. The room is filled with boxes of papers and stacks of kitchen chairs. At the far corner of the room is a long brown couch, and it makes Brian's stomach drop to see that Pete Draper is on it. He is on his back, with one arm hanging almost to the floor, his gap-toothed mouth open and his face filled with long silver stubble. But Brian decides he is asleep rather than dead, and pulls the door quietly shut.

From Draper's house it is only a short walk to Kathryn's. She lives outside the aircraft company development, her house having been built in the twenties. It is close to the Beach Club, where she and Brian played as children, never acknowledging each other's presence. The house, low and flat-roofed, sits with its back to the water. There is almost no front yard, but the backyard runs long and barely slopes to the water. Kathryn bought it from an older couple who had owned it for nearly fifty years, and she cried because she felt she was evicting them, even though the house had been for sale for two years and they were thrilled to have a buyer. Kathryn has told Brian that it is far from her dream house, but it fulfills her longing to have property by the water. She jokes that it took the settlements from two divorces to get it, and now she doesn't have anyone to share it with. She works for the school system as a computer programmer, drinks too much wine, and sees her lone child, a twelve-year-old daughter, only on birthdays. She has told Brian, through tears, that she just can't do it halfway with Tanya, and so must not live with her at all. And so she lives with her cats and dogs and spends many weekends on her small sailboat, sometimes with Brian along.

As he nears her house, Brian sees that both the car and the boat are there. But there is no sign of Kathryn or any of the animals. He walks toward the house. Along the driveway is a cluster of perhaps twenty Bud Ice bottles, abandoned, Brian assumes, by teens in the night. The bottles glisten in the late-afternoon sun like a bright, artificial litter born overnight. Brian picks them up, one by one, and sets them down into the bottom of Kathryn's empty trash can. When he is finished, he walks along East Edge Road to the Beach Club. He has not been by for more than a week even though he has wanted to keep up with the construction. Now, to extend his walk, he decides to see how far they have gotten with the new pool.

The Beach Club was built at the beginning of the 1950s, two or three years after the neighborhood itself had been completed. One day the aircraft company sent what seemed to the neighborhood residents to be hundreds of loads of clean white sand on down Bay Drive, across East Edge, and then back onto a little piece of rock road that led to a stretch of black-mud shore. They dumped the sand into two huge piles just up from the shore, and as young mothers and tiny children watched, a big yellow bulldozer smoothed out the mucky shore and then began pushing the sand out into the water, as if trying to get rid of it. But more and more sand kept coming until, toward the end of the day, there was nearly a quarter-mile stretch of white-sand beach. The scene of this transformation is among Brian's earliest memories. He stood next to a rail fence with his mother and told her about each new load as it arrived.

The mothers gravitated to this spot as if it had religious significance. They packed up lunches and young children and spent the whole day there, working on their tans and playing with their children in the clean upper-bay water, eating leisurely picnic lunches on the new wooden tables set out under the trees just up from the water. Decades later, Brian Hardin is still pulled to it, but today for a new reason. There have been rumors, over the past several summers, that the state would close the club because of water pollution. And at last, during the middle of this summer, it had happened. The beach was closed for the year during the first week in August, perhaps owing as much to poor attendance as to the water.

At the chain-link fence that surrounds the club, Brian pushes open the unlocked gate and goes in. Toward the edge of the property, silhouetted in the gathering dusk, is a bulldozer. The big concrete-slabbed patio, where in summers past at this time of day Brian would have been part of a round-robin Ping-Pong tournament, has been pushed into a chunky pile toward the fence. Several of the gums and hollies—trees native to the area and left standing when the club was built—have been pushed over to make room for the big rectangular hole made by the bulldozer. The hole will be transformed, sometime before the next swimming season, into a full-size pool. Already they have moved the picnic tables away from where the trees were, closer to the water, where they sit, incongruously it seems to Brian, on the sand where he took boyhood naps and learned to throw a Frisbee and not to be afraid of the water. Now the tall green-and-white signs, set in a row six feet apart cross the beach, tell people they *must* be afraid of it: NO SWIMMING, in huge green letters. And underneath: BY ORDER OF THE STATE DEPARTMENT OF HEALTH.

As Brian walks toward the sand, which over the years has turned dark and clumpy as the old black muck has worked its way up through it, he suddenly sees someone else on it. The figure is crouched over something at the far end of the beach. At first Brian does not recognize the person and is tempted to turn and leave, allowing privacy. But then, by her thinness and the attitude of her body, he recognizes Kathryn. He speaks her name softly into the dusk, moving toward her. She looks up, without surprise, almost as if she's been expecting him and he's just a little late.

"*Look* at Mencken," she says. She is bent over one of her dogs—a retriever she found a year ago. She holds the dog's head in her hands, presenting the face for Brian to inspect. "He's so sick," she says, and looks back at the dog.

Brian squats next to the dog and the woman. "What is it?" he says.

She looks at him blankly for a moment, as if he's only pretending not to know. "It's all this crap," she says. "It could be any of this junk." She gestures widely with her left hand, holding the dog with her right. "He could've drunk some of this poison water," she says. "Maybe he ate some of that sloppy concrete they poured today. Maybe those little assholes you play ball with fed him lye for the fun of it. I don't know." Brian follows her eye as she looks over the broken, trashy surface of the Beach Club. "What the hell kind of place is it when your dog can't walk around and not have to worry about getting sick because he takes a drink of water," she says, nearing tears. At the edge of the water, the dark foam carries a collection of small twigs and paper scraps, a motor oil container and a soft drink can. "We started out peeing in that water when our moms made us stay down here all day to get an early childhood start on our skin cancer." She looks up at Brian as she says this and lets out a sad, almost involuntary laugh. "And then they started filling it up with motorboats and sewage and even airplanes. Do you realize that there are actually airplane chunks out there that they just *left*? The damn Seamaster is still in there somewhere. Did you know that?"

"Yes, I do," Brian says softly. He rubs the back of Mencken's neck, feeling a series of tiny bones that connect his head and body. As Kathryn looks out over the water in disgust and Mencken breathes in a coarse, labored way, the scent of the oily gray water wafts to Brian, verifying what Kathryn has been saying. As he stands, he is immediately aware of a new scent from somewhere back in the middle of the peninsula. It causes his stomach to drop before he realizes what it is. And then, amid an image of his mother standing at the edge of Fourth Road with a rake while other mothers and fathers stand at identical piles all along the street, Brian drinks in the scent of leaves being burned. It is too early in the fall, and it is against the law, but it is there. The smell takes hold of Brian strongly. Kathryn seems to sense it too. Her head turns slightly upward and to the left. The scent, more intense by the moment, feels strong enough to Brian to take hold of both of them, to span the time of their lives like an arch they could walk across.

Kurt Rheinheimer is editor of *Blue Ridge Country*
magazine and lives in Roanoke, Virginia. His
fiction has appeared in *Story Quarterly, Redbook,
Michigan Quarterly Review, Playgirl*, and
elsewhere. This is his third appearance in *New
Stories from the South*. He is at work on two
collections of stories.

*T*he richest vein I have found for fiction runs
around the years when I was ten to twelve years
*old. Only after I had written eight or so stories from that time did it become
apparent that in each, it was the geography, the neighborhood — with its
all-alike houses and huge airplanes and sea turtles and other awe-inspiring
big things — that had spawned each one. So it occurred to me that it was
only right to try a story in which that neighborhood itself became the main
character.*

Andrew Alexander

LITTLE BITTY PRETTY ONE

(from *Mississippi Review*)

M y sister once ordered a monkey from the back of a comic book. She folded laundry for my mother for dimes, packed our school lunches for nickels, saving the coins in a jar underneath her bed. It took her almost a year to save enough, and then we waited for what seemed like months for the monkey to arrive. On some of those days that we waited, she and I would put the cat into the empty cage, watch her circle inside, poke her with sticks, and try to get her tail to curl around the trapeze that hung from the top of the cage, talking to her like an organ grinder to a monkey: "Dance, little one, dance."

Finally, one day, the postman brought the package and handed it to my mother, who carried it into the kitchen. Here it was at last, and it had come in a plain package no bigger than a shoe box with airholes cut into the side. For some reason, I had imagined the monkey riding in the passenger's seat alongside the postman, hopping out and tipping his cap in thanks to the driver as he walked up the front walk to join us at our house.

Using a bread knife, my mother carefully slit open the box. Inside, nestled in some dirty straw, was the monkey my sister had ordered. It looked like something cold and stillborn, the fur wet and patchy on puckered skin, the face pinched and ugly. Beside the monkey, half-buried in the straw, was a newsprint pamphlet, *Your New*

Friend: Caring for Your Squirrel Monkey. The monkey did not move, and, for a moment, we wondered if it had survived the journey to Atlanta.

My mother poked the thing with the blunt end of the bread knife, the lids lifted sleepily, one of the tiny hands shook, as if with palsy.

"Quick, honey," my mother said to my sister, "get the paper towels." Using the towels, my mother carried the monkey (so small she only had to use one hand) upstairs to its cage in the guest bathroom.

He lay on the bottom of the cage for days and days. Sometimes we would take him outside for sunshine, hold bananas in his face, show him our beds, our attic, our swimming pool, carry him in his box to show him our modern conveniences—dishwasher, television, disposal—as if explaining these things to a visitor from another century. My father, a doctor, would pretend to examine the monkey when we asked him to. "Have you been a good little boy?" he would say to the monkey over and over, and then answer in a high monkey-voice, "Yes, I've been a good little boy." My sister and I would put Barbie in the cage to keep the monkey company. But always he did nothing but lie in that same curled position, sometimes moving his vague, unblinking eyes to watch us. That look scared me, silenced me; it was as if he were about to ask some question, a question that I could not answer.

He had a name, Hazel I think, but no one but my sister ever called him that or anything besides "that monkey." His fur, though clean, was the color of sewer water and smelled like a sneeze. He ate a mixture of seed and dried fruit that my sister blended with yogurt and spoon-fed him every morning. As promised, she kept the cage spotless. The monkey, however, stayed on the bottom of the cage, sometimes curled up on his side, sometimes sitting up and watching us.

"Do you think he misses the jungle?" my sister asked one night as we watched him in his cage.

"No," I said, trying to imagine how my parents might answer such a question. "No, he's happy here with us."

One afternoon, when my parents were out, my sister pretended to be a pirate and held the monkey on her shoulder. I was lying on her bed. That was when I saw it, a gesture so delicate my sister never noticed it. The monkey lifted a tired hand, grabbed a fistful of her blonde hair, and stroked it. The sunlight shone so brightly through her windows that when my sister walked in front of them, she and the monkey seemed to glow like things plucked from a fire.

A few weeks later, on a rainy Saturday, my sister and I took the sparkling gown off a Cinderella doll. When we got to the guest bathroom to put it on the monkey, we found the door open and the cage empty. Someone had left the latch on the cage undone: the monkey was gone.

I thought it by far the most fun thing the monkey had done yet, but my sister cried that he might have climbed outside and gotten hit by a car. We told our mother, and she shut the windows and doors of the house so we could search for him. We looked in the laundry bin, the kitchen pots and pans, the medicine cabinet, the bedrooms, everywhere.

After a long time we went back to the guest bathroom which is where we finally found him, crouched behind the shower curtain in a corner of the bathtub, looking up at us with a pleading look, trembling. My sister shrieked with delight and picked him up by his tail to put him back in his cage. Faster than I had ever seen him move before, he slithered out of her grasp. He landed in the bathtub on his back with a sickening crunch.

"Don't touch him," my mother said when my sister reached down to pick him up again. "I think his bones are broken." The monkey lay in the tub, an arm and a leg splayed at impossible angles. He looked at us with a ridiculous calm; his eyes seemed to know nothing and everything all at once. "He's in shock," said my mother.

My mother went to phone my father at his office. The monkey

shivered, so my sister and I covered him with a towel to keep him warm. His head poked out from underneath the yellow towel. "It's OK," my sister said over and over. "It'll be OK."

My father came home that afternoon with a syringe. He carried the monkey in the towel out to the patio table where he laid him down. He told my sister and me that it wouldn't hurt the monkey at all, and then he gave him the shot. After a few seconds the monkey went limp. The head lolled lazily to one side, and his limbs, his whole body sagged lifeless on the patio table.

My sister and I went to her room, crying. She took out a sheet of paper and drew a headstone with "I'm sorry" written in fancy script, filling the page with pen-and-ink flowers. I wrote a little poem on the page: "It was fun, but now it's done." We folded the sheet and put it into the box the monkey came in, the box he was to be buried in. My father used the posthole digger and made a tall, skinny hole deep in the woods of our backyard.

"I buried that monkey straight up and down," my father said that night at dinner and laughed. "Upside down. Straight up and down." The thought of it would tickle him for days to come. That night and many nights more my sister would leave the table in tears.

"Well, all I know is that that monkey seemed sick when he got here," my mother would say after my sister had slammed the door to her room. "They should really give you kids your money back."

When my sister left I would just stare down at my plate, poke at my food with my fork. I would think about how the monkey had once stroked her hair. The gesture probably meant nothing, but at the time—although I could not say why—it was the most infuriating thing I had ever seen coming from something so weak and degraded. In silence I had watched my sister dance and pirate-sing; I felt as if I had witnessed something obscene.

The cage was moved to the attic, where it stayed for a long time, a vague and dusty accusation. Its presence there made me avoid the attic for months. When we moved to our new house, we sold

the cage to a neighborhood kid at a garage sale. A few weeks before we left, I went out with a shovel and tried to dig up the box
to see if the monkey had turned to a skeleton, but I guess I looked
in the wrong place because I dug and dug but never found it.

Andrew Alexander has studied at the University
of Southern Mississippi, Vassar College, and
Harvard University and is a recipient of the
Henfield Prize. He currently lives and writes in
Atlanta.

ANNEMARIE POYO

*When I was very young, people would ask me
what I wanted to be when I grew up, and
I would answer: a monkey. I had seen a chart
showing the evolution of mankind in stages from ape
to human, and — not understanding exactly what it was — I imagined that
I could go the other way, backwards. I would slowly give up life as a human, I
thought, and transform back into a monkey, living in the trees, hopping from
limb to limb, eating bananas, and gripping things with a prehensile tail and
agile toes. I soon learned that "monkey" was not a viable option like "fire-
man" or "doctor." The world quickly and casually strips us of such pretty mis-
conceptions, which is, in a way, what the story is about.*

*I admit we never ordered a monkey, but the story-monkey and its fate
closely resemble the pets my sisters and I did have: Sandy the dog was always
being asked if she had been a good little girl; Patsy the gerbil was dropped in
the bathtub, then put to sleep by my father; and Happy the cat was buried
straight up and down.*

Janice Daugharty

NAME OF LOVE

(from *Story*)

Midway up the ladder, Horace moans and clings like a lizard.

"Here we go again!" Sunny shoves at the seat of his gray twill pants.

"Snake!" Horace muffles a whimper.

"Just a old rat snake." The red-checked snake lies crinkled across the loose hay on the edge of the dim loft.

Horace skiffles up the top rungs and lumbers toward the window. Sunny kicks at the snake flowing beneath the hay and follows Horace to the bale where they can look out. He starts to cry in a spit-thick yodel.

"See, yonder's the house," she says, "yonder's Mama."

"Mama," he sobs and juts his long warped face. His blue eyes are teary, frozen in an upturned gaze. Mouth eternally sprung.

Sunny chews on a slip of hay. "Mama ain't studying you."

"Mama," Horace says, same way he says "snake," another word he now knows to name off another madness.

"Old man might not even come in for all you know," says Sunny.

Horace hangs his head and croaks—his new way of crying since he turned twenty. Used to, he bleated like a calf.

"You keep that up and I'm gone leave you."

He cries louder. She looks north over the greening pasture toward her granny's ranch house, then south toward the shotgun shack where her mama, Mattie Sue, is taking in clothes. A frieze of sunset along the west pinewoods casts a saffron glow over the dirt yard, coloring Mattie Sue's pale face.

"Now, hush!" Sunny sprinkles a handful of hay out the window and watches it scatter to the spring grass. "See that roan yonder?" She knows talking horses will get his mind off today being Saturday and their daddy coming home and a fight starting up. "I'm gone put you on that roan one of these days." She points across the pasture between the two houses where the herd of horses grazes and starts to say *Soon as you're big enough,* but thinks better of it—he's nearly twice her height and half her mental age. She is twelve. Horace is watching his mama bundle the stiff dried clothes in her arms as she walks toward the doorsteps.

"I'll saddle up that stallion," says Sunny, "and you can ride clear across the flatwoods."

"Okefenoak?" he says in a phlegmy yawn.

"To the Okefenoak," she says.

"Sunny ride the nag?"

She laughs. "Sunny ride the nag, uh-huh." He's not as dumb as they think—knows a nag when he sees one, knows the Okefenokee Swamp is out there. They should have sent him to school.

Horace smiles, showing pegs of rotted teeth. The screen door of the shack slams and he stares at his mama lifting her nose as if she smells smoke. She crosses the yard to the wire fence and rakes scraps from a blue bowl to the daisy wheel of yellow cats. He mewls and hunches his close-set shoulders. He has the long, lean arms of the Lamberts—tall, bronze, and tense men—though stringy fleshed and hairless pink as a baby.

"Ain't no call for all that bellering." Sunny gets up as if she is leaving, but stops at the snake by the ladder to give Horace another chance. "He might not even come, I tell you. If he does, I ain't gone let him put you away."

* * *

At supper, Horace keeps bellering, sitting up at the square white table with his hands in his lap, while Sunny and her mama eat.

"Son, here," says Mattie Sue, "eat some peas." She tries to spoon the green mush into his mouth.

"He ain't hungry," says Sunny. "Shut up, Horace."

"Don't rile him no worse, sugar." Her mama is smiling—always smiling—a smile Sunny knows to be a tic, a twitch of her formless lips.

"He can't get no worse," Sunny says.

"Could be coming down with something."

"Huh-uh. Knows the old man's coming in is what it is."

"Horace don't know what's going on from Adam." Mattie Sue gets up and takes her plate to the metal sink-and-cabinet unit.

"He does so; I got him to where he can just about talk."

"Sunny!" Her mama clacks her tongue.

Sunny takes another puffed biscuit from the platter and pokes a hole in the top and pours it full of cane syrup. She tries to hand it to Horace. "Eat this. Good, say *good.*"

He turns his face up to the bare bulb over the table, bleating as if he's unlearning what little he's learned.

"Just taste it." Sunny presses the syrupy spout of the biscuit to his lips. He takes it in his blade-white hands.

The screen door screaks and Sunny's daddy stands in the frame of dark. Skin annealed now, more from the whiskey inside than the sun outside. He tosses his cap to the floor at Mattie Sue's feet, laughs, ruffs his shaggy brown hair and staggers in. "Ain't ever man got a good-looking woman waiting at home, huh?" Getting no response, he shrugs and trips toward the table. "Far as that goes, ain't ever man's got a house neither," he adds, winking at Sunny, "and two grown younguns." He smells like hog slop.

Horace bawls with his mouth full and gets strangled—watery eyes bulging and veins raveling like yarn on his forehead.

"Drink you some tea, buddy." Sunny forces her glass to his lips.

"Wait!" says her mama. "You gone strangle him worse." She

hurries over and beats Horace on the back and the wad of biscuit shoots across the table.

"A fine howdy-do," says her daddy. "Man comes in after working all week on the highway to watch his grown son puke like a baby."

"Shut your face!" shouts Sunny.

"Sunny!" scolds her mama and flaps her with the dish towel.

"Come on, Horace," says Sunny, "let's me and you go set on the porch."

Her daddy hollers out, "You sass back one more time, missy, and I'm gone wallop you."

"Got too much on her at her age," says her mama. "Needs somebody to take aholt."

"Needs to be shed of that big baby you won't let me put away."

Sunny shoves open the screen door for Horace to shamble out. "Don't pay him no mind," she says. "You ain't going nowheres, not without me. I ain't let him haul my old mare off to the dog-food plant yet, have I?" She seats him on the doorsteps overlooking the woods where frogs throb with the turning of the creek.

"Hear them frogs?" she says. "Well, you got just as much right on this place as them. And Granny says so, too." Not true: what her Granny had said was *We've never had a cripple born a Lambert, but he's ours, right?* Same way she'd said *We've never had a girl born a Lambert* when Sunny was born. But if Sunny can only keep Horace from underfoot till after Monday—deadline for the opening at Milledgeville State Hospital—maybe they'll forget about sending him off or never have the chance again.

"I gotta study harder, Horace," she tells him, "so everbody'll quit blaming you." One ear is timing the voices in the kitchen, about to accelerate into arguing. In the runner of light from inside, she notices the blonde stubble of beard along Horace's jaw. "You a man now, Horace," she whispers, as if saying it might instill manlike power. "You're twenty, going on twenty-one. Can't use the excuse of being a baby no more with me and Mama to nuss you."

"Man," he says, same as "snake," same as "Mama."

"Sometimes, Horace," Sunny says, "I think you got it all stored in your head, waiting to come out when you're ready."

"Man," he repeats and smiles, whimpering like a sacked puppy.

All day Sunday, Sunny keeps Horace in the loft. She doesn't go down for dinner and she doesn't ride her splotchy gray mare. She watches the horses graze the sun-gilded pasture in the morning and her uncles and boy cousins ride in the evening. Now and then Sunny's mama calls her name, and finally, to keep anybody from looking for them, she yells from the loft window that they're not hungry, they're playing. She has brung two apples and two bologna sandwiches and she halves them so Horace will have enough to last till sundown.

She finds it hard to stay in the loft with only Horace and the rat snake while her cousins and uncles ride. Harder yet to shed the worry of what's coming tomorrow. "I gotta do good, Horace," she says. "I gotta bring up my grades before school lets out for the year."

Horace is terrified of the snake that keeps to the right of the loft. Now and then a rat squeaks, dwindling to a muffled silence like time swallowed. "Got him one," she says, hoping to acquaint Horace with the benefit and necessity of the snake.

He continues to cry, knowing he might get sent off. Her mama says he can't possibly understand, that he's always cried, but Sunny knows it's deeper than usual and wishes Horace could be more like the lunchroom lady's retarded son at school who always laughs.

"Can't depend on Mama," Sunny says, and he says "Mama," gazing at the snake laced in the hay. "You keep on like this and you're gone."

The late sun filters through cracks in the wide board walls and sows orange straws of light across the hay, the smothery air floating with an updraft of neighs and leathery creaks. Screen doors slam, somebody laughs. All sounds gathering in a confetti of dust specks. A rat shrieks and dies and the fat snake waits.

Horace sprawls on the hay and sleeps with his mouth gaped.

Sunny lies beside him. Thinking about another Sunday when all the Lamberts had gathered at Granny's for dinner, how she'd overheard her mama saying she wondered if Sunny wasn't more sorry for Horace than eager to play with him, that maybe Sunny had pity all mixed up with love. Granny had said something like *What difference does it make? What's love anyhow but compassion?*

That night, after her mama falls asleep, Sunny waits in the bedroom till Horace's breathing settles into its awful rhythm of puffs and sighs, then goes outside. She follows a horse path through the pasture toward the big house with a light burning in the south window. So good to be away from crying for a while, to hear the nothingness keening of katydids, the echo hark of a whippoorwill. She climbs the creosote-board fence, marching toward the light, and knocks on the wall.

The old lady peeps through the curtains, her cheeks sucked in without her teeth. "Sunny . . . what? Come on in the back way."

Sometimes Granny scares Sunny, who can see herself growing old and corpselike too, not so afraid of losing her Lambert glow as losing her right to the horses and woods, her rambling freedom. Over the years she's watched her granny turn from the horses to the house, watching life from the windows and porches.

"Granny, they gone try to send Horace off tomorrow, ain't they?"

"Looks like it." Granny stoops low behind the screen.

"You gotta stop 'em. I would but . . ."

"Ain't much you can do about it, Sunny."

"I can run away with him. I can take care of him, I *been* doing it."

"Not by yourself, Sunny. More to it than just play." Granny slaps at a mosquito on the screen. "Your mama could fill you in on a lot."

"She don't do nothing but bathe him; I can do that."

"Yeah? You're almost grown now, fixing to have a life of your own."

"I don't want no life."

"You're going through a change, honey, might find on the other side you do."

"He's the one, Granny. Horace is just about a man."

"He's done all the growing he's going to do and trying to make him more than he is ain't kind."

Sunny gets still, watching clouds spirit across the moon. "How you guess he'd take to the nuthouse, Granny?"

"Same as he takes to everything else."

"Cry, huh? Reckon they can help him?"

"No. Not but just so much he can do, just so much brain." Granny sighs. "Truth is, Horace is more animal than human in some ways."

"I'm sick and tired of people putting him down."

"They won't up yonder."

"Think they'll be good to him?" Sunny feels the tears start as the pause lingers. "Well, do you or don't you?"

"I'll say this—right at first, I couldn't stand the idea of him going off either. But at least in Milledgeville, there'll be other people like him. He won't be different like he is here. Sometimes it's kinder to let people go."

"You're just tired of him, all of y'all are."

"Ain't no enemies, Sunny; all made up in your head. But say I *am* tired of him, say your mama's tired of him—what about you? I could hear him up in the loft crying the livelong day. No worse sound in the world, but most of the time people get a letup. Aren't you tired of watching his misery?"

"If he's gotta be miserable, I don't reckon it'll hurt me."

"But what purpose does it serve?"

"Ask God."

"That's not what . . . What's the point in you being miserable? You've never played half a day with anybody but Horace."

"I don't like to play." Sunny socks her fists into her jeans pockets. "You're just selfish—all of y'all are."

"Maybe, but life's for living"—Granny leans close, talking through the screen—"so if you get the chance, you better take it. Even eighty years goes by fast."

Sunny starts to sob. "Granny, I might not never stop crying if I let him go."

"But you will. I've laid two babies and a husband to rest and I've overed crying. Laughing's what's natural. As much sadness as there is in this old world, we go the long way around to get to laugh. How come people go to fairs and stuff?"

"Granny, he would die locked up, I know he would."

"Doctor says he won't live long anyway, you know that."

"Well, I'd rather see him free."

Sunny winds back along the horse path, toward the shack at the other end of the pasture. Then she angles across to where her mare grazes obliviously. "Hey, you old bag of bones," Sunny says. The mare snorts, lifts her head, jellied eyes brimming with moonlight. "I ain't letting the old man ship you off to no dog-food plant, don't you worry." She buries her face in the furry spring coat, smelling the dead sweat of winter struggle.

Now that Sunny has made up her mind, she has to hurry. Come daylight, her mama will be making breakfast for her daddy. And his lunch. Sunny has used the entire pack of luncheon meat and a whole loaf of white bread for sandwiches. No lunch meat, and she can imagine what her daddy will think about that. What will he say when he finds Sunny and Horace gone? What will her mama say?

In the living room, she stares at the round white clock on the mantel. The ticking sounds loud in the small square room with moonlight shafts on the wide board floor that make it look like daybreak, Monday, and doom.

She tiptoes through the living room toward the front porch and pushes open the screen door and places the plastic jug of water and the bag of sandwiches on the slat wood chair by the door. Then she goes inside, to the front bedroom to wake Horace.

Leaning over him, Sunny whispers, "Wake up, Horace. We going riding."

He whimpers and rolls to the other side of the bed with his back to her.

"Shh!" she says, following him. "You wake Mama and she won't let us go."

"Go with Mama." He sits up.

Sunny clamps one hand over his mouth and the other at the back of his sweaty head. "You make the least bit of racket, and I'm going to the Okefenoak without you."

She waits till his head tilts down and his wet lips close. "Now come on. Let Sunny get you dressed and we'll go."

"Go," he whispers.

"Good boy." She dresses him—shirt, pants, shoes—then takes the olive drab wool blanket from the chest at the foot of the bed, and leads him into the moonlight.

Sunny rides the old mare into the east woods. Horace sitting behind her, whining because she had promised to let him ride the roan stallion—that's how smart he is. Not that it matters now.

"Give me about thirty minutes, Horace," she says, "and you can bawl your eyes out." Behind her, she can still hear traffic on the highway between her house and the woods.

"Sunny ride the nag," he says and tightens his arms about her waist.

At least she is keeping part of her promise.

The jug of water hangs from a length of hay string tied to the saddle horn, along with the bag of sandwiches. The blanket is folded behind the saddle on the bony rump of the mare for Horace to sit on.

Sunny lets the mare pick her way through the honeysuckle and bamboo vines, around pines, palmettos, and myrtle bushes, heading toward the taller pines.

The mare plods indifferently, as if suspecting this is another of Sunny's games—any minute Sunny might saw back on the reins and yank them left or right. But she doesn't, and the mare keeps moving with her anvil head swinging low to the ground. Keeping time like a pendulum to the sucking of hooves in the peat bog.

The sun is at ten o'clock, and Sunny has quit trying to shush Horace, just keeps riding, eyes on the mare's bobbling head and the spaced pines between the sharp, scooped ears. Crows caw. She dozes and dreams that she is still awake, still listening to the crows caw and gazing between the horse's ears, but wakes to find that her head is bobbling like the mare's and looks up to see that the sparse trees have thickened with scrub oaks and reeds, that the rosy light of morning has blanched to midday and the sun is shining behind her. Birds are singing and the horse's shadow has switched sides. But Horace is still crying and latching on to her waist. She has never heard him cry so close, for so long.

Suddenly, she lets go of the reins and the gray mare stops. Unfastening Horace's hands from her waist, Sunny swings her left leg over the head of the horse and drops to the dirt. While she coaxes Horace down, the mare cuts her murky brown eyes back at Sunny. She feeds Horace water from the jug and a sandwich from the bag. The smell of doughy bread, mayonnaise, and meat makes her hungry, but she doesn't eat and doesn't let Horace have another sandwich. Doesn't let him wander off when he tries—not yet.

She strips leaves from the branches of a waxberry myrtle bush and crushes them between her palms and rubs the wax on Horace's arms to repel mosquitoes.

On the horse again, she keeps riding deeper into the woods and doesn't talk to Horace except to point out a giant redheaded woodpecker, called a "lord god," that looks stuck sideways by its feet to a scaly brown pine trunk. "See the lord god, Horace," she says. But realizes even she cannot reach him, and anyway he can't understand, and she is talking only to hear somebody talking. No point in trying to teach him to say "lord god" either.

She stops to feed Horace again when the sun lays long shadows across the forest floor. The russet pine straw is torched by the setting sun.

Nearby is a black-water slew surrounded by towering cypresses with flat bristly tops and pop-bellied tupelos. A blue heron unfolds its great wings and flies up from the deepening shadows. Sunny spreads the blanket on the pine straw and makes Horace sit, then hands him a sandwich. He grips it with both fists and bites and keeps biting till about half of it is gone. He chokes, coughs, his face turns red as the sun. She doesn't try to help him, just watches him choke, but when he is done with the first sandwich she hands him another; she drinks from the jug first, then passes it to him. His teary blue eyes lock on hers while he drinks and drools water on his shirt. After he has gobbled the last sandwich, he lies on his side and closes his eyes.

"You're free now, Horace," Sunny says and sits beside him, watching the hippy mare graze the water grass along the mud banks of the slew, alternately glancing back at Sunny and down at her own reflection in the water. Sunny had planned to ride farther, but now she won't, though she fears she's not quite in the heart of the Okefenokee—alligators, snakes, and bears. She should have taught Horace about fire ants—look out for fire ants. Instead she has taught him about birds and butterflies.

When the moon rises, half full, she goes to the mare and un-buckles the girth on her belly, slides it from her swayed back, and tosses it aside. Then she unbuckles the bridle on the mare's neck and lifts the bit from between her ground-down teeth and slips the jingling rig over her head, then hurls it out into the palmettos and huckleberry bushes. As she starts up the bank, the mare swings her head around and steps in behind her. "Stay," Sunny says and holds out both hands, walking backwards till the horse stops, then she turns and heads toward home.

For Angie

Janice Daugharty's latest novel is *Like a Sister.* She
is writer-in-residence at Valdosta State University
in Georgia. Her short fiction has been published
in numerous journals, including *Story, Georgia
Review, Denver Quarterly, The Oxford American,*
and *Ontario Review.*

HERB PILCHER

*O*ur son Frank was born with strawberry curls,
*and for the first five years of his life, what he
mostly heard was how adorable he was. But when he
started school, his classmates teased him about his red hair. His sister Angie,
older by two years, quickly took up for Frank, in much the same way that
Sunny in "Name of Love" takes up for Horace. I used this hair episode to
inspire the conflict of the story, and Angie's love of horses and a good fight to
give Sunny an edge.*

Tony Earley

QUILL

(from *Esquire*)

As Thompson stared at Quill, the oxygen tube protruding from Quill's nostrils, curving up and back over his cheeks, took on the appearance of tusks; Quill's immaculate brush cut swept back from his widow's peak in a broad, white stripe; when he frowned he looked fierce.

"What?" Quill said. "What do you think you're looking at?"

"I just realized," said Thompson, "that, with that thing sticking out of your nose, you look like a pig."

"That's a hell of a thing to say," said Quill. "To come in here, to come into intensive care and tell a man in my condition, to tell a man with a *heart* condition, that he looks like a pig."

"A *wild* pig," Thompson said. "A boar. A big old wild boar."

"If I get up out of this chair."

"Full of piss."

"You've had the lick now, boy."

"And vinegar. With a big old pork pecker. A big old pork pecker dragging through the leaves. Digging a ditch through the woods. You could lay pipe in it. Balls like mushmelons."

"You," said Quill. His eyes closed and he opened them again. "Have always been full of it."

Thompson grinned. Remembered a Sunday in 1946. Fall. School clothes. Shoes. Quill would not get off the bicycle. He rode around and around the yard. Thompson yelled, Quill! It's my turn! Quill threw back his head and brayed the Lone Ranger song. *Da da duh. Da da duh. Da da duh duh DUH!* Thompson picked up an apple, a horse apple big as a softball, and let it fly. It caught Quill in the ear. Bad wreck. Quill climbed out from under the bike, the rear wheel still spinning, and tried to beat the dirt off his shirt; he was always funny about his clothes. Thompson could hear him breathing all the way across the yard. I know what I'll do, Quill said. I'll just kill you. Thompson lit out across the pasture; Quill sprinted for the house and the gun. The hackberry tree seemed a mile or more away. Thompson panted, Tree, Tree, Tree, Tree, while he ran. He heard the screen door bang open. Thompson dove behind the tree. Quill shot the whole tube. Eighteen rounds. Thompson heard the bullets slapping into the wood. Then it was over. Quill threw down the rifle and ran across the pasture. He brushed off Thompson's clothes. Cried and kissed Thompson all over the face. Told him how much he loved him, how sorry he was. Thompson didn't feel anything at all. He wasn't mad. He wasn't afraid. Nothing. They buried the shell casings behind the barn.

"Quill," Thompson said, "you remember that time you tried to kill me?"

Quill blinked. His eyes grew indistinct, as if sinking behind a surface of bright water. The water in each eye squeezed itself into a ball and rolled down his cheeks until the oxygen tube stopped it like a clam. "I tried to shoot you, Teenie," he said. "I tried to shoot my little brother."

"You missed me," said Thompson. "You missed me, Quill. Hey."

Quill began to sob. "And now I'm going to die, Teenie. I tried to shoot my little brother, and now I'm going to die."

Thompson glanced up at Quill's monitor.

"They said I've got damage. Teenie, they said part of my heart is dead."

Quill's hands were soft and warm. Thompson could feel *that,* although when he looked at his own hands they did not seem part of him. He stared at them as if they belonged to a stranger. He thought, on purpose, Quilly. My Quilly. My big Quilly is dying, but could not produce a single tear. He thought, Cry, Jesus, please let me cry, but what he said was, "Quill. Seriously. You cannot shoot. Worth. A. Lick."

Tony Earley's fiction and nonfiction have appeared in *The New Yorker, Harper's, Esquire,* and *The Oxford American,* where he is a contributing writer. He is the author of two books: the story collection *Here We Are in Paradise* and a novel, *Jim the Boy,* which will be published in 2000. He teaches English and Creative Writing at Vanderbilt University.

"*Q*uill" had its origins in a family story I've heard all my life: an apple was thrown, a bicycle wrecked, shots were fired. I changed the names in order to protect the identities of the apple-thrower and the shooter, both of whom are still alive and, so far as I know, well armed.

Tom Franklin

POACHERS

(from *Texas Review*)

At dawn, on the first day of April, the three Gates brothers
banked their ten-foot aluminum boat in a narrow slough
of dark water. They tied their hounds, strapped on their rifles, and
stepped out, ducking black magnolia branches heavy with rain
and Spanish moss. The two thin younger brothers, denim overalls
tucked into their boots, lugged between them a Styrofoam cooler
of iced fish and coons and possums. The oldest brother—bearded,
heavyset, twenty years old—carried a Sunbeam Bread sack of eels
in his coat pocket. Hooked over his left shoulder was the pink
body of a fawn they'd shot and skinned, and, over the right, a stray
dog to which they'd done the same. With the skins and heads gone
and the dog's tail chopped off, they were difficult to tell apart.

The Gateses climbed the hill, clinging to vines and saplings, slipping in the red clay, their boots coated and enormous by the time
they stepped out of the woods. For a moment they stood in the
road, looking at the gray sky, the clouds piling up. The two younger
ones, Scott and Wayne, set the cooler down. Kent, the oldest, removed his limp cap and squeezed the water from it. He nodded
and his brothers picked up the cooler. They rounded a curve and
crossed a one-lane bridge, stopping to piss over the rail into creek
water high from all the rain, then went on, passing houses on either side: dark warped boards with knotholes big enough to look

through and cement blocks for steps. Black men appeared in doors and windows to watch them go by—to most of these people they were something not seen often, something nocturnal and dangerous. Along this stretch of the Alabama River, everyone knew that the brothers' father, Boo Gates, had married a girl named Anna when he was thirty and she was seventeen, and that the boys had been born in quick succession, with less than a year between them.

But few outside the family knew that a fourth child—a daughter, unnamed—had been stillborn, and that Boo had buried her in an unmarked grave in a clearing in the woods behind their house. Anna died the next day and the three boys, dirty and naked, watched their father's stoop-shouldered descent into the earth as he dug her grave. By the time he'd finished it was dark and the moon had come up out of the trees and the boys lay asleep upon each other in the dirt like wolf pups.

The name of this community, if it could be called that, was Lower Peachtree, though as far as anybody knew there'd never been an Upper Peachtree. Scattered along the leafy banks of the river were ragged houses, leaning and drafty, many empty, caving in, so close to the water they'd been built on stilts. Each April floods came and the crumbling land along the riverbank would disappear and each May, when the flood waters receded, a house or two would be gone.

Upriver, near the lock and dam, stood an old store, a slanting building with a steep, rusty tin roof and a stovepipe in the back. Behind the store the mimosa trees sagged, waterlogged. In front, beside the gas pump, long green steps led up to the door, where a red sign said OPEN. Inside to the right, like a bar, a polished maple counter covered the entire wall. Behind the counter hung a rack with wire pegs for tools, hardware, fishing tackle. The condoms, bullets, and tobacco products, the rat poison and the Old Timer knife display were beneath the counter.

The store owner, old Kirxy, had bad knees, and this weather settled around his joints like rot. For most of his life he'd been married and lived in a nice house on the highway. Two-story. Fireplaces in every bedroom. A china cabinet. But when his wife died two years ago, cancer, he found it easier to avoid the house, to keep the bills paid and the grass mowed but the door locked, to spend nights in the store, to sleep in the back room on the army cot and to warm his meals of corned beef and beef stew on a hot plate. He didn't mind that people had all but stopped coming to the store. As long as he served a few long-standing customers, he thought he'd stick around. He had his radio and one good station, WJDB of Thomasville, and money enough. He liked the area, knew his regulars weren't the kind to drive an hour to the nearest town. For those few people, Kirxy would go once a week to Grove Hill to shop for goods he'd resell, marking up the price just enough for a reasonable profit. He didn't need the money, it was just good business.

Liquor-wise, the county was dry, but that didn't stop Kirxy from selling booze. For his regulars, he would serve plastic cups of the cheap whiskey he bought in the next county or bottles of beer he kept locked in the old refrigerator in back. For these regulars, he would break packages of cigarettes and keep them in a cigar box and sell them for a dime apiece, a nickel stale. Aspirins were seven cents each, Tylenol tablets nine. He would open boxes of shotgun shells or cartridges and sell them for amounts that varied, according to caliber, and he'd been known to find specialty items: paperback novels, explosives, and—once—a rotary telephone.

At Euphrates Morrisette's place, the Gates brothers pounded on the back door. In his yard a cord of wood was stacked between two fenceposts and covered by a green tarp, brick halves holding the tarp down. A tire swing, turning slowly and full of rainwater, hung from a white oak. When Morrisette appeared—he was a large, bald black man—Kent held out the fawn and dog. Morrisette put on glasses and squinted at both. "Hang back," he said, and closed the door. Kent sat on the porch edge and his brothers on the steps.

The door opened and Morrisette came out with three pint jars of homemade whiskey. Each brother took a jar and unscrewed its lid, sniffed the clear liquid. Morrisette set his steaming coffee cup on the windowsill. He fastened his suspenders, looking at the carcasses hanging over the rail. The brothers were already drinking.

"Where's that girl?" Kent asked, his face twisted from the sour whiskey.

"My stepdaughter, you mean?" Morrisette's Adam's apple pumped in his throat. "She inside." Far away a rooster crowed.

"Get her out here," Kent said. He drank again, shuddered.

"She ain't but fifteen."

Kent scratched his beard. "Just gonna look at her."

When they left, the stepdaughter was standing on the porch in her white nightgown, barefoot, afraid, and rubbing the sleep from her eyes. The brothers backed away clanking with hardware and grinning at her, Morrisette's jaw clenched.

Sipping from their jars, they took the bag of eels down the road to the half-blind conjure woman who waited on her porch. Her house, with its dark drapes and empty parrot cages dangling from the eaves, seemed to be slipping off into the gully. She snatched the eels from Kent, squinting into the bag with her good eye. Grunting, she paid them from a dusty cloth sack on her apron and muttered to herself as they went up the dirt road. Wayne, the youngest, looked back, worried that she'd put a hex on them.

They peddled the rest of the things from their cooler then left through the dump, stumbling down the ravine in the rain, following the water's edge to their boat. In the back, Kent wedged his jar between his thighs and ran the silent trolling motor with his foot. His brothers leaned against the walls of the boat, facing opposite banks, no sound but rain and the low hum of the motor. They drank silently, holding the burning whiskey in their mouths before gathering the will to swallow. Along the banks, fallen trees held thick strands of cottonmouth, black sparkling creatures dazed and slow from winter, barely able to move. If not for all the rain, they might still be hibernating, comatose in the banks of the river or beneath the soft yellow underbellies of rotten logs.

Rounding a bend, the brothers saw a small boat downriver, its engine clear, loud, and unfamiliar. Heading this way. The man in the boat lifted a hand in greeting. He wore a green poncho and a dark hat covered with plastic. Kent shifted his foot, turning the trolling motor, and steered them toward the bank, giving the stranger a wide berth. He felt for their outboard's crank rope while Scott and Wayne faced forward and sat on the boat seats. The man drawing closer didn't look much older than Kent. He cut his engine and coasted up beside them, smiling.

"Morning fellows," he said, showing a badge. "New district game warden."

The brothers looked straight ahead, as if he wasn't there. The warden's engine was steaming, a flock of geese passed overhead. Wayne slipped his hands inside the soft leather collars of two dogs, who'd begun to growl.

"You fellows oughta know," the warden said, pointing his long chin to the rifle in Scott's hands, "that it's illegal to have those guns loaded on the river. I'm gonna have to check 'em. I'll need to see some licenses, too."

When he stood, the dogs jumped forward, toenails scraping aluminum. Wayne pulled them back, glancing at his brothers.

Kent spat into the brown water. He met the warden's eyes, and in an instant knew the man had seen the telephone in the floor of their boat.

"Pull to the bank!" the warden yelled, drawing a pistol. "Y'all are under arrest for poaching!"

The Gateses didn't move. One of the dogs began to claw the hull and the others joined him. A howl rose.

"Shut those dogs up!" The warden's face had grown blotchy and red.

The spotted hound broke free and sprang over the gunnel, slobber strung from its teeth, and the man most surprised by the game warden's shot was the game warden himself. His face drained of color as the noise echoed off the water and died in the bent black limbs and the cattails. The bullet had passed through the front dog's neck and smacked into the bank behind them, missing Wayne by inches. The dog collapsed, and there was an instant of silence before the others, now loose, clattered overboard into the water, red-eyed, tangled in their leashes, trying to swim.

"Pull to the goddamn bank!" the warden yelled. "Right now!"

Scowling, Kent leaned and spat. He laid his thirty-thirty aside. Using the shoulders of his brothers for balance, he made his way to the prow. Scott, flecked with dog blood, moved to the back to keep the boat level. At the front, Kent reached into the water and took the first dog by its collar, lifted the kicking form and set it streaming and shivering behind him. His brothers turned their faces away as it shook off the water, rocking the whole boat. Kent grabbed the rope that led to the big three-legged hound and pulled it in hand over hand until he could work his fingers under its collar. He gave Wayne a sidelong look and together they hauled it in. Then Kent grabbed for the smaller bitch while Wayne got the black and tan.

The warden watched them, his hips swaying with the rise and fall of the current. Rain fell harder now, spattering against the aluminum boats. Kneeling among the dogs, Kent unsnapped the leash and tossed the spotted hound overboard. It sank, then resurfaced and floated on its side, trailing blood. Kent's lower lip twitched. Wayne whispered to the dogs and placed his hands on two of their heads to calm them—they were retching and trembling and rolling their eyes fearfully at the trees.

Scott stood up with his hands raised, as if to surrender. When the man looked at him, Kent jumped from his crouch into the other boat, his big fingers closing around the game warden's neck.

Later that morning, Kirxy had just unlocked the door and hung out the Open sign when he heard the familiar rattle of the Gates truck. He sipped his coffee and limped behind the counter, sat on his stool. The boys came several times a week, usually in the afternoon, before they started their evenings of hunting and fishing. Kirxy would give them the supplies they needed—bullets, fishing line, socks, a new cap to replace one lost in the river. They would fill their truck and cans with gas. Eighteen-year-old Wayne would get the car battery from the charger near the woodburning stove and replace it with the drained one from their boat's trolling motor. Kirxy would serve them coffee or Cokes—never liquor, not to minors—and they'd eat whatever they chose from the shelves, usually candy bars or potato chips, ignoring Kirxy's advice that they ought to eat healthier: Vienna sausages, Dinty Moore, or Chef Boyardee.

Today they came in looking a little spooked, Kirxy thought. Scott stayed near the door, peering out, the glass fogging by his face. Wayne went to the candy aisle and selected several Hershey Bars. He left a trail of muddy boot prints behind him. Kirxy would mop later.

"Morning, boys," he said. "Coffee?"

Wayne nodded. Kirxy filled a Styrofoam cup then grinned as the boy loaded it with sugar.

"You take coffee with your sweetener?" he said.

Kent leaned on the counter, inspecting the hardware items on their pegs, a hacksaw, a set of Allen wrenches. A gizmo with several uses, knife, measuring tape, awl. Kirxy could smell the booze on the boys.

Y'all need something?" he asked.

"That spotted one you give us?" Kent said. "Won't bark no more."

"She won't?"

"Naw. Tree 'em fine, but won't bark nary a time. Gonna have to shoot her, I expect."

His mouth full of chocolate, Wayne looked at Kirxy. By the door, Scott unfolded his arms. He kept looking outside.

"No," Kirxy said. "Ain't no need to shoot her, Kent. Do what that conjure woman recommends. Go out in the woods, find you a locust shell stuck to a tree. This is the time of year for 'em, if I'm not mistaken."

"Locust shell?" Kent asked.

"Yeah. Bring it back home and crunch it up in the dog's scraps, and that'll make her bark like she ought to."

Kent nodded to Kirxy and walked to the door. He went out, his brothers following.

"See you," Kirxy called.

Wayne waved with a Hershey bar and closed the door.

Kirxy stared after them for a time. It had been a year since they'd paid him anything, but he couldn't bring himself to ask for money; he'd even stopped writing down what they owed.

He got his coffee and limped from behind the counter to the easy chair by the stove. He shook his head at the muddy footprints on the candy aisle. He sat slowly, tucked a blanket around his legs, took out his bottle and added a splash to his coffee. Sipping, he picked up a novel—Louis L'Amour, *Sackett's Land*—and reached in his apron pocket for his glasses.

Though she had been once, the woman named Esther wasn't much of a regular in Kirxy's store these days. She lived two miles upriver in a shambling white house with magnolia trees in the yard. The house had a wraparound porch, and when it flooded you could fish from the back, sitting in the tall white rocking chairs, though you weren't likely to catch anything. A baby alligator maybe, or sometimes bullfrogs. Owls nested in the trees along her part of the river, but in this weather they seemed quiet; she missed their hollow calling.

Esther was fifty. She'd had two husbands and six children who were gone and had ill feelings toward her. She'd had her female parts removed in an operation. Now she lived alone and, most of the time, drank alone. If the Gates boys hadn't passed out in their truck somewhere in the woods, they might stop by after a night's work. Esther would make them strong coffee and feed them salty fried eggs and greasy link sausages, and some mornings, like today, she would get a faraway look in her eyes and take Kent's shirt collar in her fingers and lead him upstairs and watch him close the bathroom door and listen to the sounds of his bathing.

She smiled, knowing these were the only baths he ever took.

When he emerged, his long hair stringy, his chest flat and hard, she led him down the hall past the telephone nook to her bedroom. He crawled into bed and watched her take off her gown and step out of her underwear. Bending, she looked in the mirror to fluff her hair, then climbed in beside him. He was gentle at first, curious, then rougher, the way she liked him to be. She closed her eyes, the bed frame rattling and bumping, her father's old pocket watch slipping off the nightstand. Water gurgled in the pipework in the walls as the younger brothers took baths, too, hoping for a turn of their own, which had never happened. At least not yet.

"Slow, baby," Esther whispered in Kent's ear. "It's plenty of time . . ."

On April third it was still raining. Kirxy put aside his crossword to answer the telephone.

"Can you come on down to the lock and dam?" Goodloe asked. "We got us a situation here."

Kirxy disliked smart-assed Goodloe, but something in the sheriff's voice told him it was serious. On the news, he'd heard that the new game warden had been missing for two days. The authorities had dragged the river all night and had three helicopters in the air. Kirxy sat forward in his chair, waiting for his back to loosen a bit. He added a shot of whiskey to his coffee and gulped it down as he shrugged into his denim jacket, zipping it up to his neck because he stayed cold when it rained. He put cotton balls in his ears and set his cap on his bald head, took his walking cane from beside the door.

In his truck, the four-wheel-drive engaged and the defroster on high, he sank and rose in the deep ruts, gobs of mud flying past his windows, the wipers swishing across his view. The radio announcer said it was sixty degrees, more rain on the way. Conway Twitty began to sing. A mile from the lock and dam Kirxy passed the Grove Hill ambulance, axle-deep in mud. A burly black paramedic wedged a piece of two-by-four beneath one of the rear tires while the bored-looking driver sat behind the wheel, smoking and racing the engine.

Kirxy slowed and rolled down his window. "Y'all going after a live one or a dead one?"

"Dead, Mr. Kirxy," the black man answered.

Kirxy nodded and speeded up. At the lock and dam, he could see a crowd of people and umbrellas and beyond them he saw the dead man, lying on the ground under a black raincoat. Some on-looker had begun to direct traffic. Goodloe and three deputies in yellow slickers stood near the body, with their hands in their pockets.

Kirxy climbed out and people nodded somberly and parted to let him through. Goodloe, who'd been talking to his deputies, ceased as Kirxy approached and they stood looking at the raincoat.

"Morning, Sugarbaby," Kirxy said, using the childhood nick-name Goodloe hated. "Is this who I think it is?"

"Yep," Goodloe muttered. "Rookie game warden of the year."

With his cane, Kirxy pulled back the raincoat to reveal the white face. "Young fellow," he said.

There was a puddle beneath the dead man. Twigs in his hair and a clove of moss in his breast pocket. With the rubber tip of his cane, Kirxy brushed a leech from the man's forehead. He bent and looked into the warden's left eye, which was partly open. He no-ticed his throat, the dark bruises there.

Goodloe unfolded a handkerchief and blew his nose then wiped it. "Don't go abusing the evidence, Kirxy." He stuffed the hand-kerchief into his back pocket.

"Evidence? Now, Sugarbaby."

Goodloe exhaled and looked at the sky. "Don't shit me, Kirxy. You know good and well who done this. I expect they figure the law don't apply up here on this part of the river, the way things is been all these years. Them other wardens scared of 'em. But I reckon that's fixing to change." He paused. "I had to place me a call to the capitol this morning. To let 'em know we was all outta game wardens. And you won't believe who they patched me through to."

Kirxy adjusted the cotton in his right ear.

"Old Frank David himself," the sheriff said. "Ain't nothing ticks him off more than this kind of thing."

A dread stirred in Kirxy's belly. "Frank David. Was he a relation of this fellow?"

"Teacher," Goodloe said. "Said he's been giving lessons to young game wardens over at the forestry service. He asked me a whole bunch of questions. Regular interrogation. Said this here young fellow was the cream of the crop. Best new game warden there was."

"Wouldn't know it from this angle," Kirxy said.

Goodloe grunted.

A photographer from the paper was studying the corpse. He glanced at the sky as if gauging the light. When he snapped the first picture, Kirxy was in it, like a sportsman.

"What'd you want from me?" he asked Goodloe.

"You tell them boys I need to ask 'em some questions, and I ain't fixing to traipse all over the county. I'll drop by the store this evening."

"If they're there, they're there," Kirxy said. "I ain't their damn father."

Goodloe followed him to the truck. "You might think of getting 'em a lawyer," he said through the window.

Kirxy started the engine. "Shit, Sugarbaby. Them boys don't need a lawyer. They just need to stay in the woods, where they belong. Folks oughta know to let 'em alone by now."

Goodloe stepped back from the truck. He smacked his lips. "I don't reckon anybody got around to telling that to the deceased."

Driving, Kirxy turned off the radio. He remembered the Gates brothers when they were younger, before their father shot himself. He pictured the three blond heads in the front of Boo's boat as he motored upriver past the store, lifting a solemn hand to Kirxy where he stood with a broom on his little back porch. After Boo's wife and newborn daughter had died, he'd taught those boys all he knew about the woods, about fishing, tracking, hunting, killing. He kept them in his boat all night as he telephoned catfish and checked his trotlines and jugs and shot things on the bank. He'd given each of his sons a specific job to do, one dialing the rotary phone, another netting the stunned catfish, the third adjusting the chains which generated electricity from a car battery into the water. Boo would tie a piece of clothes line around each of his sons' waists and loop the other end to his own ankle in case one of the boys fell overboard. Downriver, Kent would pull in the trotlines while Wayne handed him a cricket or cockroach or catalpa worm for the hook. Scott took the bass, perch, or catfish Kent gave him and slit its soft, cold belly with a fillet knife and ran two fingers up into the fish and drew out its palmful of guts and dumped them overboard. Sometimes on warm nights cottonmouths or young alligators would follow them, drawn by blood. A danger was catching a snake or snapping turtle on the trotline, and each night Boo whispered for Kent to be careful, to lift the line with a stick and see what he had there instead of using his bare hand.

During the morning they would leave the boat tied and the boys would follow their father through the trees from trap to trap, stepping when he stepped, not talking. Boo emptied the traps and rebaited them while behind him Kent put the carcass in his squirrel pouch. In the afternoons, they gutted and skinned what they'd brought home. What time was left before dark they spent sleeping in the feather bed in the cabin where their mother and sister had died.

After Boo's suicide, Kirxy had tried to look after the boys, their ages twelve, thirteen, and fourteen—just old enough, Boo must've thought, to raise themselves. For a while Kirxy let them stay with him and his wife, who'd never had a child. He tried to send them to school, but they were past learning to read and write and got expelled the first day for fighting, ganging up on a black kid. They were past the kind of life Kirxy's wife was used to living. They scared her, the way they watched her with eyes narrowed into black lines, the way they ate with their hands. The way they wouldn't talk. What she didn't know was that from those years of wordless nights on the river and silent days in the woods they had developed a kind of language of their own, a language of the eyes, of the fingers, of the way a shoulder moved, a nod of the head.

Because his wife's health wasn't good in those days, Kirxy had returned the boys to their cabin in the woods. He spent most Saturdays with them, trying to take up where Boo had left off, bringing them food and milk, clothes and new shoes, reading them books, teaching them things and telling stories. He'd worked out a deal with Esther, who took hot food to them in the evenings and washed and mended their clothes.

Slowing to let two buzzards hop away from a dead deer, Kirxy lit a cigarette and wiped his foggy windshield with the back of his hand. He thought of Frank David, Alabama's legendary game warden. There were dozens of stories about the man—Kirxy had heard and told them for years, had repeated them to the Gates boys, even made some up to scare them. Now the true ones and the fictions were confused in his mind. He remembered one: A dark, moonless night, and two poachers use a spotlight to freeze a buck in the darkness and shoot it. They take hold of its wide rack of horns and struggle to drag the big deer when suddenly they realize that now three men are pulling. The first poacher jumps and says, "Hey, it ain't supposed to be but two of us dragging this deer!"

And Frank David says, "Ain't supposed to be none of y'all dragging it."

The Gates boys came in the store just before closing, smelling like the river. Nodding to Kirxy, they went to the shelves and began selecting cans of things to eat. Kirxy poured himself a generous shot of whiskey. He'd stopped by their cabin earlier and, not finding them there, left a quarter on the steps. An old signal he hadn't used in years.

"Goodloe's coming by tonight," he said to Kent. "Wants to ask if y'all know anything about that dead game warden."

Kent shot the other boys a look.

"Now I don't know if y'all've ever even seen that fellow," Kirxy said, "and I'm not asking you to tell me." He paused, in case they wanted to. "But that's what old Sugarbaby's gonna want to know. If I was y'all, I just wouldn't tell him anything. Just say I was at home, that I don't know nothing about any dead game warden. Nothing at all."

Kent shrugged and walked down the aisle he was on and stared out the back window, though there wasn't anything to see except the trees, ghostly and bent, when the lightning came. His brothers took seats by the stove and began to eat. Kirxy watched them, remembering when he used to read to them, *Tarzan of the Apes* and *The Return of Tarzan*. The boys had wanted to hear the books over and over—they loved the jungle, the elephants, rhinos, gorillas, the anacondas thirty feet long. They would listen intently, their eyes bright in the light of the stove, Wayne holding in his small, dirty hand the Slinky Kirxy had given him as a Christmas present, his lips moving along with Kirxy's voice, mouthing some of the words: *the great apes; Numa the lion; La, Queen of Opar, the Lost City*.

They had listened to his Frank David stories the same way: the game warden appearing beside a tree on a night when there wasn't a moon, a tracker so keen he could see in the dark, could follow a man through the deepest swamp by smelling the fear in his sweat, by the way the water swirled: a bent-over shadow slipping between the beaver lairs, the cypress trees, the tangle of limb and vine, parting the long, wet bangs of Spanish moss with his rifle barrel, creeping toward the glowing windows of the poacher's cabin, the deer hides nailed to the wall. The gator pelts. The fish with their grim smiles hooked to a clothes line, turtle shells like army helmets drying on the window sills. Any pit bull or mutt meant to guard the place lying with its throat slit behind him, Frank David slips out of the fog with fog still clinging to the brim of his hat. He circles the cabin, peers in each window, mounts the porch. Puts his shoulder through the front door. Stands with wood splinters landing on the floor at his feet. A hatted man of average height, clean-shaven:

no threat until the big hands come up, curl into fists, the knuckles scarred, blue, sharp.

Kirxy finished his drink and poured another. It burned pleasantly in his belly. He looked at the boys, occupied by their bags of corn curls. A Merle Haggard song ended on the radio and Kirxy clicked it off, not wanting the boys to hear the evening news.

In the quiet, Kirxy heard Goodloe's truck. He glanced at Kent, who'd probably been hearing it for a while. Outside, Goodloe slammed his door. He hurried up the steps and tapped on the window. Kirxy exaggerated his limp and took his time letting him in.

"Evening," Goodloe said, shaking the water from his hands. He took off his hat and hung it on the nail by the door, then hung up his yellow slicker.

"Evening, Sugarbaby," Kirxy said.

"It's a wet one out there tonight," Goodloe said.

"Yep." Kirxy went behind the counter and refilled his glass. "You just caught the tail end of happy hour. That is, if you're off the wagon again. Can I sell you a tonic? Warm you up?"

"You know we're a dry county, Kirxy."

"Would that be a no?"

"It's a watch your ass." Goodloe looked at the brothers. "Just wanted to ask these boys some questions."

"Have at it, Sugarbaby."

Goodloe walked to the Lance rack and detached a package of Nipchee crackers. He opened it, offered the pack to each of the boys. Only Wayne took one. Smiling, Goodloe bit a cracker in half and turned a chair around and sat with his elbows across its back. He looked over toward Kent, half-hidden by shadow. He chewed slowly. "Come on out here so I can see you, boy. I ain't gonna bite nothing but these stale-ass cheese crackers."

Kent moved a step closer.

Goodloe took out a notepad and addressed Kent. "Where was y'all between the hours of four and eight A.M. two days ago?"

Kent looked at Scott. "Asleep."

"Asleep," Scott said.

Goodloe snorted. "Now come on, boys. The whole dern county knows y'all ain't slept a night in your life. Y'all was out on the river, wasn't you? Making a few telephone calls?"

"You saying he's a liar?" Kirxy asked.

"I'm posing the questions here." Goodloe chewed another cracker. "Hell, everybody knows the other game wardens has been letting y'all get away with all kinds of shit. I reckon this new fellow had something to prove."

"Sounds like he oughta used a life jacket," Kirxy said, wiping the counter.

"It appears—" Goodloe studied Kent "—that he might've been strangled. You got a alibi, boy?"

Kent looked down.

Goodloe sighed. "I mean—Christ—is there anybody can back up what you're saying?"

The windows flickered.

"Yeah," Kirxy said. "I can."

Goodloe turned and faced the storekeeper. "You."

"That's right. They were here with me. Here in the store."

Goodloe looked amused. "'They was, was they. Okay, Mr. Kirxy. How come you didn't mention that to me this morning? Saved us all a little time?"

Kirxy sought Kent's eyes but saw nothing there, no understanding, no appreciation. No fear. He went back to wiping the counter. "Well, I guess because they was passed out drunk, and I didn't want to say anything, being as I was, you know, giving alcohol to young-uns."

"But now that it's come down to murder, you figured you'd better just own up."

"Something like that."

Goodloe stared at Kirxy for a long time, neither would look away. Then the sheriff turned to the boys. "Y'all ever heard of Frank David?"

Wayne nodded.

"Well," Goodloe said. "Looks like he's aiming to be this district's game warden. I figure he pulled some strings, what he did."

Kirxy came from behind the counter. "That all your questions? It's past closing and these young'uns need to go home and get some sleep." He went to the door and opened it, stood waiting.

"All righty then," the sheriff said, standing. "I expect I oughta be getting back to the office anyhow." He winked at Kirxy. "See you or these boys don't leave the county for a few days. This ain't over yet." He put the crackers in his coat. "I expect y'all might be hearing from Frank David, too," he said, watching the boys' faces. But there was nothing to see.

Alone later, Kirxy put out the light and bolted the door. He went to adjust the stove and found himself staring out the window, looking into the dark where he knew the river was rising and swirling, tires and plastic garbage can lids and deadwood from upriver floating past. He struck a match and lit a cigarette, the glow of his ash reflected in the window, and he saw himself years ago, telling the boys those stories.

How Frank David would sit so still in the woods waiting for poachers that dragonflies would perch on his nose, gnats would walk over his eyeballs. Nobody knew where he came from, but Kirxy had heard that he'd been orphaned as a baby in a fire and found half-starved in the swamp by a Cajun woman. She'd raised him on the slick red clay banks of the Tombigbee River, among lean black poachers and white trash moonshiners. He didn't even know how old he was, people said. And they said he was the best poacher ever, the craftiest, the meanest. That he cut a drunk logger's throat in a juke joint knife fight one night. That he fled south and, underage, joined the Marines in Mobile and wound up in Korea, the infantry, where because of his shooting ability and his stealth they made him a sniper. Before he left that country, he'd registered over a hundred kills, communists half a world away who never saw him coming.

Back home in Alabama, he disappeared for a few years then

showed up at the state game warden's office, demanding a job. Some people heard that in the intervening time he'd gotten religion.

"What makes you think I ought to hire you?" the head warden asked.

"Because I spent ten years of my life poaching right under your goddamn nose," Frank David said.

The Gates boys' pickup was the same old Ford their father had shot himself in several years earlier. The bullet hole in the roof had rusted out but was now covered with a strip of duct tape from Kirxy's store. Spots of the truck's floor were rusted away, too, so things in the road often flew up into their laps: rocks, cans, a kingsnake they were trying to run over. The truck was older than any of them, only one thin prong left of the steering wheel and the holes of missing knobs in the dash. It was a three-speed, a column shifter, the gear-stick covered with a buck's dried ball sack. The windows and windshield, busted or shot out years before, hadn't been replaced because most of their driving took them along back roads after dark or in fields, and the things they came upon were easier shots without glass.

Though he'd never had a license, Kent drove; he'd been doing this since he was eight. Scott rode shotgun. Tonight both were drinking, and in the back Wayne stood holding his rifle and trying to keep his balance. Below the soles of his boots the floor was soft, a tarry black from the blood of all the animals they'd killed. You could see spike antlers, forelegs and hooves of deer. Teeth, feathers, and fur. The brittle beaks and beards of turkeys and the delicate, hinged leg bone of something molded in the sludge like a fossil.

Just beyond a NO TRESPASSING sign, Kent swerved off the road and they bounced and slid through a field in the rain, shooting at rabbits. Then they split up, the younger boys checking traps—one on each side of the river—and Kent in the boat rebaiting their trotlines the way his father had shown him.

They met at the truck just before midnight, untied the dogs, and tromped down a steep logging path, Wayne on one end of four leashes and the lunging hounds on the other. When they got to the bottomland, he unclipped the leashes and loosed the dogs and the brothers followed the baying ahead in the dark, aiming their flashlights into the black mesh of trees where the eyes of coons and possums gleamed like rubies. The hounds bayed and frothed, clawed the trunks of trees and leaped into the air and landed and leaped again, their sides pumping, ribs showing, hounds that, given the chance, would eat until their stomachs burst.

When the Gateses came to the river two hours later, the dogs were lapping water and panting. Wayne bent and rubbed their ears and let them lick his cheeks. His brothers rested and drank, belching at the sky. After a time, they leashed the hounds and staggered downstream to the live oak where their boat was tied. They loaded the dogs and shoved off into the fog and trolled over the still water.

In the middle, Scott lowered the twin chains beside the boat and began dialing the old telephone. Wayne netted the stunned catfish —you couldn't touch them with your hand or they'd come to— and threw them into the cooler, where in a few seconds the waking fish would begin to thrash. In the rear, Kent fingered his rifle and watched the bank in case a coyote wandered down, hunting bullfrogs.

They climbed up out of the woods into a dirt road in the misty dawn, plying through the muddy yards and pissing by someone's front porch in plain sight of the black face inside. A few houses down, Morrisette didn't come to his door, and when Kent tried the handle it was locked. He looked at Scott, then put his elbow through the glass and reached in and unlocked it.

While his brothers searched for the liquor, Wayne ate the biscuits he found wrapped in tin foil on the stove. He found a box of Corn Flakes in a cabinet and ate most of them, too. He ate a plate of cold fried chicken liver. Scott was in a bedroom looking under the bed. In the closet. He was going through drawers, his dirty fingers among the white cloth. In the back of the house Kent found a door, locked from the inside. He jimmied it open with his knife, and when he came into the kitchen, he had a gallon jar of whiskey under his arm and Euphrates's stepdaughter by the wrist.

Wayne stopped chewing, crumbs falling from his mouth. He approached the girl and put his hand out to touch her, but Kent pushed him hard, into the wall. Wayne stayed there, a clock ticking beside his head, a string of spit linking his two opened lips, watching as his brother ran his rough hands up and down the girl's trembling body, over the nipples that showed through the thin cloth. Her eyes were closed, lips moving in prayer. Looking down, Kent saw the puddle spreading around her bare feet.

"Shit," he said, a hand cupping her breast. "Pissed herself."

He let her go and she shrank back against the wall, behind the door. She was still there, along with a bag of catfish on the table, when her stepfather came back half an hour later, ten gallons of whiskey under the tarp in his truck.

On that same Saturday Kirxy drove to the chicken fights, held in Heflin Bradford's bulging barn, deep in woods cloudy with mosquitos. He passed the hand-painted sign that'd been there forever, as long as he could remember, nailed to a tree. It said JESUS IS NOT COMING.

Kirxy climbed out of his truck and buttoned his collar, his ears full of cotton. Heflin's wife worked beneath a rented awning, grilling chicken and sausages, selling Cokes and beer. Gospel music played from a portable tape player by her head. Heflin's grandson Nolan took the price of admission at the barn door and stamped the backs of white hands and the cracked pink palms of black ones. Men in overalls and baseball caps that said CAT DIESEL POWER or STP stood at the tailgates of their pickups, smoking cigarettes, stooping to peer into the dark cages where roosters paced. The air was filled with windy rain spits and the crowing of roosters, the ground littered with limp, dead birds.

A group of men discussed Frank David, and Kirxy paused to listen.

"He's the one caught that bunch over in Warshington County," one man said. "Them alligator poachers."

"Sugarbaby said two of 'em wound up in the intensive care," another claimed. "Said they pulled a gun and old Frank David went crazy with a axe handle."

Kirxy moved on and paid the five dollar admission. In the barn, there were bleachers along the walls and a big circular wooden fence in the center, a dome of chicken wire over the top. Kirxy found a seat at the bottom next to the back door, near a group of mean old farts he'd known for forty years. People around them called out bets and bets were accepted. Cans of beer lifted. Kirxy produced a thermos of coffee and a dented tin cup. He poured the coffee then added whiskey from a bottle that went back into his coat pocket. The tin cup warmed his fingers as he squinted through his bifocals to see which bird to bet on.

In separate comers of the barn, two bird handlers doused their roosters' heads and asses with rubbing alcohol to make them fight harder. They tightened the long steel curved spurs. When the referee in the center of the ring indicated it was time, the handlers entered the pen, each cradling his bird in his arms. They flashed the roosters at one another until their feathers had ruffled with blood-lust and rage, the roosters pedalling the air, stretching their necks toward each other. The handlers kept them a breath apart for a second, then withdrew them to their corners, whispering in their ears. When the referee tapped the ground three times with his stick, the birds were unleashed on each other. They charged and rose in the center of the ring, gouging with spur and beak, the handlers circling the fight like crabs, blood on their forearms and faces, ready to seize their roosters at the referee's cry of "Handle!"

A clan of Louisiana Cajuns watched. They'd emerged red-eyed from a van in a marijuana cloud: skinny, shirtless men with oily ponytails and goatees and tattoos of symbols of black magic. Under their arms, they carried thick white hooded roosters to pit against the reds and blacks of the locals. Their women had stumbled out of the van behind them, high yellow like gypsies, big-lipped, big-chested girls in halter tops tied at their bellies and miniskirts and red heels.

In the ring the Cajuns kissed their birds on the beaks, and one tall, completely bald Cajun wearing gold earrings in both ears put his bird's whole head in his mouth. His girl, too, came barefoot into the ring, tattoo of a snake on her shoulder, and took the bird's head into her mouth.

"Bet on them white ones," a friend whispered to Kirxy. "These ones around here ain't ever seen a white rooster. They don't know what they're fighting."

That evening, checking traps in the woods north of the river, Wayne kept hearing things. Little noises. Leaves. Twigs.

Afraid, he forced himself to go on so his brothers wouldn't laugh at him. Near dark, in a wooden trap next to an old fence row, he was surprised to find the tiny white fox they'd once seen cross the road in front of their truck. He squatted before the trap and poked a stick through the wire at the thin snout, his hand steady despite the way the fox snapped at the stick and bit off the end. Would the witch woman want this alive? At the thought of her he looked around. It felt like she was watching him, as if she were hiding in a tree in the form of some animal, a possum, a swamp rat. He stood and dragged the trap through the mud and over the land while the fox jumped in circles, growling.

A mile upstream, Scott had lost a boot to the mud and was hopping back one-footed to retrieve it. It stood alone, buried to the ankle. He wrenched it free then sat with his back against a sweet gum, to scrape off the mud. He'd begun to lace the boot when he saw a hollow tree stump, something moving inside. With his rifle barrel, he rolled the thing out—it was most of the body of a dead catfish, the movement from the maggots devouring it. When he kicked it, they spilled from the fish like rice pellets and lay throbbing in the mud.

Downstream, as night came and the rain fell harder, Kent trolled their boat across the river, flashlight in his mouth, using a stick to pull up a trotline length by length and removing the fish or turtles and rebaiting the hooks and dropping them back into the water. Near the bank, approaching the last hook, he heard something. He looked up with the flashlight in his teeth to see the thing un-twirling in the air. It wrapped around his neck like a rope, and for an instant he thought he was being hanged. He grabbed the thing. It flexed and tightened, then his neck burned and went numb and he felt dizzy, his fingertips buzzing, legs weak, a tree on the bank distorting, doubling, tripling into a whole line of fuzzy shapes, turning sideways, floating.

Kent blinked. Felt his eyes bulging, his tongue swelling. His head about to explode. Then a bright light.

His brothers found the boat at dawn, four miles downstream, lodged on the far side in a fallen tree. They exchanged a glance then looked back across the river. A heavy gray fog hooded the water and the boat appeared and dissolved in the ghostly limbs around it. Scott sat on a log and took off his boots and left them standing by the log. He removed his coat and laid it over the boots. He handed his brother his rifle without looking at him, left him watching as he climbed down the bank and, hands and elbows in the air like a believer, waded into the water.

Wayne propped the second rifle against a tree and stood on the bank holding his own gun, casting his frightened eyes up and down the river. From far away a woodpecker drummed. Crows began to collect in a pecan tree downstream. After a while Wayne squatted, thinking of their dogs, tied to the bumper of their truck. They'd be under the tailgate, probably, trying to keep dry.

Soon Scott had trolled the boat back across. Together they pulled it out of the water and stood looking at their brother who lay across the floor among the fish and turtles he'd caught. One greenish terrapin, still alive, a hook in its neck, stared back. They both knew what they were supposed to think—the blood and the sets of twin fang marks, the black bruises and shrivelled skin, the neck swollen like mumps, the purple bulb of tongue between his lips. They were supposed to think *cottonmouth*. Kent's hands were squeezed into fists and they'd hardened that way, the skin wrinkled. His eyes half open. His rifle lay unfired in the boat, as if indeed a snake had done this.

But it wasn't the tracks of a snake they found when they went to get the white fox. The fox was gone, though, the trap empty, its catch sprung. Scott knelt and ran his knuckles along the rim of a boot print in the mud—not a very wide track, not very far from the next one. He put his finger in the black water that'd already begun to fill the track: not too deep. He looked up at Wayne. The print of an average-sized man. In no hurry. Scott rose and they began.

Above them, the sky cracked and flickered.

Silently, quickly—no time to get the dogs—they followed the trail back through the woods, losing it once, twice, backtracking, working against the rain that fell and fell harder, that puddled blackly and crept up their legs, until they stood in water to their calves, rain beading on the brims of their caps. They gazed at the ground, the sky, at the rain streaming down each other's muddy face.

At the truck, Wayne jumped in the driver's seat and reached for the keys. Scott appeared in the window, shaking his head. When Wayne didn't scoot over, the older boy hit him in the jaw then slung open the door and pulled Wayne out, sent him rolling over the ground. Scott climbed in and had trouble getting the truck choked. By the time he had the hang of it, Wayne had gotten into the back and sat among the wet dogs, staring at his dead brother.

At their cabin, they carried Kent into the woods. They laid him on the ground and began digging near where their sister, mother, and father were buried in their unmarked graves. For three hours they worked, the dogs coming from under the porch and sniffing around Kent and watching the digging, finally slinking off and crawling back under the porch, out of the rain. An hour later the dogs came boiling out again and stood in a group at the edge of the yard, baying. The boys paused but saw or heard nothing.

When the dogs kept making noise, Scott got his rifle and fired into the woods several times. He nodded to his brother and they went back to digging. By the time they'd finished, it was late afternoon and the hole was full of slimy water and they were black with mud. They each took off one of Kent's boots and Scott got the things from his pockets. They stripped off his shirt and pants and lowered him into the hole. When he bobbed to the top of the water, they got stones and weighted him down. Then shoveled mud into the grave.

They showed up at Esther's, black as tar.

"Where's Kent?" she asked, holding her robe closed at her throat.

"We buried him," Scott said, moving past her into the kitchen. She put a hand over her mouth, and as Scott told her what they'd found she slumped against the door, looking outside. An owl flew past in the floodlights. She thought of calling Kirxy but decided to wait until morning—the old bastard thought she was a slut and a corruption. For tonight she'd just keep them safe in her house.

Scott went to the den. He turned on the TV, the reception bad because of the weather. Wayne, a bruise on his left cheek, climbed the stairs. He went into one of the bedrooms and closed the door behind him. It was chilly in the room and he noticed pictures of people on the wall, children and a tall man and younger woman he took to be Esther. She'd been pretty then. He stood dripping on the floor, looking into her black-and-white face, searching for signs of the woman he knew now. Soon the door opened behind him and she came in. And though he still wore his filthy wet clothes, she steered him to the bed and guided him down onto it. She unbuckled his belt, removed his hunting knife, and stripped the belt off. She unbuttoned his shirt and rubbed her fingers across his chest, the hair just beginning to thicken there. She undid his pants and ran the zipper down its track. She worked them over his thighs, knees and ankles and draped them across the back of a chair. She pulled off his boots and socks. Pried a finger beneath the elastic of his underwear, felt that he'd already come.

He looked at her face. His mouth opened. Esther touched his chin, the scratch of whiskers, his breath on her hand.

"Hush now," she said, and watched him fall asleep.

Downstairs, the TV went off.

When Goodloe knocked, Esther answered, a cold sliver of her face in the cracked door. "The hell you want?"

"Good evening to you, too. The Gateses here?"

"No."

Goodloe glanced behind him. "I believe that's their truck. It's kinda hard to mistake, especially for us trained lawmen."

She tried to close the door but Goodloe had his foot in it. He glanced at the three deputies who stood importantly by the Blazer. They dropped their cigarettes and crushed them out. They unsnapped their holsters and strode across the yard, standing behind Goodloe with their hands on their revolvers and their legs apart like TV deputies.

"Why don't y'all just let 'em alone?" Esther said. "Ain't they been through enough?"

"Tell 'em I'd like to see 'em," Goodloe said. "Tell 'em get their boots."

"You just walk straight to hell, mister."

Wayne appeared behind her, naked, lines from the bed linen on his face.

"Whoa, Nellie," Goodloe said. "Boy, you look plumb terrible. Why don't you let us carry you on down to the office for a little coffee? Little cake." He glanced back at one of the deputies. "We got any of that cinnamon roll left, Dave?"

"You got a warrant for their arrest?" Esther asked.

"No, I ain't got a warrant for their arrest. They ain't under arrest. They fixing to get questioned, is all. Strictly informal." Goodloe winked. "You reckon you could do without 'em for a couple of hours?"

"Fuck you, Sugarbaby."

The door slammed. Goodloe nodded down the side of the house and two deputies went to make sure nobody escaped from the back. But in a minute Wayne came out dressed, his hands in his pockets, and followed Goodloe down the stairs, the deputies watching him closely, and watching the house.

"Where's your brothers?" Goodloe asked.

He looked down.

Goodloe nodded to the house and two deputies went in, guns drawn. They came out a few minutes later, frowning.

"Must've heard us coming," Goodloe said. "Well, we got this one. We'll find them other two tomorrow." They got into the Blazer and Goodloe looked at Wayne, sitting in the back.

"Put them cuffs on him," Goodloe said.

Holding his rifle, Scott came out of the woods when the Blazer was gone. He returned to the house.

"They got Wayne," Esther said. "Why didn't you come tell him they was out there?"

"He got to learn," Scott said. He went to the cabinet where she kept the whiskey and took the bottle. She watched him go to the sofa and sit down in front of the blank TV. Soon she joined him, bringing glasses. He filled both, and when they emptied them he filled them again.

They spent the night like that, and at dawn they were drunk. Wearing her robe, Esther began clipping her fingernails, a cigarette smoking in the ashtray beside her. She'd forgotten about calling Kirxy.

Scott was telling her about the biggest catfish they'd ever called up: a hundred pounds, he swore, a hundred fifty. "You could of put your whole head in that old cat's mouth," he said, sipping his whiskey. "Back fin long as your damn arm."

He stood. Walked to the front window. There were toads in the yard—with the river swelling they were everywhere. In the evenings there were rainfrogs. The yard had turned into a pond and each night the rainfrogs sang. It was like no other sound. Esther said it kept her up at night.

"That, and some other things," she said.

Scott heard a fingernail ring the ashtray. He rubbed his hand across his chin, felt the whiskers there. He watched the toads as they huddled in the yard, still as rocks, bloated and miserable-looking.

"That catfish was green," Scott said, sipping. "I swear to God. Green as grass."

"Them goddamn rainfrogs," she said. "I just lay there at night with my hands over my ears."

A clipping rang the ashtray.

He turned and went to her on the sofa. "They was moss growing on his nose," he said, putting his hand on her knee.

"Go find your brother," she said. She got up and walked unsteadily across the floor and went into the bathroom, closed the door. When she came out, he and the bottle were gone.

Without Kent, Scott felt free to do what he wanted, which was to drive very fast. He got the truck started and spun off, aiming for every mud hole he could. He shot past a house with a washing machine on the front porch, two thin black men skinning a hog hanging from a tree. One of the men waved with a knife. Drinking, Scott drove through the mountains of trash at the dump and turned the truck in circles, kicking up muddy roostertails. He swerved past the Negro church and the graveyard where a group of blacks huddled, four warbling poles over an open grave, the wind tearing the preacher's hat out of his hands and a woman's umbrella reversing suddenly.

When he tired of driving, he left the truck in their hiding place, and using trees for balance, stumbled down the hill to their boat. He carried Kent's rifle, which he'd always admired. On the river, he fired up the outboard and accelerated, the boat prow lifting and leveling out, the buzz of the motor rising in the trees. The water was nearly orange from mud, the cypress knees nothing but knobs and tips because of the floods. Nearing the old train trestle, he cut the motor and coasted to a stop. He sat listening to the rain, to the distant barking of a dog, half a mile away. Chasing something, maybe a deer. As the dog charged through the woods, Scott closed his eyes and imagined the terrain, marking where he thought the dog was now and where he thought it was now. Then the barking stopped, suddenly, as if the dog had run smack into a tree.

Scott clicked on the trolling motor and moved the boat close to the edge of the river, the rifle across his knees. He scanned the banks, and when the rain started to fall harder he accelerated toward the trestle. From beneath the cross ties, he smelled creosote and watched the rain as it stirred the river. He looked into the gray trees and thought he would drive into town later, see about getting Wayne. Kent had never wanted to go to Grove Hill—their father had warned them of the police, of jail.

Scott picked up one of the catfish from the night before. It was stiff, as if carved out of wood. He stared at it, watching the green blowflies hover above his fist, then threw it over into the cattails along the bank.

The telephone rig lay under the seat. He lifted the chains quietly, considering what giant catfish might be passing beneath the boat this very second, a thing as large as a man's thigh with eyes the size of ripe plums and skin the color of mud. Catfish, their father had taught them, have long whiskers that make them the only fish you can "call." Kirxy had told Scott and his brothers that if a game warden caught you telephoning, all you needed to do was dump your rig overboard. But, Kirxy warned, Frank David would handcuff you and swim around the bottom of the river until he found your rig.

Scott spat a stream of tobacco into the brown water. Minnows appeared and began to investigate, nibbling at the dark yolk of spit as it elongated and dissolved. With his rifle's safety off, he lowered the chains into the water, a good distance apart. He checked the connections—the battery, the telephone. He lifted the phone and began to dial. "Hello?" he whispered, the thing his father had always said, grinning in the dark. The wind picked up a bit, he heard it rattling in the trees, and he dialed faster, had just seen the first silver body bob to the surface when something landed with a clatter in his boat. He glanced over.

A bundle of dynamite, sparks shooting off the end, fuse already gone. He looked above him, the trestle, but nobody was there. He moved to grab the dynamite, but his cheeks ballooned with hot red wind and his hands caught fire.

When the smoke cleared and the water stopped boiling, silver bodies began to bob to the surface—large mouth bass, bream, gar, suckers, white perch, polliwogs, catfish—some only stunned but others dead, in pieces, pink fruit-like things, the water blooming darkly with mud.

Kirxy's telephone rang for the second time in one day, a rarity that proved what his wife had always said: bad news came over the phone. The first call had been Esther, telling him of Kent's death, Wayne's arrest, Scott's disappearance. This time Kirxy heard Goodloe's voice telling him that somebody—or maybe a couple of somebodies—had been blown up out on the trestle.

"Scott," Kirxy said, sitting.

He arrived at the trestle, and with his cane hobbled over the uneven tracks. Goodloe's deputies and three ambulance drivers in rubber gloves and waders were scraping pieces off the cross ties with spoons, dropping the parts in Ziploc bags. The boat, two flattened shreds of aluminum, lay on the bank. In the water, minnows darted about, nibbling.

"Christ," Kirxy said. He brought a handkerchief to his lips. Then he went to where Goodloe stood on the bank, writing in his notebook.

"What do you aim to do about this?" Kirxy demanded.

"Try to figure out who it was, first."

"You know goddamn well who it was."

"I expect it's either Kent or Scott Gates."

"It's Scott," Kirxy said.

"How do you know that?"

Kirxy told him that Kent was dead.

"I ain't seen the body," Goodloe said.

Kirxy's blood pressure was going up. "Fuck, Sugarbaby. Are you one bit aware what's going on here?"

"Fishing accident," Goodloe said. "His bait exploded."

From the bank, a deputy called that he'd found most of a boot. "Foot's still in it," he said, holding it up by the lace.

"Tag it," Goodloe said, writing something down. "Keep looking." Kirxy poked Goodloe in the shoulder with his cane. "You really think Scott'd blow himself up?"

Goodloe looked at his shoulder, the muddy cane print, then at the storekeeper. "Not on purpose, I don't." He paused. "Course, suicide does run in their family."

"What about Kent?"

"What about him?"

"Christ, Sugarbaby—"

Goodloe held up his hand. "Just show me, Kirxy."

They left the ambulance drivers and the deputies and walked the other way without talking. When they came to Goodloe's Blazer, they got in and drove without talking. Soon they stopped in front of the Gates' cabin. Instantly hounds surrounded the truck, barking viciously and jumping with muddy paws against the glass. Goodloe blew the horn until the hounds slunk away, heads low, fangs bared. The sheriff opened his window and fired several times in the air, backing the dogs up. When he and Kirxy got out, Goodloe had reloaded.

The hounds kept to the edge of the woods, watching.

His eye on them, Kirxy led Goodloe behind the decrepit cabin. Rusty screens covered some windows, rags of drape others. Beneath the house, the dogs paced them. "Back here," Kirxy said, heading into the trees. Esther had said they'd buried Kent, and this was the logical place. He went slowly, careful not to bump a limb and cause a small downpour. Sure enough, there lay the grave. You could see where the dogs had been scratching around it.

Goodloe went over and toed the dirt. "You know the cause of death?"

"Yeah, I know the cause of death. His name's Frank fucking David."

"I meant how he was killed."

"The boys said snakebite. Three times in the neck. But I'd do an autopsy."

"You would." Goodloe exhaled. "Okay. I'll send Roy and Avery over here to dig him up. Maybe shoot these goddern dogs."

"I'll tell you what you better do first. You better keep Wayne locked up safe."

"I can't hold him much longer," Goodloe said. "Unless he confesses."

Kirxy pushed him from behind, and at the edge of the woods the dogs tensed. Goodloe backed away, raising his pistol, the grave between them.

"You crazy, Kirxy? You been locked in that store too long?"

"Goodloe," Kirxy gasped. The cotton in his left ear had come out and suddenly air was roaring through his head. "Even you can't be this stupid. You let that boy out and he's that cold-blooded fucker's next target—"

"Target, Kirxy? Shit. Ain't nothing to prove anybody killed them damn boys. This one snake-bit, you said so yourself. That other one blowing himself up. Them dern Gateses has fished with dynamite their whole life. You oughta know that—you the one gets it for 'em." He narrowed his eyes. "You're about neck deep in this thing, you know. And I don't mean just lying to protect them boys, neither. I mean selling explosives illegally, to minors, Kirxy."

"I don't give a shit if I am!" Kirxy yelled. "Two dead boys in two days and you're worried about dynamite? You oughta be out there looking for Frank David."

"He ain't supposed to be here for another week or two," Goodloe said. "Paperwork—"

He fired his pistol then. Kirxy jumped, but the sheriff was looking past him, and when Kirxy followed his eyes he saw the dog that had been creeping in. It lay slumped in the mud, a hind leg kicking, blood coloring the water around it.

Goodloe backed away, smoke curling from the barrel of his pistol.

Around them the other dogs circled, heads low, moving sideways, the hair on their spines sticking up.

"Let's argue about this in the truck," Goodloe said.

At the store Kirxy put out the Open sign. He sat in his chair with his coffee and a cigarette. He'd read the same page three times when it occurred to him to phone Montgomery and get Frank David's office on the line. It took a few calls, but he soon got the number and dialed. The snippy young woman who answered told Kirxy that yes, Mr. David *was* supposed to take over the Lower Peachtree district, but that he wasn't starting until next week, she thought.

Where was he now? Kirxy wanted to know.

"Florida?" she said. "No, Louisiana. Fishing." No sir, he couldn't be reached. He preferred his vacations private.

Kirxy slammed down the phone. He lit another cigarette and tried to think.

It was just a matter, he decided, of keeping Wayne alive until Frank David took over the district. There were probably other game wardens who'd testify that Frank David *was* over in Louisiana fishing right now. But once the son-of-a-bitch officially moved here, he'd have motive and his alibi wouldn't be as strong. If Wayne turned up dead, Frank David would be the chief suspect.

Kirxy inhaled smoke deeply and tried to imagine how Frank David would think. How he would act. The noise he would make or not make as he went through the woods. What he would say if you happened upon him. Or he upon you. What he would do if he came into the store. Certainly he wasn't the creature Kirxy had created to scare the boys, not some wild ghostly thing. He was just a man who'd had a hard life and grown bitter and angry. Probably an alcoholic. A man who chose to uphold the law because breaking it was no challenge. A man with no obligation to any other men or a family. Just to himself and his job. To some goddamned game warden code. His job was to protect the wild things the law had deemed worthy: dove, duck, owls, hawks, turkeys, alligators, squirrels, coons, and deer. But how did the Gates boys fall into the category of trash animal—wildcats or possums or armadillos, snapping turtles, snakes? Things you could kill any time, run over in your truck and not even look at in your mirror to see dying behind you? Christ. Why couldn't Frank David see that he—more than a match for the boys—was of their breed?

Kirxy drove to the highway. The big thirty-ought-six he hadn't touched in years was on the seat next to him, and as he steered he pushed cartridges into the clip, then shoved the clip into the gun's underbelly. He pulled the lever that injected a cartridge into the chamber and took a long drink of whiskey to wash down three of the pills that helped dull the ache in his knees, and the one in his gut.

It was almost dark when he arrived at the edge of a large field. He parked facing the grass. This was a place a few hundred yards from a fairly well-traveled blacktop, a spot no sane poacher would dare use. There were already two or three deer creeping into the open from the woods across the field. They came to eat the tall grass, looking up only when a car passed, their ears swiveling, jaws frozen, sprigs of grass twitching in their lips like the legs of insects.

Kirxy sat watching. He sipped his whiskey and lit a cigarette with a trembling hand. Both truck doors were locked and he knew this was a very stupid thing he was doing. Several times he told himself to go home, let things unfold as they would. Then he saw the faces of the two dead boys. And the face of the live one.

When Boo had killed himself, the oldest two had barely been teenagers, but it was eleven-year-old Wayne who'd found him. That truck still had windows then, and the back windshield had been sprayed red with blood. Flies had gathered at the top of the truck in what Wayne discovered was a twenty-two caliber hole.

Kirxy frowned, thinking of it. Boo's hat still on his head, a small hole through the hat, too. The back of the truck was full of wood Boo'd been cutting, and the three boys had unloaded the wood and stacked it neatly beside the road. Kirxy shifted in his seat, imagining the boys pushing that truck for two miles over dirt roads, somehow finding the leverage or whatever, the goddamn strength, to get it home. To pull their father from inside and bury him. To clean out the truck. Kirxy shuddered and thought of Frank David, then made himself think of his wife instead. He rubbed his biceps and watched the shadows creep across the field, the treeline dim and begin to disappear.

Soon it was full dark. He unscrewed the interior light bulb from the ceiling, pulled the door lock up quietly. Holding his breath, he opened the door. Outside, he propped the rifle on the side mirror, flicked the safety off. He reached through the window, felt along the dash for the headlight switch, pulled it.

The field blazed with the eyes of deer—red, hovering dots staring back at him. Kirxy aimed and squeezed the trigger at the first pair of eyes. Not waiting to see if he'd hit the deer, he moved the gun to another pair. He'd gotten off five shots before the eyes began to disappear. When the last echo from the gun faded, at least three deer lay dead or wounded in the glow of his headlights. One doe bleated weakly and bleated again. Kirxy coughed and took the gun back into the truck, closed the door, and reloaded in the dark. Then he waited. The doe kept bleating and things in the woods took shape, detached and whisked towards Kirxy over the grass like spooks. And the little noises. Things like footsteps. And the stories. Frank David appearing in the bed of somebody's *moving* truck and punching through the back glass, grabbing and breaking the driver's arm. Leaping from the truck and watching while it wrecked.

"Quit it," Kirxy croaked. "You damn schoolgirl."

Several more times that night he summoned his nerve and flicked on the headlights, firing at any eyes he saw or firing at nothing. When he finally fell asleep just after two A.M., his body numb with painkillers and whiskey, he dreamed of his wife on the day of her first miscarriage. The way the nurses couldn't find the vein in her arm, how they'd kept trying with the needle, the way she'd cried and held his fingers tightly, like a woman giving birth.

He started awake, terrified, as if he'd fallen asleep driving.

Caring less for silence, he stumbled from the truck and flicked on the lights and fired at the eyes, though now they were doubling up, floating in the air. He lowered the gun and for no good reason found himself thinking of a time when he'd tried fly fishing, standing in his yard with his wife watching from the porch, *Tarzan of the Apes* in her lap, him whipping the line in the air, showing off, and then the strange pulling you get when you catch a fish, Betty jumping to her feet, the book falling, and her yelling that he'd caught a bat for heaven's sake, a *bat!*

He climbed back into the truck. His hands shook so hard he had trouble getting the door locked. He bowed his head, missing her so much that he cried, softly and for a long time.

Dawn found him staring at a field littered with dead does, yearlings, and fawns. One of the deer, only wounded, tried to crawl toward the safety of the trees. Kirxy got out of the truck and vomited colorless water, then stood looking around at the foggy morning. He lifted his rifle and limped into the grass in the drizzle and, a quick hip shot, put the deer out of its misery.

He was sitting on the open tailgate trying to light a cigarette when Goodloe and a deputy passed in their Blazer and stopped.

The sheriff stepped out, signaling for the deputy to stay put. He sat beside Kirxy on the tailgate, the truck dipping with his weight. His stomach was growling and he patted it absently.

"You old fool," Goodloe said, staring at Kirxy and then at the field. "You figured to make Frank David show himself?" He shook his head. "Good lord almighty, Kirxy. What'll it take to prove to you there ain't no damn game warden out there? Not yet, anyhow."

Kirxy didn't answer. Goodloe went to the Blazer and told the deputy to pick him up at Kirxy's store. Then he helped the old man into the passenger seat and went around and got in the driver's side. He took the rifle and unloaded it, put its clip in his pocket.

"We'll talk about them deer later," he said. "Now I'd better get you back."

They'd gone a silent mile when Kirxy said, "Would you mind running me by Esther's?"

Goodloe shrugged and turned that way. His stomach made a strangling noise. The rain and wind were picking up, rocking the truck. The sheriff took a bottle of whiskey from his pocket. "Medicinal," he said, handing the bottle to Kirxy. "It's just been two freak accidents, is all, Kirxy. I've seen some strange shit, a lot stranger than this. Them Gateses is just a unlucky bunch. Period. I ain't one to go believing in curses, but I swear to God if they ain't downright snake-bit."

Soon Goodloe had parked in front or Esther's and they sat waiting for the rain to slack. Kirxy rubbed his knees and looked out the windows where the trees were half-submerged in the rising floodwaters.

"They say old Esther has her a root cellar," Goodloe said, taking a sip. "Shit. I expect it's full of water this time of year. She's probably got cottonmouths wrapped around her plumbing." He shuddered and offered the bottle. Kirxy took it and sipped. He gave it back and Goodloe took it and drank then drank again. "Lord if that don't hit the spot."

"When I was in the service," Goodloe went on, "over in Thailand? They had them little bitty snakes, them banded kraits. Poison as cobras, what they told us. Used to hide up under the commode lid. Every time you took you a shit, you had to lift up the lid, see was one there." He drank. "Yep. It was many a time I kicked one off in the water, flushed it down."

"Wait here," Kirxy said. He opened his door, his pants leg darkening as the rain poured in, cold as needles. He set his knee out deliberately, planted his cane in the mud and pulled himself up, stood in water to his ankles. He limped across the yard with his hand blocking the rain. There were two chickens on the front porch, their feathers fluffed out so that they looked strange, menacing. Kirxy climbed the porch steps with the pain so strong in his knees that stars popped near his face by the time he reached the top. He leaned against the house, breathing hard. Touched himself at the throat where a tie might've gone. Then he rapped gently with the hook of his cane. The door opened immediately. Dark inside. She stood there, looking at him.

"How come you don't ever stop by the store any more?" he asked.

She folded her arms.

"Scott's dead," he said.

"I heard," Esther said. "And I'm leaving. Fuck this place and every one of you."

She closed the door and Kirxy would never see her again.

At the store, Goodloe nodded for the deputy to stay in the Blazer, then he took Kirxy by the elbow and helped him up the steps. He unlocked the door for him and held his hand as the old man sank in his chair.

"Want these boots off?" Goodloe asked, spreading a blanket over Kirxy's lap.

He bent and unlaced the left, then the right.

"Pick up your foot."

"Now the other one."

He set the wet boots by the stove.

"It's a little damp in here. I'll light this thing."

He found a box of kitchen matches on a shelf under the counter among the glass figurines Kirxy's wife had collected. The little deer. The figure skater. The unicorn. Goodloe got a fire going in the stove and stood warming the backs of his legs.

"I'll bring Wayne by a little later," he said, but Kirxy didn't seem to hear.

Goodloe sat in his office with his feet on his desk, rolling a cartridge between his fingers. Despite himself, he was beginning to think Kirxy might be right. Maybe Frank David *was* out there on the prowl. He stood, put on his pistol belt, and walked to the back, pushed open the swinging door and had Roy buzz him through. So far he'd had zero luck getting anything out of Wayne. The boy just sat in his cell wrapped in a blanket, not talking to anybody. Goodloe had told him about his brother's death, and he'd seen no emotion cross the boy's face. Goodloe figured that it wasn't this youngest one who'd killed that game warden, it'd probably been the others. He knew that this boy wasn't carrying a full cylinder, the way he never talked, but he had most likely been a witness. He'd been considering calling in the state psychologist from the Searcy Mental Hospital to give the boy an evaluation.

"Come on," Goodloe said, stopping by Wayne's cell. "I'm fixing to put your talent to some good use."

He kept the boy cuffed as the deputy drove them toward the trestle.

"Turn your head, Dave," Goodloe said, handing Wayne a pint of Old Crow. The boy took it in both hands and unscrewed the lid, began to drink too fast.

"Slow down there, partner," Goodloe said, taking back the bottle. "You need to be alert."

Soon they stood near the trestle, gazing at the flat shapes of the boat on the bank. Wayne knelt and examined the ground. The deputy came up and started to say something, but Goodloe motioned for quiet.

"Just like a goddern bloodhound," he whispered. "Maybe I ought give him your job."

"Reckon what he's after?" the deputy asked.

Wayne scrabbled up the trestle, and the two men followed. The boy walked slowly over the rails, examining the spaces between the cross ties. He stopped, bent down and peered at something Picked it up.

"What you got there, boy?" Goodloe called, going and squatting beside him. He took a sip of Old Crow.

When Wayne hit him, two-handed, the bottle flew one way and Goodloe the other. Both landed in the river, Goodloe with his hand clapped to his head to keep his hat on. He came up immediately, bobbing and sputtering. On the trestle, the deputy tackled Wayne and they went down fighting on the cross ties. Below, Goodloe dredged himself out of the water. He came ashore dripping and tugged his pistol from its holster. He held it up so that a thin trickle of orange water fell. He took off his hat and looked up to see the deputy disappear belly-first into the face of the river.

Wayne ran down the track, toward the swamp. The deputy came boiling ashore. He had his own pistol drawn and was looking around vengefully.

Goodloe climbed the trestle in time to see Wayne disappear into the woods. The sheriff chased him for a while, ducking limbs and vines, but stopped, breathing hard. The deputy passed him.

Wayne circled back through the woods and went quickly over the soft ground, half-crawling up the sides of hills and sliding down the other sides. Two hollows over, he heard the deputy heading the wrong direction. Wayne slowed a little and just trotted for a long time in the rain, the cuffs rubbing his wrists raw. He stopped once and looked at what he'd been carrying in one hand: a match, limp and black now with water, nearly dissolved. He stood looking at the trees around him, the hanging Spanish moss and the cypress knees rising from the stagnant creek to his left.

The hair on the back of his neck rose. He knelt, tilting his head, closing his eyes, and listened. He heard the rain, heard it hit leaves and wood and heard the puddles lapping at their tiny banks, but beyond those sounds there were other muffled noises. A mockingbird mocking a bluejay. A squirrel barking and another answering. The deputy falling, a quarter mile away. Then another sound, this one close. A match striking. Wayne began to run before opening his eyes and crashed into a tree. He rolled and ran again, tearing through limbs and briars. He leapt small creeks and slipped and got up and kept running. At every turn he expected

Frank David, and he was near tears when he finally stumbled into his family graveyard.

The first thing he saw was that Kent had been dug up. Wooden stakes surrounded the hole and fenced it in with yellow tape that had words on it. Wayne approached slowly, hugging himself. Something floated in the grave. With his heart pounding, he peered inside. A dog.

Wary of the trees behind him, he crept toward their back yard, stopping at the edge. He crouched and blew into his hands to warm his cheeks. He gazed at the dark windows of their cabin, then circled the house, keeping to the woods. He saw the pine tree with the low limb they used for stringing up larger animals to clean, the rusty chain hanging and the iron pipe they stuck through the back legs of a deer or the rare wild pig. Kent and Scott had usually done the cleaning while Wayne fed the guts to their dogs and tried to keep the dogs from fighting.

And there, past the tree, lay the rest of the dogs. Shot dead. Partially eaten. Buzzards standing in the mud, staring boldly at him with their heads bloody and their beaks open.

It was dark when Kirxy woke in his chair, he'd heard the door creak. Someone stood there, and the storekeeper was afraid until he smelled the river.

"Hey, boy," he said.

Wayne ate two cans of potted meat with his fingers and a candy bar and a box of saltines. Kirxy gave him a Coke from the red cooler and he drank it and took another one while Kirxy got a hacksaw from the rack of tools behind the counter. He slipped the cardboard wrapping off and nodded for Wayne to sit. The storekeeper pulled up another chair and faced the boy and began sawing the handcuff chain. The match dropped out of Wayne's hand but neither saw it. Wayne sat with his head down and his palms up, his wrists on his knees, breathing heavily, while Kirxy worked and the silver shavings accumulated in a pile between their boots. The boy didn't lift his head the entire time, and he'd been asleep for quite a while when Kirxy finally sawed through. The old man rose, flexing his sore hands, and got a blanket from a shelf. He unfolded it, shook out the dust and spread it over Wayne. He went to the door and turned the dead bolt.

The phone rang later. It was Goodloe, asking about the boy.

"He's asleep," Kirxy said. "You been lost all this time, Sugarbaby?"

"That I have," Goodloe said, "and we still ain't found old Dave yet."

For a week they stayed there together. Kirxy could barely walk now, and the pain in his side was worse than ever, but he put the boy to work, sweeping, dusting, and scrubbing the shelves. He had Wayne pull a table next to his chair, and Kirxy did something he hadn't done in years: took inventory. With the boy's help, he counted and ledgered each item, marking them in his long green book. The back shelf contained canned soups, vegetables, sardines, and tins of meat. Many of the cans were so old that the labels flaked off in Kirxy's hand, so they were unmarked when Wayne replaced them in the rings they'd made not only in the dust but on the wood itself. In the back of that last shelf, Wayne discovered four tins of Underwood Deviled Ham, and as their labels fell away at Kirxy's touch, he remembered a time when he'd purposely unwrapped the paper from these cans because each label showed several red dancing devils, and some of his Negro customers had refused to buy anything that advertised the devil.

Kirxy now understood that his store was dead, that it no longer provided a service. His Negro customers had stopped coming years before. The same with Esther. For the past few years, except for the rare hunter, he'd been in business for the Gates boys alone. He looked across the room at Wayne, spraying the windows with Windex and wiping at them absently, gazing outside. The boy wore the last of the new denim overalls Kirxy had in stock. Once, when the store had thrived, he'd had

many sizes, but for the longest time now the only ones he'd
stocked were the boys'.

That night, beneath his standing lamp, Kirxy began again to
read his wife's copy of *Tarzan of the Apes* to Wayne. He sipped his
whiskey and spoke clearly, to be heard over the rain. When he
paused to turn a page, he saw that the boy lay asleep across the row
of chairs they'd arranged in the shape of a bed. Looking down
through his bifocals, Kirxy flipped to the back of the book to the
list of other Tarzan novels—twenty-four in all—and he decided to
order them through the mail so Wayne would hear the complete
adventures of Tarzan of the Apes.

In the morning, Goodloe called and said that Frank David had
officially arrived—the sheriff himself had witnessed the swearing-
in—and he was now this district's game warden.

"Pretty nice fellow," Goodloe said. "Kinda quiet. Polite. He
asked me how the fishing was."

Then it's over, Kirxy thought.

A week later, Kirxy told Wayne he had to run some errands in
Grove Hill. He'd spent the night before trying to decide whether
to take the boy with him but had decided not to, that he couldn't
watch him forever. Before he left he gave Wayne his thirty-ought-
six and told him to stay put, not to leave for anything. For himself, Kirxy took an old twenty-two bolt action and placed it in the
back window rack of his truck. He waved to Wayne and drove
off.

He thought that if the boy wanted to run away, it was his own
choice. Kirxy owed him the chance, at least.

At the doctor's office the young surgeon frowned and removed
his glasses when he told Kirxy that the cancer was advancing, that
he'd need to check into the hospital in Mobile immediately. It was
way past time. "Just look at your color," the surgeon said. Kirxy
stood, thanked the man, put on his hat, and limped outside. He
went by the post office and placed his order for the Tarzan books.
He shopped for supplies in the Dollar Store and the Piggily Wig-

gily, had the checkout boys put the boxes in the front seat beside him. Coming out of the drug store, he remembered that it was Saturday, that there'd be chicken fights today. And possible news about Frank David.

At Heflin's, Kirxy paid his five dollar admission and let Heflin help him to a seat in the bottom of the stands. He poured some whiskey in his coffee and sat studying the crowd. Nobody had mentioned Frank David, but a few old-timers had offered their sympathies on the deaths of Kent and Scott. Down in the pit the Cajuns were back, and during the eighth match—one of the Louisiana whites versus a local red, the tall bald Cajun stooping and circling the tangled birds and licking his lips as his rooster swarmed the other and hooked it, the barn smoky and dark, rain splattering the tin roof—the door swung open.

Instantly the crowd was hushed. Feathers settled to the ground. Even the Cajuns knew who he was. He stood at the door, unarmed, his hands on his hips. A wiry man. He lifted his chin and people tried to hide their drinks. His giant ears. The hooked nose. The eyes. Bird handlers reached over their shoulders, pulling at the numbered pieces of masking tape on their backs. The two handlers and the referee in the ring sidled out, leaving the roosters.

For a full minute Frank David stood staring. People stepped out the back door. Climbed out windows. Half-naked boys in the rafters were frozen like monkeys hypnotized by a snake.

Frank David's gaze didn't stop on Kirxy but settled instead on the roosters, the white one pecking out the red's eyes. Outside, trucks roared to life, backfiring like gunshots. Kirxy placed his hands on his knees. He rose, turned up his coat collar, and flung his coffee out. Frank David still hadn't looked at him. Kirxy planted his cane and made his way out the back door and through the mud.

Not a person in sight, just tailgates vanishing into the woods.

From inside his truck, Kirxy watched Frank David walk away from the barn and head toward the trees. Now he was just a bow-legged man with white hair. Kirxy felt behind him for the twenty-two rifle with one hand while rolling down the window with the other. He had a little trouble aiming the gun with his shaky hands. He pulled back the bolt and inserted a cartridge into the chamber. Flicked the safety off. The sight of the rifle wavered between Frank David's shoulders as he walked. As if an old man like Kirxy were nothing to fear. Kirxy ground his teeth: that was why the bastard hadn't come to his deer massacre—an old storekeeper wasn't worth it, wasn't dangerous.

Closing one eye, Kirxy pulled the trigger. He didn't hear the shot, though later he would notice his ears ringing.

Frank David's coat bloomed out to the side and he missed a step. He stopped and put his hand to his lower right side and looked over his shoulder at Kirxy, who was fumbling with the rifle's bolt action. Then Frank David was gone, just wasn't there, there were only the trees, bent in the rain, and shreds of fog in the air. For a moment, Kirxy wondered if he'd even seen a man at all, if he'd shot at something out of his own imagination, if the cancer that had started in his pancreas had inched up along his spine into his brain and was deceiving him, forming men out of the air and walking them across fields, giving them hands and eyes and the power to disappear.

From inside the barn, the rooster crowed. Kirxy remembered Wayne. He hung the rifle in its rack and started his truck, gunned the engine. He banged over the field, flattening saplings and a fence, and though he couldn't feel his toes, he drove very fast.

Not until two days later, in the VA hospital in Mobile, would Kirxy finally begin to piece it all together. Parts of that afternoon were patchy and hard to remember: shooting Frank David, going back to the store and finding it empty, no sign of a struggle, the thirty-ought-six gone, as if Wayne had walked out on his own and taken the gun. Kirxy could remember getting back into his truck He'd planned to drive to Grove Hill—the courthouse, the game warden's office—and find Frank David, but somewhere along the way he passed out behind the wheel and veered off the road into a ditch. He barely remembered the rescue workers. The sirens. Goodloe himself pulling Kirxy out.

Later that night two coon hunters had stumbled across Wayne, wandering along the river, his face and shirt covered in blood, the thirty-ought-six nowhere to be found.

When Goodloe had told the semi-conscious Kirxy what happened, the storekeeper turned silently to the window, where he saw only the reflected face of an old, failed, dying man.

And later still, in the warm haze of morphine, Kirxy lowered his eyelids and let his imagination unravel and retwine the mystery of Frank David: it was as if Frank David himself appeared in the chair where Goodloe had sat, as if the game warden broke the seal on a bottle of Jim Beam and leaned forward on his elbows and touched the bottle to Kirxy's cracked lips and whispered to him a story about boots going over land and not making a sound, about rain washing the blood trail away even as the boots passed. About a tired old game warden taking his hand out of his coat and seeing the blood from Kirxy's bullet there, feeling it trickle down his side. About the boy in the back of his truck, handcuffed, gagged, blindfolded. About driving carefully through deep ruts in the road. Stopping behind Esther's empty house and carrying the kicking boy inside on his shoulder.

When the blindfold is removed, Wayne has trouble focusing but knows where he is because of her smell. Bacon and soap. Cigarettes, dust. Frank David holds what looks like a pillowcase. He comes across the room and puts the pillowcase down. He rubs his eyes and sits on the bed beside Wayne. He opens a book of matches and lights a cigarette. Holds the filtered end to Wayne's lips, but the boy doesn't inhale. Frank David puts the cigarette in his own lips, the embers glow. Then he drops it on the floor, crushes it out with his boot. Picks up the butt and slips it into his shirt pocket. He puts his hand over the boy's watery eyes, the skin of his palm dry and hard. Cool. Faint smell of blood. He moves his fingers over Wayne's nose, lips, chin. Stops at his throat and holds the boy tightly but not painfully. In a strange way Wayne can't understand, he finds it reassuring. His thudding heart slows. Something is struggling beside his shoulder and Frank David takes the thing from the bag. Now the smell in the room changes. Wayne begins to thrash and whip his head from side to side.

"Goddamn, Son," Frank David whispers. "I hate to civilize you."

Goodloe began going to the veteran's hospital in Mobile once a week. He brought Kirxy cigarettes from his store. There weren't any private rooms available, and the beds around the storekeeper were filled with dying ex-soldiers who never talked, but Kirxy was beside a window and Goodloe would raise the glass and prop it open with a novel. They smoked together and drank whiskey from paper cups, listening for nurses.

It was the tall mean one.

"One more time, goddamn it," she said, coming out of nowhere and plucking the cigarettes from their lips so quickly they were still puckered.

Sometimes Goodloe would wheel Kirxy down the hall in his chair, the IV rack attached by a stainless steel contraption with a black handle the shape of a flower. They would go to the elevator and ride down three floors to a covered area where people smoked and talked about the weather. There were nurses and black cafeteria workers in white uniforms and hair nets and people visiting other people and a few patients. Occasionally in the halls they'd see some mean old fart Kirxy knew and they'd talk about hospital food or chicken fighting. Or the fact that Frank David had surprised everyone and decided to retire after only a month of quiet duty, that the new game warden was from Texas. And a nigger to boot.

Then Goodloe would wheel Kirxy back along a long window, out of which you could see the tops of oak trees.

On one visit, Goodloe told Kirxy they'd taken Wayne out of intensive care. Three weeks later he said the boy'd been discharged.

"I give him a ride to the store," Goodloe said. This was in late May and Kirxy was a yellow skeleton with hands that shook.

"I'll stop by and check on him every evening," Goodloe went on. "He'll be okay, the doctor says. Just needs to keep them bandages changed. I can do that, I reckon."

They were quiet then, for a time, just the coughs of the dying men and the soft swishing of nurses' thighs and the hum of IV machines.

"Goodloe," Kirxy whispered, "I'd like you to help me with something."

Goodloe leaned in to hear, an unlit cigarette behind his ear like a pencil.

Kirxy's tongue was white and cracked, his breath awful. "I'd like to change my will," he said, "make the boy beneficiary."

"All right," Goodloe said.

"I'm obliged," whispered Kirxy. He closed his eyes.

Near the end he was delirious. He said he saw a little black creature at the foot of his bed. Said it had him by the toe. In surprising fits of strength, he would throw his water pitcher at it, or his box of tissues, or the *TV Guide*. Restraints were called for. His coma was a relief to everyone, and he died quietly in the night.

In Kirxy's chair in the store, Wayne didn't seem to hear Goodloe's questions. The sheriff had done some looking in the Grove Hill library—"research" was the modern word—and discovered that one species of cobra spat venom at its victim's eyes, but there weren't such snakes in southern Alabama. Anyway, the hospital lab had confirmed that it was the venom of a cottonmouth that had blinded Wayne. The question, of course, was who had put the venom in his eyes. Goodloe shuddered to think of it, how they'd found Wayne staggering about, howling in pain, bleeding from his tear ducts, the skin around his eye sockets dissolving, exposing the white ridges of his skull.

In the investigation, several local blacks including Euphrates Morrisette stated to Goodloe that the youngest Gates boy and his two dead brothers had molested Euphrates' stepdaughter in her own house. There was a rumor that several black men dressed in white sheets with pillowcases for hoods had caught and punished Wayne as he lurked along the river, peeping in folks' windows and doing unwholesome things to himself. Others suggested that the conjure woman had cast a spell on the Gateses, that she'd summoned a swamp demon to chase them to hell. And still others attributed the happenings to Frank David. There were a few occurrences of violence between some of the local whites and the blacks—some fires, a broken jaw—but soon it died down and Goodloe filed the deaths of Kent and Scott Gates as accidental.

But he listed Wayne's blinding as unsolved. The snake venom had bleached his pupils white, and the skin around his eye sockets had required grafts. The doctors had had to use skin from his buttocks, and because his buttocks were hairy, the skin around his eyes grew hair, too.

In the years to come, the loggers who clear-cut the land along the river would occasionally stop in the store, less from a need to buy than from a curiosity to see the hermit with the milky, hairy eyes. The store smelled horrible, like the inside of a bear's mouth, and dust lay thick and soft on the shelves. Because they'd come in, the loggers would feel obligated to buy something, but every item was moldy or stale beyond belief, except for the things in cans, which were all unlabeled so they never knew what they'd get. Nothing was marked as to price, either, and the blind man wouldn't talk. He just sat by the stove. So the loggers paid more than what they thought a can was worth, leaving the money on the counter by the telephone, which hadn't been connected in years. When plumper, grayer Goodloe came by on the occasional evening, he'd take the bills and coins and put them in Kirxy's cash drawer. He was no longer sheriff, having lost several elections back to one of his deputies, Roy or Dave. Now he drove a Lance truck, his routes including the hospitals in the county.

"Dern, boy," he cracked once. "This store's doing a better business now than it ever has. You sure you don't want a cracker rack?"

When Goodloe left, Wayne listened to the sound of the truck as it faded. "Sugarbaby," he whispered.

And many a night for years after, until his own death in his sleep, Wayne would rise from the chair and move across the floor, taking Kirxy's cane from where it stood by the coat rack. He would go outside, down the stairs like a man who could see, his beard nearly to his chest, and he would walk soundlessly the length of the building, knowing the woods even better now as he crept down the rain-rutted gullyside toward the river whose smell never left the caves of his nostrils and the roof of his mouth. At the riverbank, he would stop and sit with his back against a small pine, and lifting his white eyes to the sky, he would listen to the clicks and hum and thrattle of the woods, seeking out each noise at its source and imagining it: an acorn nodding, detaching, falling, its thin ricochet and the way it settles into the leaves. A bullfrog's bubbling throat and the things it says. The soft movement of the river over rocks and around the bases of cattails and cypress knees and through the wet hanging roots of trees. And then another sound, familiar. The soft, precise footsteps of Frank David. Downwind. Not coming closer, not going away. Circling. The striking of a match and the sizzle of ember and the fall of ash. The ascent of smoke. A strange and terrifying comfort for the rest of Wayne Gates's life.

Tom Franklin grew up in Dickinson, Alabama, and received an MFA from the University of Arkansas. His stories and essays have appeared in *The Nebraska Review, The Chattahoochee Review, Quarterly West, Smoke,* **and elsewhere. He recently published his first collection,** *Poachers,* **and his first novel,** *Hell at the Breech,* **is forthcoming. He is married to the poet Beth Ann Fennelly and teaches at the University of South Alabama in Mobile.**

DON H. FULLER

I wrote and rewrote "Poachers" several times over three and a half years,
trying to make it work. Among other problems, I couldn't figure out how
to kill the third brother. Then one July day my wife (fiancée then) and I were
hiking in the Sierra Nevadas; we'd spent the afternoon retracing our steps
from the evening before, looking for my lost Swiss Army knife and talking
about the story. The knife had been Beth Ann's first Christmas present to me,
and I loved it. I remember crawling under bushes and climbing behind big
rocks, anxious to find the knife but also complaining about not being able to
finish "Poachers." "Maybe," I said, "I should just give up."

Suddenly Beth Ann looked at me and said, "Why does the last brother
have to die? You don't need to murder everybody, you know. Maybe the game
warden just hurts him."

"Or blinds him," I said, and we stared at each other for what felt like a
long time. Back at the car, we found the pocketknife under the driver's seat,
which seemed appropriate.

That evening, celebrating at a restaurant, I was wondering aloud what
would happen if you dripped snake venom in someone's eyes when the couple
at the next table exchanged a look, paid quickly, and hurried away.

APPENDIX

A list of the magazines currently consulted for *New Stories from the South: The Year's Best, 1999,* with addresses, subscription rates, and editors.

Agni
Boston University Writing Program
236 Bay State Road
Boston, MA 02215
Semiannually, $18
Askold Melnyczak

American Literary Review
University of N. Texas
P.O. Box 311307
Denton, TX 76203
Semiannually, $15
Fiction Editor

American Short Fiction
Parlin 14
Department of English
University of Austin
Austin, TX 78712-1164
Quarterly, $24
Laura Furman

The American Voice
Kentucky Foundation for
    Women, Inc.
332 W. Broadway, Suite 1215
Louisville, KY 40202
Triannually, $15
Frederick Smock, Editor
Sallie Bingham, Publisher

The Antioch Review
P.O. Box 148

Yellow Springs, OH 45387
Quarterly, $35
Robert S. Fogarty

Apalachee Quarterly
P.O. Box 10469
Tallahassee, FL 32302
Triannually, $15
Barbara Hamby

The Atlantic Monthly
745 Boylston Street
Boston, MA 02116
Monthly, $17.94
C. Michael Curtis

Black Warrior Review
University of Alabama
P.O. Box 862936
Tuscaloosa, AL 35486-0027
Semiannually, $14
Christopher Chambers

Boulevard
4579 Laclede Ave., Suite 332
St. Louis, MO 63108-2103
Triannually, $12
Richard Burgin

The Carolina Quarterly
Greenlaw Hall CB# 3520
University of North Carolina
Chapel Hill, NC 27599-3520

Triannually, $10
Fiction Editor

The Chariton Review
Truman State University
Kirksville, MO 63501
Semiannually, $9
Jim Barnes

The Chattahoochee Review
Georgia Perimeter College
2101 Womack Road
Dunwoody, GA 30338-4497
Quarterly, $16
Lawrence Hetrick, Editor

Cimarron Review
205 Morrill Hall
Oklahoma State University
Stillwater, OK 74078-0135
Quarterly, $12
Fiction Editor

Columbia
415 Dodge Hall
Columbia University
New York, NY 10027
Semiannually, $15
Lori Soderlind

Confrontation
English Department
C.W. Post of L.I.U.
Brookville, NY 11548
Semiannually, $20
Martin Tucker, Editor

Conjunctions
Bard College
Annandale-on-Hudson, NY 12504
Semiannually, $18
Bradford Morrow

Crazyhorse
Department of English
University of Arkansas at Little Rock
2801 South University
Little Rock, AR 72204
Semiannually, $10
Judy Troy, Fiction Editor

The Crescent Review
P.O. Box 15069
Chevy Chase, MD 20825-5069
Triannually, $21
J. Timothy Holland

Crucible
Barton College
College Station
Wilson, NC 27893
Annually, $6
Terrence L. Grimes

Denver Quarterly
University of Denver
Denver, CO 80208
Quarterly, $20
Bin Ramke

The Distillery
Division of Liberal Arts
Motlow State Community College
P.O. Box 88100
Tullahoma, TN 37388-8100
Semiannually, $15
Niles Reddick

DoubleTake Magazine
Center for Documentary Studies
1317 W. Pettigrew Street
Durham, NC 27705
Quarterly, $24
Robert Coles

Epoch
251 Goldwin Smith Hall

Cornell University
Ithaca, NY 14853-3201
Triannually, $11
Michael Koch

Esquire
250 West 55th Street
New York, NY 10019
Monthly, $15.94
Adrienne Miller

Fiction
c/o English Department
City College of New York
New York, NY 10031
Triannually, $20
Mark J. Mirsky

Fish Stories
3540 N. Southport Ave., Suite 493
Chicago, IL 60657
Annually, $12.45
Amy G. Davis

Five Points
GSU
University Plaza
Department of English
Atlanta, GA 30303-3083
Triannually, $15
Pam Durban

The Florida Review
Department of English
University of Central Florida
Orlando, FL 32816
Semiannually, $7
Russ Kesler

Gargoyle
c/o Atticus Books & Music
1508 U Street, NW
Washington, DC 20009
Semiannually, $20

Richard Peabody and Lucinda
  Ebersole

The Georgia Review
University of Georgia
Athens, GA 30602-9009
Quarterly, $18
Stanley W. Lindberg

The Gettysburg Review
Gettysburg College
Gettysburg, PA 17325-1491
Quarterly, $24
Peter Stitt

Glimmer Train
812 SW Washington Street, Suite 1205
Portland, OR 97205-3216
Quarterly, $29
Susan Burmeister-Brown and Linda
  Davis

GQ
Condé Nast Publications, Inc.
350 Madison Avenue
New York, NY 10017
Monthly, $20
Ilena Silverman

Grand Street
131 Varick St., Room 906
New York, NY 10013
Quarterly, $40
Jean Stein

Granta
250 W. 57th Street
Suite 1316
New York, NY 10017
Quarterly, $34
Ian Jack

The Greensboro Review
Department of English

University of North Carolina
Greensboro, NC 27412
Semiannually, $8
Jim Clark

Gulf Coast
Department of English
University of Houston
4800 Calhoun Road
Houston, TX 77204-3012
Semiannually, $12
Fiction Editor

Gulf Stream
English Department
Florida International University
North Miami Campus
North Miami, FL 33181
Semiannually, $7.50
Lynne Barrett

Harper's Magazine
666 Broadway
New York, NY 10012
Monthly, $18
Lewis H. Lapham

Habersham Review
Piedmont College
Demorest, GA 30535-0010
Semiannually, $12
Frank Gannon

High Plains Literary Review
180 Adams Street, Suite 250
Denver, CO 80206
Triannually, $20
Robert O. Greer, Jr.

Image
P.O. Box 674
Kennett Square, PA 19348
Quarterly, $30
Gregory Wolfe

Indiana Review
465 Ballantine Ave.
Indiana University
Bloomington, IN 47405
Semiannually, $12
Fiction Editor

The Iowa Review
308 EPB
University of Iowa
Iowa City, IA 52242-1492
Triannually, $18
David Hamilton

The Journal
Ohio State University
Department of English
164 W. 17th Avenue
Columbus, OH 43210
Semiannually, $8
Kathy Fagan and Michelle Herman

Kalliope
Florida Community College
3939 Roosevelt Blvd.
Jacksonville, FL 32205
Triannually, $12.50
Mary Sue Koeppel

The Kenyon Review
Kenyon College
Gambier, OH 43022
Quarterly, $22
Fiction Editor

The Literary Review
Fairleigh Dickinson University
285 Madison Avenue
Madison, NJ 07940
Quarterly, $18
Walter Cummins

The Long Story
18 Eaton Street

Lawrence, MA 01843
Semiannually, $9
R. P. Burnham

Louisiana Literature
P.O. Box 792
Southeastern Louisiana University
Hammond, LA 70402
Semiannually, $10
David Hanson

Lullwater Review
Box 22036
Emory University
Atlanta, GA 30322
Semiannually, $12
Fiction Editor

Meridian
P.O. Box 5103
Charlottesville, VA 22905-5103
Semiannually, $10
Ted Genoways

Mid-American Review
106 Hanna Hall
Department of English
Bowling Green State University
Bowling Green, OH 43403
Semiannually, $12
Robert Early, Senior Editor

Mississippi Review
Center for Writers
University of Southern Mississippi
Box 5144
Hattiesburg, MS 39406-5144
Semiannually, $15
Frederick Barthelme

The Missouri Review
1507 Hillcrest Hall
University of Missouri

Columbia, MO 65211
Triannually, $19
Speer Morgan

Modern Maturity
601 E Street, NW
Washington, DC 20049
Six times a year
John Wood

The Nebraska Review
Writers Workshop
Fine Arts Building 212
University of Nebraska
   at Omaha
Omaha, NE 68182
Semiannually, $9.50
Art Homer

Negative Capability
62 Ridgelawn Drive East
Mobile, AL 36608
Triannually, $15
Sue Walker

New Delta Review
English Department
Louisiana State University
Baton Rouge, LA 70803-5001
Semiannually, $8.50
Erika Solberg

New England Review
Middlebury College
Middlebury, VT 05753
Quarterly, $23
Stephen Donadio

The New Yorker
20 W. 43rd Street
New York, NY 10036
Weekly, $36
Bill Buford, Fiction Editor

Nimrod International Journal
The University of Tulsa
600 South College
Tulsa, OK 74104-3189
Semiannually, $17.50
Francine Ringold

The North American Review
University of Northern Iowa
Cedar Falls, IA 50614-0516
Six times a year, $22
Robley Wilson

North Carolina Literary Review
English Department
East Carolina University
Greenville, NC 27858-4353
Semiannually, $17
Alex Albright and Thomas E.
    Douglas

Northwest Review
369 PLC
University of Oregon
Eugene, OR 97403
Triannually, $20
John Witte

The Ohio Review
290-C Ellis Hall
Ohio University
Athens, OH 45701-2979
Semiannually, $16
Wayne Dodd

Ontario Review
9 Honey Brook Drive
Princeton, NJ 08540
Semiannually, $12
Raymond J. Smith

Other Voices
University of Illinois at Chicago
Department of English (M/C 162)
601 S. Morgan Street

Chicago, IL 60607-7120
Semiannually, $10
Fiction Editor

The Oxford American
P.O. Box 1156
Oxford, MS 38655
Bimonthly, $19.95
Marc Smirnoff

The Paris Review
541 E. 72nd Street
New York, NY 10021
Quarterly, $34
George Plimpton

Parting Gifts
March Street Press
3413 Wilshire Drive
Greensboro, NC 27408
Semiannually, $8
Robert Bixby

Pembroke Magazine
Box 60
Pembroke State University
Pembroke, NC 28372
Annually, $5
Shelby Stephenson, Editor

Playboy
680 N. Lake Shore Drive
Chicago, IL 60611
Monthly, $29
Alice K. Turner, Fiction Editor

Ploughshares
Emerson College
100 Beacon Street
Boston, MA 02116-1596
Triannually, $19
Don Lee

Prairie Schooner
201 Andrews Hall

University of Nebraska
Lincoln, NE 68588-0334
Quarterly, $24
Hilda Raz

Puerto del Sol
Box 30001, Department 3E
New Mexico State University
Las Cruces, NM 88003-8001
Semiannually, $10
Kevin McIlvoy

Quarterly West
317 Olpin Union Hall
University of Utah
Salt Lake City, UT 84112
Semiannually, $12
M. L. Williams

River Styx
634 N. Grand Blvd., #12
St. Louis, MO 63103-1002
Triannually, $20
Richard Newman

Salmagundi
Skidmore College
Saratoga Springs, NY 12866
Quarterly, $18
Robert Boyers

Santa Monica Review
Santa Monica College
1900 Pico Boulevard
Santa Monica, CA 90405
Semiannually, $12
Lee Montgomery

Shenandoah
Washington and Lee University
Troubadore Theater
2nd Floor
Lexington, VA 24450
Quarterly, $15
R. T. Smith

Snake Nation Review
110 #2 W. Force Street
Valdosta, GA 31601
Triannually, $20
Roberta George

The South Carolina Review
Department of English
Strode Tower Box 341503
Clemson University
Clemson, SC 29634-1503
Semiannually, $10
Frank Day

South Dakota Review
Box 111
University Exchange
Vermillion, SD 57069
Quarterly, $18
Brian Bedard

Southern Exposure
P.O. Box 531
Durham, NC 27702
Quarterly, $24
Pat Arnow, Editor

Southern Humanities Review
9088 Haley Center
Auburn University
Auburn, AL 36849
Quarterly, $15
Dan R. Latimer

The Southern Review
43 Allen Hall
Louisiana State University
Baton Rouge, LA 70803-5005
Quarterly, $20
James Olney

Southwest Review
307 Fondren Library West
Box 750374
Southern Methodist University

Dallas, TX 75275
Quarterly, $25
Willard Spiegelman

Sou'wester
Dept. of English
Box 1431
Southern Illinois University at
  Edwardsville
Edwardsville, IL 62026-1438
Semiannually, $10
Fred W. Robbins

Story
1507 Dana Avenue
Cincinnati, OH 45207
Quarterly, $22.00
Lois Rosenthal

StoryQuarterly
P.O. Box 1416
Northbrook, IL 60065
Quarterly, $12
Diane Williams

Sundog: The Southeast Review
406 Williams Building
Florida State University
Tallahassee, FL 32306-1036
Semiannually, $8
Fiction Editor

Tampa Review
Box 19F
University of Tampa Press
401 W. Kennedy Boulevard
Tampa, FL 33606-1490
Semiannually, $10
Richard Mathews, Editor

Texas Review
English Department
Sam Houston State University
Huntsville, TX 77341

Semiannually, $10
Paul Ruffin

The Threepenny Review
P.O. Box 9131
Berkeley, CA 94709
Quarterly, $16
Wendy Lesser

TriQuarterly
Northwestern University
2020 Ridge Avenue
Evanston, IL 60208
Triannually, $24
Reginald Gibbons

The Virginia Quarterly Review
One West Range
Charlottesville, VA 22903
Quarterly, $18
Staige D. Blackford

WV Magazine of the Emerging
  Writer
5 West 63rd St.
New York, NY 10023

West Branch
Bucknell Hall
Bucknell University
Lewisburg, PA 17837
Semiannually, $7
Robert Love Taylor

Whetstone
Barrington Area Arts Council
P.O. Box 1266
Barrington, IL 60011
Annually, $7.25
Sandra Berris

William and Mary Review
College of William and Mary
P.O. Box 8795

Williamsburg, VA 23187
Annually, $5.50
Forrest Pritchard

Wind Magazine
P.O. Box 24548
Lexington, KY 40524
Semiannually, $10
Charlie G. Hughes

The Yalobusha Review
P.O. Box 186
University, MS 38677-0186
Annually, $8
Fiction Editor

Yemassee
Department of English
University of South Carolina
Columbia, SC 29208
Semiannually, $15
Stephen Owen

Zoetrope
126 Fifth Avenue, Suite 300
New York, NY 10011
Triannually, $15
Adrienne Brodeur

ZYZZYVA
41 Sutter Street
Suite 1400
San Francisco, CA 94104-4903
Quarterly, $28
Howard Junker

Previous Volumes

Copies of previous volumes of *New Stories from the South* can be ordered through your local bookstore or by calling the Sales Department at Algonquin Books of Chapel Hill. Multiple copies for classroom adoptions are available at a special discount. For information, please call 919-967-0108.

NEW STORIES FROM THE SOUTH: THE YEAR'S BEST, 1986

Max Apple, BRIDGING

Madison Smartt Bell, TRIPTYCH 2

Mary Ward Brown, TONGUES OF FLAME

Suzanne Brown, COMMUNION

James Lee Burke, THE CONVICT

Ron Carlson, AIR

Doug Crowell, SAYS VELMA

Leon V. Driskell, MARTHA JEAN

Elizabeth Harris, THE WORLD RECORD HOLDER

Mary Hood, SOMETHING GOOD FOR GINNIE

David Huddle, SUMMER OF THE MAGIC SHOW

Gloria Norris, HOLDING ON

Kurt Rheinheimer, UMPIRE

W. A. Smith, DELIVERY

Wallace Whatley, SOMETHING TO LOSE

Luke Whisnant, WALLWORK

Sylvia Wilkinson, CHICKEN SIMON

NEW STORIES FROM THE SOUTH: THE YEAR'S BEST, 1987

James Gordon Bennett, DEPENDENTS

Robert Boswell, EDWARD AND JILL

Rosanne Coggeshall, PETER THE ROCK

John William Corrington, HEROIC MEASURES/VITAL SIGNS

Vicki Covington, MAGNOLIA

Andre Dubus, DRESSED LIKE SUMMER LEAVES

Mary Hood, AFTER MOORE

Trudy Lewis, VINCRISTINE

Lewis Nordan, SUGAR, THE EUNUCHS, AND BIG G.B.

Peggy Payne, THE PURE IN HEART

Bob Shacochis, WHERE PELHAM FELL

Lee Smith, LIFE ON THE MOON

Marly Swick, HEART

Robert Love Taylor, LADY OF SPAIN

Luke Whisnant, ACROSS FROM THE MOTOHEADS

NEW STORIES FROM THE SOUTH: THE YEAR'S BEST, 1988

Ellen Akins, GEORGE BAILEY FISHING

Rick Bass, THE WATCH

Richard Bausch, THE MAN WHO KNEW BELLE STAR

Larry Brown, FACING THE MUSIC

Pam Durban, BELONGING

John Rolfe Gardiner, GAME FARM

Jim Hall, GAS

Charlotte Holmes, METROPOLITAN

NEW STORIES FROM THE SOUTH: THE YEAR'S BEST, 1989

New Stories from the South: The Year's Best, 1990

Tom Bailey, CROW MAN

Rick Bass, THE HISTORY OF RODNEY

Richard Bausch, LETTER TO THE LADY OF THE HOUSE

Larry Brown, SLEEP

Moira Crone, JUST OUTSIDE THE B.T.

Clyde Edgerton, CHANGING NAMES

Greg Johnson, THE BOARDER

Nanci Kincaid, SPITTIN' IMAGE OF A BAPTIST BOY

Reginald McKnight, THE KIND OF LIGHT THAT SHINES ON TEXAS

Lewis Nordan, THE CELLAR OF RUNT CONROY

Lance Olsen, FAMILY

Mark Richard, FEAST OF THE EARTH, RANSOM OF THE CLAY

Ron Robinson, WHERE WE LAND

Bob Shacochis, LES FEMMES CREOLES

Molly Best Tinsley, ZOE

Donna Trussell, FISHBONE

New Stories from the South: The Year's Best, 1991

Rick Bass, IN THE LOYAL MOUNTAINS

Thomas Phillips Brewer, BLACK CAT BONE

Larry Brown, BIG BAD LOVE

Robert Olen Butler, RELIC

Barbara Hudson, THE ARABESQUE

Elizabeth Hunnewell, A LIFE OR DEATH MATTER

Hilding Johnson, SOUTH OF KITTATINNY

Nanci Kincaid, THIS IS NOT THE PICTURE SHOW

Bobbie Ann Mason, WITH JAZZ

Jill McCorkle, WAITING FOR HARD TIMES TO END

Robert Morgan, POINSETT'S BRIDGE

Reynolds Price, HIS FINAL MOTHER

Mark Richard, THE BIRDS FOR CHRISTMAS

Susan Starr Richards, THE SCREENED PORCH

Lee Smith, INTENSIVE CARE

Peter Taylor, COUSIN AUBREY

NEW STORIES FROM THE SOUTH: THE YEAR'S BEST, 1992

Alison Baker, CLEARWATER AND LATISSIMUS

Larry Brown, A ROADSIDE RESURRECTION

Mary Ward Brown, A NEW LIFE

James Lee Burke, TEXAS CITY, 1947

Robert Olen Butler, A GOOD SCENT FROM A STRANGE MOUNTAIN

Nanci Kincaid, A STURDY PAIR OF SHOES THAT FIT GOOD

Patricia Lear, AFTER MEMPHIS

Dan Leone, YOU HAVE CHOSEN CAKE

Karen Minton, LIKE HANDS ON A CAVE WALL

Reginald McKnight, QUITTING SMOKING

Elizabeth Seydel Morgan, ECONOMICS

Robert Morgan, DEATH CROWN

Susan Perabo, EXPLAINING DEATH TO THE DOG

Padgett Powell, THE WINNOWING OF MRS. SCHUPING

Lee Smith, THE BUBBA STORIES

Peter Taylor, THE WITCH OF OWL MOUNTAIN SPRINGS

Abraham Verghese, LILACS

NEW STORIES FROM THE SOUTH: THE YEAR'S BEST, 1993

Richard Bausch, EVENING

Pinckney Benedict, BOUNTY

Wendell Berry, A JONQUIL FOR MARY PENN

Robert Olen Butler, PREPARATION

Lee Merrill Byrd, MAJOR SIX POCKETS

Kevin Calder, NAME ME THIS RIVER

Tony Earley, CHARLOTTE

Paula K. Gover, WHITE BOYS AND RIVER GIRLS

David Huddle, TROUBLE AT THE HOME OFFICE

Barbara Hudson, SELLING WHISKERS

Elizabeth Hunnewell, FAMILY PLANNING

Dennis Loy Johnson, RESCUING ED

Edward P. Jones, MARIE

Wayne Karlin, PRISONERS

Dan Leone, SPINACH

Jill McCorkle, MAN WATCHER

Annette Sanford, HELENS AND ROSES

Peter Taylor, THE WAITING ROOM

NEW STORIES FROM THE SOUTH: THE YEAR'S BEST, 1994

Frederick Barthelme, RETREAT

Richard Bausch, AREN'T YOU HAPPY FOR ME?

Ethan Canin, THE PALACE THIEF

Kathleen Cushman, LUXURY

Tony Earley, THE PROPHET FROM JUPITER

Pamela Erbe, SWEET TOOTH

NEW STORIES FROM THE SOUTH: THE YEAR'S BEST, 1995

Dale Ray Phillips, EVERYTHING QUIET LIKE CHURCH

Elizabeth Spencer, THE RUNAWAYS

New Stories from the South: The Year's Best, 1996

Robert Olen Butler, JEALOUS HUSBAND RETURNS IN FORM OF PARROT

Moira Crone, GAUGUIN

J. D. Dolan, MOOD MUSIC

Ellen Douglas, GRANT

William Faulkner, ROSE OF LEBANON

Kathy Flann, A HAPPY, SAFE THING

Tim Gautreaux, DIED AND GONE TO VEGAS

David Gilbert, COOL MOSS

Marcia Guthridge, THE HOST

Jill McCorkle, PARADISE

Robert Morgan, THE BALM OF GILEAD TREE

Tom Paine, GENERAL MARKMAN'S LAST STAND

Susan Perabo, SOME SAY THE WORLD

Annette Sanford, GOOSE GIRL

Lee Smith, THE HAPPY MEMORIES CLUB

New Stories from the South: The Year's Best, 1997

PREFACE *by Robert Olen Butler*

Gene Able, MARRYING AUNT SADIE

Dwight Allen, THE GREEN SUIT

Edward Allen, ASHES NORTH

Robert Olen Butler, HELP ME FIND MY SPACEMAN LOVER

NEW STORIES FROM THE SOUTH: THE YEAR'S BEST, 1998

Stephen Marion, NAKED AS TANYA

Jennifer Moses, GIRLS LIKE YOU

Padgett Powell, ALIENS OF AFFECTION

Sara Powers, THE BAKER'S WIFE

Mark Richard, MEMORIAL DAY

Nancy Richard, THE ORDER OF THINGS

Josh Russell, YELLOW JACK

Annette Sanford, IN THE LITTLE HUNKY RIVER

Enid Shomer, THE OTHER MOTHER

George Singleton, THESE PEOPLE ARE US

Molly Best Tinsley, THE ONLY WAY TO RIDE